A TALE OF TWO URGENCIES:

SAVING THE PLANET
and SAVING YOUR SOUL

JAY MENNENGA

outskirtspress
DENVER, COLORADO

A Tale of Two Urgencies:
Saving the Planet and Saving Your Soul
All Rights Reserved.
Copyright © 2014 Jay Mennenga
v2.0 r1.1

Dr. Heidi Pearson, Assistant Professor of Marine Biology, University of Alaska Southeast, Juneau, for reviewing Chapter VII, "Arctic Animals," for animal accuracy.

Photographs on front cover purchased from PHOTOS.COM.

Author photograph courtesy of Main Street EFX Photography, Laurel, Montana.

Scripture in the body of A Tale of Two Urgencies taken from the HOLY BIBLE, NEW INTERNATIONAL VERSION. Copyright © 1973, 1978, 1984 International Bible Society. Used by permission of Zondervan Publishing House.

Scripture in Appendix B taken from THE MESSAGE Copyright © 1993,1994,1995,1 996,2000,2001,2002. Used by permission of Nav Press Publishing Group.

Outskirts Press, Inc.
http://www.outskirtspress.com

ISBN: 978-1-4787-0819-3

Outskirts Press and the "OP" logo are trademarks belonging to Outskirts Press, Inc.

PRINTED IN THE UNITED STATES OF AMERICA

Excellent editing by Mark Reisetter, Lewiston, Minnesota.
(minnesotatrout.com)

Photograph of original oil painting of the Editor titled, "Matching the Hatch,"
courtesy of the artist, Gene Stevens, Altura, Minnesota, and courtesy of
"Wild Wings," Lake City, Minnesota.

Table of Contents

⤞✧⤝

I. North to Alaska

Brice Sutherland and his son Blaine waited expectantly on the dock near the airport in Kotzebue, Alaska, for their transportation to arrive to carry them on the last leg of their journey to Katooska. Spud, their Karelian Bear Dog, excitedly paced up and down the dock, occasionally trying to lap the incoming waves.

"This should be fun," exclaimed Blaine. "What do you think, Spud? Several piercing barks followed. Brice stood silently scanning the skies for the approaching plane.

Finally the red and white seaplane hit the waves and bounced to the dock as the pilot killed the engine. Out jumped a grizzled man wearing a blaze life jacket and an "Arctic Adventure" cap. Without saying a word he helped the men cram their supplies into the back of the plane; then the trio, with Spud lying on the equipment, climbed in and buckled their seat belts.

The pilot turned his head 90 degrees to the right and shouted to the back seat, "You're now north of the Arctic Circle, where the sun won't set for 37 days. This could be a loud and bumpy ride. We've got a storm coming in off the ocean. It used to be the ice would still be on the sound until now to protect us from these storms. I'll try to beat it, and get you safely to your destination. Prayers are welcome," as the plane bobbed and taxied out to sea.

"What kind of guy is this?" thought Brice. "Does he really believe God can help us? Is that his crutch? I hope he knows what he's doing."

The plane's one engine revved up, and the pontoons plowed through the waves until it was finally airborne. Brice and Blaine breathed a sigh of relief, as Spud pressed his nose against the window, trying to stick his head out in typical dog fashion. With a dip of his wing, the pilot headed north along the coast.

Farther out to sea Brice could see the whitecaps pounding the shore. "How's the pilot going to land on these rough waters?" he mused.

"There's where we're going to land," yelled the pilot, pointing to a small cove surrounded by evergreen trees. Hang on! Here we go! The trick is to hit the wave just right and ride it to shore. It's like surfing."

The pilot started descending to find the right wave. He was about to land when he suddenly veered sharply upward, and circled for another try. After another try at landing – without success – he checked his fuel gauge, and again shouted, "This is it! We've got to hit it right this time. The waves are becoming fiercer and the winds are picking up."

As Blaine and Brice hung on for dear life, the pilot throttled the engine down for his approach. Just as he was ready to touch down on a wave, a gust of wind swept under one wing, flipping the plane into the sea 100 feet from the dock – in five feet of water.

Spud jumped out a window and swam ashore, panting heavily on the sandy shore, wondering where his masters were. The pilot, with blood flowing from a deep cut on his face, shouted, "Unfasten your seat belts and swim ashore. Your life vests will keep you afloat."

With the waves crashing on the shore, they didn't have to swim, but were carried to the dock – crashing into it. Before the undertow could sweep them out to sea, all three men managed to grab a post and pull themselves to safety. Finally their supplies and equipment were washed ashore, and grabbed by Professor Paul Plankton and several of his interns waiting on the dock.

"Are you guys OK?" the professor asked.

"Do you have a first aid kit handy?" asked the pilot. "I need to stop this bleeding," as he looked down at his hand bloodied from touching his face.

"What about you, Brice?" asked Dr. Plankton. "And how's your son?"

"Other than a few bumps and bruises, I think we're OK," replied Brice. "How are our supplies?"

"We retrieved what we could," answered one of the interns.

"Don't worry about it," said Paul. "We'll replace anything you lost."

In the meantime another one of the interns ran to get a first aid kit, and returned to treat the pilot. "You never know when your Boy Scout training comes in handy," he stated proudly.

"I'll give you a merit badge, and recommend you to the Red Cross," said the pilot wryly. "It's a good thing I said my prayers. We must have had a guardian angel protecting us."

Another intern, overhearing the conversation, interjected, "You mean like Clarence in *It's A Wonderful Life*? "He didn't even have wings."

"Yea, but he sacrificed his life to save George," replied the pilot.

"OK, enough of that," interrupted Dr. Plankton. "You guys were just lucky. We've got to dry out your supplies and get you folks settled. The pilot can stay with us until they send another plane for him. Turning to Brice, the professor said, "What a way to begin your practicum, Brice. Anyway, welcome to the International Polar Year in Alaska. Blaine and you will be meeting many famous climate scientists who are here to study this 'canary in the coal mine.' Sorry about the rough landing."

As the shaken Sutherlands, with Spud happily trotting by their side, climbed into Professor Plankton's van to head to their yurt, Brice muttered to Blaine, "Well, we wanted an adventure, and that seaplane landing was certainly it. I wonder what else is in store for us up here."

Overhearing their conversation the professor replied with a smile, "Wait and see," as they headed toward Katooska - home of the International Polar Year of 2021.

The Plains of Nebraska

Brice Sutherland, born and raised in the Sandhills of Nebraska, had made a name for himself as a running back with the Cornhuskers during their heydays of the 1990s under legendary coach Tom Osborne. After completing his major in Environmental Science at the University of Nebraska in Lincoln, Brice was content to return to the family homestead, and manage their vast herd of cattle on their 3,000 acre ranch. Starting to show a little gray in his thick brown hair, he was tall, trim, fit, and muscular with only a slight midriff bulge. And he wasn't limping from knee injuries like many of his colleagues. Now Brice was chasing calves instead of footballs, at only a slightly slower speed.

Lately he noticed something disturbing. The huge Ogallala Aquifer, upon which the ranches depended for irrigation, was drying up. At the turn of the century scientists had warned of this depletion. And now their predictions were coming true. What would happen to the vast ranches? What about the cattle and corn crops? Would farm families have to move to try to find jobs in the many small towns or few large cities that were suffering water shortages from the extended drought on the prairie?

After discussing their dire situation with his wife, Tricia, and their only son, Blaine, a "spitting image" of his father, the family decided to take a vacation out West to see the scenery and explore possible avenues of employment for Brice and Tricia, a petite brunette with a ready smile and pleasant personality, who was now a school secretary in a small rural school. At ages 46 and 42, respectively, both parents were loath to make mid-career changes, but they didn't seem to have any other viable options. However, for Blaine, soon to be a graduating senior from his small school, it was an opportune time. He, typical of many small town kids, wanted to "stretch" his long legs and "see the world."

Traveling the National Parks

The Sutherlands had never visited any national parks, but remembered watching a spectacular documentary about U.S. National Parks by famous filmmaker Ken Burns. They still had vivid pictures in their minds of the geysers of Yellowstone, the majestic mountains of the Grand Tetons, and the glaciers and Alps of Glacier National Park. So they decided to take in all three national parks in one vacation.

With the three of them squeezed into their Honda Hybrid, their first stop was Grand Teton National Park. Having read a little about each park before they left, Brice chuckled when he saw the protruding Tetons. "I know what those French trappers were thinking. They had women's breasts on their minds when they named these peaks. And I can see why."

Tricia retorted, "Get your mind out of the gutter, and admire their awesome beauty."

Blaine entered the fray. "Do you know French, Dad?"

"Just enough to be dangerous, son," as he cackled under his breath.

After passing the National Elk Refuge in Jackson, Wyoming, and enjoying the panorama of the mountains one more time, they headed toward America's first national park – Yellowstone, home to the largest free-roaming bison herd in the world, a thriving wolf population, grizzly bears, elk, and the most concentrated geyser activity in the world.

What trip to Yellowstone would be complete without seeing Old Faithful spew her hot, gaseous plume close to 200 feet in the air, and right on schedule? While driving by beautiful, blue Yellowstone Lake – North America's largest alpine lake – they noticed acres and acres of red evergreens – an oxymoron.

Stopping the car Brice hopped out. "Here's an interpretive trail. Let's get out and see what we can learn."

Blaine, the unofficial travel guide, read the first sign on the trail. "Those of you who have been to Yellowstone years ago probably noticed something different about the evergreens – they're not that color anymore. You may also have noticed hotter temperatures in the summer, more forest fires, less rainfall, milder temperatures, and less snow in the winter. Many climate scientists attribute these changing conditions to global warming. These factors have all converged to weaken the trees' resistance to disease, giving a foothold to the Mountain Pine Beetle, which literally sucks the life-giving sap from these trees. This is a serious problem that park biologists are addressing. Enjoy your visit."

"Who wants to drive a thousand miles to see dead trees," queried Brice. "Not me. I'll go back to the treeless prairie."

"Yea, Dad. Enjoy your visit."

With that pessimistic assessment, the family was ready for their last national park, bordering the Canadian border in Montana.

"Maybe we'll see green trees, glaciers, and mountains the way God created them," chimed in Tricia.

"Or the way they evolved," countered Brice.

The scenery stopped round two of the tit-for-tat conversation. Glacier was indeed impressive, with its blue, serene, sun-glittering lakes, and swift mountain streams silhouetted by rugged, jagged peaks.

"Where are all the glaciers?" wondered Blaine. "Isn't that why people come here?"

There were patches of snow hugging the shady side of some mountains, especially along the Going-to-the-Sun Highway. But where were the glaciers? Finally they stopped to read an interpretive sign along the highway. Profiling a picture of the Shepherd Glacier directly above them, it recounted the history of the park. This time they all read silently: "In 1850 there were 150 glaciers, but today only ten remain. The projections by climate scientists are that by 2030 no glaciers will remain. Disappearing glaciers are the "canary in the coal mine." Enjoy your visit."

Once again Blaine popped up, "So are they going to change the name of the park?" Will anyone still visit?"

As the Sutherland's headed home to a lower elevation and hotter climate, the beauty of their trip was marred by the many red trees and sobering signs. They reflected in their minds the following questions: "Who and what can be done to keep America and the world beautiful?" (Blaine). "How can God's Creation be protected?" (Tricia). "Will the planet evolve to correct the abuses caused by global warming?' (Brice).

Brice Makes a Crucial Decision

What had started out to be a scenic vacation, turned out to be a time of soul searching for the family. The signs in the national parks explaining the deadly changes to the evergreens and the disappearing glaciers haunted them even as they went back to their busy summertime ranch work.

Then one September night after supper, the family was sitting on the porch watching the sun set as it cast its lengthening rays over the brown countryside, illuminating patches of their pasture. Brice, in a reflective mood, said, "I've been thinking a lot about our trip out West. I've also been doing some reading in my spare time to try to understand what's going on. One time, while surfing the Internet, I found a website that listed schools offering graduate degrees in climate change. One of them, the University of Alaska, even offers this program through an interactive web feed. This means I could sit right here at home and watch the professor's lectures, and even ask him questions – just like being in a regular classroom at UNL. What do you think of that?"

"Think about what?" wondered Tricia.

"About me taking a course like this. That's what I think."

"Brice, you haven't been to school since you left Lincoln years ago. Can you teach an old dog new tricks?" chided Tricia.

"Interests change as you grow older, and besides our trip may have sparked more than an interest – a passion for me," stated Brice resolutely.

"Go for it, Dad," echoed Blaine.

Linking with Alaska

And so, the long winter nights found Brice hunched over his computer, soaking in a new world of charts, graphs, and scientific explanations of why the world is warming – fortunately translated into layman's terms by his patient professor. And student Sutherland was not afraid to ask questions, such as, "How do we know this isn't just an evolutionary cycle of variations in the earth's temperature?"

On the screen popped another chart comparing previous warming climates with those of today. "We are off the chart with temperature increases. It looks like a hockey stick. The rise is that steep," emphasized the professor holding his right arm straight up for Brice to see. "And furthermore, we have met the enemy, and it's us with our increasing use of fossil fuels."

Talking through his computer, Brice asked the professor, "Didn't a guy named Al Gore become famous many years ago with his famous 'dog and pony show' of charts and graphs?"

"Yes, you're right, and he said back then we have about ten years to turn this crisis around to avoid catastrophe for the planet. Guess what? Time is up. It's more **urgent** than ever we act now."

But this course was not all about facts that would bore most students, but not Brice. What he really liked was the live web cam shots depicting some of the effects of global warming in the Arctic. One link filmed researchers flying over the open sea, with tiny ice floes dotting the blue waters, formerly frozen solid only 15 years ago. And then a close up view showed a scrawny polar bear straddling two pieces of floating ice, wistfully scouting the open water for seals. The caption on the screen read, "The first casualty of melting sea ice. How long will the bears last?"

Another view showed an oil tanker gliding through the open water without being accompanied by an icebreaker – a feat unimaginable ten years ago. Again the caption, "Lewis and Clark failed to find the Northwest Passage through America, but these tankers are sailing through it now. Can the ships and animals coexist on these waterways?"

The most dramatic shot showed the former tiny Alaskan village of Kivalina, a narrow 600 foot strip of eroded land sandwiched between the sea and river which used to house 400 indigenous hunters. Now this ghost town is a junkyard of ramshackle houses, crumbling foundations which used to support children and worshippers, and rusted oil tanks. The sea has reclaimed the land and dispossessed the villagers.

Shocked to see this sight Brice quizzed the professor, "What happened to the people?"

The professor began, "Because of rising temperatures and melting ice, no protection remained on the shore when the fierce sea buffeted the land during storms. Therefore, more and more land was washed out to sea. Finally the land was completely flooded, and the native peoples had to abandon their homes where they had lived for centuries, and relocate inland. You are seeing America's first climate refugees, and you'll see more like this. Kivalina is the "canary-in-the-coal- mine" and it's the coal that is to blame."

Finally, in the spring Brice persevered and finished the academic portion of the course. He took the final exam in his home, under the watchful eye of his professor from afar, and passed with flying colors! But there was one final hurdle to earning his Master's Degree: A practicum in Alaska in the summer of 2021 to study the effects of climate change "up close and personal" on site in the Arctic in conjunction with the International Polar Year. Would he be heading up North?

A Family Conference

Meanwhile, things weren't going well on the ranch. The cattle prices were still low, the cost of diesel and fertilizer was continuing to rise, and sparse snowfall meant little water for irrigation. Even the grass in the Sandhills, green in the spring, started browning earlier than usual. The drought showed no signs of abating. The venerable Farmer's Almanac was predicting an unusually dry and hot summer.

"It's bound to be cooler in Alaska," expressed Brice confidently. "And besides, there are more national parks to explore. Trish, you have the summer off. Blaine, you're undecided about college or work in the fall, and I need the practicum to complete my degree. What do you say? Let's all head to Alaska."

"OK, I'll go Dad. Just don't sing that song. You're not a bass."

"Trish, what about you?" wondered Brice.

"What kind of accommodations are up there?"

"Well, it's not the Holiday Inn. We'll be in yurts. Doesn't that sound fun?" quipped Brice.

"I'm not amused at all. You men go and play in the wilds. I'll try to hold the ranch together if we can still get water. Besides, I'd like to hunt for another job. I'm hearing rumors our school may be consolidated with another because of declining enrollment. And who knows where this adventure will lead you, Brice?"

Brice, secretly getting his wish, stated confidently, "Well, it's settled then," as he "high-fived" Blaine. "We're heading to the 'Last Frontier' and my lady holds down the fort," as he smiled slyly at his wife.

Trish, outmanned, turned briskly, and headed into the house, pondering her next move.

Preparing for the Journey

With a month before his practicum started, Brice and Blaine decided to drive their truck up the Alaska Highway and camp along the way. Waxing philosophical, Brice stated, "It's the journey and not the destination, son."

"Whatever, Dad. Can we take Spike with? He could chase the bears away. I've seen on YouTube there's even a species of bear that attacks humans."

"No, Spike needs to stay on the ranch. He's a herding dog. Tricia will need him."

"Hey, Dad, I read on Wikipedia there's a dog that is bred especially to hunt bears. It's called a Karelian Bear Dog from Finland, where they are a national treasure. They have quick reflexes, are fearless, and will even sacrifice their lives for their master."

"Well son, why don't you see if you can find one around here that we can buy and take with us? Maybe having another dog on the ranch isn't such a bad idea."

With that command Blaine got on the Internet and found a breeder in Laramie, Wyoming, specializing in Karelians. He sent pictures of a three year old black and white shorthaired male. Brice and the breeder settled on a price of $500, and agreed to meet in Sidney, Nebraska.

Their new acquisition was apprehensive and skittish when meeting his new masters. Spud circled around the Sutherland's truck as if it were a bear, and then finally jumped in the bed, and the three of them headed back to the ranch. When they drove down their lane, Spike came out barking at the strange dog. Spud, showing no fear, immediately jumped out as Spike, protecting his turf, attacked with teeth bared and hair standing on his back. Spud circled and charged Spike from behind, biting his tail. Spike yelped and ran away as Trish came out to see the commotion. Spud wasted no time in claiming his new territory, and proving he was now the alpha dog at the Sutherland ranch.

The weekends found Brice and Blaine camping close to home – in the artificial Nebraska forest near Halsey – a Depression era experiment that had worked. The dogs had established the pecking order, and had their own space in the campsite. The humans were now getting used to hiking with a backpack, pitching a tent, sleeping in it, and cooking over a campfire. Each time they camped they learned to jettison more supplies, and finally pronounced themselves "happy campers," ready for the long trip.

Back at the ranch the three of them worked to plant crops and mend fences for their cattle. They also worked with their hired hand, Blake, who would manage the ranch with Tricia during the men's absence.

Late one spring evening, after chores, Brice and Tricia asked Blake to sit on their porch, share a beer, and talk about the summer's work. Brice spoke up first, "Blake, you're fitting nicely into our operation here. We hired you because of your experience, work ethic, and honesty. We trust you will stay in the bunkhouse and give Tricia the privacy she wants."

Knowing what Brice was thinking, Blake promised, "You can count on that."

Early the next day, their truck packed with camping supplies and extra diesel, Brice and Tricia hugged a long time. They gave each other a passionate goodbye kiss. With a tear in one eye Tricia said, "I know you're following your passion up North, but don't forget about your passion here."

"I won't, honey," promised Brice. "I'll call and text you when I can."

Tricia replied softly, "Don't worry about me. I'll be fine. We have a good hired hand."

Blaine also hugged his mother, saying, "I'll keep Dad on the 'straight and narrow.'"

"Load up," Brice barked, and Spud obediently jumped into the back of the truck reserved for him. The two men slid inside the cab, Tricia waved goodbye, and Spike ran alongside, barking as the vehicle motored out of sight; and with a toot of the horn, they were off – headed toward a new adventure.

On the Road

With Willie Nelson's famous song on their radio, the three males headed north to catch I-90 in South Dakota. They passed the Badlands, named for its desolate but colorful formations of red and pink hues.

"And we think the Sandhills of Nebraska are dry and barren, particularly with the drought," commented Brice.

Continuing west through Rapid City and the Black Hills, they crossed Wyoming, catching a glimpse of the rounded Big Horn Mountains, with a tinge of red – the telltale sign of the pine beetle. And then it was into Montana, which appropriately means mountains. And for these flatlanders it was a real treat to drive from the Beartooths in the central part of the state north to Glacier National Park – again.

"Let's camp here tonight," stated Brice.

Since it was crowded, they found an isolated site in the national forest. While Spud checked and marked his territory, the two humans proceeded to raise their tent, gather wood, and start a fire. It was still cold in June, with snow on the ground. On the picnic table was this sign: "Beware of the bears. They are just coming out of hibernation, and are hungry. Be sure you store your food in your vehicle, in the bear proof containers provided, or in a bear bag in a tree at least 10 feet high and 10 feet from the trunk. Keep your campsite clean. Enjoy your visit."

As they cooked their deer meat, fried potatoes, and baked beans over their fire, they reminisced about their trip last year. "I wonder if the glaciers are still melting," said Blaine, "and if we'll see the same thing in Alaska?"

"In my class I learned that global warming is happening twice as fast in Alaska than in any other place in the world," answered his father. "So we'll probably see lots of effects up there."

After a long day on the road they were ready to "turn in" as the red sun set over the snow-covered mountain peaks, producing the characteristic Alpenglow. They stored their food and toiletries in the bear bag, tied it tightly shut, flung it over a tall branch like a cowboy with his rope, and secured the rest around the trunk.

"There. That should keep the bears away," predicted Brice confidently. Spud, you watch for the bears." Understanding his job, the faithful dog settled down in front of their tent, looking intently at the bear bag while the humans grabbed some "shut eye."

Suddenly, after several hours, the starry silence was broken by a loud crash. Instantly Spud leaped up and ran toward the bear bag, now on the forest floor. Brice woke up with a start and shined his flashlight toward his dog. He saw Spud barking furiously and encircling a large black form. As both men stumbled from their tent, Brice's light illuminated a hump on the animal – the telltale sign of a Grizzly.

The bear ran toward the bear bag but Spud stood his ground. The Grizzly then turned around and charged the bear dog, and suddenly stopped short of him, retreating into the woods. By the time Brice arrived on the scene with his bear spray ready, the commotion was over. Spud had stood his ground, and proved his mettle in his first test.

"Good dog, Spud," shouted Brice as he ran over to pet him on the head. Blaine was not far behind and flung his arms around his panting pet. "Spud, you saved our bacon – literally. I'm glad I found you. You'll do well in Alaska."

Brice was more reflective. "How could that bear get our bag? We followed the instructions. I guess we learned our lesson tonight. We'll have to do better next time."

The rest of the short night was uneventful, but Spud was still vigilant.

Into Canada

Anticipating going through customs in Canada, the Sutherland's were ready with their passports. After 9/11 this was no longer the longest unfortified border in the world. They were even ready with Spud's vaccination record – with which the Border Patrol didn't bother. But they did spot wood in their truck.

"Pull over pal," said the official gruffly. "You can't take it in. You may be bringing disease that could further damage our trees. They're already weakened by the Mountain Pine Beetle – another effect of global warming. Put your wood over there in that bin," he said pointing to the right. Besides, we furnish disease-free wood at our parks."

As the Americans, with Spud enjoying more room in the truck bed, drove away, Blaine commented, "I thought Canadians were friendly, laid-back people."

"Not this one," replied Brice. "But at least they believe in global warming, and I learned in my class that British Columbia has a carbon tax, and it's working."

And soon they saw the evidence – miles and miles of red and dead pine trees. Brice, glancing at Blaine in the cab, "Does this remind you of anything?"

"Yea, our trip to Yellowstone, only here it's worse. I wonder how it will be in Alaska."

And then they both smelled a whiff of smoke, and looked around to see the gray haze in the distance. As they continued driving, they saw more pine trees blackened by the forest fires on both sides of the road. The smoke was so thick in places that Brice had to turn on his truck headlights – in broad daylight. If the smoke didn't hide the mountains, the scenery was beautiful (the motto on the residents' license plates is "Beautiful British Columbia").

As dusk approached they found a provincial park, pulled in and set up camp. Blaine, walking Spud, found the wood box. "Yep, he's right. There's wood in this bin. Maybe it's the same wood we had to leave. But at least we're legal."

After finishing their campfire cooking, including "s'mores" for dessert, they retired to their camp chairs to relax after a long day of driving. Spud was crouched by their side, ever vigilant.

All of a sudden Blaine pointed to the sky and shouted, "Dad, look at those weird colors. They look like streamers of green, orange, and red, and they're moving. What's going on?"

"Haven't you heard of the Northern Lights? Usually you don't see them this time of the year with the long days. The sun's solar flares must be strong. Maybe the gods are mad."

"Whatever it is, it's pretty awesome. I wish Mom were here to see them. She'd be talking about God's Creation."

"Yea, and she'd ask me how something that beautiful could just evolve from cosmic dust, and we'd get into that religion 'thing' again. Maybe it's a good thing she isn't here. Let's "hit the hay" and hope our bear bag hangs tight tonight. Spud, you have the night watch. Goodnight," and the men crawled into the tent and sleeping bags, dreaming of a quiet night.

Only Spud's barking at the strange sky disturbed them this time. Was it the motion of the Aurora Borealis? Or was it his wolf instincts coming through? At least it wasn't a bear this time.

On the Alcan

On the third day of their pilgrimage North, the trio reached the southernmost terminus of the Alaska Highway, or Alcan (Alaska-Canada Highway) at Dawson Creek, BC.

"Hey, Dad, I read in my guide book that most of the 1,390 miles of the Alaska Highway are actually in Canada, so why do they call it the Alaska Highway?"

"Don't know, Son." Not wanting to be bothered, Brice said curtly, "Why don't you keep reading in your guide book." "That kid of mine has lots of questions," he thought as the silence resumed until they reached Whitehorse, a seemingly huge town in the Yukon Territory – still more isolated but stunningly beautiful with towering mountain peaks. This time they camped in a commercial camp with a hot shower and entertainment by the "Yukon Yuks," a local rock band thoroughly enjoyed by Blaine but not his tired father. And guess what? Spud was "off duty." No bears around tonight!

Back in the USA

Day four found the trio seeing the towering 18,000 foot snow-capped mountains welcoming them to the forty-ninth state. Playing tourists, Brice and Blaine jumped from the truck, as did Spud. Brice set his iPhone on automatic, and joined Blaine, holding Spud in front of him, for a group picture in front of the sign, "Welcome to Alaska – The Last Frontier." At the border crossing, music was blaring Bruce Springsteen's "Back in the USA" – quite a contrast from the Canadian crossing.

Their first hint of civilization, after miles of red pines, was Tok, a military construction camp that helped build the Alaska Highway as a defense against a possible Japanese attack during World War II.

The Japanese only captured two Aleutian Islands, which were liberated by American troops at a great cost of lives.

Another 110 miles of trees, with occasional glances at the majestic mountains, found them at Delta Junction – a good time to stretch and walk Spud, who chased something black into the forest. Was it the bear that they heard stalks humans? And then it was on to Fairbanks – Alaska's second largest city and home to the University of Alaska where Brice's professor taught his virtual classes.

They pulled into a campus parking lot, and Brice pulled up the professor's e-mail with instructions for taking the next mode of transportation – a commercial flight from Fairbanks to Kotzebue, and then a seaplane from Kotzebue to Katooska. Free parking would be provided for their truck at the Fairbanks airport.

Locking their truck and unloading their gear, including a kennel for Spud, the trio hopped a shuttle to the terminal. As long as Spud would be in a kennel – the first time for him – he could ride coach class like a human. "Having Spud with us is a better deal than sticking him with the baggage," concluded Brice. "I've heard horror stories of dogs freezing to death at high altitudes. Not our dog."

The plane taxied down the runway and was airborne for the two-hour flight to the Alaskan West Coast. No terrorists on this plane – only Inuits, fishermen, hunters, scientists, and students like Brice. The plane circled over the Chukchi Sea, giving the passengers a glimpse of the night sun that was still above the horizon, reflecting on the glimmering and choppy water. And then they saw something unsettling from their window – the runway that they were approaching was partially submerged by the sea.

As they descended, the pilot explained, "You see on your right that the runway we will be landing on has water on it. Because of global warming, the sea level is rising, and the water is creeping inland. You also see construction of a sea wall at the East end. They are extending the runway farther inland – just in case the sea keeps rising. There is no reason for concern. The runway is plenty long. We will be landing soon. Thank you for choosing Explorer Airlines. Enjoy the land of the midnight sun, and welcome to Kotzebue. Your connecting flight to Katooska should be arriving at the dock momentarily.

II. Northwest to Alaska

Independence Day in Iceland

As they have every year since 1944 in Iceland, the entire village of Reykjafjordur turns out on June 17th for their Independence Day celebration - this one the 76th. Among the throngs of people flocking to the waterfront is the Steffansson family – Niels – a rugged, ruddy lifelong fishermen; Lara – the loyal, plain homespun housewife; and their son Magnus, an articulate creative college student.

As the most Northerly settlement in Iceland, this tiny fishing village is bathed in 24 hour sunlight. But there's only one problem - you can't wait until sundown to explode the traditional fireworks. The creative solution is to explode them anytime during the festivities.

The state contracts with a private company to construct a huge black sail of fire retardant material just for this "sound and light" show. At a predetermined time the biggest and most modern trawler of the fishing fleet sets sail for a laser-generated "x" visible 500 feet offshore in the Norwegian Sea. At precisely midnight, with the sun still much above the horizon, the fireworks skyrocket toward the black sail, which has been pre-programmed to be hoisted 200 feet into the bright sky. The contrast between the bright flashes of red, white, and blue - the colors of the Icelandic flag - against the dark fabric again achieves the desired effect - Icelandic "ohs" and "ahs." Another Icelandic innovation goes off without a hitch.

Next is a patriotic poem, "My Iceland," read by Poet Ingvar Rasmussen:

Land of fire and ice,
Where the people are so nice.
Where living in the winter means survival,
But in the summer there's always a revival.
We are a nation isolated and small,
But in the world we stand proud and tall.
After all, we lead the world in poets,
And we want everyone to know it.

After seeing and hearing this reading on the "black screen," a cheer erupts from the people on the shoreline and in their boats - horns blaring - they spontaneously sing their national anthem, "O God of our country."

Every celebration must have a parade – but on the sea? The theme this year is "Climate: It Is Changing." Three fishing trawlers are "decked out" with red, white, and blue streamers and flowers, and Icelanders in authentic period dress - each portraying one aspect of the theme. The action on each trawler is projected from the shore onto a huge black mast, so the onlookers - crowding the shore or in dinghies along the coast - can follow the drama.

The first trawler depicts Iceland as settled by the Norse from 870 to 930 during the Little Climatic Optimum warm period from about 500 to 1100. The "black screen" shows the fearsome Vikings coming, not to rape, pillage, and plunder, but to settle this fertile land, abundant with foilage and birch trees. They get to work clearing the land, planting crops, raising hay, building their longhouses of wood and sod, and raising livestock. The climate is conducive to bumper crops, long wool sheared from the sheep, and luscious steaks from their cattle. The people, their livestock, and their crops thrive. This is one of their best times in history.

The next trawler unfurls a huge banner on its side with the heading, "The Little Ice Age: 1500-mid1800s." Now the scene changes dramatically, focusing on the hardships brought about by the colder climate. Bedraggled settlers are shown leaving their farms, with brown, eroded, barren land in the background. They head on foot and on horseback to the sea, crossing ice patches and frozen rivers – even in the summer. Helga turns to her husband Olaf and says, "At least the sea isn't frozen yet. Maybe we can start a new life of fishing in Reykjajordur."

Another dramatic scene shows videos of polar bears reaching Iceland by crossing the sea ice, which had encroached on land. Because of the colder waters, beached whales are shown on the shore, with hungry citizens eager to eat their meat and use the whale blubber for their lamps. These were the worst of times - hay couldn't be grown, animals died from disease, fishing stocks dried up, and smallpox infected humans - a perfect storm for disaster. Even though the population decreased, most survived, and with Icelandic optimism, conditions much improved over time.

The third and final ship hoists her sail with "The Great Warming" banner - this time the black is outlined with a flickering orange glow. The first scene presents a chart indicating the gradual increase in global temperatures since the 1850s. Starting in 2000 and continuing until 2100, the line takes a steep upward climb. The caption reads: "Can you see the hockey stick?" "Yes, shouts an onlooker from the shore, but where's the ice"?

Next we go into a house where a family is comfortably seated around the dining room table. Jon looks out the dark window, trying to peer into the cold winter night. "You know, I never get cold inside ever since the city installed geothermal heat in our house. It's toasty warm, and even too."

"Yes, chimes in his wife Olga, "and I go barefoot all through our house. The floor is always warm."

In the background belches white, non-polluting steam from one of Iceland's many state-of-the-art geothermal plants. In the background you can see steam rising above the sails. In the foreground many people are soaking in the pure blue thermal waters of the Blue Lagoon, Iceland's most famous tourist attraction - in the shadow of another geothermal plant surrounded by black lava cliffs.

Gunner says to his girlfriend Katrin, "You look funny with that white stuff on your face."

"Here, have some," as she throws a piece of silica mud that sticks on Gunnar's face. Now, we're even."

This tranquil setting closes with the caption: "Iceland is fighting global warming. We're now carbon-free! We're waiting for the rest of the world to do its part."

Now the music turns from festive to somber as the next scene appears. A huge wall of water is shown rushing down the hillside into the ocean. Above is a conglomeration of ice, ash, and molten lava. The ice and red hot lava cascade into the sea; the ash darkens the sky. A volcano has just erupted underneath one of Iceland's massive glaciers - shrunk and weakened by warmer temperatures. Down by the ocean lies the now devastated town of Vik. The residents were warned and evacuated safely, but the buildings were demolished. Boards, steel siding, and trees are floating everywhere. Even the beautiful church on the hill was lifted from its foundation and thrown into the depths of the sea. Once again the caption: "This could happen if the earth continues to warm."

The last scene pans the City of Reykjavik from the 75 meter tall Hallgrimskirkha, Iceland's famous state Lutheran church. Around Rekjavik Harbor is a 20 foot high sea wall of metal alloys, buttressed by reinforced concrete. The water is rising and constantly lapping on the seaward side. Drivers on the highway ringing the harbor have to look up to see the tops of the ships sailing by. It is indeed a strange sight, but for now the city is safe. The caption: "How long will the wall hold?"

In the midst of the fireworks and fun on this special day, the festivities end on a somber note about the climate of the future. The villagers quietly disperse to their warm and safe homes, but Magnus is heard saying, "What can we do to protect our town from global warming?"

Inside the Ministry of Sustainability

As one of the scenes in the Independence Day pageant depicted, Iceland's goal is to become the world's first carbon-free society. To implement this audacious goal, the government in 2010 created the Ministry of Sustainability. Every year during the long summer days the minister and her staff retreat to Thingvellier National Park to assess their progress. Returning to Iceland's democratic roots, this time in a geothermally-heated chalet overlooking clear blue Lake Pingvallavatn, Minister Olga Jonsdottir opens the meeting by asking her staff for progress reports in each of their departments.

"Madam Minister," starts Chief Engineer Fridrik Olafsson, "we've made good progress, as you can see on the 3-D screen, by building another three geothermal plants. Now 95% of all homes in Iceland are heated by this abundant hot water coming from the ground on which we live." Shifting gears, Mr. Olafsson continues, "And I'm happy to report that our expertise in geothermal technology is being recognized, even in the USA, where we signed five contracts in Montana, California, and Oregon to help them develop this carbon-free energy. They're finally showing leadership in combating climate change. And we could use their money!"

"Let's hear from the transportation sector", suggested the Minister."

"Thank you, Madam Minister." We are progressing toward phasing out all vehicles using fossil fuels, and replacing them with hydrogen vehicles. Our goal of installing hydrogen fueling stations all around the Ring Road is 90% completed. Within a year anyone with a hydrogen vehicle could drive completely around our island. No other country even comes close to this accomplishment. We are even powering our whale-watching ships and fishing vessels with hydrogen fuel cells. This means we will not have to import foreign oil or drill for it off our shores. Let the other nations fight wars in the Middle East. We don't need their oil."

"Thank you, Mr. Rasmussen, complimented the minister. That is indeed encouraging. However, there's one statistic in which we lead the world that I'm not proud of. As you know, we lead the world in per capita energy use, with the USA second. Sure, almost all of our energy is pollution-free, but where's our conservation ethic? We need to show the world we want to be carbon-free, but also energy-wise. How can we do this?"

"I have a crazy suggestion," said Ms. Gunnarsdottir.

"Let's here it," said the minister. "That's what this retreat is for."

"OK, but don't laugh. Let's see what our citizens can come up with to save energy. We're a literate society, with the highest per capita of writers. Let's sponsor a nation-wide contest for all citizens over 18 to suggest ways to reduce their energy use. We could draft rules and post them on our web site. What do you think?"

"I like the idea," chimed in Mr. Rasmussen. "But we need a prize to motivate them. What could be a fitting reward for their essay or poem?"

"I got it!" exclaimed Mr. Olafsson. Next year the International Polar Year is in Alaska, where scientists will be studying the effects of climate change in the Arctic. We could send the winning entry, and their family, to be observers. Maybe we could learn something from them."

"Is there a consensus on Mr. Olagsson's contest idea?" asked the minister.

(Silence ensued). Hearing no objections, I'll go ahead and ask our staff to draft rules for your review, and with your approval, I'll make sure it's promoted nation-wide. Let's harness the creative juices of Icelanders, and show the world we're concerned about saving energy, too.

This has been a good and productive retreat. Thank you for your reports, and your work toward becoming a sustainable society - the envy of the world. God willing, we will achieve our goal. Retreat adjourned. See you back in Reykjavik."

Magnus Calculates His Carbon Footprint

Meanwhile, back at Rekjafjordur, the village with the spectacular Independence Day celebration, Magnus is still pondering what he can do to combat global warming already affecting his country. He has completed his first two years at the University of Iceland in Reykjavik, and is now home for the summer, working on a hydrogen-fueled fishing trawler. He's taking a summer course via satellite, picking up the professor's audio and video presentations on his laptop, which he uses during his down time on the sea.

Part of his course on "The Science of Climate Change in Iceland," is a requirement for each student to calculate their carbon footprint, using a formula provided by the professor. Magnus types on his laptop www.carbonfootprint.com/calculator.aspx. After inputting his country and region, the formula asks him for the following information:

* For his house - the number of residents and type of energy used
* For any plane flights – their destination, number taken, and class traveled)
* For automobile use – the year, model, make, transmission, and miles driven)
* For other modes of transportation such as motorbike, bus, and rail
* For secondary sources such as types of food eaten, clothes purchased, packaging, recycling, recreation, finances and other services

After this thorough inventory, Magnus clicks the results button to reveal the total tons of $CO2$ he uses for 2020 at 20 tonnes (a figure larger than the US ton). This figure is about the same as the average for the USA, but is more than the average for the industrialized world. But the really revealing figure is that to reduce the effects of the most serious effects of global warming the average has to come down to only 2 tonnes per person. Maybe Iceland isn't as energy efficient as he thought. What can he do about it?

After finishing his college course, he stopped at a local convenience store for gas and Skyr (Icelandic yogurt). As he returned to his car and started to peel off the cover on the deliciously sour yogurt, he noticed a sticker on the lid that read: "Make a difference in the world. Win an essay contest and a trip to Alaska to see the polar bears before they are gone. For entry information, go to www. skyr.com." He finished his yogurt and shoved the label in the glove compartment as he drove away – he had other things on his mind, and Alaska wasn't one of them.

The Contest

After eating a supper of codfish, boiled potatoes, tomatoes grown in the local greenhouse - heated by geothermal steam - and homemade bread baked in a geothermal oven in the ground, Magnus, along with his parents, turned on their flat screen HDTV to watch "Iceland Today" on their state-owned channel. And there it was again: a commercial co-sponsored by the Ministry of Sustainability and Styr, showing an Icelander driving a gas-guzzling SUV, leaving his car idling while he runs into a grocery store. All the while the automobile is vacant, no one attempts to steal it, but the camera is trained on the polluting exhaust, creating a black cloud of smoke. The announcer states: "We don't worry about thieves here, but we don't like polluters. Help create a cleaner environment and save energy. Enter the essay contest sponsored by Skyr. Details at skyr.com."

After seeing the commercial Niels turns to Magnus and says, "Would you like to see the polar bears in Alaska?"

"Sure, Dad, but I'd have to win the contest first, you know."

"Didn't you learn about protecting the environment in your class?" asked Lara.

"Yea, a little bit, but the class was mostly charts and graphs."

"Well, why don't you think and pray about entering the contest. Maybe the Lord will give you ideas. After all, He'd like to protect His Creation, too you know," stated Niels.

With the deadline approaching Magnus still hadn't decided on whether or not to enter the contest, let alone formulating any creative ideas. And then one autumn afternoon, while walking along the beach, with the setting sun sending rays of red ribbons over the ocean, it hit him! He silently thanked the Lord, ran home, immediately fired up his laptop, wrote 250 words, and e-mailed his entry on the last day of the contest. And then he went about his business as a first semester junior majoring in Environmental Science, and forgot about the contest. And he continued to eat Skyr! He also kept calculating his carbon footprint while away from home, seeing if living in the dorm and riding his bike would lower his carbon footprint – which it did.

Then one late February afternoon the Steffansson family was in a local restaurant celebrating the return of the sun with "Solar Coffee" and conversation. Since the restaurant had Wi-Fi Magnus brought his laptop to check his e-mail. He scrolled down his Inbox and opened an e-mail from the Department of Sustainability, which read," Congratulations! You have won our essay contest on creative ideas to protect and preserve the environment." The notice further stated, "We would be pleased if you would read your essay on the public cable channel. Instead of requesting your appearance in Reykjavik, and to save CO_2s, we will telecast you at home, using our webcam link. You will be provided further information regarding the trip for your family and yourself to Alaska in the summer of 2021. Congratulations!"

Magnus interrupted the casual conversation with, "Remember that contest I entered about the environment? Well, I won! I get to go to Alaska! I even get to read my essay over TV! Thank you, Lord!"

"Congratulations, son," said Niels. "See, prayer does work."

"Do we get to go too?" asked Lara.

"Of course, that's part of the deal," reaffirmed Magnus. "They're going to give us more details on the trip next summer. So don't pack your bags quite yet." With that the other patrons in the restaurant clapped for Magnus and assured him they would be watching him on TV.

The Broadcast

The day for Magnus' live broadcast arrived. He even put on a sport coat and tie for the first time since he was in his cousin's wedding party at church. And yes, he even cleaned his room, since the broadcast would be beamed there. Before the actual broadcast, a representative from the Department of Sustainability came on Magnus' computer screen to check the audio and video, together with instructions for Magnus - relax and read your essay distinctly, periodically looking at your screen.

And then the countdown began from Reykjavik: "10,9,8,7,6,5,4,3,2,1, your on." A laser red light came on Magnus' screen, and he began: "Iceland is on track to become the first carbon-free nation in the world. We also have the highest mobile phone use per capita. Combining these two firsts, I am proposing a high-tech method to monitor, and hopefully reduce, the emissions of carbon dioxide - the leading cause of greenhouse gases and global warming.

Nearly all of us carry our cell phones with us wherever we go. Why not put them to use to help save our glaciers? Here's how my plan will work. First, the mobile phone companies in Iceland will manufacture phones that will have special buttons for inputting carbon dioxide emissions, including a CO_2 calculator. The Department of Sustainability will initiate a trade - your present phone for the "Enhanced CO_2 Phone" free of charge. Second, you will have an app to calculate your emissions in real time in the following areas: Home energy use; Transportation; and Food Consumption. Follow the prompts for each category to total your CO_2 usage.

"This voluntary program will run for a year, after which the Department of Sustainability will record the total CO_2 emissions for each participating individual in order to obtain an average per person. Then the third part of my plan will be implemented that will provide incentives to reduce your CO_2 emissions."

Here Magnus pauses briefly and looks directly into his screen for an extended period. "The next year will operate as described above. However, for this period a "cap and trade" system will be implemented. If you find that your total CO_2 use for the second year is below the individual average, you will receive a carbon credit that you can sell to someone using more than the average amount of CO_2. The theory is that the market will encourage all individuals to lower their carbon footprint, thereby assisting the Department of Sustainability to reach its goal of carbon neutrality by 2025.

"Icelanders are hardy people that have been through tough times before, and we are optimistic things will work out this time - God helping us. Thank you, and good night."

The red light went off from his screen, and Magnus fell on his bed, exhausted, but gratified that he had helped inspire the nation to protect their beautiful country. Immediately he received a congratulatory e-mail from the Department of Sustainability, complimenting him on his speech. Now he'd have to wait and see if his far-reaching plan will actually be put into practice – and if it will work.

A Hot Hike

Magnus, needing to get away from all the publicity after winning the contest, headed with his close friend, Erik, to attempt a challenging hike for the first time up Mt. Hekla. They drove to the base of the snow-covered mountain, and, with a partly cloudy sky, started their ascent up the trak on the northeastern side. Their goal was to reach the 1,491 meter summit, traveling southwest to see the crater of the last volcanic eruption, still hot and smoldering with a thick cloud of smoke. The entire hike, if all goes well, would be an eight hour round trip. They both carried a day pack with plenty of water, sandwiches, fruit, energy bars, and their survival gear of cell phones, flashlights, knives, extra clothes, rain gear, and binoculars.

After only a few hundred meters up the trak they read their first sign: "THE HISTORY OF HEKLA: You are approaching Iceland's most active volcano, having erupted 15 times since the settlement era. Several of them, including the first one in 1104, caused considerable damage, as did the eruptions of 1947 and 1970. The most recent ones, occurring every ten years, have done little damage. WARNING: Hekla can erupt with only 38 minutes warning. If you start to feel small tremors under your feet, turn around immediately, and run or walk speedily to your vehicle, and vacate the premises. Enjoy your hike."

Erik turned to Magnus with a worried look, "Are they just trying to scare us, or what?"

"It's a liability thing. Let's go," as Magnus headed upward.

After about two kilometers up the steep black volcanic trak, they came to another sign, "THE GATES OF HELL: 16th Century literature recorded this mountain as the entrance to hell, with groaning sounds coming from the damned, and vultures and ravens carrying more souls to this hot place. Science has confirmed this mountain as a very active volcano, with hell a matter of conjecture. Enjoy your hike."

After reading this sign Erik turned to Magnus, "Do you believe in a real hell?"

"Yes, I do, and I'm glad I won't be going there."

"How do you know? How can anyone know?"

"Do you believe in the Bible," asked Magnus.

"I don't know, but I read it sometimes. There are some good stories."

"Do you believe what Jesus said in the Bible?"

"I believe he was a good man and wouldn't lie," answered Erik.

"Can I tell you a story about heaven and hell?"

"I suppose so."

Magnus began, "This is a story about a poor man named Lazurus who goes to heaven and a rich man who ends up in hell. Jesus describes hell as a place of fire and torment. Anyway, this rich man sees Lazurus in heaven, but can't get there because of a huge chasm. Jesus is the only one who can bridge that gap, but you have to ask him to forgive you for your sins, which we've all committed, accept what He did by dying for you on the cross, and come into your life to guide you. And he promises you'll be in heaven forever if you believe in Him. There's no purgatory or second chance. Think about it."

As they started up again they were both quiet. Maybe Erik was pondering the parable. But they both noticed the clouds becoming increasingly black and thick – but they thought nothing of it. They were determined to reach the summit by noon, and eat their lunch while peering down into the smoking crater. And this they did – right on schedule.

Packing up and checking the gathering clouds again, Magnus suggested, "Lunch break's over. We'd better head down. Sometimes the toughest part is down. We've seen the crater, and it's still hot, so we'd better not go there."

About an hour down the trak Erik looked around, nose in the air, and wondered, "Do you smell something funny?"

"You mean like rotten eggs?"

"Yeah."

"That's sulfur," confirmed Magnus. "It must be coming from the crater we saw. It's probably nothing to worry about."

About an hour later they both felt something shaking beneath their boots. This time they didn't need to wonder what it was.

"We'd better get going," yelled Magnus. "If these tremors continue and get stronger, it's gonna blow! Let's step it up. You remember what that sign said. We've got only a half hour to get outta here."

"I hear you bro."

Their gait now turned into a run, with both men panting and stumbling down the rocky path. Magnus didn't take time to turn around and look at the thickening black smoke rising high above the summit. He remembered what happened to Lot's wife. He didn't want to be turned into a pillar of salt right now!

And then the first chunk landed beside them – a red-hot piece of lava about the size of a soccer ball. They both held their backpacks over their heads to shield them from the "lava bombs" thudding behind them. They found a rock outcropping with a cave underneath it, and crouched down to hide from the heavenly onslaught.

"We're going to have to make a run for it," ordered Magnus. "I figure we're only about 15 minutes from our car. Lord, protect us."

Then they noticed water coming down the trail.

Erik, turning around, asked, "Where's the water coming from?"

"It must be from the melting snow caused by the heating up of the volcano. Let's step it up!"

And then they noticed something more ominous – red-hot molten lava creeping down the cliff above them. It was just starting to pick up speed and depth, covering the volcanic rock behind them and coming closer!

"OK, let's make a break for it," yelled Magnus. Follow me. I'll try to dodge the lava and water and run close to the trees to dodge the "bombs." Watch your footing. It can get slippery, and hot."

Like a couple of stallions leaping from their stalls, Magnus, with Erik close behind, sprinted down the trail, breathing falling ash, and brushing off small particles of lava dropping on them. At one point on the trail they had to jump over the ever-thickening lava and an ever-rising creek.

As they reached the parking lot – both panting like dogs – a "lava bomb" the size of a grapefruit landed on the right fender of Magnus' Hybrid Honda, causing a deep dent. They both clamored inside the vehicle as another missile landed on the roof with a thud.

"Wow, that was close," sighed Erik. "Thanks for praying."

As they left the parking lot, still dodging the "bombs" bigger than most fruits, they noticed other cars parked down the hill on the road. People were getting out, hoping they wouldn't get a "hit from heaven," and taking their cell phone pictures and relaying them to their friends. Magnus had one thing on his mind – to get away from the traffic to a place of safety.

And he wanted to relax?

Through the Northwest Passage

The Icelandic hydrogen-powered research icebreaker, the *SS Sustainability*, silently sped through the relatively calm M'Clure Strait on its journey through the Northwest Passage. As she headed into the open water of the rougher Beaufort Sea, Magnus checked an old travel guide for Alaska to find that the Chukchi Sea, west of Barrow, is usually ice bound, even in July. And the place is frequented by polar bears.

'So where's all the ice and the polar bears?' muttered Magnus to himself.

As the ship passed Barrow, the world's northernmost city, all eyes on deck were trained on a strange creature floating on a small chunk of ice ahead of them. "Look," said Jon, pointing to the starboard side, "there's an animal on that chunk of ice, but I can't tell what kind it is."

Kristin, peering through her binoculars, took a closer look. What she saw was a scientific surprise! The animal was definitely a bear of some kind, with a coat of dark gray, interspersed with flecks of black. A hump on its back behind her outstretched neck was visible, along with a snout that was more flat than long. Her front claws were wide and her body insulated with the odd looking fur.

"Here's my hypothesis," boldly state Sigga. "With the scarcity of ice, the polar bears have been forced to retreat to land, where they have been mating with grizzly bears in order to survive. What you're looking at is a hybrid bear. It'd be interesting to see what the cubs look like when they emerge from their dens in the spring."

Had the three Icelandic scientists, heading to the International Polar Year, made an original discovery? They would soon find out as their 200 foot ice-reinforced research vessel neared their destination – the Katooska Research Station.

The Steffansson family, along with the Icelandic scientists were to witness other surprises as they embarked on their seven day, 4,000 nautical mile voyage from Rekjavik through the long sought after route to the Arctic – the Northwest Passage – now virtually ice-free in the summer. Norwegian explorer Roald Amundson, the first person to navigate the ice-bound passage in 1903-1906, would be shocked to see what the crew, scientists and the Steffanssons were now witnessing.

The first surprise was to see Prime Minister Jonsdottir on the dock of Rekjavik Harbor, congratulating Magnus. "Congratulations, Magnus. I'm pleased to meet you and your parents as she shook hands with the trio. Our research department is working on your cell phone idea and it looks promising. Maybe we'll have a role to play for you upon your return. Feel free to ask our climate scientists about their research and shadow them at the IPY. And we want to learn from the other climate scientists how we can continue to lead the world in our use of carbon-free energy. Bon voyage!"

After churning through the sometimes rough North Atlantic, the *SS Sustainability* reached the southern tip of Greenland on Day 2. To their surprise they saw green grass, hay, and fields of potatoes growing next to the shore! The scientists took thermal imaging pictures, comparing land temperatures with those previously recorded when the land was glaciated. This time the mapping depicted more magenta coloring indicating the land was indeed warming. This dramatic change is good news for the indigenous Inuit population – now able to grow crops.

The Vikings who originally settled Iceland deliberately mis-named it and Greenland to keep settlers away from the former country. Even they would be surprised to see the "greenness" of Greenland today! But this seemingly positive effect of global warming must be juxtaposed against the rapid melting of Greenland's glaciers. Wanting to see this phenomenon "up close and personal" the ship docked at quaint and colorful Ilulissat, Greenland's largest fishing port. It was now Day 3.

South of this port lies the Jakobshavn Glacier, the largest of Greenland's ice cap, and retreating faster with each passing year. The scientists, and the Steffanssons, disembarked and rented a land rover to view this magnificent glacier. They brought their telescopes and measuring devices, set them on a hill across from the bay, and sat in amazement at what they were seeing and hearing. As the glacier continues its plunge into the sea, huge pieces break from the main mass (calving), careening into the fjord with a thundering noise, creating huge waves that could sink fishing vessels that strayed too close. But they also saw some surfers trying to ride the waves – and wiping out.

The icebergs are huge, irregular shapes reminding viewers of medieval castles, with streaks of blue ice illuminated by the summer sun. Some have capsized and overturned, exposing their undersides, which have been made smooth by the water. Tourist ships are venturing into the fjord to see this spectacle of Nature – accentuated by humans. But the scientists are measuring the mass of the icebergs, their coloring, and the frequency of calving. They want to determine if the rate of melting is increasing, and project their findings into the future.

After spending a full day at the glacier the SS Sustainability left Ilulissat on Day 4 and headed North up the West coast of Greenland. The scientists were trying to spot more glaciers calving. They didn't see anything of the magnitude of Jakobshavn, but they did see several huge icebergs bobbing, weaving, and even turning upside down in the rough seas. The waves splashed over the bow, sending the scientists and their telescopes to the lower deck. No more observations, but a chance for the scientists to digest what they had seen.

"From all accounts the calving of all glaciers is increasing, especially the Petermann Glacier – Greenland's largest," concluded Kristin.

"And not only that," added Sigga, "but the mass of the glaciers is also rapidly diminishing."

"Well, soon we'll find out what the other IPY scientists have found out. We've seen the evidence first-hand," related Jon

Now it was time to "hunker down" as the ship was tossed by the wind whipping the 20 foot waves. The Steffansons and the scientists experienced sea sickness for the first time, and stayed in their cabins close to the toilet. But the quiet hydrogen motors, with diesel backup, kept the ship on course throughout the perilous day .

When the storm finally subsided the scientists scrambled atop to find, not more icebergs, but plenty of green grass growing where the glaciers once were. They also noticed many rivulets running into the sea – evidence of more glacial melting and rising sea levels.

On Day 5 the *Sustainability* made a 90 degree turn and headed West through the Davis Strait and into large Baffin Bay. Since their vessel was relatively light they could negotiate the shallow waters of the Lancaster Sound, where they noticed something peculiar.

The passengers woke up on Day 6 to notice that the rocks on the North shore were all black. The scientists knew this was not a volcanic area so prevalent in Iceland, so it had to be from a recent oil spill. The black oily residue was spread on the shore as far as they could see. And there was an eerie silence. The native sea birds and sea otters had disappeared; no doubt victims to this smothering slim.

"I remember hearing about the huge oil spill of the Exxon Valdez back in the 1980s," mentioned Kristin. "This looks like the pictures of the shoreline I saw then."

"And now the big oil companies are already drilling in the Arctic. We've seen oil spills in the North Sea, but Norway has been quick to clean up their spills. Can the other countries do as well?" asked Jon.

"We'll probably find out soon enough. It's already crowded with commercial shipping lining up to exploit the Arctic's riches, and the animals are suffering," sighed Sigga.

No sooner had he finished speaking when one of the crew spotted something black floating on the starboard side. He motioned to the scientists to come and take a look. With binoculars raised Kristin was the first to declare, "It's a dead seal, covered with oily black tar."

"Do you think the oil from the Tar Sands is now way up here? wondered Sigga. "A bad omen for the climate and the environment."

The scientists fell silent as they pondered this new "discovery." Were there more victims to this "black gold rush" out there?

The sleek *Sustainability* now entered the narrow Barrow Strait. The captain cut their diesel engines and relied on hydrogen power to quietly coast through these shallow waters. The slower pace gave the scientists and the Steffanssons the opportunity to scour the sea for marine mammals.

They saw ringed seals swimming in the open waters – an unfamiliar environment for these animals. They need the ice to reproduce and raise their pups. The family lives under the ice, only surfacing to breathe through the holes they claw in the ice. And usually the polar bears are waiting to nab their favorite food. But where are the polar bears without the summer ice as their platform?

And then another sea creature surfaced that caught everyone by surprise. The telltale black and white colors of the Orca whale breached on the starboard side, sending a spray from his blowhole over the bow. And as quickly as the killer surfaced he dove into the murky waters in hot pursuit of his favorite food – the plentiful ringed seal.

"Well, there's a first for us – seeing an Orca this far North," said Kristin.

"Something else we can share at the IPY," added Jon.

"I wonder who will be the king of the Arctic – the new killers or the reigning bears?" pondered Sigga.

Continuing through the Bering Strait the ship encountered small chunks of thin ice that froze last summer, and is now melting under the unusually warm summer sun.

"We've all seen pictures of a solitary, thin polar bear floating on a chunk of ice about that size," said Kristin as she pointed to the closest chunk. " I wonder if we'll see that pathetic picture now."

As the ship sped up before it entered the wider and deeper Melville Sound, Sigga shouted, "My GPS picked up the North Magnetic Pole due North on Brathurst Island."

"Where's Santa and his elves?" questioned Jon sarcastically.

Without hesitation Sigga replied, "They're at the geographic North Pole, along with our little people that live in the rocks under the snow."

They're bantering died down as the wind picked up from the West, whipping the waves, now crashing against the ship's bow. The ship started pitching, sending the scientists, Steffanssons, and the crew below deck into their quarters. And then everyone on board suddenly felt a huge thud on the starboard side, sending the ship lurching to the left. Magnus looked through his porthole, gasping, "It's a large chunk of ice that hit us."

And then on the intercom came the captain's calm voice, "We just ran into an old piece of ice that seemingly came from nowhere. Stay calm and in your cabins. Our crew is checking for possible damage."

The crew clamored on deck to see a gash on the starboard side, about six feet long and a foot wide. Fortunately, it was several feet above the water line, so there was no immediate danger of the ship taking in large amounts of water, although splashes from the waves did manage to slosh into the lower deck, causing those below to climb to the top bunk in their rooms.

After consultation with the crew the captain again came on the intercom with this announcement: "After discussing the situation with the crew, we've concluded that we can continue our voyage without danger of sinking. But just to be safe, we'll travel as close to the shore as we can. I've contacted the shipyard at Prudhoe Bay, and they will be able to repair the gash, but this will delay our trip. Thank you for your understanding and patience."

"Well, thank God at least it sounds like we're safe," said Niels gratefully.

"We even get to see the Alaska pipeline," said Magnus excitedly.

The storm finally subsided, and the rest of the journey to Prudhoe Bay was uneventful, except for seeing a solitary polar bear swimming in open waters far from shore. Maybe he was looking for the ice that hit the ship. When they arrived at their unexpected stop, the welders were ready to repair the gash. However, everyone on board had to disembark. While the captain stayed at the dock to watch the repair work, everyone else headed for what was supposed to be a town to find someplace to eat, relax, and wait. Most of Day 7 would be spent on terra firma.

The scientists and Steffanssons found a rundown bar that served food and drinks. While they were eating their salmon sandwiches and sipping on their favorite beverage a rugged rough-handed rigger yelled from the bar, "Where you guys headed?

Sigga, taken by surprise, was the first to answer, "Katooska in Kotzebue Sound on the Western coast.

"What are going to do in that God-forsaken place?" asked a stocky female rigger snuggling close to the rigger. "If it wasn't for that seawall, the town would be gone."

Feeling a little braver Kristin answered, "We're climate scientists participating in the International Polar Year. We want to study the effects of global warming up here, and see how serious it is."

Rising to his feet and walking toward their table a tall slender blonde-haired rigger said defiantly, "So what are you going to do about it - shut down this oil field? I suppose you think we're responsible for your problem. So what are you going to do about it?"

Sensing the rising tension Jon finally spoke up, "I don't mean to demean your jobs up here, but we've got to switch to less polluting fuels like we have in Iceland. We're almost carbon-free now, and we're waiting for your country to take the lead. You're making progress, but we all have a long ways to go to save our planet."

Before the men at the bar could respond, a welder barged in to inform the guests that they could board their ship. Without saying a word the travelers walked briskly by the bar as those seated collectively shook their heads in disbelief.

"Good luck, you'll need it," shouted one as we left.

"Watch out for the bears," snickered another.

"And don't you buy our oil," was the last parting shot as the heavy wooden door slammed behind them.

And with these snide remarks ringing in their ears, the scientists and the Magnus family headed back to their ship to resume their voyage - now a day later than originally planned. Their greeting at the IPY would be more pleasant as the "patched up" S.S. *Sustainability* headed into Kotzebue Sound - no climate deniers there.

Part Two: The International Polar Year

☙❖❧

III. Project One:
Glaciers and the Land

Settling In: Nebraska

With Brice, Blaine, and Spud cramming their camping gear into Dr. Plankton's Land Cruiser, the Nebraska party headed to their quarters, where they would spend the next three months. On the way they noticed many dome-shaped structures rising from the melting snow. Finally they stopped in front of one, and Paul climbed out.

"This is your yurt, the one over here with the American flag. You'll find it surprisingly comfortable. Go ahead and get settled in before our meal in the mess hall. Here's a map of the grounds, and a schedule of activities for this week. I'll see you later."

As Blaine peered inside, he was impressed. "This is really neat!"

As the three of them entered by the insulated steel door, with Spud already sniffing it out, they saw a bunk bed, a cook stove, tables, and chairs resting on the hardwood floor. They even had lights and a fridge - all powered by propane. Their sink and shower would use recycled water, with their drinking water coming from a separate purified reverse osmosis system. Since the research station was equipped with Wi-Fi, their laptops would work fine. But there was no TV, and no channels to be surfed.

As they walked back out the door and onto the deck, comfortably elevated above the wet ground, they noticed their view of the Chukchi Sea, lapping against the seawall.

"Well, Spud what do you think?" asked Blaine. With his bark and tail wagging, he gave his approval. So did the men – tacitly.

Surveying the bunk beds Brice made the decision.

"Blaine, you and Spud can bunk together on the bottom. I'll hop up to the top, even though I'm not in shape anymore. Let's stash our stuff in here, and walk over to the mess hall for dinner. We'd better put Spud in the bear proof dog run that Paul mentioned. He said they've seen polar bears on shore."

Settling In: Iceland

Several hours later the *SS Sustainability* docked in Katooska, and the six passengers (Magnus, Lara, Niels, and the three scientists, Jon, Kristin, and Sigga) were greeted by one of the IPY hosts.

"Welcome to the IPY, Icelandic scientists. I'm sure you'll make a significant contribution to our Arctic research, and will also learn much during your summer stay. And you must be Magnus. We heard about your winning essay. Congratulations! And this must be your parents," the host concluded. Your whole family will not only see changes up here, due to climate change, but will be able to see our world-class scientists at work."

The host continued, "You probably noticed all the white-shaped domes from the harbor. Well, these cozy and comfortable yurts will be your home during your stay. They are made in Alaska, and can withstand extreme temperatures, all with the comforts of home."

Handing them a map he instructed them, "This map will direct you to your two yurts, the ones with the Icelandic flag on them. Each country has their own yurts for the scientists, and this map will help you recognize their flags as you walk by them. After all, this is a global village up here, dedicated to saving our planet. I'm sure you'll do your part. See you at the mess hall for dinner."

Meanwhile, the scientists were also settling in. Jon discovered that part of the dome was movable in order to observe the heavens. He commented, "That's a good idea when the sun isn't shining twenty-four hours a day. They must have scientists here the rest of the year too. Maybe they could see the Northern Lights as we can back home."

Kristin joked, "No offense, guys, but I like my private quarters."

"Don't be so sure about that," chuckled Sigga. "Just kiddin'"

At that Jon brought them back on track. "Let's get over to the mess hall before the food is all gone, and see who's here." And so they did.

They, along with the Nebraskans, feasted with acclaimed scientists on fresh salmon caught in the ever-encroaching ocean. And then the group migrated to the main meeting hall for the opening session.

"Now we'll finally find out what's going on, and what we're going to do here," predicted Brice to Blaine.

Spud and I will follow you around," said Blaine.

Magnus echoed the same sentiment as he and his family hurried to the hall.

The Opening Ceremony

Dr. Plankton met Brice and Blaine at the back door of the meeting hall, and pointed to a sign toward the back spelling, "U of Alaska Practicum." "Go find a seat in that section, and take copious notes. I'll check with you later."

Through another door walked Magnus and his parents, sitting in the section reserved for guests – also in the rear of the building. And then the festivities began.

The Presiding IPY Officer, Dr. Dimitri Pushkin from Russia, welcomed the scientists, educators, artists, the press, students, and guests to the 4th International Polar Year. He then motioned for everyone to stand while the scientists, with a representative from each country bearing their flag, walked to their respective seats. The music accompanying this procession was soft and somber, denoting the gravity of their task.

Blaine turned to Brice and said, "This looks like the opening ceremony for the Olympics, without the torch."

"Good. We don't need to warm the planet anymore, " responded Brice.

When all the scientists were seated, and the music stopped, Dr. Pushkin began: "Back in the last decade Al Gore and numerous scientists warned the world that we only have about ten years to start making major reductions in greenhouse gases to avoid the most catastrophic causes of global warming. Ladies and gentlemen, that "window" is now closed. We are now on the threshold of the "tipping point," – the 2 degree Centigrade increase in global temperatures since the Industrial Revolution. Once that point is reached there is no hope of preventing the devastating scenarios your models have been predicting.

The countries of the world have made great strides to reduce their use of fossil fuels. But the question remains, 'Are these measures too late to save the planet?' We say an emphatic, 'No.'"

Polite applause erupted, and Dr. Pushkin briefly paused before continuing.

"We are gathered in this rapidly changing environment to study and alert the world of these serious effects of climate change. But the final solution to this, the most serious threat to our planet, rests in the hands of the world's leaders. Your challenge is to conduct the most extensive studies of this problem, using the highest ethical standards, have them peer-reviewed, and ultimately published in scholarly scientific journals, which we hope the politicians will read."

At that a hushed laugh could be heard throughout the hall.

"Some of you may be called upon to testify about your findings before your government. Don't "sugar coat" your findings. Tell the truth, even if ominous, but at the end always give the people hope. Remember, you're speaking for all of Creation.

Tomorrow your work begins. The projects and participants, along with our daily schedule, are posted on our website www.IPY. org. Good night, and God bless your efforts."

As they headed back to their yurt Magnus exclaimed, "I hope our government's goal to become the world's first carbon-free country is mentioned. Surely our scientists will see to that."

"Don't worry about that, son," said Niels. "We've had a big day. Let's try out our bunk beds."

As Brice and Blaine were leaving the hall, they noticed the

sound of a ferociously barking dog, and recognized it as Spud. They ran to his dog run and found him excitedly running around, and occasionally stopping and peering to the west.

"What is it, boy," shouted Blaine. "What do you see? A polar bear? grizzly? I know you don't bark unless there's something there. At least whatever it was isn't around anymore. Good dog. You're doing your job."

Brice went inside the run, and hooked the lease on Spud, and he led them to their new home in the Arctic, with the humans wondering what the sensitive smelling Spud saw. If only he could talk.

The Projects: An Overview

The most important phase of the IPY was about to begin. So after a breakfast of steak and eggs, Brice, Blaine, (Spud was getting several walks per day in between his kennel time) Magnus, Niels, and Lara again headed to the meeting hall to see what was going on. This time there was no "pomp and circumstance," and no flags representing the sixty participating countries. Instead the scientists were grouped by their areas of expertise. They included the effects of climate change on the (1) glaciers and the land, (2) ice in the Arctic Ocean, (3) atmosphere, (4) indigenous peoples and their land and (5) animals in the Arctic Ocean.

The projects leader, Dr. Olaf Johannson from Norway, stepped to the podium and addressed the scientific groups: "Distinguished scientists from all over the world. Today we embark on the most important polar year in our history. Because the climate here is changing twice as fast as the rest of the world, our field projects will only take place near the Arctic Circle. You are already grouped by your areas of expertise, illustrated by your many published books and articles in scientific journals.

However, this time we have an **urgency** to communicate our findings to world leaders, in the hope they will take immediate action to save our planet. Members of the world press will be allowed to report on our findings, and even accompany you during your field trips and projects. Educators will be able to utilize our research in their classrooms at the appropriate levels. Artists and musicians will use their creative talents to communicate the seriousness of our research to the general public. The world awaits your latest research. I know you will up to the challenge. Best wishes for a fruitful year in the Arctic."

After these introductory remarks Magnus huddled with his parents to figure out which topics they wanted to attend first. "I'm really interested in the melting of glaciers, and their effect on our country. After all, we have the largest icecap outside the poles. I'd like to know how long our largest glacier, Vatnajokull, will last."

"Will follow you, son," said Lara. "After all, you're the reason we're here."

Meanwhile, Brice and Blaine were doing the same thing on the other side of the hall.

"Well, Dad, what are you going to do?"

"Well, we don't have glaciers in Nebraska, but I'm interested in learning how long they will be around up here. Let's go to the glacier session first."

Dr. Plankton spotted Brice in the back and asked, "Which session are you going to attend first?"

"Blaine and I are going to the glacier session first. I guess it doesn't matter, since I am required to attend them all anyway, right?

"Yes, that's right," echoed Paul. "You choose the time and with whom you may want to attend. After all, meeting scientists from all over the world is part of your practicum."

But before doing so Brice tried to call Trisha, but there was no answer. Hmmm.

Back At The Ranch

With the summer solstice near, things were heating up at the Sutherland Ranch. The continual drought was already taking effect, making it difficult to grow their crops. In addition the "ditch rider" reduced their irrigation allotment. This meant the hay was growing slower – if at all – and couldn't be cut until later in the summer. Where they formally harvested hay twice, this year it would only be cut once. And the prices were skyrocketing.

Blake, the hired hand, was still doing as good a job as expected under the adverse conditions. He repaired fences, fixed machinery, and herded the cattle from one pasture to another on horseback – and thought of Trisha, who was absent much of the time – looking for another job in town.

One night after Trisha returned from town, she asked Blake to come to the porch for their weekly progress report. After going through the ranch details she asked, "Has Brice ever tried to call you?"

"No, I figured if he wanted to tell me something, he would go through you. Why do you ask?"

"He said he would be in touch with me, but the only time was when he showed me a web cam shot of their seaplane that crash landed, and then he made fun of the pilot who prayed and then crashed."

"Well, maybe he's having too much fun up there with the Eskimos. Just remember, Trisha, I'm here 24-7."

"What do you mean by that?"

"Nothing much. Remember that saying, 'A bird in the hand is worth two in the bush.'"

"OK, our meeting is over. You'd better head back to your bunkhouse."

As Blake left he couldn't help thinking, 'She's getting lonely already.'

Project One: Glaciers and the Land

Greenland's ice sheet could melt at much lower temperatures than previously thought, according to a study published in the *Journal of Nature Climate Change.*
Potsdam Institute for Climate Impact Research

Research into the speed at which Greenland's glaciers are slipping into the ocean suggests that previously predicted rises in sea levels are unlikely. The study provides a lot of rich detail about the variability in ice sheet dynamics, but does not dramatically change our overall understanding. This work shows the situation is not as bad as the worst possible case, but it is still serious for future sea level rise and is certainly more complex than many of the models suggest.
University of Washington, University of Bristol.

An up tick in seismic activity in southern Alaska followed the retreat of glacial ice.
NASA and the U.S. Geological Survey

Iceland's Snaefellsjokull glacier is currently thinning and retreating so fast, particularly since 2000 with unusually warm weather, that it could completely disappear within a few decades.

Icelandic Met Office

The next day Magnus, Niels, and Lara hurried over to the meeting hall to grab a seat for the session dealing with glaciers and the land. Every seat was occupied with scientists, the media, and the teachers. At the back there was a special section for artists, who had their easels and brushes with them to capture the visual aspects of this popular presentation.

The presenter was Dr. Leslie Swensen with the Nordic Institute in Greenland. She came prepared with her Power Point Presentation, and a sound and light show on three screens around the room. On the screen behind her podium were the following topics she was to address:

1. The changing glaciers in the Arctic
2. Where is the melt water going?
3. Effect on the sea levels?
4. Effect on the land?
5. Can the shrinking glaciers be halted?

Before uttering a word, Dr. Swenson clicked her remote and on the surround sound screens appeared a picture of a huge glacier – not pure white as you would expect, but covered with dirt, mud, and rocks. And then the calving begin, as huge chunks broke from the glacier, plunging into the adjacent waters with a deafening roar – sending a tidal wave that appeared to be coming right at those seated in the hall.

"We don't need our 3-D glasses for this," exclaimed Magnus. "I even ducked."

After this dramatic glacial depiction, Dr. Swensen began:

"You have just witnessed the calving of the Jacobshavn Glacier in Greenland. We have measured its mass every year, and it's losing ice at an alarming rate. I've sat on the top of a hill overlooking Disco Bay and viewed huge icebergs criss-crossing the ocean. Their eerie shapes remind you of castles coated in ice blue vertical streaks throughout, floating out to sea. And many of them are much larger than Manhatten."

Seated toward the front were the Icelandic scientists Jon, Kristin, and Sigga. Jon whispered to Kristin, "She doesn't have anything on us. That's exactly what we saw when we sailed past this glacier."

Dr. Swensen continued, "Their mass is measured in gigatons. For you mathematicians that's a billion metric tons. The latest calculations for 2020 estimated a total ice loss from Jacobshavn of 80 gigatons – twice that of 2010. And the projections in the future will probably accelerate.

"We've also measured how fast this glacier was moving. It's now moving twice as fast as ten years ago – a phenomenal 260 feet per day, or over 10 feet per hour, or 2 inches per minute. That means you can stand on it – if you're brave enough – and actually see it move! The old adage, 'Slow as a glacier' may not be true anymore.'"

With that startling fact, a few "Wows" and "Oohs" were heard in the audience of sophisticated scientists.

A scientist from Finland asked, "With this glacier moving at that speed, how long will it be before it completely breaks up in the sea?"

Dr. Swenson thought a moment and then responded, "We can't really project a date – it could be hundreds of years, or sooner. All we really know is the trend is toward acceleration. A related question that I'll mention is, 'Can this rapid glacial melt be stopped?' I'll answer that question during my next topic.

"A mystery that has only recently been solved is, 'Where is all the melt water going?' Researchers visiting Greenland in the summer have noticed water flowing on top of the glaciers. Sometimes it disappears into moulins, holes in the ice where the water rushes down into the abyss with a loud gurgling like a waterfall. And then they noticed something else. The melt water collected into lakes, and then sometimes disappeared overnight, or sooner. Where was it going? Scientists discovered something shocking. This water was somehow draining all the way to the bottom of the glacier, 'lubricating' it so it could slide more easily over the rocks and soil, and hastening its trip to the ocean. Also, when warm ocean water runs under the part of the glacier protruding into the ocean, this speeds up the glacier. Because of these feedback loops, there's very little you can do to stop these glaciers "run" to the sea."

"Another startling discovery is that the Greenland Ice Cap is starting to melt, due to the warmer summers. This massive ice sheet, if completely melted, could raise sea levels by 20 feet. But it would probably take hundreds of years."

Magnus whispered to his father, "I hope we can actually go out on a glacier. I'd like to see what she's talking about."

"Go ahead. Your mother and I will stay back here."

Dr. Swenson continued, "I'll briefly touch on two other related issues: the effect of this rapid glacial melt on the sea level rise, and on the land. As far as the former, the seas will definitely rise because of this phenomenon. The questions are: "How high and how fast?" Once again the projections run the full gamut of gradual to disastrous, and are related to the warming of the earth and snowfall amounts that may actually be greater with warmer temperatures. What I believe to be a realistic scenario is the sea level rise during this century caused by three components, each contributing one foot: the warming oceans, the melting of mountain glaciers, and the melting of the Greenland and Antarctic Ice, for a total of three feet. This rise, even though gradual, could have serious consequences for low-lying countries like the Netherlands, which is already reinforcing its sophisticated system of seawalls and pumps. Also, over 150 million people live along the coasts on ground no higher than three feet above sea level. And the many low elevation islands are especially vulnerable. Coastal cities throughout the world will have to spend billions of dollars to prepare for this, but thankfully they should have time if they start to act now. We're already seeing the consequences of sea level rise on communities on the Alaska coasts, forcing the indigenous peoples to move inland."

Dr. Swenson summarized her talk with comments on the land after the glaciers have melted. "We usually don't think that melting glaciers would affect the land after they leave, but they do in three important ways. One, because the ice no longer reflects the sun back to the atmosphere, the darker land absorbs the sun's rays, contributing to a rising temperature. Two, the land that was once covered by brown tundra is now sprouting trees and shrubs, which are darker in color than the tundra. These plants, which do absorb carbon dioxide also absorb more of the sun's rays, and so the feedback cycle continues. And finally, the melting of these huge masses of ice can actually cause the land to rise. Maybe that would throw off the altimeters a little bit. Just a little humor here."

But no one laughed.

Using her laser pointer Dr. Swenson continued, "You notice on the screen how much of Greenland is shaded red and orange – meaning warm temperatures – by our thermal imaging mapping."

"This is exactly what we found out when we stopped in Greenland on the way here," confirmed Sigga.

"Yea, it's nice that we scientists can agree on our research results," chimed in Kristin.

Dr. Swenson concluded, "I hope this presentation dramatically illustrates how many variables are affected by the melting of glaciers in the Arctic. And we really didn't dwell on the melting in the Antarctic, which could have far more serious consequences for the world. That's a whole other session. It's not a pretty picture, but our job is to present the findings. Hopefully, you members in the press will get the word out to the policy makers. They are the ones who can do the most to halt this alarming trend. I'm not one of them. I'll stick to the cryosphere. Thank you."

Her presentation garnered a smattering of applause. The seriousness of the situation was sinking in – and it was only the first topic.

On The Columbia Glacier

The second part of this session was to allow interested participants to see up close the disintegration of a glacier. The closest glacier equivalent to Jacobshavn in size was the Columbia Glacier near Valdez in south central Alaska. The IPY had available a chartered plane to ferry scientists and other interested parties to this melting glacier.

Since this field trip was part of Magnus' contest prize, he boarded the plane for the two hour flight. As the plane descended he noticed how massive this glacier was – stretching back from the bay as far as he could see. They passed many weird-shaped icebergs on their way to a skied landing on the glacier. No need for rubber tires here.

As the passengers deplaned they noticed a host of dog sleds, with the Siberian Huskies yapping with excitement. The glacier guide greeted Dr. Swenson, "I bet you thought we'd have big land rovers for your tour. The glacier is too soft for that now. These dogs know the terrain and can smell danger. You can trust them. They're used to pulling heavy loads," as he looked around at the several plump scientists, who spent too much time in front of their computers in their offices. You could tell the field researchers from the armchair scientists – the former fit, lean, and muscular.

The guide continued, "You're looking at the largest contributor to sea level rise in North America. The Columbia, once 3,000 feet thick, is now down to only 1,000 feet in some places. It is traveling 100 feet per day in its slide to the sea. We'll be seeing and hearing its calving. We need to be careful when traveling to watch out for crevasses. You can't see them until you're right on top of them. We'll probably also see moulins, and maybe even lakes filling from the melt water. Have your cameras ready, and hold on to the sides of your sled. Your dogsled driver knows the route." With these instructions the group headed from the edge of the glacier in a convoy of dogsleds, with the canines barking as they went.

The "road," if you can call it that, was bumpy as the sled rails skimmed over the small rocks scooped up by the glacier's relentless march to the sea. The dogs, who had been on this route before, were pretty good at dodging the bigger rocks and boulders. Periodically, the sled driver would stop so the passengers could get out and survey the scenery. With the dogs now quietly resting, the guide asked everyone to be quiet for a few minutes to enjoy the solace and take pictures. The only noise was the sound of the wind and the water running atop the glacier. This reminded Magnus of the times he would hike alone on one of Iceland's many glaciers. It also reminded him of one of his favorite Bible verses, "Be still and know that I am God." But the restless dogs, eager to continue the trek, again interrupted this time of silence.

The sleds continued, sometimes going through running water that was running into a distant lake. Their next stop was to view a moulin, with water gurgling down a deep crevasse. Since the passengers were not roped together, they didn't dare peer straight down.

However the guide, who had a rope connected to a rod driven deep into the solid portion of the glacier, walked to the edge of the moulin, and with his crampons firmly set, descended about 100 feet. With his video camera he caught the sight of the rushing water before it disappeared out of sight. He then climbed back to the surface, explaining to the awe-struck spectators, "Don't try this at home. This water is falling all the way from the surface to the bedrock of the glacier, "greasing its skids" so it travels faster. It's another one of those feedback loops that accentuates the problem of glacial disintegration. I'm sure Dr. Swenson covered that in your session."

The group headed back to their sleds to continue their journey on the glacier. The farther toward the sea they went, the more water they drove through. At times it was even mushy in the summer sun. You could even see the slush that the dogs' feet hurled back at the sled, splattering the passengers.

Then suddenly Magnus' sled veered to the right and nearly overturned, skidding along on one runner. Finally it came to an abrupt stop with loud high-pitched screams in the distance. The two lead dogs were nowhere to be found. What had gone wrong with these sure-footed canines?

The driver jumped from the sled, and ran to the front yelling "Ho" to the rest of the dogs, who immediately stopped. He looked down in front of the sled and found his two lead dogs trapped in a deep crevasse – hanging in mid-air by their harnesses, yelping wildly. The other dogs braced themselves - acting as a tether to keep the lead dogs from plunging farther into the hole. And they held their ground – temporarily.

Immediately two scientists jumped from the sled and ran to the front to assist the driver, who was reaching down in the crevasse and furiously pulling the harnesses. But with two dogs, he couldn't lift both of them to the surface. So the scientists formed a human chain, with the one closest to the driver locking his hands around his waist, as did the other to the one in front of him. On the count of "3" they all dug in their heels in the solid part of the snow and pulled with all their strength – grunting and groaning. The lead scientist lost his footing and, like a row of dominoes, the three of them slumped in the snow with their heels still dug in – panting and pondering their next move. And then the chain started slowing moving toward the crevasse, with the sound of the dog's panic barking becoming louder.

Meanwhile, Brice and Blaine and another scientist from a near-by sled sprang into action. Reminiscent of his football days, Brice, with Blaine and the scientist following, sprinted to the scene. The other three members of the human chain stood up, regained their strength, and now the six humans, linked together with their arms, tried again. This time the chain moved backwards ever so slowly- as if in a choreographed dance. Finally first one front paw and then another of the first dog appeared on the soft snow surface. After a few more steps backwards by the straining men the second set of front paws appeared. The rescue was successful!

The driver ran to his dogs. "Duke, are you OK? Scout, how about you?" Duke was licking his left hind paw, signaling something was wrong. The driver went over to try to touch it, and Duke tried to nip him, but the driver pulled back in time. The driver then went back to his sled, pulled out a plastic stretcher, and brought it back to Duke.

He gingerly placed Duke on it, and pulled it back to the sled. In the meantime Scout was up on all fours, and ready to go – unhurt.

"Duke might have a broken leg, so he can't run anymore. Who wants to volunteer to carry him on your lap till we get back to the trucks? I think he's settled down now."

"I will," said Magnus. "I left my dog home, and I miss him. Maybe this will help me, and Duke, too."

"Thank you," said the driver. "But be careful not to touch his sore leg," he said, pointing to Duke's left rear leg. "Just pet him and try to keep him calm. He's "in the boot" now. That's what they do with tired dogs in the Iditirod." The driver handed Duke to Magnus, who licked his face – a sign they were buddies already.

"You were a brave dog, Duke, said Magnus. "You were just about a "goner," but you'll be OK. Just rest in my lap and enjoy the ride. Your work is through for awhile."

Brice and Blaine, overhearing the conversation, slowly walked over to Magnus' sled.

"Thanks for the help," expressed Magnus. You two came to the rescue just in time."

"We have a dog up here named Spud. "I wonder if he could've survived that fall," as Brice pointed to the crevasse.

"He's a tough dog, Dad," chimed in Blaine. "He chased a bear away, you know."

Walking toward Magnus' sled, but not reaching out to pet Duke, Brice introduced himself. "By the way, I'm Brice from Nebraska and this is my son, Blaine. I'm finishing my Master's degree in Climate Change here. We'll probably see you around."

"And I'm Magnus from Iceland." I'm here with my parents and our scientists. We'll probably meet again," as the sled again slowly moved over the crunching snow. Not wanting to brag Magnus didn't mention his contest. That could come later, if the three of them got better acquainted. Right now Duke's welfare came first.

The sleds rolled on for a while until they came within sight of the receding edge of the glacier. With the command from the driver, the dogs stopped and the passengers disembarked – gazing at Columbia's calving spectacular. The guide came over with this warning, "Don't walk any farther to the edge. We don't want another crisis. You never know when another big chunk of ice will break loose and tumble into the sea. It's enough just to hear the tremendous sound of these crashes. With your binoculars you can see the waves created by this phenomenon that is occurring more frequently with global warming."

The guide continued, "Something you may be able to see and feel under your feet is the glacier actually moving. Its current "speed" of 100 feet per day calculates to a little under an inch per minute. Don't worry, you won't get dizzy, but how many people can actually experience a glacier moving?"

For the next 15 minutes the spectators were treated to exactly what the guide described. The cameras and the recorders were clicking, including those of the press. In the distance they could see waves arising above the glacier as a huge chunk fell into the sea. Every so often they looked down to see if they could see the glacier moving. Since they didn't have a reference point to mark its progress, no one knew for sure. They would have to trust the scientists' measurements for a longer period of time.

Then the guide beckoned them back to the sleds. "We'd better get going. We have to get Duke back to a vet to see how he is. How's he doing, Magnus?"

"Other than a little whimpering, he's calm. We're good "buds" now.

As if understanding Magnus, Duke gave him an affectionate lick on his face.

Then the sleds headed back, taking a circuitous route past the lake they had seen at the beginning of their trip. When they reached the lake, they again stopped, but didn't get out. One of the passengers asked, "Is this the same lake we saw in the distance before? It's empty now. What happened?"

"Yes, it's the same lake," said the guide. "It's drained all the way to the bedrock, and, as Dr. Swenson pointed out, this feedback loop is causing the glacier to move even faster. You are fortunate. Not everyone sees the same lake full and then empty in a single day. OK, this is our last stop. Let's head back to the trucks, and your plane back to Katooska. I hope what you saw today reinforced what you learned in your presentation. Thank you for coming out. We only had one casualty today," as the guide looked at Duke, now limping toward the truck.

IV. Project Two:
Ice in the Arctic Ocean:
Will it Disappear?

The ice of Greenland and the rest of the Arctic is melting faster than expected and could help raise global sea levels by as much as five feet this century, dramatically higher than earlier projections.

Arctic Monitoring and Assessment Program

The Arctic Ocean could be essentially free of summer ice only a decade from now.

National Snow and Ice Data Center

As much as 25 percent of the world's remaining untapped oil deposits and 30 percent of its gas lie under the fast-receding Arctic icecap.

US Geological Survey

The Arctic nations are in a new gold rush to stake their claim to the previously inaccessible huge reserves of petroleum, natural gas, and mineral deposits, posing national security risks.

Christian Science Monitor

Brice and Blaine, accompanied by Dr. Plankton, hurried to the assembly hall to get a seat for the next session entitled "Ice in the Arctic Ocean: Will It Disappear?" The presenter was Dr. Steven Rasmussen from the University of Alaska, Fairbanks, and a colleague of Paul's.

"This should be a good session," predicted Paul. "I know he's a thorough researcher with up-to-the date information. He doesn't just sit in front of his computer in his office, but has spent much time on the ice as long as it's safe."

Without further ado Dr. Rasmussen stepped to the podium and asked, "How many of you came to Katooska by ship?" A few hands went up, including the delegation from Iceland - Magnus and his family, and the three scientists.

Dr. Rasmussen again asked, How many of you saw ice through the Northwest Passage?" This time only the hands of Jon, Kristin, and Sigga were raised.

Sigga politely raised his hand, waited for an acknowledgement from Dr. Rasmussen, and began, "Our ship was hit by a large piece of old ice, and we had to stop in Prudhoe Bay for repairs. So the ice isn't gone yet."

"Thank you, Iceland. Did anyone else experience ice first-hand?" This time no hands went up, so Dr. Rasmussen began his Powerpoint.

"My outline will consist of three sets of summer sea ice data: past and present, mapping measurements, and future projections. It goes without saying, but I'll say it anyway, that the Arctic will always be frozen over in the winter. What I'll be illustrating is the mass and depth of the ice at the end of the summer, in September. That's what we look at to determine the effects of climate change on the ice melt.

"Back in the 1980s satellite pictures showed a smaller area of ice left at the end of each summer. In the space of a little over a decade the ice had shrunk from 2.9 million to 2.4 million square miles, a decline of half a million square miles. But this pattern isn't consistent. Sometimes the ice increases for several years, but the overall trend has been downward to the tune of 10 percent per decade. The most dramatic decline occurred between 2006 and 2007, from 2.3 to 1.7 million square miles, a loss in one year that previously happened in 11 years. Was this year a "tipping point," after which the ice would inevitably decline in subsequent years?"

Dr. Rasmussen paused to see if anyone would answer his rhetorical question. Seeing no response – only silence – he continued again. "Since the catastrophic ice loss year of 2007, we have seen consistently smaller ice masses at the end of each summer. But in 2015 there was another significant decline to an even 1 million square miles. Since then the ice loss has continued to where it is today at .5 million square miles. This computes to a total ice loss of over 80% since 1983, or over 20 percent per decade - far greater than the previous decades' decline. We are now using robotic submarines that measure the depth of the ice from underneath, and it too is decreasing. So both the area and the mass are melting rapidly.

"A few more numerical projections for you mathematicians. The biggest guessing game in town is when, not if, will the Arctic be ice-free in the summer? The projections by climate scientists have been all over the board, from the earliest at 2010, which obviously didn't happen, to 2050. Virtually no one is predicting the end of this century, postulated by the IPCC back in the early 2000s. All the models then had to be recalibrated to encompass the fast changes occurring here. Those of you who traveled here no doubt noticed the oceans in the Arctic are basically ice-free except for some old pack ice that takes longer to melt. Our latest models now show that by the end of next summer this ice will also disappear. And then the race for the oil and gas under the waters will begin. It will be a different and more crowded world up here, so enjoy this year of relative solace."

Magnus turned to his parents and commented, "He must've known our ship hit the pack ice she was talking about."

"That's right, son," replied Niels. "I guess were famous for that!"

Dr. Rasmussen, pausing briefly while looking at the Icelandic delegation, began again. "There are many interrelated factors behind my hypothesis: the more the ice melts, the less the sun's rays are reflected back into the atmosphere by the white color. Instead the darker water in the ocean absorbs the sun's rays, which in turn heats up the ocean, which in turn causes more storms, which drop snow on the ice. This snow serves to insulate the ice from growing, making it easier for the ice to melt in the summer, which in turn leaves more open water, and the positive feedback loop repeats itself.

"And if that isn't enough, try adding methane - a greenhouse gas about 20 times more potent than carbon dioxide – into the mix. Scientists in the last decade made a startling discovery that methane was seeping from the permafrost underneath the Arctic Ocean, and bubbling up into the atmosphere. This is another consequence of the feedback loop I just mentioned. This phenomenon is continuing throughout this decade, and, if unchecked, has the potential to throw off our previous models, and, more importantly, the climate. We previously thought methane would only be released when the permafrost on land melts, so were getting a "double whammy." This doesn't bode well for the Arctic ice, nor its icon, the polar bear. We'll continue to monitor this development. We scientists get surprises all the time, and this was a big one.

"And if you want more feedback, here's another one. It's called the Arctic Oscillation that's been particularly strong recently."

Dr. Rasmussen's Powerpoint now showed an animated sound graphic of sea ice being driven by high winds from the Arctic to the Atlantic Ocean. As a thermometer on the screen showed the mercury gradually rising, the ice gradually broke into pieces and disappeared in the water.

"That's cool," exclaimed Blaine.

"Yea, but what he's showing is more warming," concluded Brice. "I'm beginning to get this stuff."

Dr. Rasmussen concluded, "I hope you can see what is happening now. The open water absorbs more heat, which melts more ice, and so on. On this note, we are adjourned. On our field trip tomorrow we will fly over the remaining ice so you can see the changes for yourself. Thank you."

As the session ended Paul asked Brice what he thought of the presentation. Realizing he was answering his professor the Nebraskan replied, "He gives you a lot to think about with his facts and figures. I liked him." But Brice was thinking, "I hope I can understand this stuff. It's not about 'X's' and 'O's.'"

Over The Ice

The sun, still high in the sky, greeted those from Dr. Rasmussen's session who waited early in the morning to board several large US Army helicopters – on loan from the Alaska National Guard. Dr. Rasmussen stood underneath the stationary rotor blades checking the names as the passengers boarded. Filling the last three seats were Brice, Blaine, and, directly across the aisle, Magnus.

Brice turned to Blaine and reminded him, "The last time we flew we had Spud with us. I hope this flight goes better than the last one."

Magnus, overhearing their conversation, piped up, "You're the ones that helped rescue the sled dogs on the ice, aren't you?"

Looking across the aisle Brice and Blaine nodded simultaneously in the affirmative.

"You said you had a dog. What kind is it?"

"He's a Karelian bear dog," answered Blaine. "We thought we needed a dog that would protect us from the bears, and he already has."

Brice, shouting over the roar of the blades, picked up the conversation. "Blaine and I drove up here on the Alaska highway. One night while we were camping, Spud chased a bear away, and we felt safe after that. You'll have to come over to our yurt and see him.

The "chopper's" noise drowned another further conversation as it took off and headed north along the coast of the Chukchi Sea, looking for ice. Since they each had headsets, they could hear Dr. Rasmussen's narration.

He begin, "Usually at this time of the year you would sea ice along the shore, starting to melt. Now you don't see any there, since it melted over a month ago. We'll head up the coast to what was once Kivalina. Since the lack of ice left them vulnerable to the ocean's storms, the villagers finally had to evacuate. After much litigation, the State of Alaska released some of its minerals' trust funds to pay for this relocation. And they were just the first victims of climate change up here. We'll fly over other "ghost towns" that suffered the same fate. Look for decaying ruins in the rising water."

The helicopter turned from the coast and headed out to sea, looking for ice chunks. Magnus thought as he looked through his binoculars, 'I wonder if I can see the chunk that hit our ship.' He did see some old ice, but not as large as the one he experienced on board the S.S. Sustainability. 'Maybe these chunks have melted since we last sailed past them,' he again mused.

Dr. Rasmussen again came on the headsets, "What you're seeing below is a mixture of thin ice and old pack ice. The former will be melting much more quickly than the latter type of ice, which is more dangerous for shipping. But if the projections are accurate pretty soon the pack ice will also be gone."

Magnus turned to Blaine and shouted over the roar of the motor, "Our ship got hit by one of those chunks that Dr. Rasmussen just mentioned. Thank God, it wasn't serious, and after stopping in port for repairs, we made it safely here."

"Good," said Blaine.

Dr. Rasmussen motioned to the pilot to descend in order to obtain a closer view of the ocean. After dropping down to about 100 feet above the water, Dr. Rasmussen, looking through his binoculars and pointing exclaimed, "There's bubbles on the water. That must be methane coming to the surface from the melting permafrost on the ocean floor, like I mentioned in my presentation." He then motioned to the pilot to hover over the area so we could see if anything else would develop.

After a few minutes the water was interrupted by the breaching of an Orca Whale, displaying the full length of his beautiful black and white body glinting in the bright sunlight. As quickly as he surfaced he was gone, with his massive tail the last to be submerged.

"This is a different kind of whale watch," exclaimed Magnus.

"Yea, we got a 'birds' eye view. Pretty cool," said Blaine.

Dr. Rasmussen again got on the intercom. "In previous years you would've seen polar bears on the ice instead of this whale, who is now at the top of the food chain. The polar bears have had to retreat to land to find their prey, and they're hungry. Our government finally declared them a threatened species, due to climate change. I don't know how much protection they'll get with that status. In my opinion, they should be listed as an endangered species, but I'm not a politician."

Dr. Rasmussen gave the high sign to the pilot and they ascended to their former altitude and turned back toward the coast, heading north to Point Hope, jutting out into the sea. They expected to see a community of around 700 people, but instead saw another "ghost town," – another victim of the sea's rise.

Again the pilot descended for a closer look. Maybe there were still brave villagers fighting the flood, but they needed more than sandbags. The passengers could see a half-built seawall that must not have held back the waters - but no residents. What happened to them? Did Alaska use her oil revenues to bail them out, and relocate them? If so, where are they now? There was no sign of civilization below them. Only a silent testimonial to global warming. How many more villages will suffer this same fate?

Now the "chopper" did a "180" and headed south to Katooska. Brice thought, "I saw pictures of Kivalina during my classes, but this is the real thing. Point Hope looks the same. Alaska has a crisis on its hands, trying to fight the rising sea, and Mother Nature is winning. What can be done?"

The trip back was basically devoid of sea ice, except for a few small white chunks dotting the calm blue ocean. And then Dr. Rasmussen spotted something, and shouted through the intercom, "Look down to your right with your binoculars. What do you see?"

After a few seconds Blaine exclaimed, "I see a polar bear on that small chunk of ice!" as he pointed. "Do you see it, Dad?"

"Yes, he seems pretty thin."

"He's a pathetic looking creature, one of God's best creations, and look at him, said Magnus."

Dr. Rasmussen, pointing downward, interrupted, "He probably hasn't eaten for a long time, since his favorite food, the ring seals, are no longer around. He's probably trying to swim as far as he can in the open water looking for something to eat, and just happened to see this ice to rest on. He can't go on very long this way. Maybe he'll be able to make it back to shore, and see what he can scrounge up there. He's no longer the proud poster child of the Arctic."

Still pointing toward the bear Dr. Rasmussen continued, "And there's something else he has to worry about. See that Russian oil tanker steaming toward him? It's coming pretty close and it can't stop very fast. I hope the bear senses this new danger."

All the passengers were straining to get a view of this unfair match up. As the bear came closer to the tanker, the captain sounded his horn, which resounded in the plane's cabin.

With his binoculars focused on the incident Dr. Rasmussen shouted, "Look, the bear stopped swimming, looked around, and turned around. At least he's safe for now."

"Thank God," muttered Magnus under his breath.

And the Nebraskans uttered a sign of relief, as did the other passengers. Were they witnessing another obstacle for the polar bears?

As the helicopters heading back to Katooska, Dr. Rasmussen was still scanning the horizon with his binoculars. Suddenly he motioned to the pilot to descend. The other "choppers" followed and started circling around a large black pool floating from a large oil platform directly below them. And they saw another polar bear swimming toward this murky, sticky goo. Would he turn around in time to avoid being coated with this smothering tar?

Dr. Rasmussen explained, "We now have an Arctic Council that's supposed to respond to oil spills that are becoming more frequent with these navigable waters. And if these animals and the indigenous peoples that depend on them don't have enough to worry about, we're having more frequent and intense storms in the oceans up here. So what happens to the oil rigs when a rogue wave washes over them? Can the oil companies handle this type of disaster? It would make the Exxon Valdez and BP oil spills look innocuous by comparison. Furthermore, we have more whales and migratory birds as the ice recedes. Welcome to the new gold rush – this time on the water. Well, enough of the gloom and doom for now. The pilot said we're running low on fuel, so we'd better head back. See you on land."

As the helicopter settled down on the landing pad, Dr. Rasmussen thanked the passengers for coming on this sobering tour, and closed with this: "You've seen the rapid changes happening in the Arctic due to climate change. Some of you may want to write articles, not only in scientific journals, but also in the popular media, describing what you saw. Maybe some of you may even want to propose solutions to your elected representatives. It's going to take a worldwide effort to solve this crisis."

As the passengers disembarked Brice invited Magnus over to their yurt to see Spud, ready for a run. After sniffing the new human, the four of them were off to the ocean – this time devoid of bears, ships, and oil spills.

V. Project 3:
What's in the Atmosphere?

"Soot (black carbon), ground level ozone, and methane may account for up to 40 percent of observed global warming in the Arctic."
Arctic Council, composed of the foreign ministers of Canada, Denmark, Finland, Iceland, Norway, Russia, Sweden, and the USA

"A substantial amount of methane is being vented to the atmosphere from the Siberian seabeds, creating the possibility of a 'tipping point' being crossed whereby abrupt and unstoppable climate stabilization could be caused."
National Science Foundation, USA

"Carbon dioxide and methane are substantially more abundant now than at any time during the last 650,000 years."
Intergovernmental Panel on Climate Change

"To avoid dangerous climate change, the world must hold global average temperatures to between 3.6 and 5.4 degrees Fahrenheit."
European Union

Magnus and his parents hurried into the hall, looking for seats in the front of the hall. They wanted to see their three scientists as they presented on volcanoes. However, the main speaker was Dr. Andrea Johnsen, a climate scientist from Sweden.

Dr. Johnsen began her remarks by making reference to the environmental rankings, which were just posted on the IPY's website: "I am pleased to learn today that my country is again the world leader in protecting the environment. However, we all need to be more committed to saving the planet from the most serious effects of global warming. That's what I want to address in this session."

Dr. Johnsen was interrupted by a question from one of the members of the press seated in the rear. "Dr. Johnsen, I don't mean to be disrespectful, but you scientists can get pretty technical when talking about this subject. In order to engage my readers on climate change, they first need to understand, in layman's terms, the causes and consequences of global warming. And before that I need to understand this complex subject myself. Would you please oblige me in this matter?"

"Yes, sir, that's what this session is about. A general primer on the various greenhouse gases and their relative strengths once they reach the atmosphere. I'll also mention various temperature increase scenarios, and their likely effect on the environment. Finally, I'll discuss black carbon and methane as contributors to global warming. And then the scientists from Iceland will discuss the impact of volcanoes on an opposite concept – global cooling. I will be using charts and graphs, which you will find in your syllabus. Now, let us begin.

"When we think of greenhouse gases what immediately comes to mind?"

A unified cry of "CO2" rang throughout the hall.

"Even the average non-scientist knows this. This is the one that gets the most publicity – right, you members of the press?" as Dr. Johnsen pointed to "press row." The guy with the question nodded sheepishly. "And it's the easiest to control if we stop burning fossil fuels – a policy question I won't get into now.

"But there's actually a more potent greenhouse gas, methane – approximately 20 times as dangerous to the atmosphere as is CO2.

You've seen its destructive effect as it melts the permafrost on land, causing buildings to collapse. You also saw it seeping up from the permafrost under the Arctic Ocean – a recent discovery. And then there's all those cows chewing their cud, burping, and you know what. Is anyone here from Nebraska?

A yell went up from the back, "Go Big Red. We're proud of our cows and our football team," shouted Brice. "Don't take them away from us. Just furnish us with diapers and we'll take care of them."

A roar of laughter erupted from the hall. And then someone yelled, "Go, Sooners."

Dr. Johnsen, not a football fan, was puzzled by these outbursts, but waited patiently for the rivalry to subside.

"Another agriculturally-related greenhouse gas is nitrous oxide, commonly known as laughing gas. This comes from soils upon which too much nitrogen fertilizer has been used. So agriculture is a significant contributor to greenhouse gases.

"The largest greenhouse gas, by volume, is water vapor. However, we can't do much to control the precipitation, although we've tried seeding the clouds with limited success. We need a certain amount of water vapor to keep the earth from freezing. But adding CO_2 into the atmosphere heats up the air, causing it to soak up more water from oceans, lakes, and rivers. Thus this increased water vapor acts as an enhanced greenhouse gas, heating the earth even more – another example of positive feedback.

"So the culprit goes back to CO_2s – the leaven in the atmosphere. A little bit goes a long way toward heating up the globe."

"Scientists measure the amount of CO_2 in the atmosphere by ppm, or parts per million. Don't ask me how large a part is. It's just a common phrase, which you, the press, said you wanted. It shows the relative density of atmospheric gases relative to the saturation point, which in this case would be one million. Is that clear, you members of the press?

Another unified "Yes."

Dr. Johnsen continued, "Scientists have been rather accurate in measuring the amount of ppm in the atmosphere. For example, in 2010 the number was 390. With an increase of 2 ppm per year, the number has jumped over 400 to 412. But now the rate of increase has also been increasing, mainly due to the rapid industrialization of some of the developing countries such as China, India, and Brazil. With the ten year window for CO2s to start decreasing having passed, there is a real **urgency** to reduce this important ppm number."

At this point Magnus turned to his parents and said, "Are you getting this stuff?"

"I'm not into numbers and models," replied Lara. "I'm waiting for our scientists to talk about volcanoes."

Niels chimed in, "Me too. I understand them. After all, we live with them."

"The next number is the one that is controversial. That is the one that scientists have labeled the 'tipping point,' meaning that if this number is reached at some point in the future, the effects of global warming will cause catastrophic damage to the earth, and these consequences cannot be reversed. Some scientists advocate a higher number like 450, giving the global community a fighting chance to gradually reduce reliance on fossil fuels.

"Dr. James Hansen from the USA thinks we need to actually lower the number to 350 or less to take into account the long-term amplifying effects of warming. He says this can only be done by leaving most of the fossil fuels in the ground, sequestering the carbon from existing coal-fired plants, drastically reducing our carbon footprint, and rapidly switching to renewables. Dr. Hansen also thinks that if we make serious reductions in methane, ozone, and black soot we could ease the requirements on CO2 by 25 ppm.

"For purposes of this IPY, I'm recommending we split the difference between these two numbers, and aim to reduce the ppm to 375 by 2025 - a mere four years before it's too late.

"Too late for what?" shouted someone from the back.

Dr. Johnsen responded, "Thank you for that. That's the next part of my presentation. The various scenarios I'll show you will answer your question, and illustrate the **urgency** to act. Are the policy makers listening? You members of the press need to make sure they are. Let's take five and I'll be back. Thank you."

As the audience milled about the smorgasbord of salmon sandwiches, Magnus spotted Brice and Blaine - where else? - by the table.

"So are you getting all these numbers and this ppm stuff?"

"Well, math wasn't my strong suit in college," replied Brice.

Blaine piped up, "Yea, but I get the **urgency** thing. It's up to us to do something about it."

"Well stated," answered Magnus as they filed back to their seats for the next presentation.

With her PowerPoint on the big screen, Dr. Johnsen began again.

"I'm going to throw a lot of scenarios at you to emphasize the adverse effects of global warming, so hang on. Since the Industrial Revolution the earth has warmed by 1.5 degrees Fahrenheit. Since the CO2s stay in the atmosphere for centuries, we can't do anything about it.

"So the scenario continues upward from there. For an increase of 2 degrees Centigrade (3.5 degrees Fahrenheit), we can expect the following:

Lower crop yields, resulting in a risk of hunger to 10-30 million persons.

Increase in human health problems.

Less water availability and more droughts.

Environmental refugees fleeing the above problems.

More intense rainfall and hurricanes.

Increase in heat waves and fires.

"You may remember the world community has set a goal to not increase average global temperatures more than 3.5 degrees Fahrenheit, or 2 degrees Centigrade above the pre-industrial level. As we know by now, the above scenario is now being played out throughout the globe. In addition to the above vulnerabilities increasing, here's what will happen if we exceed this number by another degree Celsius(3) or 5.4 degrees Fahrenheit:

Bleaching of most of the world's coral reefs.

Potential sea level rise of ten feet, due to melting of the Greenland and West Antarctic ice sheets.

Loss of tropical mountain glaciers.

Significant reduction in monsoon rains caused by a weakening of the ocean conveyer belt which carries currents throughout the world.

Serious threat of inundating low-lying coastal areas and islands, which is already happening right here in Alaska.

Between 20 and 30 percent of all species risk extinction.

"Once again the above harmful effects are cumulative, with an additional one degree Celsius (4) or 7.2 degrees Fahrenheit adding the following new vulnerabilities:

A sea level rise of forty feet due to the almost complete melting of the Greenland and West Antarctic ice sheets.

Major species extinction.

Widespread death of coral reefs.

"This scenario I have just explained would happen if the ppm reached the higher limit of 450 that some scientists see as the "tipping point." As you can see, there will be some pretty serious consequences for our world.

Dr. Johnsen continued: "There's one last scenario that would happen at a ppm level of 550, the highest our models have predicted. Do you want to hear it?"

A member of the press shouted, "Go for it. The public thinks we like to print the bad news. Maybe we can shock the decision-makers into taking action."

"OK, here it is. Remember you include all of the above scenarios, plus the following:

Plummeting global food production, leading to riots in many countries.

Shutdown of the ocean circulation system and a major release of carbon from the thawing permafrost, which we are already seeing in the Arctic.

Up to one-fifth of the world's population affected by flooding.

Up to 160 million more people at risk of hunger.

Up to 3.2 billion people suffering from increased water scarcity.

Almost all the boreal forests and large tracts of the Amazon rain forest gone.

Major ecological changes over forty percent of the world's land masses.

Very substantial increases in human deaths from malnutrition, infectious diseases, heat waves, droughts, and floods.

Dr. Johnsen concluded her remarks with, "Not a pretty picture, indeed, but this is what the science sees. Hopefully the world will wake up and take action to reduce CO2s to at least 375 before we see any of the above scenarios."

Because of the seriousness of her remarks, Dr. Johnsen only received a smattering of applause. And she suggested a break before the next topic, so the audience could digest the seriousness of her talk.

As Magnus milled around the hall, Blaine and Brice saw him at the refreshment table, drinking juice and chomping on a cookie.

Brice struck up a conversation with Magnus, "Pretty sobering stuff, huh?"

"Yea, it makes you wonder how long this world will be around."

"What do you mean, we've been around for billions of years, and we'll probably be around for billions more," stated Brice proudly.

"Have you ever read the Bible?" asked Magnus.

"No, I don't believe in it. Besides, what's that got to do with today?"

"Well, it says someday the earth will be destroyed by fire. That's global warming to the extreme. I bet the scientists haven't factored this into their models."

Magnus didn't pursue the "debate." 'I'll pray for a better time,' he thought.

Changing the subject, Magnus asked Blaine, "How's Spud doing up here?"

"He's getting used to it. I take him on long walks every day. I feel safe with him. He's better protection than my bear spray."

Brice, overhearing the conversation, replied, "Yea, the other day we took him down by the sea and he was acting strange."

Blaine finished with, "I had him on the leash, and he started running into the water, and was barking furiously, but I pulled him back before the waves hit him. Don't know what he smelled."

"Maybe it was a polar bear coming to shore," concluded Brice. "We'll never know."

Global Cooling, Compliments of Volcanoes?

Project director Olaf Johannson from Norway stepped to the podium to introduce his neighboring Icelandic scientists with these words: "We will now hear from the world experts on volcanoes, where else but from the land of fire and ice, appropriately named Iceland. Since Icelanders are listed in their phone book by their first names, I will introduce these scientists as Sigga, Katrin, and Jon. Applauding loudly in the front were Magnus, Niels, and Lara.

Sigga began: "You've probably heard the off-hand remark, 'All we need to cool the planet are a few good volcanoes. Bring them on!'"

With no further introduction the hall darkened and three screens simultaneously showed spewing red-hot lava and black and gray ash clouds from a series of volcanoes. Some of them were accompanied by surround sound thunder and electrifying lightning bolts streaking across the darkened sky. This dramatic sound and light show lasted for perhaps ten minutes, and then the lights were again lit.

It was now Katrin's turn, "You have just witnessed a composite of our volcanoes over the years, including our most active, Hekla, which erupted last year, and is due for an eruption every ten years.

Magnus whispered to his mother, "Erik and I can vouch for that. By the grace of God we escaped that eruption."

Katrin continued, "Those of you who have flown on Icelandair may have noticed we name our planes after our volcanoes. Has anyone traveled on Hekla? Was it a wild ride?"

The audience looked a little puzzled and amused at the same time. Finally one person asked, "Can you choose to fly on a dormant volcano and be guaranteed a smooth ride?" Laughter erupted (no pun intended).

Katrin continued, "Iceland's most devastating display was the Laki eruption of 1783-85, which produced the largest lava flow in historical times. It was responsible for killing one-fourth of the population through famine and disease, as well as a loss of 70% of the livestock. Some even blame these harsh conditions for starting the French Revolution. And more relevant to our discussion, the volcanic cloud lowered the temperature in the Northern Hemisphere by about 2 degrees Celsius, or 3.5 degrees Fahrenheit."

Now it was Jon's turn again. "In the 20th Century there have been three major volcanic eruptions - Mount Agung, El Chichon, and Mount Pinatubo. Even though Mount St. Helens wasn't as big as these three, I'll mention it to make my point. I'll also factor in all the volcanoes that have erupted in Iceland since 1750, including all of Hekla's eruptions, and the infamous Eyjafjallajokull of 2010 - can you pronounce it?

A non-Icelander from the middle of the hall shouted, "I won't even try, but I know it means 'island mountain glacier,' which certainly makes sense."

"You're right," continued Jon. "This volcano, which if you remember disrupted air travel during 2010, was a prelude to the much bigger Katla, which has erupted 16 times since our settlement era, and which erupted again in 2014. And our civilization still survived, contrary to the Mayan calendar predicting the end of the world in that year.

"Fortunately, before the Katla eruption, Icelandair, with the help of German technology (a modest cheer was heard from the German delegation), developed a jet engine that can safely fly through volcanic ash. These engines now use infrared sensors to detect an active volcano up to 100 miles away. Today most European and North American airlines have adopted this revolutionary engine, which has solved the flight delay problem. On our field trip tomorrow we'll be testing these sensors on our plane.

"Even though volcanoes do influence portions of the globe by cooling it, this effect is short-lived. At most the climate may be altered for a few years before again heating up, due to greenhouse gases, which have a much longer life span in the atmosphere. Only a long period of volcanism would significantly cool the planet, and act as a brake on the greenhouse effect now accelerating climate change.

"If you think our country has had a restless past, you're absolutely right. But here's something even scarier if the globe continues to warm. Because our glaciers are melting rapidly, their weight upon our many volcanoes will lighten, making it easier for the magma to rise to the earth's surface and erupt. So we have a vested interest in combating climate change. Why do you think we're working so hard to become carbon-free?

"In summary, the following chart illustrates the relative influences of various types of greenhouse gases compared to volcanic eruptions. As you can see," as Katrin used her laser pointer, "the total amount of CO_2 pumped into the atmosphere from 1750 to 2010 is twelve times that of all the volcanoes during the same time period.

"So, can we count on volcanoes to solve the global warming problem? Only briefly, and only on a localized scale. Iceland is using its technology in the areas of geothermal, hydroelectric, and hydrogen to reduce its greenhouse gases, and not relying on its volcanoes. So much for that myth."

And now it was Sigga's turn again. "As long as we're dispelling myths causing global warming, there's another one relating to sunspots, which are alternately hotter and cooler during their ten to twelve-year cycle. Those who debunk human-caused global warming attribute the planet's heating due to active sunspot activity. The evidence suggests otherwise. The sun has recently experienced a slight cooling trend that would be offset in seven years by our CO2 concentration. So much for that myth."

With that the three Icelandic scientists thanked their audience, and ended with "Bless, bless" (goodbye in Icelandic), and a standing ovation from Magnus, Niels, Lara and the others in the audience.

The Problem with Soot

Dr. Johannson again took the podium to introduce the final speaker for the afternoon, Dr. Ingrid Gunderson from Finland, to discuss black carbon.

Dr. Gunderson caught the attention of the restless audience (it had been a long session) by starting, "I'm holding something in my closed hand that is the third-most potent contributor to global warming after carbon dioxide and methane. What is it?"

The audience quickly quieted as they pondered this mystery.

Finally a lady from Latvia ventured a guess, "Is it ozone?"

"Good guess," responded Dr. Gunderson. "But this substance in my hand is visible, unlike ozone."

A gentleman with a high-pitched voice squeaked, "Soot."

"You're absolutely right," she said as she unfolded her hand and threw black particles into the air, landing on several people in the front row, who quickly brushed it from their clothes.

Dr. Gunderson continued, "The common name for this sub-stance is black carbon or ice dust. The scientific name is cryoconite. It comes from the burning of fossil fuels, namely coal, and biofuels, mainly wood. The good news, if you want to call it that, is that this pollutant doesn't last in the atmosphere nearly as long as does $CO2$.

"So, how, you may be thinking, does this black carbon contribute to global warming, since, as we have just heard from the Icelandic scientists, a similar substance - ash from volcanoes - can cool the planet temporarily? Good question. I'll now answer it.

"Once this pollutant enters the atmosphere, it can encircle the earth and land on the Arctic snow and ice. Being a dark color it absorbs the sun's rays, and starts to produce tiny round holes in the white Arctic, finally turning it into water. Hence, what was formerly a reflective substance - the snow and ice - is gone, leaving the dark-er water to absorb the heat, thus contributing to a warmer Arctic. Estimates have been that this type of air pollution has contributed to about a half or quarter of the overall temperature increase. This warming could trigger a positive feedback loop, whereby the snow melts earlier, causing earlier forest fires, which in turn would send more of these black particles into the atmosphere, and you know the rest of this scary story.

"Conversely, removing these aerosols through strict laws would significantly reduce this problem. Once again, we're back to the de-cision-makers having the last word. It worked to reduce the ozone layer over Antarctica, so it can work again here in the Arctic. So I'll end this serious topic on a positive note. Thank you."

During the courteous applause Dr. Olafsson again returned to the podium with these closing remarks: "So now you members of the press, the public, and scientists have a summary of the various greenhouse gases, natural and man-made, together with their potency. Now you know why the emphasis on combating global warming is on reducing CO_2s. Thank you to all the presenters of this very informative session.

"Tomorrow morning we have chartered a commercial passenger jet to fly over Mt. Redoubt. We want to see an active volcano from above, and also test the new and improved safety detection sensors. After all, we're here to be on the cutting edge of research. Those of you who signed up for this trip will meet at the Katooska airport. You will notice the seawall protecting the runway is now complete - just in time. The ocean is still rising. See you then."

As the crowd was dispersing, Brice and Blaine found Magnus and congratulated him on the Icelandic scientists' presentations.

"You folks certainly know your volcanoes," complimented Brice.

"We're known as the most restless place on earth," replied Magnus. "Maybe someday you can visit me there. I'd love to show you our fire and ice."

"I hope we can," Brice affirmed as he gave a thumbs up to Blaine.

Little did they know that hope would turn into reality soon.

Blaine, Magnus, and Spud

Spud was ready to run by the time Magnus reached Blaine's yurt. The human-canine pair had their usual route around the compound and extending along the shores of the Arctic Ocean. With the summer sun never setting, they couldn't see the sun setting over the ocean, but it was beautiful with the sun glistening on the ever-melting summer ice. Spud didn't care. With his leash removed, he was looking for anything that moved - from bears to sea gulls.

"Do you have a dog back home?" asked Blaine.

"Sure do. Since our family raises the Icelandic sheep I showed you on my cell phone, we got the best sheep dog, a red and white Border Collie. They're the smartest dog, you know. We trained Sally ourselves."

"Spud's pretty smart, too," countered Blaine. He knows where the bears are, and flushes them out of the trees. And then they run away."

"Has he done that here?"

"Not yet, but I know he's caught their scent, and barked at them. Since the ice on the ocean here is melting and disappearing, there are hungry polar bears coming on the shore. Look, there's one now! Spud, go get him!" yelled Blaine.

Sure enough, Spud headed toward the ocean, barking at the thin polar bear swimming toward the shore. When the bear heard Spud's bark, he started to circle in the water, and then changed his course and headed out to sea, looking for any ice floe upon which he could land.

"See what I mean," Blaine stated confidently. "He just protected us."

As Spud returned toward the pair, Magnus bent down and petted his wet fur. "Thanks, Spud, you're a brave dog."

The rest of the walk was uneventful as they headed back to the yurt, with Magnus thinking, "I wonder if Sally would protect me like that from the coyotes around our farm?"

Brice Makes the Call

As the boys were romping with Spud, Brice was again seated on his favorite stool at his favorite "watering hole," the "Midnight Sun Saloon." He found this spot when first walking around Katooska, and had been frequenting it ever since. Although not much of a drinker back home, he fell into this habit in his new and strange surroundings. Besides, he was away from Tricia and the ranch responsibilities.

"I suppose you want the usual shot," said Sara the familiar bartender.

"Make it a double this time," requested Brice. "I need to get up the courage to call home."

"Why? Somethin' wrong?" asked Sara.

"I hope not. It's just that I promised Tricia I would call her regularly, and I haven't been very faithful with that. Besides, she hasn't texted me for several days. Maybe she's given up on me way up North."

"Well, I haven't given up on you," said Sara seductively as she leaned forward in her skimpy cocktail outfit.

With a quick glance down, Brice, faking like in football, stammered, "Wha wha what do you mean by that?"

"You know what I mean?" as Sara came closer.

"Now you're getting me all flustered, and I need to call home," said Brice nervously.

"Here, have another drink on me. That'll calm you down."

"Thanks, Sara. You've been good for me," said Brice as he grabbed her hand and kissed it. "See, chivalry is still alive, even in Alaska." As he pulled out his cellphone, he motioned to Sara to wait on the couple coming in the door.

Brice then stumbled from his stool, staggered to the corner by the window, shielded his phone from the bright sun, hit autodial, and waited. . .

On the other end, checking her caller ID, Tricia said sarcastically, "Well, it's about time."

"Time for what?" feigned Brice.

"For your regular call?"

"Honey, I've been busy up here. Remember, you didn't want to come up here with me," Brice reminded Tricia.

"Who have you been busy with?"

"What do you mean by that?" asked Brice, faking innocence.

"The loud music and talking in the background doesn't sound like you're working very hard on your practicum," surmised Tricia.

"Well, I gotta relax after a hard day, you know."

Finally Tricia got up the nerve to ask Brice point blank, "So, did you find a floozy up there?"

"Sara's just a good friend," said Brice slyly as he hit the "Speaker On" button on his phone, and went back to the bar, holding his phone to Sara's mouth.

"You bet, Mr. Cornhusker," she replied romantically as she moved closer to Brice.

Tricia thought about hanging up after that remark but came back with, "Well, two can play that game. Blake and I are handling the ranch quite well. We have nightly conferences on our porch. You don't seem to care about it anymore. Anyway, say "hi" to our son. He's called me more than you have. He wonders where you go at night. Isn't it hard to hide from the midnight sun?"

With that Tricia pushed the disconnect button on her cell phone. She'd heard enough. And Blake would certainly want to know what was going on "way up North." Tricia was losing her patience with Brice, and getting lonely on the prairie. How would Blake handle that?

And how would Brice handle Sara, now that his fans weren't around? He finished his drink, gave Sara a nice tip and a goodnight kiss, and again staggered out the door and headed back to their yurt, hoping Blaine wouldn't see him try to climb into his bunk. But Spud would, and wouldn't say a thing!

Seeing a Volcano up Close

Their day had started routinely - to view the 10,192 foot Mt. Redoubt volcano in the Aleutian Range of southwestern Alaska. The three, along with IPY scientists, boarded an Icelandic Express two-engine prop-jet, flown from their island country especially for this trip. The three Icelandic scientists (Jon, Kristin, and Sigga) who presented previously on volcanoes were now leading this trip. Assisting them were three Alaskan scientists knowledgeable about this active volcano, which has erupted five times since 1900. Now it was showing signs of another eruption, with hot gases steaming from its caldera.

John Peterson from the University of Alaska Volcanic Research Center explained, via wireless intercom, the purpose of this field trip to the passengers:

"Today's flight will attempt to get the closest to an active volcano of any commercial flight in history. Our plane is outfitted with the latest volcanic ash sensors that were developed in the wake of the two Icelandic volcanoes - Eyjafjallajokull in 2010 and Katla in 2014. Although the "Eyja" eruption grounded 150,000 flights in Europe, Katla - even though a much more powerful volcano - caused little airline disruption because of this technological breakthrough. This safety device is now standard on all jet engine flights likely to encounter volcanoes. And our plane, in addition to having these sensors, also has propellers as an added safety feature in conjunction with its two jet engines. There has never been an accident involving these planes when crossing active volcanoes. We'll be circling the volcano several times, giving you an excellent bird's-eye view. So relax and enjoy the up close views of Mt. Redoubt."

As the five of them, together with the scientists, buckled up in preparation for take-off, Brice turned to Magnus seated across the aisle: "I suppose seeing volcanoes is no big deal for you, since you live in one of the world's hotspots?"

"Oh, no. Every volcano is different. You can't predict when an eruption will occur, or how long it will be. Our scientists are working on that."

Blaine chimed in, "How close have you been to a volcano in Iceland?"

"Too close. A buddy and I were hiking up our most active volcano when it started to erupt. We had to literally run for our lives, jumping over flooded creeks and dodging lava bombs. Thank God we made it down safely."

The 50-passenger plane taxied down the runway made shorter by the ever encroaching sea seeking to seep over the floodwall. Since it was a smaller plane, it easily cleared the wall. The passengers settled back for the 600 mile flight to Redoubt, enjoying the smooth and sunny ride.

Their relaxing flight was interrupted by turbulence - not uncommon in the Arctic. But this seemed worse. As the passengers started waking up, John Peterson again came on the wireless, this time not sounding routine: "The turbulence you are experiencing is coming from Mt. Redoubt, which suddenly has increased in intensity. You can see the volcanic cloud thickening and darkening from this newer eruption, which was not predicted by our scientists. We're still going to circle the volcano, and hopefully avoid the worst of this eruption. Hang on!"

"Well, here we go again," said Brice, remembering his crash landing upon arriving in Katooska. "Blaine, are you ready for this?"

"As ready as I'll ever be, Dad."

As the small plane neared the volcano, it started to pitch up and down as explosions from deep inside the caldera were catapulted upward into the atmosphere. Now it was the Icelandic scientists' turn to explain what was happening. Since Jon and Sigga were seated in the same row, with Kristin across the aisle, they tried to communicate with each other in the still-shaking plane.

"What we're experiencing is a pyroclastic flow," shouted Jon.

"Yea, I know," responded Kristin. "These rock particles and gases can hurl at us at 130 kilometers per hour, and reach a temperature of 800 degrees Centigrade."

"We better tell the pilots not to go any closer. Maybe they can still circle but in ever-widening circles until we see how serious this is," suggested Sigga.

After taking a few seconds to digest the seriousness of the situation, John relayed this information to the pilots. While he was still speaking and looking out his window, John saw several small rock particles hit the underside of the right wing, leaving small holes.

John warned the pilots, "You'd better be on the lookout for rocks hitting the plane. I just saw several of them hit my wing, leaving small holes. Do you have any detection devices for this?"

One of the pilots answered back, "No, we don't. We'll have to rely on visual sightings like the early pilots did. But if there's damage to the fuselage, our systems will detect the loss of air pressure in the cabin."

John continued, "You'd better make an announcement, but don't scare them."

As the plane made a sharp turn away from Redoubt, the captain, in a somewhat excited voice, said, "After discussing the situation with several of the scientists on board, and in order not to endanger you and our plane, we are heading away from the volcano, but will still fly in ever-expanding concentric circles so you can still get a look at this unexpected cloud of rocks and gas. The turbulence should subside the farther from the volcano we are. Remember, your safety is our utmost goal. Thank you for your understanding."

Immediately after this announcement the captain headed the plane away from the volcano, all the while dodging the "jet-propelled particles." Magnus looked back to see the billowing cloud, reminding him of when he encountered Hekla last spring. Only this time he was above it, and not below the fiery darts. He wondered, "What are Brice and Blaine thinking? They've never seen an active volcano before. Are they afraid?" Just in case, he shot up a quick prayer for protection for them and all the passengers. He saw trembling lips moving, and figured these were the so-called "foxhole prayers" - from even the atheists aboard.

Magnus was jolted back to reality by a sharp piercing sound toward the rear of the cabin. Another rock particle had opened a four inch hole in the floor, causing shrieks from the nearby passengers. Since the plane was full, they had nowhere to flee, but could only look at the black ash from the volcano entering the fuselage. Could these left-brained unemotional scientists stay calm in this time of crisis?

And suddenly, just as the stewardess' instructions stated, oxygen masks from all over the cabin dropped in front of the beleaguered passengers. Only this time it was not a drill! This would test if the passengers had paid attention to these instructions, which some of them had heard hundreds of times.

Brice, the tough former Cornhusker, frantically grabbed his mask, and smashed it on his face. When no air would come out, he clumsily pulled the mask forward, finally feeling the flow of air. If he were on the football field, he would've "fumbled the ball." He then looked over to see how Blaine was doing. Calm and collected, and breathing normally, he gave the "thumbs up" sign to his Dad. Magnus gave two thumbs up to both of them. They were safe for now.

Since the plane was only flying at 12,000 feet - too close to the volcano - there really wasn't a need for the oxygen masks. Nevertheless, the passengers kept them on as instructed by the stewardesses. At least that quieted the cabin to a few muffled voices heard above the turbulence, including some "Hail, Marys."

Brice recalled seeing disaster movies where passengers and their possessions were sucked through gaping holes in the fuselages, due to the change in air pressure. Nothing like that was happening here. However, in the cockpit it was not so tranquil.

The co-captain was frantically radioing the Anchorage Airport, explaining their precarious situation, and requesting permission to land. Meanwhile, the captain was giving up his concentric circle plan, trying to combat the turbulence, while keeping the aircraft aloft. As the hole in the cabin increased in size to a foot in diameter, the plane started losing altitude, and was now down below 10,000 feet.

Finally the control tower in Anchorage got back to the captains: "You are about 100 miles out, and we have cleared a runway for you, and foamed it, in case you lose your landing gear. We'll talk you through this. Good luck."

The glide path to Anchorage was anything but smooth. The plane kept dropping faster and was now down to 5,000 feet at 50 miles out. The Cook Inlet, with its many fishing vessels, became clearer the closer they came to the airport.

From the control tower came this warning: "You're losing altitude too rapidly. That could compromise your landing gear. Suggest a belly landing. We will recoat the runway with more foam. Fire trucks are on standby. Good luck."

The captain mentally rehearsed his flight simulator experience for this emergency landing procedure, and told the co-captain to notify the passengers to expect a rough landing, and to take one of the brace positions in the safety card found in the seat in front of them.

Once again Brice frantically grabbed the card, and Blaine and he quickly agreed to protect their heads by bracing their arms on the seats in front of them. They looked across the aisle to see Magnus,

Niels, and Lara in the same positions. Only Magnus was looking up, as if to heaven.

After what seemed an eternity in these positions, they heard a scraping noise as the plane bumped down on the runway, sliding from side to side in the thick, white foam. Finally after turning completely around, the plane came to a stop, and the passengers heard the sirens of the fire trucks racing down the runway. The firemen jumped from their trucks and ran to the plane's exits, grabbing the doors from the outside, and instructing the passengers to jump onto the evacuation slides they had wheeled to each exit. It looked like a free-for-all, but all the passengers were evacuated safely, and whisked away from the plane. And none too soon.

As they looked back, a ball of flame erupted where the hole had been. The firemen quickly trained their hoses on the spot and extinguished the flame before any more outbursts. But this plane wasn't going anywhere - a victim of Mt. Redoubt's unpredictable volcanic fury.

After experiencing Mt. Redoubt's fury as it brought down their plane, Brice, Blaine, Magnus and the scientists were forced to take another plane back to Katooska. As these passengers filed silently up the ramp to board their prop-jet at the Ted Stevens International Airport in Anchorage, Brice was trying to make sense of this latest crisis. Was this real or was he experiencing the "fog" after being hit head-on by a burly lineman on the football field?

This was the second close call for Blaine and him upon their arrival at the IPY. At least Spud wasn't on this plane. He was safely back in his pen at the yurt. But what about the humans?

As their second plane climbed and then leveled to their flight path, Alaska Air treated their scientists to a meal of freshly-caught salmon from the Cook Inlet. And there was another surprise – each tray had a Bible verse inscribed on top – a Christian version of fortune cookies!

Brice's verse was from Isaiah 43, verse 2: "When you pass through the waters, I will be with you, and when you pass through the rivers they will not sweep over you. When you walk through the fire you will not be burned; the flames will not set you ablaze." He stared at it thinking, "God, if you exist, did you really protect me when our seaplane crashed into the sea, and now another plane? Are you trying to tell me something?"

Magnus' verse was from the same chapter of Isaiah, the last half of verse 1: "Fear not, for I have redeemed you; I have summoned you by name; you are mine." Magnus said a prayer of thanks for Jesus dying for him on the cross and "saving" him by grace, and that he would be a good witness to Brice and Blaine.

Blaine's verse was also from Isaiah, the 41st chapter, verse 10: "So do not fear, for I am with you; do not be dismayed, for I am your God. I will strengthen you and help you; I will uphold you with my right hand." He thought, "I hope you are my God. How can I know for sure?"

With all the excitement, Brice finally relaxed, closed his eyes, and relived the horrendous events of his airborne day. His seatmates, Blaine and Magnus were chatting away, enjoying a smooth flight back "home."

Later, as the plane landed safely on the Katooska runway, Brice finally awoke. As they taxied to a stop, Brice was glad to be back on terra firma. It had been another adventure for the Nebraskans and Magnus. What would the next field trip bring?

VI. Project Four:
Effect of Climate Change
on Indigenous Peoples
and Their Lands

Because of the rise in the oceans, due to increases in CO2, nitrous oxide, methane, and the accelerated melting of the Greenland and Antarctic icecaps, 200 million men, women, and children will be forced into exile by the end of this century.

IPCC Report (International Panel on Climate Change)

"The state (Alaska) will never pay for the extra cost (to relocate). We'll have to find other funding. If we fail, we'll disappear. Our special culture, our community traditions like sharing and respect for our ancestors, our subsistence economy - everything that makes us a unique community will perish in a city like Nome, which is foreign to Inupiaq culture."

Jonathan Weyiouanna, Shishrmaref resident

"I can't think of any technology that would allow us to continue living on our islands if the sea level continues to rise. We can only hope that the developed countries will step up and do their part by considerably reducing their greenhouse gas emissions."

Mohanned Zahir, Haveeru Daily journalist, Male, Maldives

As the participants ambled into the assembly hall for their next session, several conversations were coalescing around the same topic: "Did you see the news reports about our close call with Redoubt? After seeing replays of our belly landing in Anchorage, it's amazing we all survived."

Brice, in overhearing some of these conversations, turned to Blaine and said, "Are you ready for more adventures today?"

"Sure, Dad. Isn't this why we came up here?"

"Yea, but I'd like to get outta here alive?"

Magnus, right behind them, overheard Brice's comments, and thought, "Maybe one more adventure will do it."

As the three of them took their seats together, the project director Dr. Johannson again took the stage to introduce this session.

He began, "Ladies and gentlemen, our previous sessions have inundated you with empirical data from charts and graphs illustrating the seriousness of global warming on the glaciers, sea ice, and the atmosphere. This session will provide a refreshing change as we hear first-hand reports of local indigenous peoples directly affected by climate change. Their stories may sometimes be emotional as they relate how their villages have tried to cope with the ravages of the sea and the melting permafrost.

"The villagers portrayed by today's speakers are the first of many climate refugees. According to U.N. projections, by the middle of this century as many as 150 million people will join this new kind of displaced group, fleeing from the effects of climate change. Today you will be getting a first-hand glimpse of what some of your models are projecting for the future, unless policy makers take bold steps to stem this trend.

"When listening to these stories, consider the following factors: Will these people's lifestyle and culture be irrevocably changed? Who will pay for their relocation, and what will be its effect on their future? Is there a moral issue with the biggest greenhouse gas emitters affecting those least likely to use fossil fuels?

"And now to the speakers, each from a different village on the West coast of Alaska."

The crowd hushed as two men and one woman entered the stage, all attired in their native dress. One of the men stepped silently forward to the podium in his seal skin boots, fur seal pants and shirt, topped off by his white polar bear hat.

Kivalina

He began by greeting his audience in his Inupiaq tongue and then quickly switching to English: "Good morning, ladies and gentlemen. I am Simon Metuq, formerly from the small village of Kivalina, once located about 100 miles north of where you are now, and north of the Arctic Circle. My village was the most northerly of the ones you will hear about today.

"I've said formerly, because my village no longer exists. If I want to brag about being first, I can say that we were the first climate refugees in Alaska. And we will not be the last. But I'm getting ahead of myself. Let me tell you about our village, and what happened to it, and where I am living now.

"My ancestors have lived in Kivalina for generations, living off the land and the animals that surround us. Our location between the Chukchi Sea and the Kivalina Lagoon made it easy for us to take our dogsleds over the frozen ice almost all year to hunt seals, whales, and polar bears.

What's more, we had a natural freezer. We could store our meat in underground caves without fear of spoiling in the cold climate, where it sometimes got down to - 40 degrees Fahrenheit. It was a tough life during the long, cold, and dark winters, but at least we could pass these survival skills on to the next generation. And we could count on the solid ice to provide protection from the storms hitting our coastline. But all that changed gradually starting in the 1980s. And this is what I want to talk about now.

"We started noticing that the winter ice melted earlier in the summer and didn't return until later in the fall. We didn't worry much about it until the fall storms coming from the ocean started wearing away our coastline. We thought "this too will pass," but it didn't. In fact every year more and more of our land was washed out to sea - never to return. Since our land between the waters was only 600 feet wide, it would only be a matter of time before we had to do something to protect our village.

Simon then turned to the audience and asked, "If you were living in my village, what would you do?"

The listeners were surprised, but after a few moments several shouted answers:

"Look for a new location," came an answer from a man in the front.

"Build a seawall," came another answer.

"Sue the biggest contributors to global warming," demanded a lady with a determined voice, not from China or the U.S.

Simon smiled when he said, "Good ideas. We tried all three, and they didn't work out. We wanted to stay in our village, and continue our traditional ways. So we decided we could build a seawall to hold back the ocean. We built a 2.5 million dollar wall, ten feet high, made of baskets of sand that were reinforced with wire. Then we had a celebration thinking we were safe again. And, wouldn't you know it, that very day we had a bad storm that started to pull the sand back into the water. Within a month the whole seawall had vanished into the ocean. Strike one on that idea.

"So then we realized we couldn't stay in our village. The Army Corps of Engineers started looking around for new sites for our village, but didn't come up with anything. Besides they said it would cost the government about $400 million dollars. That's a million dollars for each of our 400 villagers. I didn't realize we were worth that much," Simon said sarcastically. "The U.S. Government didn't want to add that much to their huge deficit, so that idea was dropped. Strike two.

"But I bet they would've spent that amount to relocate the residents of the American Gulf Coast, with their problems with more hurricanes. After all, those people have money and nice houses that the government wants to protect. And they vote! I guess we don't count way up here," declared Simon dejectedly.

"So, out of desperation, we decided to try the legal route. We pooled our meager resources and hired a lawyer to bring a lawsuit against the largest coal, oil, and gas companies, accusing them of contributing to global warming that has wrecked our village. This got a lot of attention in the press. Pointing to the tables in the back reserved for the press, Simon looked directly at them and asked, "Did any of you cover this story?"

After the reporters looked at each other, they collectively shook their heads from side to side, signifying "No."

"Well, I hope you cover this story. We're just the first of many villages that are facing these same problems."

One reporter did have a question for Simon. "What happened to your lawsuit?"

"The court threw it out. They said we didn't have standing – whatever that means," answered Simon. "Strike three, and we're out."

Another spontaneous question came from the audience. "So where are you living now?"

Simon began his answer in a subdued voice, barely audible even with his microphone. "You've heard and seen pictures of refugee camps all over the world. Many of you probably know about Indian reservations in America. Well, that's what they're like, except now they're called climate refugee camps. That's where most of our former villagers are now living. The government says they are only temporary until funding is available to again return us to a safer village, but you know how that promise is. Just ask the Native Americans about that.

"Our people are nomads that follow the animals we hunt. Because the climate is warmer now, and the sea ice is gone most of the year, our animals are also gone. So we stay in our camps, wishing we could return to the sea. Some of us work on oil rigs drilling for the oil they have now discovered. Others help load and unload their oil tankers, since they can now travel through the virtually ice-free Northwest Passage.

"When you think of it, it's really ironic. The companies, because of the melting ice, are finding the oil and gas that contribute to the same global warming that destroyed our villages. Maybe you people can do something about it. That's why I came here to tell you the story of our people. Thank you."

With that Simon received a standing ovation. Maybe that would cheer him up.

Newtok

And now it was Aggalak Tom's turn to add to what Simon said.

"I am Aggalak Tom, an Inuit who used to live in our little village of Newtok, about 500 miles, as the crow flies, south of where Kivalina used to be. Newtok was located on the western coast in Alaska facing the Bering Sea. The sea used to be our friend, bringing us plenty of ice so we could take our dogsleds out to hunt walruses, seals, and polar bears. And then it became our enemy when the storms battered our ice-free coast most of the year. Each year, after the ice melted, we lost about 130 feet of our coastline. And as Simon mentioned, we also lost our animals and our source of food and clothing. Our very survival as a proud people was in danger, due to climate change. Since we couldn't stop the erosion, we decided to move.

"I'll give you two examples to illustrate how dangerous living in Newtok was. Because of warmer weather, the permafrost started melting. Some of our houses actually collapsed into the mud and tilted on their sides. One house was completely swallowed up by the soft ground. Fortunately, no lives were lost. Another house was teetering on the edge of the eroded ground, and it was ready to fall into the sea. So the villagers rounded up their pickups and chains and pulled the house away from the brink to a safer location - at least for a while.

"Another story comes from my experience traveling on the ice. I now use a snowmobile to get to my fishing shack. One day I was going out there, and when I got to where I thought it was, all I could see was a large hole in the ice. I lost everything - stove, bed, chairs, equipment, and all my fishing tackle. The ice melted two months earlier than during normal times. But these times are not normal anymore. Maybe what we are experiencing now with the warmer temperatures, melting permafrost and sea ice, and fewer animals to hunt is now the new normal. I hope not.

"The Alaska Permanent Oil Fund, which pays its residents a yearly bonus from the oil revenue, paid for our relocation to the tune of $300 million dollars. Maybe with all the new oil and gas discoveries in the Arctic, the state will have money for more re-locations. But as of now most other villages suffering from the same fate as Simon and I have, will end up in the climate refugee camps.

"My people are the sentries for the world. We are living in the North, where the temperature is warming two times more than the rest of the world. What's happening to our villages is only a preview of what the rest of the world will experience - unless you scientists convince the leaders of the world to get serious about saving, not just us, but our planet. But we don't have much time. The doomsday clock is ticking closer to midnight. Thank you."

Again a standing ovation. The seriousness to these people is sinking in.

Shishmaref

The third villager stepped to the podium, not in her native Inuit dress but in American "street clothes" (red and blue skirt with a white blouse) and introduced herself as Sheila Swan. And then she began.

"You may wonder why I'm not dressed like Simon and Aggaluk. Well, for one thing, I'm not of their gender."

The ensuing laughter was a good relief after the seriousness of the previous two speakers.

"The other reason is that, because of what's happening to our villages, our people are becoming more 'Americanized,' and blend-ing in with other Alaskans. We dress just like you. We've lost our identity as an Inupiaq culture. That's the worst part of what is happening to us.

"My former village of Shishmaref is located about 150 miles southwest of Kivalina on the Chukchi Sea, close to Russia. But we couldn't see it from our little houses! No, we don't live in igloos anymore.

"Our young people have adopted your modern ways with their cell phones, iPods, video games, computers, and TV. Since they can't hunt any more, it gives them something to do during the long winter nights. And because of this, the obesity rate is increasing - another bad side effect of climate change.

"Most of us have traded in our dogsleds for snowmobiles, which emit CO2s into the atmosphere. So we aren't completely carbon neutral. But one boy in our village, when we were living there, found out they can be dangerous on the ice. One day in late spring he went to check his fishing hole when he heard a loud cracking noise. He knew what was happening, and jumped off his snowmobile just before it sank into the ocean. If he would've had a dogsled, and one dog went through the ice, the others could have pulled him to safety, and saved everything. He was lucky this time. He learned not to trust the thickness of the ice as his parents and grandparents had done for years.

"Our village had several other close calls like this one. One lady was woken up by her house tilting. She looked out the window, and shined her flashlight on the ground, only to find it had eroded under her house. It was teetering on the edge, and about ready to fall into the sea. She ran out the back door just as the whole house plunged down the bank. All she could hear were the boards being pounded into smithereens by the raging storm. All her possessions and family pictures were lost at sea. She stood there and cried and cried before some of the villagers took her to one of their houses - for how long she didn't know. She also didn't know where she was going to live next. She had no family there. But in times like these we pull together to help each other. That's what's important about keeping our culture.

"We got together and formed the Shishmaref Relocation Committee, and voted to relocate by 2022. We tried raising the money from private sources, so as not to depend on the government for help. Besides, the Permanent Alaska fund that paid to relocate Newtok doesn't have the money for any more relocations. The Alaska citizens want to keep their yearly bonus. They would agree to a reduced rate, but that won't be enough to relocate all the villages in danger. We tried the legal route, and that didn't work either. So now we're going to the U.N. After all, global warming is an international problem. CO_2s and other pollutants don't stay in the countries that produce them. The wind carries them wherever it blows.

"Our committee has launched a petition drive, not only for us, but for the more than 200 indigenous villages affected by this **urgent** problem. We are calling on the U.N. Commission on Human Rights to solicit contributions from the biggest emitters of greenhouse gases - you know who you are - to establish a series of climate refugee camps by 2022 - the year we voted to relocate. These camps would be located at a safe distance from the sea, and would include several villages in the area. They would be located as close to where the whales, seals, walruses, polar bears, and caribou now live - if they are still around. These animals have migrated farther north to try to find sea ice. These camps would allow the residents to come and go to continue their fishing and hunting and subsistence living.

"I would urge you to support this effort to preserve our culture and way of life. After all, we're probably one of the least-polluting societies. If global warming continues as you scientists predict, you may be forced to live like us. We want to be around to help you, if it comes to that. Thank you."

Amid cheers and shouts of, "We'll help you, we'll help you, yes, we can," the crowd again took to their feet for a prolonged ovation for all three native Alaskans. Would the scientists shed their lab coats for the pinstriped suits in the halls of government? Simon, Aggaluk, and Sheila gave them a challenge to do just that.

Dr. Johannson thanked the three as he again came to the podium to explain the field trip. "Tomorrow you will have the opportunity to see the climate refugee camp that Simon mentioned. This is the first camp of its kind in the world, and is operated by the United Nations High Command for Refugees. The U.N. extended the definition of refugees to include peoples displaced by global warming. This is another dubious first for Alaska.

"And this time we will travel by coach rovers. See you tomorrow at 8:00 AM sharp."

"Thank God, if you exist, that we don't have to fly again," said Brice.

"Are you getting paranoid, Dad?" asked Blaine.

"No, but maybe this time there won't be a crisis."

A Letter from Tricia

After the session Brice walked over to the temporary post office established just for the IPY. Even in this age of e-mails, videophones, and text messages, some people still send old-fashioned letters. This time he found one in his mailbox. "Who would be sending me a letter without a return address? It must be from someone around here," he thought.

Curiously he opened it to find a handwritten letter from Tricia. "How odd," he again thought. "She put a lot of effort into this. It must be important." He turned over the one-page letter to see how she signed it ("Trish" - not "Love, Trish.")

"Oh, oh. Something must be wrong."

He finally mustered up the courage to start reading it. It began simply, "Brice,"

"You haven't kept your promise to stay in touch with me; and when you did call me, you were with that floozy Sara. Besides that you don't seem concerned about what's going on at the ranch with Blake and me. Well, it's about time I tell you.

"The ranch isn't doing very well. Because of our drought (you probably think it's because of global warming) the Ogallala Aquifer is low, so we can't irrigate any more. All our crops and hay have dried up, so we have nothing to feed our cattle, so Blake and I decided to sell them to get what we could from them, which wasn't much. Besides, Blake was getting fresh with me, so I fired him. I'm still trying to be faithful to you, but now I'm wondering why. So now it's just Spike and I on the ranch.

"And another thing. I found a teaching job in Lincoln, so I'll be moving there in August. There's no point in staying at the ranch any longer. Maybe the government will help us out. Anyway, I'm fleeing to the big city. I feel like a refugee from the rigors of the ranch. I decided I needed to get a life for myself, since you don't seem to care for me anymore.

"I don't believe in divorce. Maybe this is a temporary separation, and it will all work out when you return. Remember, Blaine has to start college this fall.

"I'll send you my new address.

Trish."

Brice was glad he was alone when he read the letter. He needed time to think about it. So he went back to the yurt. Blaine was gone, but Spud was in his dog run, so he leashed him up, and the two of them went for a walk down by the ocean, which was calm for a change.

Once on the beach, he let Spud off the leash, and threw sticks in the water. Spud eagerly jumped in after them, each time bringing them back to Brice. He could've done this for hours, but Brice had another agenda.

He had Tricia's letter in his hand, making sure it didn't get wet from Spud shaking the water from his fur. He read it again, this time slowly, pondering his options. "I could go home now to try to patch things up, but I would lose my practicum credits, and the degree I badly want. Or I could call Tricia and try to 'sweet talk' her, but she'd see through that. Or should I just concentrate on my sessions here, and worry about the home situation when I return? And Trish was right; I do have to get Blaine home in time to enroll in college. I won't tell him about this, unless Tricia already has. At least we as parents try to work together when it comes to our only son. That's one good thing about our marriage - if it will last."

During his long walk with Spud, the last option was the one he would choose. As the old maxim says, "Time heals all." He would be putting it to the test. Even though the sun was still high in the sky, it was getting late. He and Spud, headed back to camp. Blaine would be wondering where they were. Better cheer up and get ready for another trip.

America's First Climate Refugee Camp

At 8:00 AM, with a bright sun shining, several 30-passenger

coach rovers pulled up to the assembly hall - impressing the waiting crowd. These vehicles were especially outfitted with oversized mud and snow tires for their trip along the western coast of Alaska. During July the weather could turn from cold and snow to rain and sleet to hot sun - all in one day. With the permafrost melting because of the warmer temperatures, drivers had to be ready to travel cross-country to find firm footing for their vehicles.

Each coach rover had an indigenous guide, who now lived in the climate refugee camp to which the group is traveling. Since Simon was one of yesterday's speakers, he hopped a ride back to the camp, and would be available for tours upon arrival. The camp is located about 20 miles inland from Katooska in a formerly deserted and barren area that used to be home to thousands of caribou. These nomadic animals have now moved north in search of a cooler climate.

During the short trip to the camp, each guide related their stories of how their village had been ravaged by a sea that was no longer held in check by the sea ice. In each case, erosion claimed their land until houses had no yards, and stores no places to park. Usually the "last straw" was when a house teetered and then tumbled into the ocean, forcing the family to either move in with friends or relatives, or to leave the village entirely.

Upon hearing the story of their guide, Magnus said to his parents, "This sounds like the three speakers we heard yesterday. I wonder how many more villagers will be forced to leave? I guess we'll find out today."

Meanwhile in another coach rover Brice was staring out the window, not taking in the scenery, but still thinking about Tricia's letter. "Maybe I should go home and try to settle things with her. But then this whole trip will be wasted. No, I gotta stick this out. This is my last course. I'll never have another chance like this. Maybe Tricia will come back to the ranch."

Blaine was also looking across the aisle to the window on the other side, and thinking "Who would want to live out here? From my history books I learned that's what we whites did to our Native Americans. You'd think we would've learned something from history. But maybe there's no other choice. Things are pretty bad for these people up here."

As the coaches approached the camp, they were greeted by a sign which read: "Welcome to America's First Climate Refugee Camp, operated by the U.N. High Command on Refugees. Enjoy your visit." One thing that the passengers immediately realized was the absence of fences. After all, the camp was built for nomadic peoples who are free to hunt and fish, and return to the camp with their catches. This is not a prison camp. The inhabitants are not to blame for the loss of their villages. The culprit is the invisible CO_2 being spewed into the atmosphere by the developed nations.

The usual five (Brice, Blaine, Magnus, Niels, and Lara) that had been traveling together on field trips were in the lead coach guided by Simon. Upon their arrival Simon was met by a team of residents who would show the passengers around the camp. As the delegation walked down the boardwalk covering the muddy main street, they noticed rows and rows of trailers.

Simon, anticipating their questions, quickly answered, "You may remember seeing these types of trailers set up for victims of natural disasters. Well, FEMA, the U.S. Federal Emergency Management Authority, has furnished these as well. In fact they are better than what most Alaska Natives lived in at their former villages. But as you can see, they all look the same. Not much room for individuality here."

As they followed Simon down the main road, they also noticed several stations where there were long, stainless-steel tables with hoses connected to pumps. Under each table was a large steel barrel dug partially into the ground. With the permafrost gone, digging in the soil was relatively easy.

As they passed the first station Niels asked, "What are these tables for?"

Simon responded, "I figured someone would ask that. The camp tries to be as much like what these people were used to when living in their villages. They survived on hunting and fishing, which they can still do. Notice the many pickups, snowmobiles, and four-wheelers parked here. No dogsleds anymore. When they return with their catches of salmon, halibut, seals, or other small marine animals, they need a place to clean them. That's what these stations are for. We also furnish community freezers to keep their meat until they eat it. There aren't any ice caves anymore. The climate is too warm now."

The group now stopped in front of a white building with a bell on the roof, and a playground with swing sets, sandboxes, teeter totters, and a wooden maze with tunnels, stairs, and walking paths.

Simon continued, "This school is for the native children, and the lessons are taught in their original language and English. The teachers reside here, and are available as tutors for those students needing extra help or enrichment in subjects they are good at. Just like all schools in Alaska, the students have to take tests to see if they can move to the next grade, which is easy in a one-room school. They get a lot of individual attention that way."

They continued their tour and stopped in front of another building with one large room with many tables and chairs.

Simon opened the front door, and the tour walked in.

"This is the place where the women gather to make clothes and crafts from the hunts done by the men. They make anything from boots and jackets from sealskin to necklaces from walrus teeth. They leave the camp to sell their wares to the tourists, and are a big hit in their native dress."

"Do they get to keep the money they make from their sales?" asked Lara.

"Only half of it. The rest goes back to the camp to help with the overall expenses. The residents here get their trailer free, but have to pay their own utilities. We also have a mess hall, which we will pass shortly. So the camp takes care of their basic necessities. Anything else is up to them."

"How do they pay for their other expenses, like TVs, computers and iPhones if they use them?" asked Blaine.

"Oh, yes, they use them. They're modern now. We have an employment service here that helps men and women find a job that matches their skills. Many of the men are working for the oil and gas companies. You see more oil rigs now that the Northwest Passage is almost ice-free during the summer. These companies provide busses to take workers from here to their work site."

Magnus interjected, "It's really ironic that these people that have had to leave their villages because of climate change caused by these companies are now working for them. Doesn't that bother them?"

"I don't know," wondered Simon. "I suppose if it pays well, that's what the workers want. I remember reading about the bad oil spill off the U.S. Gulf Coast in 2010. Many of those fishermen that couldn't go out to the sea instead ended up working with the same oil company that put them out of work. These people needed the money, too."

"Is there a problem with unemployment here?" asked Brice.

"Look around," said Simon. "You see many young men sitting on the steps of their trailer, smoking and drinking in the middle of the day. What does that tell you?"

"Is there a problem with violence and abuse?" asked Lara.

"Well, we don't have a jail, but we could use one sometimes."

"What happens if someone gets hurt in a fight?" asked Blaine.

"We have an **urgent** care clinic over there," said Simon pointing to our left. "It is staffed by medical personnel from the surrounding area. If anything is serious, we fly them to the nearest hospital."

"Do you have a church here?" asked Magnus.

"We have a chaplain that comes for weekly services, but not too many attend," said Simon. "They think church is boring."

"It's not, if you have a personal relationship with Jesus, interjected Magnus. "He gives you a reason for living and strength to deal with your problems. Maybe that's what these people need."

After that the group walked in silence until they came to a row of people holding signs. And these Inuits were conveying a message - also in silence.

"What's this all about?" asked Brice.

"I don't know. This certainly wasn't on our tour. Read the signs. That'll tell you what's going on."

These native Alaskans stood in rows of about 12, about 10 feet apart, and on both sides of the main road on which the tour was walking. Each of them held a sign about 2 feet by 4 feet down in front of them. As the tour approached them, everyone from both rows raised their signs in unison. Each sign had only one letter, and was colored either red, white, or blue on a rotating basis.

The whole group stopped suddenly, moving their heads from left to right to read the letters. In patriotic American colors the message was:

"PLEASEHELPUS"

While they were still trying to figure out this message, the person holding the last "P" sign on each side of the road suddenly switched it to a new sign that read: "P,". Now the changing message read:

"PLEASEHELP, US"

"I get it," said Blaine excitedly. "They want our country to help them. Is that right, Simon?"

"I don't know. I didn't know anything about this. Someone must've organized this in a hurry."

This caught the attention of the members of the press who were also on the tour. Several of them ran up to the demonstrators- microphone in hand and cameras blazing - asking them why they did this, and what they hoped to accomplish.

A lady named Nancy, who was the spokeswoman for the protestors, answered: "We were forced here after our village eroded away. With more villages suffering the same fate, more and more Inuits are coming here. It's getting crowded, and will only get worse. We want the American government to give more aid to the U.N. so they can construct more camps for the refugees. We know you are a generous people, and have responded to crises in the past. We want you to do the same thing now."

The lady from the press thanked her, and assured her they would get their message to the "lower 48." After that interview the press and the tour headed back to the busses that would take them back to a place that was not yet endangered by the rising sea levels. How long they would be safe would depend on the accuracy of the climate models. And maybe it was time for the scientists to take their own signs to Washington.

VII. Project Five: Effect of Climate Change on Arctic Animals

"Pictures of an unhappy (polar) bear perched on a tiny, melting ice floe floating on a blue sea have become the symbol of an Arctic under threat. The pictures highlight the strange irony that the region's top predator, a terrifying and powerful hunter, is helpless without ice."

Alun Anderson, *After the Ice: Life, Death, and Geopolitics in the New Arctic*

"I think all the ice-dependent species (polar bear, ringed seal, walrus, and beluga, bowhead, and narwhal whales) are in trouble, in quite big trouble if we lose the ice."

Steven Ferguson, University of Manitoba

"I've seen killer whales swim right up to the edge of the ice in summer. It seems that it is part of the new Arctic that these big predators are here very early."

Kit Kovacs, Norwegian Polar Institute

It was now early August and the long, summer days were starting to become noticeably shorter. The sun was hovering lower in the sky and soon it would set for the first time since the IPY began. The scientists, many of whom had teaching responsibilities at their universities for the fall semester, were anxious to head home. The same could be said for Magnus and Blaine, one a returning college student and the other an incoming freshman, respectively.

Even Brice was wondering what things would be like when he returned to his vacant ranch, and if he still had a life with Tricia. But as he learned as a Cornhusker, the game "isn't over till it's over." It was the fourth quarter but there was still one more session to go, and then his Master's Degree would be completed. So he slogged on to the goal line.

As the delegations filed into the assembly hall for the last session, the din of chatter was several decibels higher than when they first arrived the first part of June. Many friendships, both professional and personal, had developed during the ensuing time in the Arctic. Many business cards were exchanged, and iPhone numbers given out. And even though there was no assigned seating, these friendship groups gravitated together. And the same could be said for the Icelandic and Nebraska connection. The five of them were seated together again.

Dr. Johannson also seemed more informal as he took the podium for the last session. He started out, "Well, we made it." And before he could continue he was interrupted by applause, each person cheering himself or herself for having persevered.

After a long pause he continued, "If the rest of the world would be as enthusiastic as you in learning about climate change, then we may be able to save it. But the jury is still out. I guess that makes your missions at home all the more important.

"This session will integrate aspects of the land, sea, and atmosphere as they affect the animals in the Arctic, some of them which you have seen up here. I suppose you all want to hear about the fate of the polar bear, but there are many other animals at risk, as well as new ones inhabiting our territory. Our presenters will share their experiences in studying these creatures that depend on the ice for their survival. Our first presenter is Dr. Bill Hanson from the University of Winnipeg in Manitoba, Canada. His province encompasses Churchill, still considered the polar bear capital of the world.

Dr. Hanson has seen many of them down there as he ventured beyond the sign with the warning: "Danger: Polar bears beyond here. Do not proceed."

Polar Bears

Dr. Hanson began: "Well, I'm still alive, even though, as Dr. Johannson stated, I trespassed - for research purposes, of course (muted laughter from some of the scientists). What I'd like to do today are four things: First, to separate fact from fiction regarding the habitat of the polar bears, using my latest data; second, to project the fate of these bears; third, to share a sad experience while studying these magnificent creatures; and finally to touch briefly on two other marine mammals threatened by the loss of sea ice.

"You've all seen the pathetic picture of a solitary polar bear haplessly drifting on an ice floe hardly bigger than his skinny body, gazing intently into the open blue water, searching for seals that he can catch. This poster child of global warming has been used to stir the emotions of people so they will contribute to environmental organizations dedicated to protecting this species.

In an informal move Dr. Hanson asked, "Has anyone seen a polar bear either on your journey here, or while here?"

With raised hand Jon, one of the Icelandic scientists, exclaimed, "While sailing through the Northwest Passage we saw what looked like a cross between a grizzly and a polar bear on a small chunk of ice."

Katrin continued, "Yea, it was a blackish-grey with a hump on its back, a flat snout, and front paws that were insulated with fur."

Sigga, with tongue-in-cheek, "And we named it "grizzlar bear." This time the laughter was palpable.

Dr. Hanson, smiling broadly, said, "You stole one of my points. What you saw has been confirmed by observations in other parts of the Arctic. With the summer ice basically gone, the survival rate of the cubs has declined dramatically, since they can't hunt seals who also depend on the ice for breeding. So, in order to perpetuate their species the males have come ashore to mate with female grizzlies, resulting in what you have described. That's Darwin's "survival of the fittest" in action. You can make up names for these hybrid bears, as you have already done. "Polies" is another term I've heard. In fact, this phenomenon is so new we don't even have a scientific term for this new species. But I'm confident we'll be seeing more of whatever you want to call them. Thank you for your observation."

While this exchange was going on Brice was thinking, "I wonder if that's what Spud saw the day we were walking by the ocean?"

Dr. Hanson continued: "Now, back to my question about the bear on the ice floe. That doesn't necessarily mean they're in trouble. They may be riding these chunks of ice as a means of locomotion to find seals on other larger ice floes. They are excellent swimmers with their huge paws, and have been spotted 60 miles from any other ice. But if there is no ice to be found, they will eventually drown from exhaustion. I have observed polar bear corpses floating in the open ocean with no ice in sight. That would be a more dramatic poster than the ones you've seen.

"As far as the fate of these bears - let's start with current numbers. As of a decade ago there were an estimated 25,000 polar bears worldwide, with 2/3 of them residing in my country, and also here in Alaska, Russia, Greenland, and Norway. Since this census was taken, there has been an overall decrease in the polar bear population. The USA now classifies them as threatened under the Endangered Species Act. In my country they have a concern status which gives them special protection.

"Researchers have found a correlation between the breakup of the sea ice and the survival rate of cubs. For every week earlier that the ice breaks up - a trend that is continuing - 3 to 8 percent of the cubs don't survive. With less ice, the bears are forced to give up their choice prey, the ringed seal, and forage for food on land. As a result they come ashore at a lighter weight, which increases the mortality rate of their cubs."

Dr. Hanson concluded this part of his presentation with these rhetorical questions, "So what are the projections for the survival of the polar bear? The main question seems to be not will they become extinct, but when. Here the projections vary depending upon where the bears reside. If they are in the narrow, frozen channels in the northern Canadian islands, they may survive until the end of the century. If any ice that is left in the summer stays closer to the shore, they may last until 2080. The consensus seems to be that two-thirds of the polar bears will be gone by 2050 - and that's only a human generation away. If the summer ice keeps melting faster than the models have projected, the bears' fate may be sealed sooner than mid-century. Will your grandchildren be living at the same time as these icons of the Arctic? Once again there is an **urgency** for the world to take collective action to prevent yet another species from becoming extinct."

A Dramatic Encounter

Dr. Hanson began, "I'll bring my presentation to a close by relating a harrowing experience I had recently while researching the polar bear. For the past ten summers I have been studying the cubs when they come ashore to look for food. I tranquilize them with my 'drug gun,' and then, when they are fast asleep, I weigh them on my portable scale. As I mentioned earlier, I'm trying to see if the mortality rate of the cubs is increasing. If the mother is still with her cubs, I tranquilize her also, but don't weigh her. My scale is not big enough for her.

"Even though Churchill has lost only two of its residents to polar bears since its founding in 1717, I am well aware of the danger in running into a hungry bear, particularly a mother with her cubs. That was the case a year ago this month. A gaunt mother with two cubs, evidently exhausted from swimming in the open water, came ashore scrounging for food. I dutifully walked within range of the three bears and tranquilized them all with one shot each. After stumbling around for several seconds they all collapsed into a deep sleep, which usually lasts about an hour. This generally gives me adequate time to perform my duties - but not this time! I had never before tried to weigh two bears when a third, in this case the mother, had also been tranquilized. Obviously, to get to the cubs I had to also sedate her.

"Anyway, I worked rapidly to weigh the two cubs, but I had problems with my scale. For some reason - maybe it was the rain we had with the warmer temperatures that day - the LED digital readout would not show on my screen, so I had to reweigh the cubs several times before the numbers were visible. This took about twenty minutes of extra time.

"Since I was concentrating on the cubs, I didn't see the mother beginning to stir from her sleep. By the time I did, she was already up on all fours and was fixing to protect her cubs. With one shake of her massive head she shook off the effects of the drug, and charged me with a ferocious growl. I ran to the other side of the cubs, thinking she would stop when she saw them, which she did - about 20 yards from me. This gave me time to pull out my 50 caliber pistol loaded with 1 special blank and 5 live cartridges.

"The mother briefly sniffed her cubs, and then proceeded to continue her charge toward me. With fear and trembling, I fired the blank that made a deafening noise. That momentarily stopped her, and I took off running and looked for cover. There was none in the white flat landscape. I could hear her heavy breathing as she gained ground on me. As a last resort, I stopped, turned around, and fired 3 shots at point blank range. With blood soaking her beautiful white fur, she took a few more steps and fell at my feet with one last cry. I stood there, my gun hand shaking, making sure she was dead, and then turned my attention to the still-sedated cubs. And then I picked up my equipment and made a "bee line" to the truck, and then collapsed.

"You know in the cowboy movies when someone is jumping from a building onto his horse, it's usually done in slow motion. That's how this experience felt for me. I even saw buttons popping from my jacket as I ran. And I still have scary dreams about this encounter.

"But the worst part was I had to kill a threatened animal, even if it was in self-defense. I was the one who made the mother extinct. It wasn't the greenhouse gases this time. This incident won't be in my journal articles, but I will remember it for the rest of my life. So pay attention to the warning signs if you are ever in Churchill. If there are no signs where you are hiking, be aware of your surroundings. A hungry polar bear is a dangerous bear. If you are their only source of food, they'll try to have you for lunch. Thank you."

A standing applause greeted Dr. Hanson. After about a minute the clapping subsided, and Dr. Hanson began again: "Two other marine mammals are also endangered by the rapidly melting sea ice. They may not make the posters, and are more numerous than the polar bear, but are both considered threatened under the Endangered Species Act. I am referring to the ringed seal and the walrus.

Seals and Walruses

"The ringed seal is also in danger because of a lack of ice needed to give birth to their young. These 150 pound adults, with their gray coat and silver circles, or rings, need eight weeks with which to raise their young on stable ice. If the ice starts to break up before they are weaned, the pups have to leave their mother for the sea, lowering their survival rate. This doesn't bode well for the perpetuation of their species.

"And finally the strange-looking walrus, with its blubbery body that can weigh up to 3,000 pounds, huge tusks, and I am told, its horrendously bad breath. They, like the seals, depend on the ice to raise their young, which takes about a year. When the mother dives for clams to feed her pups, she leaves them on the ice as a moving platform.

"As the ice retreats, the mother may be forced to abandon her pups and swim ashore to try to find food. These stranded pups are not ready to fend for themselves, and may drown at sea. If the mother can't care for them in shallow waters, the species will decline significantly.

Dr. Hanson closed with these thoughts, "This isn't a pretty picture for the future of these bears, seals, and walruses, but that's what the models project if the summer ice melt is complete. Thank you again."

Again, a hearty applause.

During the break Dr. Hanson happened to pass by where Brice and Blaine were standing, drinking their pop and eating their salmon crackers. Brice took the initiative,

"That was quite a story about you having to shoot that polar bear. Did you have any training in how to protect yourself against their attacks?"

"Not really. I've been a hunter all my life, so I guess it came instinctively. It was either me or the bear, and my weapon was my last resort. I'm not happy about what I had to do, but at least I'm here to try to protect the bears from their unseen enemy - CO2.

Dr. Johannson again took the podium to introduce the next speaker.

He began, "How many of you have been up close to a whale in the open ocean, not at Sea World?"

What seemed like a majority raised their hands.

"Then you will be interested in our next speaker's experiences with the world's largest mammal. Dr. Heidi Hill from the University of Alaska at Juneau has been studying these gentle giants for ten years, but has found out they always aren't so docile. Please welcome Dr. Hill."

Whales and Seabirds - on and under the Ocean

After the usual polite applause Dr. Hill began, "Before I share some of my 'whale-of-a-story' experiences, I want to give you a perspective on what's happening to these creatures in the Arctic as the ice continues to melt at an accelerated rate. It may surprise you.

"It's an open research question as to whether Arctic sea ice is a help or hindrance to whales. It depends on the type of whale. The three most common whales historically seen in the Arctic are the bowhead, beluga, and minke. All three use the ice as cover from predators, which include the Inuit hunters. Less ice makes them more vulnerable to a new type of whale in these waters.

"Orcas, commonly called killer whales, have been more frequent in the ice-free Arctic since I began researching them. I first tracked them around the Shetland Islands, north of Scotland at 60 degrees latitude. Several years later I spotted them 1,200 miles north of the

Shetlands at 80 degrees north latitude around the Norwegian island of Svalbard. Furthermore, they were arriving earlier each year - in the spring instead of the summer. And last summer I was surprised to find them as far north as the geographic North Pole at 90 degrees north latitude! With the waters around this pole now usually ice-free in the summer, it is no surprise these opportunists have arrived at the top of the world. These killers are causing problems for the other whales that have resided in the Arctic for thousands of years, as I will illustrate.

"Orcas see other species of whales as part of their prey. The bowhead doesn't migrate, so is a permanent resident in the Arctic. This 20-meter long whale, with the largest mouth of any mammal, can put up the strongest resistance to a killer whale attack. They are adept at using their huge head, comprising 30 percent of its body length, to break the surface ice and hide from predators. Bowheads will stand and fight killers, and sometimes win. They are an endangered species, not because of the killer whales, but because of human hunting.

"Not so with the beluga, a five meter long, all-white whale. They are highly social and known for their vocal chirping. But with the preponderance of the killers, these "canaries of the sea" are now strangely silent. I've tracked them with my underwater ultrasound device, and haven't been able to detect a single sound. My hypothesis is that they are intimidated by the bigger killers, who also remain silent when hunting their prey. Only when they attack is there a cacophony of sound, resulting in crushing bones.

"I will share an experience I had observing a pod of Orcas in action against the slightly smaller minke whale - 7 -9 meters long. Rather than me tell you, I brought a video I'll now project on the screen. This is a "dog-eat-dog" world, so some of the images are graphic. My research assistant and I followed this scene to the bitter end."

The video opens with the tall, triangular, sweptback fins of a pod of killer whales breaking the surface of the water together. In the center of this pack was one smaller minke whale with a smaller, sweptback fin. The killers have already drawn blubber blood, attracting a flock of excited, noisy seabirds.

The strategy of the killers was to literally drown the minke by preventing it from coming up to breathe. They did this by pressing around it to force it back below the surface. This process went on repeatedly, with the minke never able to break through the surface or the pod. Finally the helpless whale in the middle grew too exhausted, and became the prey for the top predator in the Arctic. The video ends with the drowned minke floating on the surface as the killers eat its bloody blubber.

Dr. Hill concluded, "I know this is not a pretty picture, but it represents the new Arctic and the new icon that soon will replace the polar bear. Let's take a quick break while I load two other videos of my research on and below the sea."

During the break Magnus found Brice and Blaine again imbibing on Arctic ale and salmon cookies. "Well, what did you think of Dr. Hill's presentation?"

Blaine spoke first, "It was gross to see the largest animals in the world fighting each other. But I guess they have to eat, too."

Brice chimed in, "I thought it was only us humans that killed each other, but I guess not. It really is survival of the fittest out here. Maybe that's the way it will be with us if global warming continues to cause more extreme weather. Look at what's happening with the droughts in Africa and the flooding in Asia. And we in the U.S. have had our share of extreme weather, too. Have you in Iceland, Magnus?"

"Well, we've had more volcanoes than usual, and more flooding because of the rapid melting of the glaciers. I don't think any part of the world is escaping this. It makes my task more **urgent** when I get home."

The threesome ambled toward their seats as Dr. Hill began again.

The Food Chain

"There are more plants and animals affected by global warming than the more visible marine mammals I just described. Now I want to take you to the ice-edge zone to show you the diversity of life living there. This is where the microscopic phytoplankton, which means plant drifter or wanderer, bloom in the spring sunlight when the ice melts. This bottom-of-the-food chain plant is eaten by fish, which in turn are eaten by seals, who finally end up in the stomach of polar bears and killer whales. Thus the food chain starts where the ice and water merge.

"So come along with me as my assistants and I cruise on our re-search ship, the *S.S. Empirical*, which also is equipped with a small two-person submarine to catch the food chain in action both below the ocean and on its surface."

Once again a video came up on the screen, this time with back-ground music from Jacque Cousteau's sea voyages. The first scene caught seals diving for fish. Large seabirds dive into the water in search of the same species. The next pictures were a split screen covering walruses diving to the shallow ocean bottom to grab clams, and then surfacing on the ice. The next series, all taken from the sub-marine with a telescopic lens, focused on Orcas feeding on plankton and krill. The final frame caught a solitary thin polar bear waiting for a seal to surface on a small chunk of ice.

After the lights came back up, Dr. Hill commented, "These

scenes look idyllic - the way the food chain is supposed to operate. Now I'll show you what happens to breeding birds when the ice melts."

Again the lights dimmed and the sights and sounds of thousands of birds perched on the high Arctic cliffs came into view. It looked like a scene from Alfred Hitchcock's movie of many years ago, "The Birds," except they weren't attacking anybody.

Dr. Hill again, "This is where these parent birds breed and raise their young. However, as the ice retreats farther out to sea there has been a gradual decrease in the survival rate of the chicks. Here's my working hypothesis. The adults have to fly to the ice-edge to fetch food and carry it back to their young. If the journey gets longer, two factors are in play. One, the adults will eventually become weaker because of these repeatedly longer flights. And two, the young chicks are left home unprotected for longer periods of time from predators such as the Arctic Fox and large gulls."

Dr. Hill concluded her remarks, "I hope I've demonstrated to you that the loss of sea ice affects large and small animals, and tiny plants, both on and below the surface of the Arctic Ocean. Thus the ice serves to maintain the balance of Nature. Lose the ice and we will lose this balance, and a new and scarier Arctic will be the result. And God's creatures, both great and small, will be the victims of our human excesses. Once again, I hope our political leaders are watching our sessions, and taking note of what needs to be done. Thank you."

With that challenge, she received a sustained standing ovation - a fitting conclusion for the last speaker of the last project.

After the crowd was again seated, Dr. Johannson walked onto the stage to announce the field trip.

"Our field trip will be led by Dr. Hill, who volunteered her university's research ship for this special exploration. She will be guiding us to a remote island in the ice-free Arctic where walruses and seals have been observed by her assistants. Dr. Hill hopes to also catch killer whales in action as they seek their prey. This time your experience will be in 3-D and in real time. See you on the *S.S. Empirical* tomorrow morning."

Magnus' Text Message

During the break, Magnus checked his cell phone as he always does. Usually the messages are routine, but not this time. This one was from the Ministry of Sustainability Olga Jonsdottir back in his home country. It read, "Your CO_2 cell phone is operational. Will bring a prototype to your closing ceremonies."

Magnus kept looking at the message saying, "Good timing, Lord. Thank you."

How this would play out when the Minister arrived would be interesting. "I only gave them the idea; they developed it," he thought.

Brice's Texting

During the same break, Brice was texting Tricia. He never did reply to Tricia's last message about her selling their ranch and moving to Lincoln for her new teaching job. He needed time to think about his response, which is, "Decided to divorce. You sold ranch without me. You and Blake getting fresh. Now you've moved. I'll do the same. Sara and I live here. You and Blake live there. Lawyer will contact."

Brice hesitated before pushing the "Send" key. He thought, "Is this what I really want to do? How will Tricia react? What about Blaine? I haven't told him anything. I wonder if he suspects anything." And then he rationalized, "Tricia made the first move. She literally sold the ranch and moved. And Blaine's in my way. And Sara likes me. We could be happy here. And maybe I could help save the planet right here."

After what seemed an eternity of deliberating, Brice sent the message, and waited for Tricia's reply. In the meantime, he had work to finish in the Arctic.

Looking for the Icons of the Arctic

The usual five, accompanied by the rest of the IPY delegation, met at the Katooska Harbor, where they would board the research vessel in search of the old and new icons of the seas - polar bears and killer whales, respectively. While on the dock, Magnus spotted the three Icelandic scientists that accompanied his parents and himself on the *S.S. Sustainability*.

Magnus turned to Sigga, and pointing to the *S.S. Empirical*, said, "This looks the same as ours."

"Indeed it does. But is it powered by hydrogen? We'll have to board it to find out. I bet it isn't."

Kristin, overhearing the conversation, chimed in, "If it is, it shows the USA is finally getting its act together, even in oil-rich Alaska."

As they boarded, Jon, spotting the captain on the bridge, shouted, "Are you using hydrogen to power this ship?"

"Not yet," he replied. "We're trying to catch up with you."

When everyone had boarded Dr. Hill's ship, she again greeted them with these instructions, "Welcome, again. We will be heading into the ice-free Kotzebue Sound, looking for an island where walruses are raising their young. Since the ice is completely gone, these parents and their pups have retreated to an island. My research assistants, Gretchen and Randy recently flew over the island we are about to see, and spotted a huge herd of approximately 1,000. So, hopefully they will still be there. The question is if the killer whales will also be there, waiting to snag the pups that are just getting used to the water. If we do, it will be a first for us. We've been to this island several years ago, when there was still a little ice for the walruses, and didn't see any killer whales then. Since then the summer temperatures have warmed two degrees Fahrenheit, so we'll see. As soon as we leave the harbor, you can start watching for the animals you've heard about during our presentations. If you spot them, let Gretchen, Randy, or myself know. We want to track their territory."

Dr. Hill gave the high sign to the captain, and the *S.S. Empirical* headed out into the choppy sea, with harbor porpoises following alongside with their playful dives. These intelligent animals are not dependent upon the ice for their survival, so they are the fortunate ones in the Arctic, into which they are invading.

As the *Empirical* sped along the coast, the top deck was ringed with passengers, binoculars to the ready, looking for any sign of movement under the whitecaps. After a brief time of silence, one of the scientists on the starboard side yelled, "A ringed seal at 3 o'clock, about a hundred yards out." Some of excited spectators ran from the port side to get a better look.

Gretchen, also spotting the seal, explained over the PA System, "You're looking at a pup that, because the ice is gone, had to leave his mother prematurely to look for food. They are vulnerable to predators in the open water. You'd better keep an eye on him."

Now everyone's binoculars were fixed on four seals, swimming for their lives. Again it was quiet, with only the noise of the diesel engines heard above the lapping of the waves on the bow.

As the *Empirical* veered to the right, the port side furnished the excitement. With most people still watching the seals swimming in the sea, something else appeared. Four enormous triangular fins broke the surface of the water - the telltale sign of killer whales. Before any onlooker could shout, the black-and-white predators grabbed the helpless seals and pulled them underwater.

Several people let out gasps at the swiftness of their catches.

This time the starboard side spectators ran to the other side to see if the whale would surface. Again they waited in silence, binoculars trained on the spot of the attack.

And then another surprise greeted them. Several of the whales surfaced in a circle, awaiting the next move. And then in the middle, one killer surfaced with a bleeding and headless seal in his mouth. With a flick of his head, he flung the seal into the air, to be caught by one of the encircling whales. And then the fun - for them - began. Each of the killers in the circle had their turn at seal tossing, back and forth until the whale that originally caught it now devoured it. With the "game" over, the killers all dove, with their sleek tails the last to be seen by the shocked spectators.

One of the passengers exclaimed disgustedly, "I can't believe they're tossing that seal around for sport. Why don't they just eat it and get it over with?"

Brice, overhearing the conversation, added, "That's why they're called killers. We had an incident in our country where a supposedly tame killer whale at Sea World in Florida grabbed a trainer on the side of the pool, and pulled her under, where she drowned. They're still wild animals, even in captivity."

Blaine said, "Yea, I remember hearing about that. I was only a kid then, and it spooked me. I guess I know why now."

A Sudden Storm

All of a sudden, a gale force wind blew toward the *Empirical*, carrying with it powerful waves that broke over the bow. The spectators scrambled down the stairs to seek safety in the hull. Since their ship only had a few private cabins, the passengers mingled in the open dining area, wondering what was coming next.

Dr. Hill dispelled the suspense, "We unexpectedly ran into a squall that didn't show up on our radar. We're heading right into it, so the ship is going to be pitching for a while. We've encountered these before, and they usually don't last very long. Hold onto the side railings, and use the attached bags if you must "toss your cookies." We're still heading for the walrus island that is closer to the shore, so we should find calmer waters there. I'll give you the all clear when you can come above again. Thank you for your understanding. Over and out."

Brice, hanging onto the railing like it was a football, turned to Magnus, sitting next to him, and said, "Well, here we go again. Like someone said, 'It's not an adventure until something goes wrong.'"

Magnus replied, "Don't you like challenges? Like coming from behind in the fourth quarter to win a football game?"

"Yea, but that's only a game. This could be a matter of life or death."

Magnus didn't reply, but thought "Yes, it is - spiritually."

Finally, the *Empirical* stopped pitching and settled down to an even cruise, the wind died down, and the sun shone again. This part of the latest adventure was over, and everyone's "cookies" remained with them.

This time it was Randy on the PA, "Ladies and gentlemen, as you can tell, we passed through the storm, and are on course to see the walruses. You may now return to the deck. We should be coming to their island in about 15 minutes. Thanks for riding out the brief storm."

A Swimmer in the Sea

Once again the passengers lined the deck, their binoculars searching for movement on the surface. The silence was broken by several excited voices, "There's something swimming behind us."

As other onlookers rushed to the stern of the ship, Dr. Hill, who was already standing back there, pointed to the animal, and in an animated voice, exclaimed, "That's a polar bear swimming in the open waters. With no ice around, he's probably heading to the shore. I wonder how far he's swam. They are excellent swimmers, but can become exhausted if they don't find ice or land within sixty miles."

Now everyone was crowding to the stern, looking at this pathetic creature looking for the ice that wasn't there. As the ship turned toward the walrus island, the white bear turned in the other direction, and headed toward land. Perhaps he smelled something that would sustain him there.

The Battle at Walrus Island

As the *Empirical* neared the walrus island, those watching the bear by the stern now moved to the bow to catch a glimpse of this crowded island. At first all they could see was a mass of brown. As the ship sped closer, the outlines of a mass of bodies crowded together came into view. This huge blob seemed to be moving closer together, and now agitated grunts and shrill calls were heard. There must be something going on that only a closer inspection would reveal. These usually lazy and serene animals were forming a circle. What was causing the commotion?

It was a strange-looking creature that was charging toward the circled walruses. It was definitely a polar bear of a mixed breed, with a dark gray coat interspersed with flecks of black. Behind her long outstretched neck was the telltale hump of a Grizzly Bear. Her snout was flat, and her front paws were wide and insulated, good for swimming.

Dr. Hill excitedly exclaimed over the PA, "You're looking at a hungry, hybrid bear, different than the one we saw behind our ship. Look how thin he is. He's been swimming for miles to find ice. Desperate for food, he's trying to pick off one of the pups, but you can see how the mothers are forming a circle to protect their young. If the bear gets too close to these massive animals, he'll get tusked and badly wounded."

So as to not disturb the animals, Dr. Hill called the captain to idle the engines, and announced, "Let's wait here, and see how this fight for survival plays out."

The *Empirical* came to a halt about one hundred yards from shore.

Now all the passengers scrambled to the starboard side to see if this emaciated "grizzlar" could break the walrus' defense. He also circled the circle, looking for an opening from which to drag a pup to the outside. Every time the bear found an opening and entered the circle, several large walruses charged him, trying to strike him with their lethal tusks. But the bear was more agile, and backed away.

Finally the frustrated bear jumped on one of the smaller walrus' back, and with his sharp teeth, tried to drag her away from the circle. But as soon as the bear bit into her inch-and-a-half thick skin and two-inch-thick blubber, he realized it was futile and backed off.

Driven now by his survival instinct, and his dire need for food, the bear made another attempt to break into the circle, where the pups were squealing. But again he was rebuffed by the herd. Finally, he stood up on all fours and tried to jump over the herd, but was met with a sharp tusk in mid-air. Now badly bleeding from his hip, he retreated to the outside, where, totally exhausted, he fell down - motionless. With his last hope for sustenance gone, he would breathe his last.

It wasn't really the walruses that sealed his fate, but the changing climate. How many more scenes like this will be played out in future years before these Arctic symbols become extinct?

The Killers' Turn

At Dr. Hill's command, the captain fired up the engines and the *Empirical* started circling the island, heading back to port. When the ship was in view of the other side, several spectators, holding their binoculars firmly to their eyes, exclaimed, "Look at these cute baby walruses. Where are they going?"

Randy, standing next them, answered, "They're looking for their mothers, who had to swim farther out to sea to find food for them. Without the ice as a platform, the mothers must leave their young on the island while they dive for clams. And the pups are not very good swimmers yet, so they'd better stay close to shore - if they know what's good for them."

Randy then got on the PA and announced these new visitors to the rest of the passengers, who now crowded to the port side, and waited in anticipation of what would happen next. And it wasn't long.

Pretty soon a half dozen tall, triangular swept-back fins circled the pups, and those on board knew what was coming next. This time three killers surfaced, each with a pup in its mouth. And then they pulled their prey under the water, leaving no sign of an attack. All was quiet. What was going on underneath? Were they plotting another attack?

And then up they came, one killer still with parts of the pup in her mouth. The other five whales then surfaced, and got ready for their favorite sport - this time walrus-tossing. As before, they each took turns throwing and catching this half- dead pup. The spectators, thinking this gruesome show was over, lowered their binoculars, and settled in for the ride back.

And then something strange happened that only Dr. Hill noticed. One of the killers surfaced with a pup in his mouth, with all his body parts intact! What was this, the whales' encore? And then slowly the Orca swam toward the shore, opened her mouth, and deposited the squirming pup close to the shore, and then turned her massive body and tail toward the open sea, joining the rest of the pod.

Once again the passengers were surprised, elated, and puzzled. But before anyone could ask, Dr. Hill, anticipating their question, explained,

"You just saw what seemed to be an act of mercy on the part of one Orca sparing the life of one walrus. That seems to defy the 'law of the jungle' and the 'survival of the fittest.' Researchers have been studying this phenomenon for years, and have yet to reach a definite conclusion. One hypothesis is that when their hunger has been satisfied, they simply stop eating. When they've eaten the equivalent of a seal or walrus a day, they see no need for a senseless killing. Maybe we could learn something from them about not overeating.

"A newer hypothesis is that whales actually have emotions and can empathize with a creature much smaller and more vulnerable than they - after their stomach is full. So are they showing mercy? Maybe someday we'll know for sure? Pardon the pun, but that's food for thought!"

Dr. Hill concluded the trip with this summary:

"Today you saw the old Arctic and the new Arctic in action. The polar bear, weakened from the lack of ice and the length of his swim, was unable to be the predator for which he is known. However, the killer whales, free to travel in the ice-free Arctic, demonstrated their efficiency in living up to their name. Sorry to say, the old icon will probably fade away as the new icon asserts its dominance of the seas - unless we can reverse what you just saw.

"Now go back to your yurts and get ready for the closing ceremonies. You've studied, listened to, and seen the science. Now it's time for action. Our radar has not picked up any more storms, so hopefully it will be smooth sailing back to port. Thank you again."

And so it was; and it was still an adventure.

A Bear and a Bear Dog on the Beach

Meanwhile, back on terra firma, Spud was getting restless; not having his usual walks while Brice and Blaine were on their last field trip.

"Thank God, or whoever," Brice thought. "No more crises. I've had enough adventures to last a lifetime."

Magnus came over to the Sutherland's yurt to see Spud, who recognized him, and barked and jumped excitedly when he came. Brice and Blaine greeted him, and asked Magnus if he wanted to come with them to walk Spud.

"Of course," came his answer. "That's why I came over."

Brice ran in to get Spud's leash, and the three humans and one canine were again off to the sea, where Brice and Spud had previously walked. Spud, being now off-leash, again ran toward the choppy water, and this time jumped in before being hurled back by a whitecap.

"The sea's a little rough today," commented Blaine. "Maybe there's a storm coming in."

Brice followed the conversation with, "Yea, we'd better keep an eye on Spud. He could be washed out to sea by the undertow."

Spud, oblivious to any potential danger, ran back into the water, "surfing" to shore on the whitecaps. After shaking the water from his thick fur, he would playfully plunge farther out, each time enjoying the ride to the beach.

Meanwhile, the men kept walking along the beach, keeping Spud in their sights. Suddenly they stopped in their tracks, and peered at some kind of crumpled, whitish, speckled form about 50 yards from them. They immediately knew what it was - an exhausted "grizzlar,"- awakened prematurely from a tiring swim in search of ice. And he was lean, haggard and hungry! Startled by the men, the bear slowly rose to all fours, assessing the situation with its nose in the air.

And then with a ferocious roar, the bear suddenly charged the men, moving faster as he became fully awake. Equally startled, the humans promptly did a "180," yelling for Spud as they ran as fast as they could in the soft sand. "I've never run this fast on the field," thought Brice, leading the other two up a slight hill. And the bear was gaining on them! Magnus, bringing up the rear, could hear the bear's heavy breathing close behind him.

And then the men heard another ferocious roar, this time from Spud, who ran behind Magnus, cutting off the bear from his hot pursuit. The bear turned around, and started to chase Spud, who circled the bear, who in turn whirled to try to catch Spud.

The three men stopped, and panting heavily, turned around, not knowing if they should intervene in this dangerous "game." They stood at a distance yelling, "Get him Spud." The bear was growling loudly, trying to ward Spud away, but the smaller animal was too quick for the tired bear.

This cat and mouse game continued for some time, with the bear lurching at Spud with his powerful front paws, and the dog artfully dodging them. And then something unexpected happened. The bear, figuring he may be safer in the water, turned around and headed out to sea. Spud lunged after him, only to be swept under one of the rippling waves. Surfacing again, Spud started swimming to the bear as the waves became stronger. Now the bear had the advantage.

Just as he would do to a seal, the bear suddenly turned and struck at Spud, catching him in his powerful jaws, holding him underwater. The three men, sensing Spud's predicament, rushed into the water, waving their arms and yelling, trying to scare away the bear. The bear then turned around to see the men running toward him. Not wanting to risk a confrontation with the humans, the bear, with the struggling Spud still in his mouth, flung him toward the trio, and headed out to sea - never to be seen again.

Brice, with a burst of his former speed, ran and swam to reach Spud who was bleeding and struggling to keep his head above the water. Brice grabbed him like a football, and carried him to the shore to examine his wounds, crying out, "God, if you're real, save him."

Blaine and Magnus gathered around Brice and Spud, now bleeding profusely from the bear's bite on his throat. His sides heaved as he struggled to catch his breath. And then, with one last mighty gasp and whimper, Spud went limp - his open eyes staring blankly toward the heavens.

Brice dropped his head on Spud's still warm body, and sobbed and sobbed, saying, "No, Spud, you can't go, you're a fighter." And now Blaine and Magnus fell on this pile, crying themselves, while trying to console Brice. Now there was another form on the beach - haggard and hapless.

Man's best friend was no more.

Now What?

As the men lay there for who knows how long, the rising tide started to wash over their bodies. Finally Brice picked up the bloody Spud with tender arms, and started walking aimlessly along the beach. Brice and Magnus looked at each other, not knowing what to do. As they watched Brice's blood-spattered silhouette in the lowering sun, Magnus turned to Blaine and said, "He needs our help. Let's catch up with him."

As Blaine and Magnus ran to catch up with Brice, they saw him looking up to the sky yelling, "Why, God? Why? Is this another of your tricks on me?" The football star's face was now tear-streaked and teary-eyed as Brice turned to see the boys approaching him.

With the three re-united with Spud, Magnus took the initiative. "Brice, I heard your questions, and we can talk about them later, but for now we'd better figure out what to do with Spud. Do you guys want to give him a decent burial?"

This time it was Blaine's turn to think this tragedy through.

"Look, there's a cave over there," as he pointed away from the sea. Let's put Spud in it for now, and go back to the camp, and find a box that we can use for a coffin."

Magnus interrupted, "Good thinking. Then we can come back later, and conduct our own funeral for our faithful friend that gave his life to save us."

Blaine, putting his hand on Spud's still warm body, looked up at his dad, now somewhat composed, and asked, "What do you think of that, Dad?"

Brice simply nodded, went into the cave, and found a natural small opening in the rocks. He then gently laid Spud down in his "tomb." Magnus then found a heavy rock, picked it up, and put it over the opening to protect Spud from any more predators. And then the trio headed back to camp, talking about where they would find a box that would work for their secret mission.

Brice, now engaged again, remembered, "The IPY Headquarters said they were giving out packing boxes for our trip home - one per person. Let's see what they've got. Blaine, if we have to, we can squeeze our belongings into one box, and use the other for our dear friend."

"Sure, Dad. That's the least I can do for Spud."

Upon arriving at the headquarters Brice asked if they could get their boxes early.

"No problem," said the receptionist. "I'll have them out for you when you want them."

Brice smiled meekly, thanked her, and they left to return to his yurt to plot their next move.

Epiphanies

As they were walking, Brice turned to Magnus and asked, "I know Spud is only a dog, but I'd like to have a human funeral for him with just the three of us. Do you have any ideas?"

After silently thanking God for this opening, he replied, "You see a lot of crosses in cemeteries. Tombstones always have the dates when the person was born and died. I've even seen Bible verses on the graves, and they are usually decorated with flowers, and sometimes even have pictures of the deceased."

Brice commented, "Sounds good, but why the cross?"

With the spiritual door now open, Magnus began his Socratic questioning to both Brice and Blaine,

"What do you think the cross represents?"

Blaine was the first to reply, "A terrible way to die."

Magnus, "Who died on it?"

Brice, "Many people in Roman times."

Blaine, "I've seen pictures of Jesus on a cross with some kind of wreath on his head, and blood all over. Not a pretty picture."

Magnus, "Now you're getting it. But why did Jesus die anyway?"

Brice, "Because he was a rebel against the government."

Magnus now addressed Brice, "During your football days, did you ever see anyone in the stands holding a sign that said, 'John 3:16'?"

"Of course, many times. But I didn't pay any attention. After all, I was busy scoring touchdowns."

Magnus again, "Do you know what that John 3:16 sign is?"

Blaine, "Yea, it's a verse from the Bible. I memorized it in Bible school one summer, but I don't remember it now. Do you know it, Magnus?

"Yes, it says, **'For God so loved the world that he gave his one and only Son, that whoever believes in him should not perish but have eternal life.'**"

Magnus continued, "Here's another Bible verse we could use for Spud's funeral. It goes something like this, **'Greater love has no one than this, that one lay down his life for his friends.'**"

The spiritual light bulb went on as Brice, holding back tears again, said, "That's what Spud did for us. He gave his life protecting us."

Magnus, seeing the connection, related, "And that's what Jesus did for us. He died on that cross willingly because He loved us. He did His part; now we have to do our part."

Brice, now interested, asked, "So, what's our part?"

Magnus answered, "We must believe in Jesus. Do you, Brice?"

Brice, again composed, began his thoughtful answer, "You know, I came up here not believing in God. Judging by my wise cracks, you probably knew that, didn't you Magnus?"

Magnus tacitly agreed with a slight nod of his head.

Brice continued, "But I've had several close calls up here. First our seaplane (as he looked at Blaine) crash landed before it reached the dock. Then you remember our emergency landing in Anchorage after our plane was hit by the surprise volcano erupting on Mt. Redoubt. And then Tricia left me. I guess I can't blame her. And now this. Why? Why? Why?"

Magnus, now trying to close the conversation, summarized,

"God is trying to get your attention. Sometimes He has to make things miserable for us before we'll listen to Him. But what He is really doing is showing how much He loves us. This is how personal He is. If the three of us were the only ones on Earth, Jesus still would've sacrificed His life for us. All He wants us to do, as John 3:16 says, is to believe in Him."

"So, what does that really mean?"

Magnus reached into his pocket and pulled out a twenty dollar bill, and held it out to Brice.

"Brice, I'm going to give you this bill. Do you believe I would do it?"

"Sure, I take you at your word. We've become good friends, and I can trust you to do what you say you will."

"But when does this money become yours?"

"When I take it from your hand."

To show he was serious, Magnus actually said, "Here, it's yours. I'm not bribing you, but want to contribute to the costs for Spud's funeral."

Brice, surprised, took the money, saying "Thank you."

Magnus summarized his object lesson, "And that's what 'believe' means. We have to accept what Jesus did for us on the cross by accepting His gift that is free. We can't earn it by being a good person, because we're not perfect as Jesus was. So He made a way out for us. And He even gives us the faith to believe in Him."

After waiting to see if they had more questions, Magnus, seizing the teachable moment, looked at both Sutherlands, and asked the final question, "Brice and Blaine, are you ready to accept Jesus right now?"

Another question from Brice, "Where? Here? We're not in church, you know."

Magnus answered, "That doesn't matter. Jesus is here with us, and knows your thoughts and attitudes toward Him. All you have to do is pray to Him. It's just like talking to Him. It's your sincerity He wants."

Since they both seemed hesitant, Magnus suggested, "Would it be OK if I said a prayer out loud, and you each repeated the words?"

Brice, looking at Blaine, said, "Is that cool with you?"

Blaine agreed, "Sure, Dad. I'm with you. At least this will honor Spud."

Brice again, "Go ahead, Magnus. You've got us this far. Let's score one for God."

And so, right where the three of them were seated on the bunk beds in Brice and Blaine's yurt, Magnus began:

"Dear Jesus," (Magnus waited to hear two more faint 'Dear Jesus' from Brice and Blaine) "Thank you that you loved us so much you died for us" (again the quiet words from the two), "even though we are sinners and deserve to die" (again the hesitating voices). "And thank you that you even used Spud to show us how much you sacrificed for us" (here Magnus had to wait longer for the quivering words to come).

Magnus continued his prayer, "And now, Jesus, we ask You to forgive our sins, and we accept by faith what You did for us on the cross" (now the sincerity was evident from the men's voices). "We ask You to come into our lives and give us the power to live for You for the rest of our lives - no matter what." (This long sentence took a while for Brice and Blaine to finish). Then Magnus closed with a simple, "Amen."

He looked up and saw two peaceful faces, each with moist eyes. They each did slow, sober fist bumps as a sign of solidarity. Brice and Blaine had taken the first steps of a new life with a new Master. Now things would be different for them.

A Tribute to Spud

The next day, a bright, sunny Sunday with no session, found the trio, with their "packing boxes," off on another mission by the ocean.

As they rumbled down the bumpy dirt road in Brice's truck, he, seemingly a different person, suggested, "I think it would be nice if we could carve a Bible verse on our box."

Magnus asked, "What verse?"

"The one you mentioned about giving your life for your friends."

Magnus again, "Yes, it would work. Even though it refers to Jesus' action, it could work for Spud, too."

Blaine, also interested, followed up with, "And we could carve a cross."

And then he asked a practical question, "We can't take Spud home with us in our box, so we have to have his funeral here. But who can we get to do the carving?"

After a moment of silence, Brice said, "I've seen a store downtown by the "Midnight Sun Saloon" (which he vowed not to enter again) that does wood engraving. It's run by Inuits. Maybe we could check it out."

Magnus suggested, "Why don't you two take your box to that store, and see if they can do the wood-burning we talked about - the Bible verse, the cross, and anything else you can think of."

He hurriedly wrote down the verse Brice suggested, drew a cross, and handed the paper to Brice, saying, "If that store can still do it today, maybe we can have our little funeral tomorrow. I'd better get back to my parents. I'll stop over tomorrow. It will be weird not seeing Spud there to greet me. I'll really miss him, too."

"Yes, I know," said Blaine.

Brice predicted, "Yea, it's going to take a while to get used to this."

With these concluding remarks, the men separated, to meet again tomorrow. And they were all thinking how Spud was in his tomb by the rising sea. They wouldn't want him to be washed away after they had gone home. They wanted this to be a permanent resting place for their faithful friend.

The Day of the Funeral

Since there were no more presentations until the closing ceremonies, the three men got together to plan Spud's funeral. Magnus came over to the Sutherland's yurt bright and early the next day. This time there was no friendly bark and wagging tail to greet him. It was strangely quiet.

Brice, answering the door with a cheerful smile, greeted Magnus with, "Boy, I really slept soundly last night."

"How so?," inquired Magnus.

"Well, obviously Spud's fight was the worst thing that has happened to me up here. But after I prayed that prayer with you, I had a feeling things were going to work out. What made the difference?"

Blaine was now getting up, and echoed his father's dilemma, "Yea, I feel the same way as Dad."

Here was another spiritual opening for Magnus. He wasn't proselytizing, but was only answering their sincere questions. And he had some of his own.

"When we all prayed yesterday, who were you praying to?"

"Jesus." they said in unison.

"What did you ask him to do?"

Brice this time, "To come into our lives."

Blaine added, "And to give us the power to live for him."

Magnus, "You are both correct. Good memory. Can I share another Bible verse that explains what you just said?"

"Of course," said Brice.

"OK, it goes something like this, "If you are a new creation in Christ, old things have passed away, and new things have come. That means when you asked Christ to come into your life, he starts a makeover on you. We still do wrong things, but now we want to please him by obeying him. It's a lifelong process, and I have a long ways to go. But remember, Jesus is now with you, and gives you the power to live for him. Before we leave I'll give you each a Bible so you can learn about him and how to please him. But for now you're starting down the right road, and that's exciting for us all."

Brice politely ended this "God talk" with, "Thanks for answering my question. But that's enough for now. We can't forget about Spud."

Magnus agreed, "You're right." Let's walk down to that shop and see if our box is ready."

On the way to the store, the three men approached the "Midnight Sun Saloon." Brice hesitated, thought briefly about his flings with Sara and saw the door was open. Before he would've gone in, grabbed a bar stool and a beer, and flirted with Sara. Blaine and Magnus also hesitated, and looked at each other with a quizzical stare, and then continued walking with Brice. Indeed something was different with this former Husker.

They entered "Inuit Carvings" and an old, grizzled man with rough hands and a ruddy face recognized them from yesterday. He got up from his stool, reached for two boxes on his shelf, and handed one to Brice and the other to Blaine.

They all looked at the newly decorated "boxes-turned-coffins" for what seemed like a long time. Finally the old man broke the silence,

"I know what you're thinking. I've lost many sled dogs when I used to hunt on the ice. If a polar bear is hungry, he will eat anything he can catch. I've had to shoot a few of them to protect my dogs. Now our people use snowmobiles, but they must be careful they don't fall through the thin ice. We've lost several of our best hunters to this melt."

Brice reached into his pocket, pulled out the twenty-dollar bill that Magnus gave him, matched it with his own, and gave it to the man, who nodded in approval.

As the three of them left the store, Magnus, with a puzzled look on his face, said, "I don't mean to ask a dumb question, but why two boxes?"

Blaine answered, "Dad and I talked about it, and we want to have our own funeral for Spud when we get home. Of course, we can't take his body with us, but we'll bury the box and have our own funeral again. Maybe if you ever visit Nebraska, you can see Spud's spot."

"Deal."

"Deal," echoed Brice, "but for now let's head to our spot by the sea."

Before this they stopped at the Sutherland's yurt, left one box there, grabbed some of Spud's things, put one box in the back of Brice's pickup, and headed down to the sea one last time.

As they headed down the soggy road where the permafrost had been, they noticed whitecaps on the thundering waves. Brice stopped in the middle of the road to assess the situation.

"It looks like a storm is brewing out there. Let's see if we can make it to Spud's tomb and have our ceremony before it gets worse. What do you think, guys?"

Magnus replied, "You're the driver. Go for it." Blaine nodded in approval, and they were off in a burst of mud flying from the tires.

When they arrived at their destination, the waves were lapping at the entrance to where they had laid Spud. The men hurriedly exited the truck, Brice grabbed the box, and they stumbled into the cave, now protected from the howling wind. Without saying a word, Brice removed the stone over the opening, and squeezed into the opening and gingerly picked up Spud, who was now stiff with rigor mortis. He also detected the beginning of a putrid odor as he winced and gingerly carried him from the cozy cave. He then gently wrapped him in his favorite blanket, and finally laid him carefully in the three foot by four foot cedar box, its sweet smell now competing with Spud's. Brice then held out his football-carrying hand to Blaine, who handed him Spud's collar and leash - never to be worn again. And then Brice slowly closed the coffin, stood up, and came back to stand beside the other two, as the three of them stared silently at the coffin encasing their departed friend. Even though the wind was still howling, and the waves were still lapping, they were strangely sheltered from the storm.

After what seemed like several minutes, Brice turned to Magnus and said, "Would you say a few words, and lead us in a prayer?"

Magnus replied, "I'd be honored."

The Eulogy

Magnus, looking at the coffin, started by talking to Spud: "Spud,

I've only known you for a short time, but have grown to love you like I do your masters. You were always full of energy, ready to run and please us."

Here he hesitated, swallowed deeply, and looked briefly at the moist eyes of Brice and Blaine, and then began again, "And you showed your stuff as a brave and faithful bear dog by sacrificing yourself to save us. And for that we will be forever grateful. If there are dogs in heaven, we will again see you running, jumping, and playing. And we look forward to that day. Rest peacefully by the sea you enjoyed so much, our faithful friend."

Magnus then came over and stepped between Brice and Blaine, put his arms on their shoulders and prayed loudly above the roaring ocean, "Dear Jesus, we don't always understand why things like this happen, but we claim your promise that all things work together for good to those who love you and are called according to your purpose. But please answer the why question for us sometime. Amen."

And once again they were silent, hearing only the wind and the waves. The three of them took one last look at their coffin with this inscription on the top of the tear-stained coffin:

"Spud Sutherland: Karelian Bear Dog
Born in Wyoming, February 15, 2018.
Died saving his friends in Alaska, August 15, 2021.

'Greater love has no one than this, that he lay down his life for his friends.' John 15:13"

And running along each side of the top of the coffin was an elongated cross.

And now one task remained. In the bottom of the cave was some soft sand, suitable for digging. Brice, shovel in hand, took the first turn, again entered the cave and began digging, piling the sand by one side of the rock wall. After about five minutes he handed the shovel to Blaine, who crawled in and did the same. Finally it was Magnus' turn, who finished digging deep enough to bury the coffin. When he hit a pool of sea water, he stopped shoveling.

Finally Brice crawled through the opening and grabbed the coffin, and handed it down to the two men who steadied Spud as they lowered him into his final resting place. For the last time the three men looked down at the coffin, as if they could still see Spud. This time the sound of the water gurgling in the hole competed with the wind and waves outside.

And as they did before, each man scooped several shovelfuls of sand on the coffin until it was completely buried. No trace of Spud or his coffin remained. One by one they scrambled through the opening, and looked down one last time. Finally they all picked up the large rock and rolled it in front of the opening, sealing it as tight as they could without cementing it shut. It would have to do. Hopefully Spud's tomb would be safe from predators and the rising sea. Who knows, maybe they would be back to check on him later. For now their mission was completed. Brice and Blaine would have another burial in Nebraska, but it wouldn't be quite the same.

VIII. Closing Ceremonies

There was an air of excitement as the scientists, educators, artists, musicians, students, and members of the press crowded into the assembly hall for their final session before returning to their respective countries. Whereas at the beginning there had been a formal atmosphere, now, after two months of working, relaxing, and enjoying each other's company, the mood was festive. This time there were no flags carried by representatives of each country. In fact the procession looked chaotic. People strolled in as citizens of the world, dedicated to saving the planet from the ravages of climate change, now sensitized by the presentations they had heard and experienced. Some even held hands and walked shoulder to shoulder. Also walking together were Brice, Blaine, Magnus, and his parents, waving to their new-found friends, as were the other delegations. It was a time for celebrating before the hard work at home would begin.

This time the accompanying music was distinctly American: Aaron Copeland's famous "Fanfare for the Common Man" - a song traditionally played when dignitaries were present. And they were here - representatives from governments who will see the most climatic changes if the Arctic continues its warming pace. These decision-makers came from Russia, Norway, Denmark, Greenland, United States of America, Iceland, Sweden, Finland, Canada, and Great Britain. The political leaders of each country would have their turn at the podium.

Since climate change ultimately affects the entire planet, the proceedings were being beamed by satellite to each nation's capital city, including those in the Southern Hemisphere. As the scientists had revealed, climate change is happening faster at the Poles, and this includes Antarctica - the focus of the next IPY. This world connection would allow each country's government to "be on the same page," a necessary step in building an international coalition to combat what is now being labeled as the greatest threat ever faced by humanity.

When all had taken their random seats, and the inspiring music had ended, Dr. Dimitri Pushkin, the presiding officer from Russia, stepped to the podium to address the delegations.

"Two months ago I welcomed you to this International Polar Year when you were eager to learn about climate change from the experts, and to see first-hand its effects in the Arctic. You have all survived, even though I understand some of you have had close calls."

He paused as many looked at each other and nodded in affirmation. Brice commented to Magnus, "Why was he looking at me when he said that?"

Magnus answered, "He doesn't know it was a 'God-thing.'" Brice, still trying to figure out what had happened to him after Spud's gallant fight, nodded in silent affirmation.

When the crowd quieted down, he again began, "Now you are going home to be the vanguard of teachers that will build a grassroots movement to save the planet."

A spontaneous standing ovation greeted this challenge.

Dr. Pushkin continued, "We are particularly pleased to see the political leaders from countries closest to the Arctic. Your remarks today, together with your governments' commitment to combating climate change, are being closely watched by the world. As we know, ever since the Kyoto Protocols expired in 2012, the world has been steadily warming, and the CO_2 levels increasing. Several international conferences have failed to secure binding agreements to fight global warming. We hope and pray this time it will be different."

Again a standing ovation, directed toward the nine political leaders on the podium.

Dr. Pushkin concluded, "And now we will eagerly hear from the speakers you see before you, the order having been determined by each leader pushing a numerical button on their iPhone. We don't draw numbers from a hat anymore.

Sweden

"And now I'll call on the representative from the first country chosen, Sweden, who pushed key number one on his iPad.

Rousing applause ensued from the small Swedish contingent, with politeness being the rule from the rest of the audience.

"Good morning. I am Sigmund Liefsen, Prime Minister of our environmentally-conscious country. In fact, according to the latest rankings, Sweden ranks number one in protecting the environment. It must be a coincidence that I'm the first speaker."

This time the Swedish scientists, including previous presenter Dr. Andrea Johnsen, stood up and chanted the familiar, "We're number one, we're number one," generally heard only at sports events.

Mr. Liefsen, waving his arm downward, signaled to his fellow countrymen that that was enough, and they immediately sat down again.

After the demonstration died down, he continued, "And we are proud that one of our cities, Vaxjo, has as its goal to become Europe's first fossil-free city. They're not quite there yet, but are coming close. They use a centralized heating system that uses low-emitting wood chips from our abundant forests. Other innovations include providing free parking for green vehicles, and expanding our bike paths. We even clear them of snow before the roads! Even though we are a small country, we hope to be a model for the world of what local innovation can do to combat climate change.

"Yes, we're proud of that international ranking, but we have much left to accomplish to reduce our carbon footprint. Even though we presently receive about forty percent of our energy from renewables, we're not satisfied until we become carbon-free.

"We're always looking for new ways to avoid using fossil fuels. In fact we've harnessed human body heat in our large and crowded buildings to heat adjacent buildings. That's using old technology in a new way. Why waste something we all produce naturally?"

Again the Swedes stood and started hugging one another.

Quite surprised, the Prime Minister, without missing a beat, said, "Thank you for demonstrating your body heat. Now you may sit down again," – and they did.

Brice turned to Magnus and said, "I thought the Swedes were a cold people."

"People think Icelanders are, too, but we only hug in private. Maybe we should try this type of heat along with our geothermal. We'd be warm all winter," Magnus joked.

The Prime Minister continued, "But we've also had our problems with the extreme weather, with record-setting temperatures and snowfall in recent years. It's more than naturally occurring variations. Models by our own scientists attribute it to human-induced climate change.

"But our people are resilient and can rise to the challenge of protecting the environment. We have instituted a nation-wide program to become fossil-fuel-free by 2030. The Southern half of our country has already reached that goal. The government is providing incentives and programs to encourage people to use more of our readily available mass transit instead of driving their own vehicles. We have many bike and walking paths, and wide lanes on our highways to encourage cycling by pedal power. We joined other European cities in instituting a bike rental system. Our fishing industry is expanding and encouraging more consumption of this healthy meat. Our homes are becoming more efficient with government-purchased programmable thermostats. Tax credits are available to install efficient windows and appliances.

"We cultivate a spirit of community where all citizens become involved to lower their carbon footprint. And we are on target to have the entire country carbon-free by 2030. We're only a small country leading by example, but the larger developed countries need to "step up to the plate" if we hope to save our planet from catastrophic consequences due to rapid climate change. I urge you to accept that challenge. Thank you."

This time it wasn't just the Swedes that applauded.

Brice knew he had a mission - in more ways than one - when he returned home. "Our country has to take the lead," he thought.

As the applause faded, Magnus was thinking, "I thought we were number one. Oh well, wait until they hear from us."

Denmark and Greenland

Dr. Pushkin stood briefly to welcome the second speaker in the cell phone lottery, Prime Minister Jens Christiansen from Denmark, who took the podium.

"Thank you. As the country exercising political authority over Greenland, I am representing this huge territory that holds the key to the predicted sea level rise this century. I want to thank Dr. Leslie Swensen from the Nordic Institute for her excellent presentation dealing with our glaciers - the most famous being the Jakobshavn. I have disturbing news. It's melting faster than the scientists predicted, resulting in city-sized icebergs breaking off into the ocean. In fact, our neighbor Canada has to regularly protect their shipping lanes from these monsters, and reroute their vessels to avoid *Titanic*-like collisions. Thanks to the ever-warming temperatures, the ice is melting rapidly and lubricating the glacier for a faster ride to the sea. In fact Jakobshavn is believed to be the largest contributor to sea level rise in the Northern Hemisphere, and it's the fastest moving glacier in the world.

You probably remember that every five years the Intergovernmental Panel on Climate Change - IPCC for short - has increased their projection of sea level rise. The latest report, issued in 2017, predicts a rise of four to six feet by the end of this century. If true, this could be disastrous for low lying countries as alluded to by Dr. Swensen. You've seen the devastation to some native villages right here in Alaska. And to add more **urgency** to this situation, the next IPCC Report due out next year may increase it further.

"The melting of the Greenland ice sheet is predicted by some climate scientists to reach the point of no return by 2040. However, other reports place that point between 100 and 1,000 years, so take your pick. In any scenario the melting will continue, with new water rushing into the sea.

"However, not everything is 'gloom and doom.' Green grass and fertile fields are sprouting up where the glaciers once lay. The Inuits are becoming farmers instead of hunters, raising fruits and vegetables, and even hay for their livestock. Even farmers' markets have proliferated – a welcome sign to the burgeoning tourist industry. But the rest of the world is suffering the consequences of a warmer and less icy Greenland.

"What can be done about it? I know Denmark doesn't rate as high as our other Scandinavian countries in protecting the environment. In any event I am announcing an initiative that might push the point of no return in Greenland back a decade or two, and possibly reverse the rapid melting."

A hush fell over the audience as they anticipated Mr. Christiansen's next words. Magnus, in particular, wanted to check out the country that once ruled his. Would it be a technological breakthrough, or just another goal that wouldn't be met?

"I've consulted with Dr. Ingrid Gunderson of Finland, one of your Nordic presenters, who presented about the ice dust, or black carbon problem in the Arctic. Reducing this human pollution problem would slow the glacial melting and buy us time to save the planet. She's been working on a system that would sequester the soot from the coal that is burned and released into the atmosphere. Coal plants in the larger countries, particularly the U.S. and China, are already using this technology. We still don't know if this is a permanent solution, but it's worth trying with the black carbon. This proposal won't be popular with the coal industry, but it is necessary if we are serious about saving our low-lying islands and countries."

Mr. Christiansen continued, "Therefore Denmark and Greenland are hosting an international conference in 2022 titled, 'Black Carbon: Can It Be Eradicated?' Our goal is for each participating nation to formulate guidelines, together with the technology, to remove these dangerous particles from the atmosphere, and bury them deep in the ground - never to return. Each developed country, along with the United Nations, will be expected to contribute financially to this project that will ultimately benefit the entire planet. And this conference will ask for binding commitments, unlike the unsuccessful conference we hosted in Copenhagen in '09.

"You remember the success the world had in responding to the widening hole in the ozone layer in the last century. We banned the aerosols causing this problem, and it worked. We did it once, and we can do it again. Thank you."

With the reminder of Copenhagen, the audience reaction was more subdued. Another huge task awaited the international community. But this was only part of the global strategy to save the planet. And Magnus was pleased that another Scandinavian country was taking the initiative in combating global warming.

Before Dr. Pushkin introduced the next speaker, he prefaced his remarks, "It seems we're developing a friendly competition between nations. Who can do the most to fight climate change? Can our third speaker, Prime Minister Alun Wagner from Great Britain top Sweden, Denmark, and Greenland? Let's see if he can. Welcome Mr. Prime Minister."

Great Britain

Mr. Wagner began, "What's the matter with competition if it helps save the planet?"

This time everyone stood and applauded in unison. Maybe a breakthrough was coming.

He continued, "After all, the big oil companies compete for the world's share of the market, and pollute to boot. Why shouldn't we encourage them to clean up their mess?"

Another round of rousing applause.

For the third time the Prime Minister began, "Seriously, our former Prime Minister Tony Blair called climate change the 'biggest long-term threat facing our world,' to which I agree. I now provide an overview of what, not only our country, but the European Union, is doing to combat this **urgent** threat.

"The extreme weather we've been experiencing in Europe has finally caused our people to 'get it.' BBC surveys have found an increasing percentage of our citizens to attribute climate change to human activities. Furthermore, large majorities say it is necessary to take major steps to combat it. So my question to us as political leaders is, 'Do we have the political will to lead our constituents?' This issue is now not just for our environmental ministers, but for us."

This time the politicians on the stage all arose, grasped each other's hands, and held them up in a sign of unity. But would it last this time? The previous record of international climate change conferences was not good.

Again Mr. Wagner began, "We believe our people will respond to this challenge. You may remember the severe austerity program we instituted last decade. We all pulled together, and today are a stronger nation because of it. The same thing can happen with the problems before us today.

"Great Britain led the way in Europe by adopting the world's first climate change law that fixed targets for cutting carbon emissions, monitored its progress, and established five-year carbon budgets. And I'm happy to report it is working. Although we missed our goal of a 30 percent reduction by 2020, we've set a longer-range goal of a 70 percent decrease by 2050. Scientists tell us we actually need an 80 percent reduction by 2050 to avoid the worst effects of climate change, so we might revise our reduction upward during this decade.

"And that's not all we've done. London has taken the lead in cutting its greenhouse gas emissions by 60 percent by 2025. And I'm happy to report they are on their way to meeting their goal. When the mayor of our largest city levied a congestion tax, it was initially unpopular. But now the air in the central city is cleaner, and pedestrian malls and walkways have sprung up where cars once roamed. Another success story."

This time it was the Brits' turn to "strut their stuff," and not their stuffiness.

The Prime Minister again, "And here's what we're considering. We're used to credit and debit cards. What if everyone were given a credit card that could be used for an allocated amount of carbon emissions? As you consume carbon dioxide to heat your home, drive your car, take a plane, or purchase your food, you would debit their use until you reached your weekly, monthly, or yearly allocation. We already have the carbon footprint label on all the food items in our grocery stores, so the carbon credit card could be used even when you shop.

"In other words, you would budget your energy use just like you do your personal finances.

"Does this sound too 'Big Brotherish?' Well, we seemed to have gotten used to the body scans before we fly. Serious problems sometimes require seemingly drastic solutions, for the good of the planet. Don't you agree?"

This time the applause was mixed with a few boos. Maybe he was reaching too far too quickly. Would the world wait?

Magnus, sizing up what he was hearing, was again thinking, "I bet there will be a market for our CO2 phone."

The Prime Minister closed with one more world-first. "Those of you who have traveled to our country by ship, or spent time on our shores, can attest to the power of the wind and waves. We are putting these forces of Nature to good use by harnessing them to produce electricity. So if you see huge sea snakes off our shores, don't be afraid. They don't bite. They only serve as conduits for converting wave and tidal energy into carbon-free energy.

"Some of you may be thinking, 'These innovations sound great, but how are you going to pay for them?' Thank you for asking.

"Some of you may remember the 600 page report, authored by Dr. Nicolas Stern, the head of our Economic Service. He analyzed the costs to the world economy of combating climate change with a 'business as usual' approach. His surprising conclusion was that the costs of inaction would cost more than taking aggressive action to reduce greenhouse gases 80 percent by 2100. This 'do nothing approach' would risk economic disruption on a scale of World Wars I and II or the Great Depression. Also temperatures could rise by 5 degrees C. or 9 degrees F. by the end of this century. Sir Stern concluded with this warning, and I quote, 'Even if climate change turned out to be the biggest hoax in history, the world will still be better off with all new technologies it will develop to combat it. The price of waiting for more evidence is too high. You're playing with a planet here.'"

Mr. Wagner closed with this challenge, "This report makes it all the more **urgent** to forge an international agreement, not with just the countries represented here, but with all countries. Because we are not an island. Our earth from space, beautiful to behold, doesn't have any boundaries. I believe the time is right for bold action, and it starts with you. Thank you."

This time the standing ovation was thunderous. But it will take more than applause.

Texting from Afar

During their break Brice, as usual, checked his iPhone for any messages. This time there was one from Tricia - like his previous one to her – terse and to the point. It read, "Go ahead and file. Have it your way. Remember, it's your idea. I'm making my own life here."

After taking a few minutes to soak in the message, Brice - wanting to share his "new life" with her - responded quickly with, "I'm not filing. Want to see you when I return. I've changed! Will explain later."

Tricia, now curious, also texted Brice immediately, "I'll have to see you to believe it. You have my phone number. Call me when in Nebraska."

Brice also checked immediately, but did not respond. "She'll have to see me in person, and judge for herself," he thought. Meanwhile, back to the speakers.

Canada

Dr. Pushkin welcomed the assembly back for the last half of the political presentations by introducing Canada's Prime Minister, Christina Shepherd. She began with the caveat, "We Canadians are doing more than just playing world class hockey. We are also excelling in innovative ways to combat climate change, because we've seen what warmer temperatures are doing to our environment, making it less harsh than it used to be.

"First I'll start with the melting Arctic ice. You've already addressed this topic, but I'll personalize it for our country. Some of the ice shelves, which have developed over thousands of years as the winter ice increased, are now melting and breaking off into the ocean. These free-floating islands are threatening our oil and gas platforms. Recently one of these city-sized icebergs rammed one of our drilling rigs, completely demolishing it. I guess that's one more reason to reduce our use of fossil fuels.

"Furthermore, there's a phenomenon called the Arctic Oscillation. According to climate scientists, increased warming whips up more winds that drive the sea ice from the Arctic to the Atlantic Ocean. This results in more ice shelf melting, more icebergs, and more problems for our shipping and drilling. And so the positive feedback loop goes.

"The effect of a warmer Arctic on our animals is another ecological problem we, and they, face. Dr. Bill Hanson has already discussed the problems faced by the polar bears in coping with the declining ice floes. But another animal may be threatened or endangered - our caribou. Canadian researchers have estimated their population has declined 70 percent in the last four decades. And this precipitous drop cannot be attributed only to natural fluctuations.

"Every year caribou undertake the largest migration of an ungulate in the Northern Hemisphere - a spectacle to behold. But now spring is indeed 'springing ahead,' arriving earlier, and with it come the young nutritious plants. The problem is the caribou haven't arrived yet to feed on this rich food. They may soon be on our threatened list along with the polar bear.

"Hotter summers also bring more insects, which harass the caribou with greater intensity, interrupting their feeding. The warmer winters – that even the hardy Canadians now enjoy - cause problems for the caribou. More precipitation falls as freezing rain rather than snow. The rain turns into ice on the ground, sealing in the animals' winter food source, the lichen. The ice also makes it more difficult for the caribou to walk, thereby causing them to use extra energy that eventually weakens them. And that's when the wolves come out. And they do more than howl. They are efficient and crafty predators.

"So what are we doing about these problems? We may not be number one in the environmental rankings, but we are leading in combating global warming in another way. In 2008, British Columbia became the first government entity in North America to levy a carbon tax. Now before you non-BC Canadians throw your hockey sticks at me, let me explain how it works."

Ms. Shepherd hesitated and pretended to duck behind the podium. Finally she reappeared, unscathed, and began again.

"This tax is levied on everyone who burns fossil fuels, including corporations and individuals. Seventy percent of the cost is borne by businesses and industry. You may ask, 'How did we sell this to the public?' We made it revenue neutral. Every dollar is rebated to the taxpayers through reductions in our small business tax, corporate tax, as well as low-income climate credits, and a bonus, climate-action dividend.

"You may also be wondering, 'How successful has it been?' Politically it's been popular with the voters. In fact, every prime minister that has campaigned to keep this tax has been elected. What started in BC has now spread to all our larger provinces except the Northwest Territories. It's ironic because that province is the most impacted by global warming. Our goal is to bring them on board, as well as the island provinces, by 2030. Then it would be a truly nationwide tax.

"How successful has this tax been in accomplishing its goal? Not only has it reduced carbon emissions by 50 percent since it started, the price of gas has dropped by an equivalent amount, due to the lower demand because of more energy-efficient vehicles on the road.

"In fact we now have what we call a Hydrogen Highway from Vancouver to Montreal, lined with hydrogen fueling stations. We're making the fuel of the future now, and it's 100 percent pollution free. And one of our small provinces, Prince Edward Island, has created a hydrogen-powered village, using its wind turbines to split the hydrogen from water, and then using it to power fuel cells. They use these cells for their cars, busses, cargo trucks, and excursion boats."

Magnus, upon hearing this, thought, "Wait until you hear what our Prime Minister will say. We had the world's first hydrogen fueling station, and we've been making the fuel of the future before Canada. But I'm being too nationalistic. After all, we're here to save the planet, not just a couple of countries."

The Prime Minister continued, "And we have another environmental first for North America. First it was our environmentally-conscious British Columbia, and now all of our provinces have outlawed plastic bags."

At that remark some cheered, but others hid the plastic bags they had carried into the hall.

After the mixed reaction, she began again, "And this law includes all cruise ships, whether registered in Canada or another country, from carrying these throwaways into our ports, such as Vancouver, Victoria, and Prince Rupert on the Pacific side, and Halifax and St. John's on the Atlantic Side.

"You've all seen pictures of the huge Pacific garbage patch that is mainly composed of plastics. Fish and marine mammals mistake them for food, swallow them, and realize their deadly consequences too late. This is one way to help preserve our fishing stocks. A win-win for the environment and the economy. It can be done."

Ms. Shepherd closed with this admonition, "We are anxiously waiting to hear what the U.S. has to say about this world-wide crisis. After all, CO_2, floods, droughts, fires, and diseases don't respect national boundaries. We share a 3,000 mile border with our good neighbor to the South, and want to work with them as well as the rest of the world. It will truly take a global effort if we are to succeed. I think we are up to the challenge. Thank you."

During the applause a few small Maple leaf flags were raised by proud Canadians. The competition among countries was continuing. But could they also work together?

Russia

And now it was the presiding officer's turn to talk about his country. Dr. Pushkin received a special introduction from Dr. Johannson that began, "Dr. Pushkin's country and my nation of Norway were enemies during the Cold War, but now we are working together for the sake of the planet. As the largest country in land area, Russia has seen drastic changes in their fragile environment this century. They have much to lose if the Arctic continues to warm, and are serious in combating global warming. Please welcome Dr. Pushkin."

After polite applause, Dr. Pushkin began by thanking Dr. Johannson for his introduction, and strolled across the stage to shake Olaf's hand and said, "We can't reverse history, but today we can make history by taking steps to save the planet, and Russia is willing to join the international community as a full partner."

He received a standing ovation, and spotted a few Russian flags waving, before he began again.

"As you probably know from your history, the Soviet Union was more concerned about winning wars and promoting communism than protecting the environment, so we have a long way to go to catch up with you Western countries. But our present political leaders have experienced much extreme weather the last decade to convince us climate change is real.

"You may remember the series of ravaging wildfires as a result of a devastating drought that plagued our country in 2010. This perfect storm was intensified as a result of record high temperatures, reaching close to 30 degrees Fahrenheit above normal. Most people don't have air conditioning, so the elderly were hit hard, resulting in many deaths. This served as a wake-up call to our leaders that something needs to be done.

"The ramifications of this extreme weather were felt worldwide as our wheat crop fell by one-third, sending food prices soaring. There were even food riots in many poor countries, resulting in many deaths in the scramble for survival.

"And the last several years have seen average temperatures climb even higher than those before the 2010 drought. But we're taking steps to prevent another disaster. Restrictions on campfires in the forests have been implemented. Residents living in wooded areas now must maintain fire breaks around their buildings. And we've even developed the technology to seed the clouds for rain during dry seasons. And prayer doesn't hurt either. Finally, we've upgraded our firefighting equipment to include aerial tankers, and increased the number of fire trucks and crews. And what do you call your elite fighters?

"Hot shots," came the reply from some Americans.

"Yes, that's what we call ours too," added Dr. Pushkin.

"But there's another result of global warming that could have an even greater impact on our fragile ecosystem. You've probably heard the dreaded phrase during the Stalin era, 'You're being sent to Siberia.' Not an ideal vacation spot then, and not even now. Because of the rapidly rising temperatures, the permafrost is melting there, releasing methane, a much more potent greenhouse gas than carbon dioxide. After a period of relative stability, methane is now again on the increase, and along with CO_2s, are at their highest levels in the last 650,000 years.

"You remember Dr. Andrea Johnsen's presentation on atmospheric gases, mentioning methane even seeping from the ocean floor. And you can't forget the native Inuits describing losing their houses due to the thawing permafrost. Indeed the foundations of the Arctic are crumbling.

"But the good news is that methane doesn't last very long in the atmosphere, unlike carbon dioxide. Therefore we can clamp down on these emissions quickly, and that would buy time to concentrate on the thornier problem of reducing carbon emissions. Our scientists are working on methods to capture and sequester methane in Siberia, and pump it into large geologic faults. Hopefully, it will be buried permanently in our country, never to escape and cause further damage.

"Unfortunately our President could not be here today. He is meeting with the Presidents of China and India to try to get them on board with a global climate treaty. His goal is to persuade the four largest emitters of greenhouse gases, including the USA and my country, to take the lead in convincing the other countries to support an international agreement in Reykjavik in December. So your work is crucial. Finish this IPY well. Thank you."

As the applause started, Dr.Pushkin, in a show of solidarity, walked over to where the U.S. President was sitting, and shook her hand. She, somewhat surprised, rose and they both held up their hands together.

Maybe this time something significant would come from these sessions. The whole world was watching.

Magnus' Surprise

During the break Magnus checked his cell phone as usual. This time there was a text message from the Ministry of Sustainability. It read,

"New Message
FROM: Olga Jonsdottir

You'll be pleased to know CO_2 phone you proposed is now available for distribution. During my remarks today I'll recognize your essay and present you with first phone. I'd like to talk w/ you later about new position I'm creating in our ministry. Thx for your efforts."

Upon reading this Magnus was overwhelmed. Here he was, a college student interacting with all these world-renowned scientists, and now he was going to be recognized in front of all of them. He started to swell with pride until this thought interrupted his pride, "Who do you think gave you this idea, son?" He immediately recognized the silent voice of God, and said out loud, "Sorry, God. You're the boss, not me."

Fortunately, no one was around to hear him supposedly speaking to himself.

Magnus, wanting to share this news, walked to where his parents were, at the break buffet eating salmon sandwiches and drinking fruit punch. "I don't want you to be surprised, but our Minister of Sustainability (he turned and pointed to the stage where she was seated) is going to recognize me for my cell phone idea. Do you remember meeting her before we began our trip here?"

"Of course we do, son. And we're proud to be here with you," complimented his father.

"I guess there's a reason why we're here with you. Just don't get a big head over this," cautioned his mother.

"Don't worry. I've already heard about that." That's all he would say. Now it was time for the next speaker.

Norway

This time Dr. Olaffson, the Project's Director, took the podium to introduce the next political leader. "Before I introduce our next political leader, I would like to mention Norway's commitment to the cause we all espouse. We have consistently been in the top five countries in protecting the environment. The U.N. has consistently ranked us, along with the nation you will hear from next, as the most livable country in the world. We are the fifth biggest oil exporter, and the record-high prices for this crude have made us wealthy. And we have the most sophisticated drilling equipment for use in the turbulent North Sea. Our safety record is impeccable - not one accident," he bragged as he looked at the U.S. President, who immediately looked away, with thoughts of the massive BP oil spill a decade ago still etched in her mind. But she had a response for the waiting world that they would hear shortly.

"Even though the oil industry has replaced fishing as our main exporter, we are working hard to produce two-thirds of our energy from renewables. Our goal is to become a carbon-free nation by 2030, 20 years ahead of our previous goal. We are also offsetting our present emissions by sponsoring reforestation projects in the developing world. The more trees we can plant, the more carbon is taken from the atmosphere.

"Enough about our country. Now I would like to introduce the country we originally settled. Yes, our Vikings had a notorious past of raping and pillaging, but finally they settled down and brought agriculture and babies to this uninhabited land of fire and ice. And

I must admit that we deliberately misnamed Iceland and Greenland to keep settlers from coming to our land. Judging by Iceland's low population, it has worked - at least for now. Recently it's been discovered as the best place to visit, and maybe relocate.

"Now Iceland is in a race with us to be the first carbon-free country. I'll let their Minister of Sustainability mention Iceland's other firsts. And she has a surprise in store for you. So welcome Olga Jonsdottir."

Magnus, seated in the front with his parents, Brice, and Blaine, leaned over to his mother and whispered in her ear, "The surprise must be about the phone." Lara simply smiled at her son, and winked at him. His father, overhearing the conversation, gave him the thumbs up sign as his approval. The three Icelandic scientists, Jon, Sigga, and Katrin were up and applauding loudly. The rest of the audience was not as excited – after all, it wasn't their country.

Iceland

Ms. Jonsdottir began with an introduction to Iceland,

"Thank you, Mr. Olafsson, for setting the record straight about our name. We're more than glaciers and volcanoes. And we do owe our heritage to your fertile Vikings," she said with a twinkle in her eyes.

"Seventy percent of our population can be traced to your country. I'm the exception to the blue-eyed blonde stereotype. No blonde jokes, please. They wouldn't go over well in the most feminist place in the world."

The audience started to laugh, but reverted back to silence with her last statement.

The minister continued, "To put our country in perspective, compared to Alaska our population is less than half, and our geographic size is one-fifteenth. What we lack in size we make up in world firsts. Here's the list:

"The happiest in the world [that elicited puzzled looks from the audience].

The next three firsts are all per capita. Maybe we have an advantage here with our small and homogeneous population.

* The highest Internet use
* The highest mobile phone use
* The most writers and artists
* Our longevity and literacy rates are among the highest in the world
* Thirty percent of our population has a university degree

"And now I'll give you the 'rest of the story.' Our glaciers are melting faster than at any time in our history. This allows the volcanoes underneath them to more easily rise to the surface, and blow with increasing frequency. You have heard about our recent ones, with names you cannot pronounce.

"But they have also been a blessing to our country. Back in the 1970s we made a concerted effort to convert from dirty, polluting coal to geothermal energy by harnessing the molten lava beneath our surface. As a result all the homes in Reykjavik are heated by nonpolluting geothermal energy. Our goal is to make every home in Iceland warm and cozy this way. Even our greenhouses use geothermal heat to grow tropical plants. Yes, that's right; you Americans don't have to go to Hawaii for fresh fruit. We have harnessed our glacial lakes and rivers to produce carbon-free hydroelectric power. But this has attracted aluminum smelting plants that do emit greenhouse gases. We are in the process of sequestering these pollutants, and burying them below our inactive volcanoes. This technology has never been tried, so we'll see how it works. But I have confidence it will be successful because the three scientists you heard talking about volcanoes are spearheading this project. Please stand up Sigga, Jon, and Kristin."

The three surprised scientists looked at each other, hesitated, but slowly stood in their humble way, and politely received the applause due them.

Ms. Jonsdottir continued, "As a small country we can be a laboratory of new ideas for you larger countries. One of our entrepreneurs even founded a Ministry of Ideas, a think tank for creative ideas that includes sustainable technology that can be exported to the world.

"And finally, we are harnessing the fuel of the future. Iceland built the world's first hydrogen fueling station. We now have them all around our island, so anyone with a hydrogen vehicle can circle our country on our Ring Road. When you visit Reykjavik, you can rent a hydrogen-powered Prius, or ride on a fuel cell bus. We have made them as safe as a gasoline or diesel engine. We're past the Hindenburg days as some of you Americans might remember. Our slogan is 'Never fear, hydrogen is here.'

"We now have more hydrogen, plug-in electrics, and even methane vehicles than the old-fashioned gas guzzlers. And we have plenty of public places to recharge your electric cars.

"Most of our fishing fleets are powered by hydrogen, as well as our whale watching ships. As the captain of the Elding has stated, 'When we spot a whale, I cut my noisy diesel and use the ship's fuel cells to power our electrical system. It's totally silent. When we stop the engines, we realize how loud the old generator was. And the only waste product is steam, which we use to make cappuccinos on board.'"

With that last comment Brice turned to Magnus and in jest said, "That does it. Sign me up on that boat."

"Me too," affirmed Blaine.

"Deal," said Magnus. "I like pollution-free coffee too."

Olga continued, "And the tourists love it. They can hear the whales spouting and splashing, instead of the engines sputtering.

"Our transportation sector is now 100 percent fossil-free. With all the turmoil in the Middle East lately, we're glad we don't depend on their oil," she added as she looked at the American president, who returned the glance with a wry smile thinking, "Do I have a surprise for you, sweetheart."

The minister continued, "I forgot to mention two other firsts for Iceland. Even though we have the highest proportion of energy produced by renewable sources, we also have the highest electrical power consumption per capita in the world. We're not proud of that last first. Sure, we can rationalize and say our energy is fossil-free, so what's the big deal. But we need to cultivate a conservation ethic by doing basic things such as recycling, turning off unneeded lights, and shutting off our power cords when not in use.

"Please allow me to mention two technological breakthroughs we have engineered that can combat climate change. Carbon Recycling is a joint American-Icelandic company that captures carbon from industrial emissions and converts it to synthetic methanol, which, when mixed with petrol, can be used in normal cars. This technology kills two birds with one stone: it not only takes CO_2 from the atmosphere, but it uses it to lessen our reliance on fossil fuels.

"And last year, after decades of discussion, our country installed the world's longest undersea electric cable to the U.K.," Olga stated as she turned and looked at the British Prime Minister, who applauded her politely. We have extra loads of our green geothermal and hydroelectricity that can now be transferred to the Continent which has seen its prices skyrocket, partially because of the price they have placed on carbon. And then turning to the American President, Ms. Jonsdottir stated, "And we're working on a huge undersea cable to North America, where demand is also growing for carbon-free energy.

"Let me close with two challenges. One, Iceland's goal is to become a carbon-free and oil-free country by 2025. That's a mere four years away, but we think we can make it. And I encourage the rest of you to set a challenging goal. Maybe this **urgent** competition is what we need to save the planet from catastrophe."

A round of applause greeted her appeal, particularly the Icelandic contingent. And Magnus was wondering what was coming next.

The Surprise Unveiled

The minister turned around to shake hands with Dr. Olafsson, whispered something in his ear, and then turned around and again headed for the podium, looking over the crowd for someone in particular. She held up her hands to quiet the crowd and then began again.

"I now want to introduce our latest technology that will help us all reduce our carbon footprint." She reached under the podium, pulled out a cell phone, and held it up for the audience to see.

"You all know what this is."

The audience started looking at each other, uttering sounds of, "Da," and "What else is new?"

By now Magnus knew what was coming, so he made his way to an empty chair at the end of his row.

Finally Olga continued, "I know there are many versions of cell phones on the market, but this is the prototype of the one we developed - a real-time carbon calculator."

Now the crowd was buzzing in amazement, with sounds of, "Wow, I wonder how you thought of that?"

Suddenly, an image of this phone was projected on the screen behind the Prime Minister, with several of the keys enlarged.

She continued, flashing her laser pointer on the enlarged image of the phone, "This phone has special keys to measure how many units of CO_2 you are using as it happens." Focusing her pointer on Key 1 she explained, "This key measures your transportation emissions, not including walking or biking."

Focusing the laser on each key as she explained it, the proud Prime Minister continued, "Key 2 records your home energy use, not including burning wood, which is carbon neutral; Key 3 is for your food and drink consumption, including the cost of shipping, manufacturing, and packaging; Key 4 is for electronic use, including the use of televisions, computers, peripherals and cords; Key 5 is for miscellaneous emissions, with a chip that gives examples; Key 6 is the average carbon footprint per year for each person in your country; Key 7 is your carbon footprint. Key number 8 is the overload key. A LED light flashes when your daily average is above that of your countrypersons. This annoyance will continue until you push Key 9 to either purchase a carbon offset with your credit or debit card, or lower your footprint."

Before she could continue, the crowd spontaneously stood and applauded this invention. Some even looked at their cell phones to check their keyboard against the one on the screen. And now they were truly amazed - but not Magnus.

She continued, "I should point out that this program is voluntary. Those choosing to participate will receive a free CO2 phone from our ministry. The idea is to encourage friendly competition to lower your footprint. And 'green prizes' will be given to those who lower their footprint the most. Hopefully the overall CO2 average will de-crease each year until we achieve carbon-free status."

Finally the part for what Magnus was waiting came. Looking directly at Magnus, the Minister stated, "And now to give credit to the inventor of this new gadget; allow me to introduce a fellow Icelander, Magnus Steffansson. Magnus, please come up on the stage."

Magnus slowly stood to his feet, and headed toward the front. Blaine, sitting on the aisle two rows ahead of him, reached out and gave him a "high five" as the audience stood again.

Olga extended her hand to welcome Magnus as he reached the podium, not sure if he should look at her or the audience. After all, this was all new to him, and besides, this wasn't the Academy Awards.

When the crowd quieted again the Minister explained, "Magnus entered an essay contest our department held to find the most cre-ative way to save energy. It was sponsored by Skyr, the company that produces our version of yogurt. Try it. You'll like it," and she held up a carton.

"His winning prize was a free trip to the International Polar Year with his parents, Niels and Lara. Stand up, please, and be recognized with your son."

The crowd looked around to find the two standing in the back, both slightly waving their hands. They, like Magnus, weren't used to this publicity.

Back at the podium Ms. Jonsdottir now held out her hand, and while giving Magnus the Carbon Calculator, said, "Magnus, may I present you with the first phone we have manufactured. You deserve it. Use it to set an example for all Icelanders, and the world, of what one person can do to save the world."

Once again applause erupted as Magnus sheepishly reached out to take "his" phone and held it up for all to see.

This time it was the Minister's final remarks, "Before I ask Magnus to say a few words, I would like to mention that this phone will be available commercially yet this year, sold through one of our companies. Our department will notify the appropriate distributor in each country about the purchasing details. That's my only commercial. Magnus, would you like to say a few words?"

Magnus looked down at his new phone, hesitated, and then haltingly walked toward the podium, shooting up a quick, silent prayer before he began.

"Thank you, Ms. Minister, for this phone. My parents and I also thank you for this trip. We've learned a lot here that I want to share with my friends back home. It's my peers that need to get serious about saving the world. I'll do my part, and use this phone," as he held it up again.

"And I thank God for giving me the idea and Skyr for sponsoring the contest. I'll eat it the rest of my life. Thank you."

As the applause started again, the Minister again shook hands with Magnus, who, as he left the stage, was immediately mobbed by curious "techies," always interested in the latest technology. And here it was, for the entire world to see. But would it be taken seriously by the younger generation, or just be another gadget to be used until the next one comes out?

After the curious seekers finally slinked away, Magnus' parents came up to hug him, and check out his phone. He gave it to his father, who studied it for a while, and finally said, "It looks just like my phone, except the carbon keys are green."

He then gave it to Lara, who started punching the green keys to see what would happen. Nothing did, so she returned it to Magnus, who, like a football, handed it off to Brice.

Finally Brice exclaimed, "We don't have this in Nebraska. People aren't very 'green' where we live."

Magnus butted in, "But maybe this will help them to be careful about their carbon footprint. I'll see if I can get you one when I get home. Deal?"

"Deal."

United States of America

When the commotion had settled down, Dr. Olafsson again took the podium for this announcement:

"We are eagerly waiting for the remarks from the leader of our host country. Last, but certainly not least, please welcome the President of the United States."

Taking the suggestion literally, one American was seen holding a sign that read,

"Welcome back, Sarah."

With everyone standing and applauding, all eyes were fixed on the dark-haired, slim and fit beauty with the trademark square rim glasses, who strolled confidently to the podium.

After everyone was seated, President Palin began, "Thank you. It's good to be back. I'll always call Alaska home."

And this time the American delegation stood again and applauded. The press crowded the podium for photo ops and sound bites for the evening news. She was still a celebrity in her native land, even though she didn't finish her term as governor. But her strategy eventually sent her to 1600 Pennsylvania Avenue.

The President began, "You scientists may remember my previous comments pooh - poohing global warming as a liberal plot headed by Al Gore. As our free press has frequently mentioned (she turned and looked glaringly at press row), I'm not known as an intellectual heavyweight. But I can point out every country in the world on a globe, including Russia (she again paused and looked at Dr. Pushkin), but I can't see it from here." President Palin then stopped and feigned a look to the Bering Sea, and shook her head in the negative.

Several people in the audience were shaking their heads, wondering where the leader of the free world was going with these remarks. And then they found out.

"And now to get serious. My home state isn't the same as when I was governor. The glaciers I saw from the Governor's Mansion are almost gone. There is little snow on the mountains. Our bears, moose, and caribou are dying from the warmer temperatures. The polar bears and seals are disappearing with the ice. I've seen the native villages in Alaska crumbling into the ocean, and visited with these families who have lost everything, including Simon Metug, Aggalak Tom, and Sheila Swan. They are now living in the climate refugee camps you have seen.

"On the positive side, the Northwest Passage is now open to shipping. Hopefully, we can agree on the sharing of this new oil and gas wealth. People are growing crops north of the Arctic Circle. Even though there may be benefits from climate change, the negative aspects greatly outweigh them.

"You may be asking what caused me to do an about face on this issue. Well, I've been doing my homework. Being President gives you access to the best minds in the country. The briefings I receive from our scientists on this issue all point to the **urgency** of doing something soon to save the planet. And some of you in this room have helped me understand this complex issue. When you're on the inside, you realize how serious issues are, and you grow into the office. That I have done. I'm not the same Sarah anymore. I'm a 'born-again' believer in human-caused change, and I want to do what I can to protect God's Creation. And you members of the press can quote me on this." This time she smiled at them.

Now the entire assembly erupted with applause at her last statement. No more "redoubts" about her stance anymore. But what would the leader of the free world do about it?

She continued, "And now for a little Presidential history lesson. It's possible to be a Republican and an environmentalist. Some of you from my country may remember that Richard Nixon established the EPA, which is now regulating greenhouse gases, in spite of the opposition of some Congressmen from my own party. Former President Obama, a 'green' President, couldn't convince a Republican Congress to pass meaningful climate change legislation. Now it's time for the United States of America to finally become the world leader on this issue, as we have done many times in the past."

Again thunderous applause from the audience.

Magnus turned to his parents and said, "It's about time. Lead on, USA."

President Palin continued, "This International Polar Year is the appropriate place to announce my five point 'Lead the World' plan for saving the planet."

Point One appeared on the screen behind her, as she read them to her listening audience:

"* By 2030 all coal from existing plants will be sequestered and buried in underground natural leak-proof caverns.

* Starting now there will be a moratorium on the building of new coal plants.

* The U.S. will mine no more coal after 2030"

Before she could continue, the crowd was on its feet again.

Point Two next appeared,

"* Beginning now there will be no more government subsidies for the coal and oil industries. These subsidies will instead be given to the renewable energy companies.

* Fossil-free renewable energy such as solar, wind, hydroelectric, geothermal, and wave power will constitute 60 percent of U.S. energy needs by 2030.

* Safe non-polluting nuclear plants will power 20 percent of U.S. energy needs by 2030.

* New plants will not be built on geologically sensitive sites."

This time the muted applause was interspersed with "boos." Not everyone had forgotten Chernobyl, Three Mile Island, or Japan's nuclear disasters.

Point Three now appeared on the screen:

"* With continued instability in Africa and the Middle East, our nation's energy needs can no longer depend on foreign sources of oil. By 2030 the United States will not import one drop of oil.

* We will phase out the production of domestic oil with the goal of ending production by 2040 in favor of less carbon-intensive natural gas.

* As we gradually rely more on nuclear and other renewable sources of power, we will build up the Strategic Petroleum Reserve until 2030."

Again the applause interrupted her speech. She knew how to fire up the crowd. It helped that she was following a master speech-deliverer into the White House.

Finally the crowd quieted, and she raised her high-pitched voice for Point Four,

" * The United States is still the leader in innovation and technology. By 2031 we will have ready for use, as a last resort, an array of geoengineering techniques to modify the climate by (1) blocking or reflecting sunlight and (2) removing CO_2 from the atmosphere. We will share our technological breakthroughs with the world."

This time the crowd was stunned, and didn't react.

President Palin took this time of silence to comment, "Yes, Star Wars is here. We need to be ready to meet this global challenge. John F. Kennedy challenged us to land a man on the moon in ten years. I am again throwing down the gauntlet. We did it before, and we can do it again."

This time it was the Americans who were heard saying the familiar, "Yes, we can; yes, we can."

President Palin finally lowered her arms as they quieted, and turned around to face the screen briefly, and then read Point Five,

" * Because of the seriousness of the world situation, the United States will reduce its carbon footprint by 80 percent by 2050, the goal climate scientists say is needed to prevent catastrophic climate change.

"We are ready to lead the world in this **urgent** task. Is the world ready to follow?"

A unified loud "Yes," resonated throughout the hall.

President Palin didn't go down into the audience and shake hands. Starting her second term precluded her from the need to campaign again. She also didn't pause to speak to the waiting press. She simply waved to the audience, gave double-thumbs up to the crowd as she left the stage, and was escorted from the building into her waiting seaplane with the Presidential seal affixed to both sides of the fuselage.

Now she could again see Sarah Palin's Alaska - what was left of it – and be briefed by her staff on the press reports of her surprising speech. In the meantime, she was off hunting moose - with a little help from her guides.

Another Surprise from the East

Dr. Pushkin, tired from the long day with the political leaders, was awakened early the next morning by the incessant beeping of his satellite phone. After finally realizing it was not a dream, he hastily punched the speaker and answered with a faint, "Hello, what do you want?"

On the other end was an excited Russian President exclaiming, "Dimitri, I have good news from the East."

"Don't you realize what time it is here? It's three in the morning. But now I'm awake. Go ahead."

"But this couldn't wait. The leaders from China and India listened intently to President Palin's speech. They were as surprised as I suppose your audience was. We were trying to negotiate binding agreements on carbon emissions, and were about to break off our talks with no agreement when she came on our satellite link. And that changed the whole mood here."

Dimitri, attired in his bathrobe and slippers, was now awake.

"So, what happened next?"

President Bendelev continued, "Both countries liked the idea of the U.S. sharing their geoengineering technology. They thought maybe that would partially make up for their industrialization that created this global mess in the first place. However, China doesn't want to give up its own technology as the world's leader in the manufacturing of wind and solar systems."

"Anything else?" Dimitri asked.

"Yes, there's one more point on which they agreed. Both countries have seen their Himalayan glaciers disappear, resulting in droughts and water shortages that have forced millions of their people to leave the rural areas and flock into crowded cities. And hundred-year floods have been coming every five to ten years now.

"They have finally realized, with the rest of the world, that these extreme weather events are becoming more common, and are now primarily caused by climate change. So both the Chinese and Indian governments will agree to a binding agreement to reduce their greenhouse gas emissions by the same amount as President Palin mentioned. No more rivalries between the developed and developing countries. They are now developed and want to support the Western World, and the U.S., in this commitment. They realize this is the last chance to save the world."

Dimitri paused while soaking in this surprising news. He then collected his senses, and thanked the Russian President for his successful negotiations.

"This is indeed historic; the first time the four major polluters have agreed on binding limits. Now we'll have to see if the other countries will fall into line. Now they have no excuse. As the Chinese probably told you during your talks, 'The journey of a thousand miles begins with a single step.' I guess we'll see."

And Dimitri was up the rest of the night, coffee in hand, pondering the next move at the IPY. Was an encore needed?

Part Three: Home

❧❦❧

IX. Going Home to Iceland

Packing

There remained one more time for the IPY participants to gather and deal with details before saying goodbye and departing to their warming countries. And there was yet one more surprise in store that Dimitri would soon reveal.

Meanwhile, at the Sutherland yurt, Brice and Blaine were busily cramming their belongings into their one cedar box for the long road trip home. Showing signs of melancholy, Brice pined, "Blaine, you're probably thinking the same thing I am."

"Yea, Dad, I was. Can we go down to the ocean and see him one more time?"

"I was going to suggest that. Let's do it on the way out."

And that was the end of the conversation. Both continued packing and hauling their belongings to their truck in silence, realizing they wouldn't have to save room for Spud. It would be a long trip home.

Meanwhile, across the camp, Magnus and his parents were dutifully performing the same tasks. Magnus was also thinking, 'I wonder if I get to see Spud again. I hope so.' He was also thinking about his cedar box, and the extra one they used by the sea.

The silence was broken by Niels' question, "Son, are you ready to go home?"

Magnus paused before answering, "I guess so. My prayers were answered." He didn't elaborate, but his parents knew his mission to Brice and Blaine was finished here.

This time Lara, knowing what Magnus was thinking, asked, "Would you like to invite Brice and Blaine to Iceland?"

"How did you know that was what I was thinking? Yes, I would. I wonder if they would like to see our country in the dead of winter?"

Back at the Sutherland yurt Brice was carrying out his last load for the truck. Surprisingly, he asked Blaine, "Are you looking forward to seeing your mother again?"

Blaine, with a puzzled look on his face, replied "Yea, I suppose. I'll be going off to college and all that."

"Hum, I just got a message we are to report to the assembly hall for an important announcement," an equally surprised Brice exclaimed. "Are you finished loading up?"

Blaine nodded in the affirmative.

After he said that, Brice realized that was what he always said to Spud before driving away in his truck. That would not be the last time he would be thinking Spud was still with them - now only in spirit.

As they walked into the hall with the others, they found Magnus and his parents, and sat together for the last time, wondering what this was all about. The crowd was buzzing about the same thing. But they didn't have to wait long.

The Announcement

For the last time, Dr. Pushkin took the stage, stepped to the podium, waited for the crowd to quiet, and excitedly began, "Thank you for coming back one more time before you head home. I think you'll like what I'm about to say."

The crowd was now very quiet (the "hearing-a-pin-drop" kind).

"How many of you Americans remember the campaign commercial a few years ago about the phone call at 3 AM, and which candidate was up dealing with a crisis?"

A few hands went up as one Yankee grumbled, "What's that got to do with anything?"

Dimitri continued, "Well, last night I was awakened in the middle of the night, not by bad news, but with good news for the planet. Our President Bendelev called to say that the Chinese and Indian leaders, who have been waiting for the U.S. President's proposal, have agreed to the same limits on their greenhouse gases as proposed by President Palin."

Dr. Pushkin continued, "Let's show our appreciation for President Bendelev's negotiations - truly a breakthrough."

On the other side of the world, the Russian President, via the satellite link, witnessed the standing ovation as he also took to his feet and applauded them. This was truly a fitting end to the IPY - the most successful in history. Maybe the world was finally turning the corner before the climate "tipping point" was reached. Now the hard work of convincing the other countries to go along with the biggest polluters was about to begin.

Finally, Dr. Pushkin thanked everyone, and pointed to the

sign on the same wall where they had seen many presentations. And then he read the sign, lit up with small LED twinkling lights, "RENDEZVOUS IN REYKJAVIK - DECEMBER 2021. See you in Iceland. Godspeed on your journey home."

With a thud of the gavel, Dimitri closed the IPY, and the participants milled around saying their goodbyes, leaving on an optimistic note, but knowing their work was not a done deal by any means. But maybe the world gained a little breathing space - for now.

Seeing Spud for the Last Time

Brice ran over to catch Magnus and shouted, "Let's go see Spud once more.

"Yes, I'd like that."

Magnus explained the situation to his parents, who agreed to wait for him back in their yurt. They understood this was the men's private time.

With that settled, the three men pushed through the crowd and into Brice's loaded truck to go see their male companion. They rode in silence, wondering how they would react. The finality of this visit was apparent to all.

The truck lumbered down the bumpy road, which became increasingly muddy as they approached the grave. The ocean had risen noticeably since their burial service. And they all knew the reason for the relentless encroachment of the sea. All they wanted was one more chance to see their favorite friend.

Brice parked the truck about a hundred yards from the cave, and the three of them squished through the muddy water to the tomb. They detected a faint smell, and knew what it was; but no one said anything. After all, they were walking on sacred ground.

Brice arrived at the cave first, walked in, and moved the rock they had placed over the opening. He peered in, plugged his nose to mitigate the smell, stepped back, and said, "The box is still intact, but the water is lapping on the bottom. The waves must have washed the sand away."

Magnus asked, "Can you still see the *Bible* verses and the cross on top?"

Brice nodded. He then motioned for Blaine to take a look. Blaine then stepped in his father's soft footprints, and peered inside for a long time, also plugging his nose. Silently he stepped back and motioned to Magnus, who followed suit.

Finally, Brice broke the silence, turned to Magnus and said, "It seems fitting we should say a prayer. Magnus, would you say something?"

Magnus, sensing an opportunity to help Brice, replied, "I think you should. After all, Spud is your dog, and he means more to you and Blaine.

Brice hesitated and, trying to make an excuse, replied, "But I don't know how to pray. I'm just learning this Christian stuff."

Magnus countered, "Prayer is talking to God like you would your best friend. Just tell Him what you're feeling. Go ahead. It won't hurt."

Brice, after a long pause, started in, "God, you know I haven't talked to you much in my life, but I want to now. Now you are my best friend like Spud was to Blaine and me. I know he can't go with us, but keep him safe in his grave. And if dogs go to heaven, can I see Spud again? Thank you for the good dog that he was, and the time we had with him. Amen."

Brice then turned to Blaine, and the two of them hugged in silence. Only the sound of the rising water lapping against the rocks could be heard. Magnus joined in, putting one arm around each man's shoulder, head bowed in a silent prayer.

After what seemed a long time, Brice turned and started the slow, squishy walk back to the truck. Once by the cab, he turned and looked back. Blaine, noticing a moist spot in his father's right eye, also turned around, as did Magnus, who thought of the *Bible* verse, "When you pass through the waters I will be with you." This promise was for Brice and Blaine.

It was only a matter of time before Spud would be swept out to sea. His mission was also finished. And what about the polar bear that Spud had so bravely fought in order to save his friends? Was he still alive, trying desperately to cling to a small chunk of ice? Or did the rising sea swallow him as well?

These were the unanswered questions on the men's minds as they loaded up for the ride back to their yurts for the final inspection.

The Last Goodbyes

And finally it was time for the Nebraskans and the Icelanders to part company. Magnus, on the way to the Sutherlands' yurt, walked by the kennel where Spud spent much of his time. He was carrying a small package.

Brice and Blaine, checking their yurt for the last time, spotted Magnus on the well-worn path.

Blaine, seeing the package in his left hand, asked, "What did I forget?"

"Nothing. I have a care package for you," and Magnus held it out to them.

Brice, by now the gracious host, said, "C'mon inside, let's see what you got."

Magnus hurried inside, and the three of them sat on the long bench that had been used many times throughout the summer. First, Magnus reached into his box and pulled out two small books with brown leather covers with the gold leaf letters, *Holy Bible*, embossed on the spine. He then handed them to each Nebraskan, who took them gingerly, turning over the cover and inspecting the fancy letters.

"This will help you learn more about God, Jesus, and the Holy Spirit. Try to read a little bit every day. A good place to start would be the Book of *John*."

Magnus then took each *Bible* again, and flipped through them until he came to the proper place. Then he took out two book markers from his box and placed them in the appropriate place saying, "That should help you get started."

Again he reached into his goodie box and pulled out another little paperback book entitled, *Beyond the Final Score*, and gave it to Brice.

Brice, seeing a red football on the cover, eagerly took it, quickly flipped through the pages, and turned it over to see a picture of Tom Osborne on the back, dressed in his typical red sweat suit and white football shoes.

"Where are the 'X's' and 'O's'? Isn't this coach's playbook?"

"Kind of. It's really about the Game of Life, with plays to help the Christian score with God. It goes along with your *Bible*, too."

"Gee, I didn't know coach wrote a book. And look, he even autographed it for me. Thanks, Magnus. I'll use 'em both."

Again Magnus reached into his box and pulled out a little book and handed it to Blaine saying, "This will help you when you go off to college. It's designed to get you through your first year with God's help."

Blaine took it and laughed at the catchy title, *Freshman Survival Guide: Stories to Make It Through the Year.*

"Boy, I could use this. Thanks, Pal."

Then Magnus scratched the bottom of the box and pulled out one more item. It was a 4 x 6 inch framed picture. He held it so the back was facing Brice and Blaine, and slowly turned it around to reveal a picture of Spud, his head above a wave, clutching a stick, and swimming toward the shore. Below the picture in handwritten English were the words, "Faithful Friend Forever."

Magnus handed the picture to Brice, who hesitatingly took it, looked at Blaine, then back to Magnus, and could only say, "Wow." He then handed it to Blaine, who just stared at it in silence, and then returned it to Brice.

And for the last time the three melancholy males hugged. Finally Magnus broke the silence by offering his last gift, "Remember the Rendezvous in Reykjavik. If you can make it, you have a place to stay. Iceland is a small country. I'll take care of you. Keep in touch. Have a safe trip home."

"You, too," replied Brice. "And thanks for everything. Don't be surprised if we show up on your doorstep."

With these parting remarks, Magnus turned around and headed back to join his parents and the three Icelandic scientists sailing east. Brice and Blaine stepped into their loaded truck, and pointed it south toward the Lower 48. What about the bears? Who would protect them now?

Iceland Bound

Magnus and his parents caught a glimpse of the *SS Sustainability*, visible in the harbor above the hastily-built sea wall. It looked sleek and shiny in the still high, mid-August, afternoon sun. And Magnus noticed something different.

After staring intently at the ship, he quizzed his parents, "Do you notice anything different about our ship?"

Both Niels and Lara surveyed the situation, and finally Niels observed, "The ship looks taller."

"Maybe it's because of the reflection from the sun," wondered Lara.

Magnus entered the conversation, "No, I think it looks taller because the sea level has risen since we last saw her. But maybe that's because the tide is in."

They boarded the ship, forgot their conversation, and settled in again.

A few minutes later while on deck, they noticed the three scientists aiming a laser gun at the sea wall.

Being inquisitive, Magnus asked Sigga, "What are you doing with that gun?"

Not looking up from his sighting, Sigga answered, "We're taking measurements to see if the ocean has risen since we came here over two months ago."

"Well, has it?" asked Niels, now also interested.

"After allowing for tidal changes it has, but ever so slightly," Sigga answered as he pointed to the sea wall. "You see the waves lapping over the side of the sea wall. They're going to have to raise its height shortly, or Katooska will be at risk of being flooded like the other villages we have seen."

"And that's not all," chimed in Katrin. If there's a large earthquake out to sea, a tsunami would devastate this area. The highest tsunami in history occurred in Alaska.

By this time Jon joined the other scientists and explained, "On our way home we'll be looking for any evidence of climate change since we arrived here. We have heard about it; now let's see what we can observe. After all, this area is the 'canary' for the rest of the world."

A blast from the ship's horn signaled the ship was ready to embark to their beloved country. What changes would they find there?

The research vessel slowly left the rising harbor and headed northwest into the Chukchi Sea into a slight headwind. The Steffanssons headed down to their cabin while the scientists stayed aboard to chart any changes. It was smooth sailing for the next few hours, and then the wind strengthened. The clouds became pitch black, and loud cracks of thunder and flashes of lightning filled the northern sky. Before the rain descended upon them in sheets, the scientists scrambled to the lower deck.

As Katrin looked out her cabin window, and steadied herself against the rocking motion, she noticed the waves splashing over her porthole. Since they seemed unusually high, she called Sigga on her iPhone to see if he was measuring their height and tidal energy. He replied that he was doing the calculations, and would have a report shortly. In the meantime Katrin lay on her bed, grabbed the wall bars, and waited for the storm to pass - which it didn't for some time.

Finally the captain announced, "Our radar has picked up an unexpected strong polar low heading toward Pt. Barrow. It's about two hours east of there, and we're about an hour from Barrow. We're going to put into their harbor, and let the storm pass before proceeding. In the meantime stay below deck and hang on. Seasick pills are in your cabin. Over and out."

Magnus, also hanging on for dear life, thought, "I got my wish, to step on the northernmost point of North America." And then he started humming a few bars from the song by Casting Crowns, "Praise You in the Storm." He had played it many times on his DVD player, so he knew it by heart.

On Top of the World

With the storm still raging, and the passengers "holed up" in their cabins, the *S.S. Sustainability* finally limped into the somewhat-sheltered harbor. But with no mountains to block the wind, and the open seas on three sides, the ship was still pitching as it tied up to the dock. Everyone stayed below the deck to wait out the storm.

Finally, the storm passed, the clouds cleared, and the crew and passengers were free to disembark to check out this barren community, mainly populated by Inupiats. While the three scientists stayed on board to review their calculations, Magnus and his parents strolled through the dusty streets on the way to Pt. Barrow. Before reaching a pier jutting into the ocean, they read a sign: "Warning: Bear Alert. Because of a lack of sea ice, polar, grizzly, and hybrid bears have been spotted in the area. Do not feed or approach. Make noise to alert them of your presence. They are hungry and dangerous. Report any sightings to the Alaska Fish and Wildlife Service. Thank you for your cooperation."

After silently reading the sign, Magnus turned to his parents and said, "I'd feel a lot safer if Spud was with us." After looking in all directions, they proceeded to walk out to the end of the pier - the northernmost part of North America.

As they paused to view the now calm seas, Niels, looking through his binoculars, pointed toward the water and exclaimed, "Look out at three o'clock. It looks like something swimming to shore."

Magnus took his father's field glasses, looked intently, and excitedly said, "That looks one of those hybrid bears we saw when we were coming through here before. But this time there's no ice for him to cruise on. We'd better leave and beat him to shore. I bet he'll be tired and hungry. We don't want another Spud incident."

He turned around and walked briskly back, followed closely by his parents. They reached the shore ahead of the bear, and kept walking until they found refuge in a coffee shop in town. They collapsed in a booth, and caught their breath. Certainly bears wouldn't come into the heart of town, would they?

As they sipped their coffee and ate their salmon sandwiches, they overheard a conversation in the next booth. Two men, dressed in a uniform adorned with a Russian flag were discussing their respective shipping routes.

"What route did you take to get here?" asked a stout man with a graying beard and glasses.

"I started from Vardo on the northern tip of Norway and took the northern route close to our country," answered a tall, wiry man with blonde hair.

"Did you encounter any ice?" asked the other.

"Not a bit. This is the first time that has happened. How about you?"

"Well, I took the Northwest Passage, and saw some old ice, but nothing new. Things have certainly changed in the last few years."

"You can say that again."

"Things have certainly . . ."

"OK, wise guy. I get your point."

The stout man continued, "But I did see something that disturbed me."

"What was that?" asked the wiry man.

"Evidence of a recent oil spill. The southern shore - rocks, sand, and all - of the Lancaster Strait was covered black with thick, gooey oil. And you could see dead sea birds and sea otters lying all over."

"Well, that's the price you pay for heating our homes and driving our cars."

"What's a few dead animals?" answered the tall man rhetorically.

Magnus, understanding their language, couldn't keep quiet. He interrupted the conversation, "Say, excuse me, I'm from Iceland,

and we are concerned about protecting our environment and God's creatures."

Taken aback, the stout captain retorted, "Mind your own business, buddy. We're just doing our job. What's yours?"

Now Niels, a husky man himself, stood up beside his son - his big arms folded across his chest.

Magnus continued, "We're coming from Alaska, where we heard about the effect the burning of oil has on the environment."

The two Russian got up from their table and made a move toward Magnus, but Niels stepped in front of his son, and they stopped.

The tall man looked down at Magnus and snarled, "Wait until you run out of gas. Then you'll thank us."

As they were walking up to pay, Magnus got in the last word with, "I have a hydrogen car, so I don't need your oil."

The stout man turned around with his final taunt, "I hope it blows up on you," he jeered as he walked away, laughing loudly.

After they left, Niels sat back down in the booth, "Son, I'm surprised at your boldness."

"Well, Dad, you heard what our mission is, to save the world. Their souls need saving too. We have our work cut out for us when we get home."

After this encounter the family collected themselves, and returned to their ship, which was ready to depart on the next leg of their journey to Greenland. What changes would await them there?

On To Greenland

Finally the surprise storm subsided and the Icelandic research vessel slowly chugged from the harbor into the open sea, again heading east. They saw several huge oil tankers flying the Chinese flag.

Magnus, spotting them from the bow of the *Sustainability*, commented to his father, "What's China doing here? Don't they know they're a long ways from home?"

"I don't know, son. But they are the world's largest economy now, so I guess they need all the oil they can find."

The Arctic "black gold rush" was on.

As they listened to the lapping of the waves against the ship's hull, suddenly the rhythm was interrupted by the sound of splashing on the starboard side. Magnus raised his binoculars just in time to see an Orca breaching the surface with his nose, expelling water from his blowhole, and diving back underwater. He got a good look at his magnificent black and white body before it submerged.

He turned to his parents and the three scientists who also saw the sight, reminding them, "There's the new icon of the Arctic."

Pretty soon another killer whale surfaced, this time with part of a seal in her mouth. This time the crew on deck anticipated the next "show."

True to what they had seen with Dr. Hill, several more Orcas surfaced to join in the "tossing." And when all the whales had caught and flung the hapless seal among the others, the "game" was over. And just as quickly, they all dove, looking for other prey. Even though this was the only whale sighting on their trip, the scientists were sure this scene was being played out many times in the iceless Arctic.

In order to see if any summer ice remained in the Arctic Ocean, the scientists decided to take the northern route to Greenland. This meant skirting north of the Queen Elizabeth Islands of Canada, and even north of the North Magnetic Pole. This was the farthest north the *Sustainability* had ever been, and they felt like the first explorers who reached the Geographic North Pole over a century ago. But in the case of those intrepid pioneers who traveled overland, the ice was essential for their land journey - the more the better. But the Arctic was vastly different in the summer of 2021.

After hugging the ice-free shoreline for a day, they finally spotted an old ice floe about the size of a medium-sized car. It was not nearly as large as the chunk of ice that collided with them on their route to Alaska. It was barely big enough to hold a skinny looking polar bear.

Katrin spotted it first with her binoculars and alerted everyone with a shout, "Bear at 9'oclock!"

Jon, also with binoculars raised, concluded, "Well, at least they're still adapting to their new environment by moving farther north."

"Let's dart him with a GPS to track his path," commanded Sigga.

After doing some quick calculations Jon concluded, "Yes, I think we can. Let's try it. Maybe he's heading for Greenland, and maybe even to our country if he can find ice on the way."

Sigga ran up to the bridge to ask the captain to cut the hydrogen engines and let the ship drift closer to the ice flow. After a few minutes without power, the ship closed to within a hundred feet of the bear.

At Katrin's command, Jon aimed the dart gun and fired into the bear's right shoulder. He flinched, and tried to brush the dart off with his left paw, but it sunk deep enough into his thick fur, implanting the GPS. The dart would disintegrate within a matter of seconds, leaving the sensor securely in place, with no harm done to the bear. Now they could track the bear's movements to determine his chances for survival. Would he stay on the ice, reach land, or swim to find food? Interesting possibilities for another journal article.

Seeing no more bears or ice, but several more tankers from Norway, Canada, Denmark, and the U.S., the *Sustainability* reached the northern tip of Greenland, ready for more measurements. This time they docked in Thule, home to a large American Air Force base. But the scientists were looking for glaciers and icebergs, not jet fighter planes.

Specifically, Katrin, Jon, and Sigga wanted to compare the rate of glacial melt here with that of the Jakobshavn Glacier they had seen farther south on their way to Alaska. After spending the night on their ship, they rented a fishing vessel from one of the Inuits and cruised along the coast, looking for icebergs that had calved from the glaciers.

All of a sudden they heard a loud crack that sounded like thunder, but with a clear blue sky that couldn't be. Then they looked toward the land in time to see a huge chunk falling from a glacier into the sea. The pilot of the boat, knowing the wave could capsize their small craft, gunned the motor, made a sharp 90-degree turn, and headed out to sea. The scientists looked back to see a large wave coming toward them, reminiscent of a tsunami. The five-foot wave hit the boat in the stern, pitching it, and spilling water into the bottom. The pilot pointed to three buckets strapped to the

JAY MENNENGA

sides of the boat and shouted, "Each one of you take one and start bailing!"

As Sigga grabbed one bucket, he complained, "We didn't sign up for this."

"Shut up and do as the captain says, or else we won't be doing anything else," chastised Jon.

As the stern continued to fill with water, the three traded their white-collar jobs for blue-collar survival, and bailed furiously for about five minutes. Finally, the boat leveled, and the captain cautiously turned around, and headed back toward the coast.

"Whew, that was close," panted a tired Katrin. Even the seasoned captain breathed a sigh of relief.

With calmer waters, the boat crept around the huge icebergs as the scientists lowered a thermometer to measure the water temperature. They reached the base of a large glacier, and motioned for the captain to halt the engine. Then they lowered another instrument that measured the volume of fresh water flowing from the glacier to the salty sea. These two baseline readings would be shared with other scientists returning to this same spot next year. No conclusions could be drawn at this point, but the Icelandic scientists' hypotheses pointed to a warming ocean and increasing glacial melt. Only time would tell if the warming was increasing as the models had predicted.

Back to Jakobshavn

From Thule, the research vessel headed south, staying within sight of the shoreline. Indeed the country was looking more like its namesake. Maybe it wasn't misnamed after all. The Icelanders spotted fields where potatoes and hay flourished. There were even fruit trees growing along the rugged coastline, and patches of green grass could be seen in the ravines of the cliffs.

They again came into port at Ilulissat, and wanted to get another close look at Greenland's largest glacier. But when they stepped off their ship, they were surprised to see vendors selling their wares at a farmer's market. Merchants were hawking not just souvenirs, but fruits and vegetables, grown in the warmer and fertile soil left by the receding glaciers.

While the scientists were busy comparing their observations of Jakobshavn with their previous calculations, the Steffansson family did the "tourist thing," bought Inuit bracelets and necklaces, and sampled the fresh food. Lara, upon biting into a succulent pear, commented, "They don't even have to use geothermal greenhouses like we do."

"That's right, honey," replied Niels, "but I bet their growing season is really short.

Magnus observed, "This country is beginning to look like ours. I wonder how our glaciers are doing."

He didn't have to wait long to find out.

Back Home

With the scientists concluding their last glacial observations, it was time for the last leg of their trip. The *Sustainability* left Ilulissat for the last time, and headed to Cape Farewell on Greenland's southern tip. From there it was 750 miles to the friendly confines of Reykjavik Harbor.

With the ship now in the open waters of the North Atlantic, the three scientists huddled in Jon's cabin to compare their latest findings. They all agreed that the glacial melt was increasing in velocity and the ocean temperature was continuing its warming trend. They had spotted more icebergs breaking from Jakobshavn than on their previous trip just two months ago.

Katrin spoke for the three when she said, "We have our work cut out for us. We need to publish our results to alert the world to what is going on here. Indeed, as the glaciers go in Greenland, so it is in the world."

Jon piped up, "And that includes our country. Will Iceland still be an appropriate name?"

Sigga wondered, "Let's see what we find when we return."

And the next day they found out as they sailed into Reykjavik Harbor, with water splashing against the seawall. Was it higher than when they left? And was that another volcanic eruption as they noticed a black plume rising in the interior?

As the Steffanssons headed down the gang plank, Magnus looked at the sea wall, and then at the blackening cloud, and commented to his parents, "Well, we're home. Thank the Lord for a safe trip. But it looks like there's work to be done here."

The scientists were already on the dock and headed to their offices, thinking about a new research project in their own country. Could it be that Iceland's glaciers were also melting rapidly, making it easier for volcanoes to penetrate the thinner ice? They were going to be busy indeed. First, they had to get ready to welcome the world that would be descending on their small island in December.

As Magnus and his parents disembarked, Magnus wondered, "Will Blaine and Brice be coming - without Spud?"

X. Going Home to Nebraska

Brice and Blaine, after packing and seeing Spud for the last time, climbed into their truck, leaving the IPY yurt they had called home for two months.

As they turned the last corner before heading down to the airport, Brice said, "Dad, you forgot to say something."

"What do you mean? We've said all our goodbyes."

"No, I mean you didn't say, 'Load up, Spud.'"

"That's not funny, son," as Brice looked at him sternly.

"Sorry, Dad. I won't say it again."

Better that the memories remain silent during their long trip home.

As they approached the Katooska Airport, they noticed the waves periodically splashing over the top of the sea wall - another object lesson of what they had learned.

They parked their rented truck, which they had used during the IPY, by the wall and boarded the seaplane back to Kotzebue. And they recognized the pilot as the one who had crash-landed their plane on the way in. And he recognized them also. He asked them what happened to their dog.

Brice responded, "Boy, you have a good memory. He got into a fight with a polar bear, and saved our lives. And by the way, God used that tragedy to bring me to Him."

"Yes, the Lord works in mysterious ways. Congratulations," as he heartily shook Brice's hand. And what about you?" as the pilot turned to Blaine.

"Yes, I asked Jesus into my life, too."

"Well, that makes a threesome on this plane. We should be OK now." And this time the flight was smooth all the way.

About halfway over the Kotzebue Sound, Blaine, looking down with his binoculars, pointed and said to his dad, "Look, Dad, there's a killer whale surfacing. See the ripples?"

Blaine handed his binoculars to his father, who, after a few moments, exclaimed, "Yes, I see one."

And then Brice scanned through the other window and, just as excitedly replied, "And there's a polar bear on that small ice chunk."

Now the father returned the lenses to his son, who also zeroed in on the bear.

"Wouldn't that be something if that was the same bear that Spud chased away?"

This time Brice didn't respond as he silently watched the bear disappear from sight as the plane gained altitude.

Blaine broke the silence with, "Remember what Dr. Hill said about the icons of the Arctic. Well, they're saying goodbye to us."

And as their final gesture, the humans at 10,000 feet waved to the Arctic animals at sea level, which were subject to the whims of the supposedly more intelligent beings.

As the plane landed at the Kotzebue Airport, also protected - at least for now - by a twenty foot sea wall, Dr. Plankton was there to greet them, and shuttle them to their pickup. He had good news for Brice.

"As you probably noticed, Brice, with my responsibilities at the University, I haven't attended many of the IPY sessions, but I have been streaming them in my office. I've also checked the webcams that beamed back the field trips. You had a close call cruising over Mt. Redoubt. And what about you, Blaine? Did you enjoy your time in the Arctic?"

"Yes, sir. It's a lot different than Nebraska. More stuff going on here. I hope I can use what I learned when I start college in a few weeks."

"You know," continued Paul, "the future of the planet really depends on kids your age. We old folks," as he looked at Brice, "are counting on you."

"And Brice, I've critiqued your journals and action plan, and was impressed with how much you learned. Hopefully you'll also apply what you learned here when you return home. And your diploma will be waiting for you."

When he heard that, Brice lit up, and for the first time in a while smiled and said, "Thank you, Dr. Plankton."

"Don't thank me. You earned it. And let me know how you're doing. Have a good trip home. Oh, I didn't notice, what happened to your dog?"

Brice answered, "You said I had a close call up here. Well, Spud had an even closer call with a polar bear, and came out on the short end. But it was all part of God's plan."

"Well, if that's what you think it was, I'm glad you came here. Maybe you'll be back."

As Brice and Blaine climbed into their pickup, Brice lowered the driver's side window, gave a thumbs up, and said, "We'll see. Thanks again."

And they were off, headed down the Alcan, from Delta Junction to the lower 48, over 3,000 miles from the plains of Nebraska. But first they wanted to see the highest mountain in North America - Mt. McKinley towering 20,320 feet into the sky. It's also the largest land mass in the world, and creates its own weather pattern, usually shrouded in clouds. But today they were fortunate. The flatlanders were treated to a spectacle of snow covering the summit, but Blaine noticed something unusual through his binoculars. He motioned to his father to pull off the road and take a look. Blaine was the first to exclaim, "I thought this huge mountain was covered with perpetual snow."

"Yea, so did I."

"But it looks bare in spots on the side I can see. Did the wind blow the snow away, you think?"

"No, I don't think so," replied Brice. "Remember we learned that winters are going to be less snowy, and more rainy. Maybe that explains it. The rain melted the snow, so it is probably bare on this side, even though it's facing north. Remember, climate change is happening faster here than in any other part of the world. I wonder if Paul has noticed this."

What other surprises would they find on the way?

Leaving Alaska

There's only one way from Alaska to Canada on land, through Tok again. It was the last town of any size (about 1,500 hardy residents) in Alaska, and the place to gas up before heading down the Alcan.

Leaving there the duo again reached the Alaska-Yukon Territory border. Brice jumped out of the truck, and motioned for Blaine to stand in front of the sign, "Leaving Alaska: The Last Frontier and the First Frontier for Climate Change. Come back soon." And the father took the ceremonial picture, which they had forgotten in their hurry on the way up.

As they climbed into the cab, Blaine asked, "Dad, do you think we'll be back here?"

"Don't know, son. If nothing else, I'd like to see if Spud's tomb is still where we buried him."

After crossing the border, they could barely see a series of towering mountains above the tree-lined road. Jutting above the others was Mt. Logan, Canada's highest peak at 19,850, barely below Mt. McKinley. But it also was covered by intermittent bare spots, another sign of less snow pack. But there is a positive side to the warmer temperatures. Now the tundra can grow crops, if water is available for irrigation.

And then it was on to Whitehorse, at 20,000 people, the biggest city in northern Canada. On their trip up they enjoyed the "Yukon Yuks." This time no band was welcoming them. Instead they were greeted by a dust storm blowing over the road that caused Brice to turn on his headlights in broad daylight. They also noticed bare fields where crops would normally be growing. Was a drought starting here? Is it climate change, or simply a weather cycle?

They found the same McDonald's and camped at the same place as before, but without their faithful watch dog. They woke up several times during the night to peer from their tent flap, making sure nothing was lurking in the dark night. They would've felt safer with Spud.

After a campfire breakfast of pancakes, eggs, and cowboy coffee, Brice pulled into a gas station. He noticed the gas prices were lower than those in Alaska, and inquired as to the reason.

The attendant, a burly, bearded man, explained, "It's that darn carbon tax we have. It's causing people to use less gas, and it's simple supply and demand. Can hardly make a living anymore. Maybe I'll move to Alaska. You don't have it there, do you?"

Brice answered, "Nope, not yet. But I think we should. We need to do something to protect God's Creation."

The big man huffed, took Brice's' money, and stalked away, muttering, "One of them, eh?"

As they drove away Blaine exclaimed, "Another friendly Canadian, eh?"

They checked the information sign outside the city to plan their route south. About every 300 miles there were places for gas, food, and lodging. Their next gas stop was Watson Lake, even though only 1000 in population, it seemed like more than a wide spot in the road. It was here they noticed the pine trees turning from live green to dead red - home of the ever-increasing pine beetles.

And then it was through the checkered trees to the larger Ft. Nelson, home to approximately 5,000 Canadians. Brice and Blaine found a clean and quiet provincial park close to town, prepared their campsite - including tying their bear bag securely - and had their campfire and 's'mores.' But they still kept a wary eye out for the bears. None came that night.

The next day they were up early in order to reach their destination, Mile 0 of the Alaskan Highway in Dawson Creek, BC. This time the Sutherlands took time to visit the information center to learn about the history of this famous highway. Built as a military necessity by U.S. and Canadian troops after the Japanese attack on Pearl Harbor, it was considered one of the engineering marvels of the 20th Century. But just as amazing, the 1,390 mile route was built in a little over eight months, in spite of -30 degree F. temperatures, snow, and pesky bugs. And today it remains the only overland route from the lower 48 to the 50th state. Brice bought a souvenir coffee mug, with a polar bear on one side and a map of the Alcan on the other. Maybe that was his way of remembering Spud.

This time the duo splurged by staying at a motel in this tourist town of 12,000. Brice, checking his atlas, announced, "Let's take a different route home, and check out two of Canada's premier national parks, what do you think?

"Well, Dad, we've checked out some of the best ones in the U.S., we might as well check these out, too."

So early the next morning they "saddled up" their pickup and said goodbye to the Alaska Highway, and turned East to Grand Prairie, and then south to Jasper National Park. The closer they came to the park, the more smoke they saw emanating from the tall, pine trees, already blackened by the forest fire. At times they could even see flames above the trees. A strong wind could carry this inferno across the road. Brice was watching for road detour signs.

"Boy, it must be a dry summer around here," commented Blaine. "I wonder if we can camp in the park."

"We'll find out pretty soon. I hope we can see the mountains through all that smoke."

Brice, with his eyes burning from the smoke in the air, was finally glad to reach their destination in Jasper at dusk. After driving through several campgrounds, they found a secluded site, unpacked their gear, and pitched their tent against the tall Ponderosa Pines. At least it would serve as a windbreak. The ban on open fires precluded them from having their normal reflective time around the campfire. They were tired, so they headed to their tent. No Northern Lights tonight - the sky was too hazy.

They dozed off right away, but their sleep didn't last very long. Blaine was the first to awaken. He heard a scratching sound on their pickup, and couldn't figure out what it was. He looked through the tent netting to see a black shape on the truck bed. He quickly poked his father, whispering, "Get up, Dad. There's a bear trying to get into our truck."

Brice, still half asleep, squinted through the side tent window to see the big bear actually rocking the truck back and forth, trying to get into the cab through the rear window. He kept hitting the glass with his huge paw. One solid thud and he would be inside, preying on their food and who knows what damage he would wreak.

Brice, searching for his bear spray, concluded, "He could ruin our truck. I'd better scare him away. Where's my bear spray?"

Blaine felt around the inside of the tent, and handed the canister to his dad, who was already outside the tent. "You stay inside, and say your prayers for me."

Brice, taking the safety latch off the trigger, held the spray at arm's length, and slowly walked toward the truck. Suddenly the bear smelled him, turned around, and jumped over the side of the box toward Brice. Brice froze in his tracks, and waited for the charging bear to come within range of the spray - a mere ten feet. And just as quickly, the bear stopped about ten feet from Brice, who was too frightened to squeeze the trigger. The huge grizzly turned and ran back into the forest, leaving Brice limp with exhaustion.

Blaine, seeing the "coast was clear," crawled from the tent and asked, "Dad, are you all right?"

"Thank God, he did a bluff charge. That was worse than a defensive tackle coming at me. Let's move our tent to an open area, and park our truck further away from our tent. Maybe we'll be safer that way. That's as close as I want to get to a bear."

Blaine, also shaken by the night visitor, could only say, "I wish Spud were here. He would've chased the bear away before he got close to our truck."

"Maybe this is our last night of camping without a dog."

By the time they moved everything, and set up their tent again, the full moon had broken through the hazy clouds, and they could at least see if there would be another intruder. They'd had enough excitement for one night.

On Another Glacier

The dog-less duo, exhausted from their close encounter during the night, slept in later than usual. They even decided to forego their usual breakfast. They packed up and stopped at the park visitor center, and inquired about seeing glaciers.

The friendly Canadian, with a winsome smile and pleasing voice, grabbed a map of the park and pointed to the Athabasca Glacier.

"This is the one you want to see," she said confidently. "It is the most-visited one in North America."

Brice spoke up, "We've just come from studying glaciers in Alaska. We learned how fast they are melting due to global warming. Is that happening here too?"

"Oh my, yes. It's been going on since 1844, and the rate has been increasing every year since 1980. We have records to prove it."

"Blaine jumped into the conversation, "How fast is it receding now?"

"About 20 meters per year," she said as she pointed to the head of the glacier on the map. "But more importantly, it has lost over sixty percent of its volume in the past 125 years. At that rate the glacier would be completely gone this century. It's happening to glaciers all over the world."

"Are you educating people about this problem?" asked Brice.

"We teach them 'aboat' the effects of global warming on the glaciers, and what they can do to reduce their carbon footprint. We take them 'oat' on the glacier to see the effects of melting - the crevasses, moulins, and melt water."

"Good for you," commended Brice. "That's what we saw on the Columbia Glacier. We want to do the same thing in the States, but we've got a long ways to go. You Canadians are ahead of us with your carbon tax."

"Thank you," said the park ranger. "Maybe together we can save the world. Would you like to take a snow coach 'oat' on the glacier?"

Brice and Blaine looked at each other with the same answer.

Twenty minutes later they were in the coach, bumping along the snowy and rocky surface of Athabasca. The driver stopped to allow the passengers to walk on the surface, with a warning to watch "oat" for the crevasses and moulins.

As they stepped on the mushy surface, Blaine reminded his dad of the close call the sled dogs had on the Columbia Glacier. "We'd better watch our step. We don't have harnesses like the dogs."

And then what did they see, but a sled dog pulling a park ranger close to the crevasse. He said, "Whoa," to the dogs, which stopped immediately. Then he hammered a steel peg into the ice and fastened a rope around it and tied the other around his waist. Then with crampons on his boots, and an ice pick in his left hand, he rappelled with a rope in his right hand - about 25 feet down into the crevasse.

Brice and Blaine saw the ranger disappear over the edge, and ran ahead of the rest of the tourists to see what was going on. When they reached the steel peg, they noticed it was inching its way from the surface ice, which was slushy on top. They immediately sensed the danger to the ranger on the other end of the rope. Both of them ran and grabbed the rope just as the peg freed itself from the ice.

They heard the ranger below yell, "Help. The rope is coming loose."

Brice yelled loudly down to him, "We have the other end. Hang on."

But the Nebraskans didn't have crampons, only their hiking boots, so they started sliding slowly toward the edge. They were about a foot from falling in themselves, when the rope suddenly slackened.

They looked at each other and Blaine said, "Oh, no."

Brice cautiously crept to the edge to look down, expecting to see a human lying face down at the bottom. But instead he saw the ranger precariously perched on a snow cliff about ten feet down, with his ice pick dug firmly into the ice, and hanging on for dear life.

Brice, using the quick reactions learned in his football days, yelled, "Hang on, we'll get you out."

He ran back to grab the rope with Blaine, and they dug their heels into the solid snow, and pulled with all their might. Gradually they walked backward as the ranger first set his axe above him, and then stair-stepped his way to safety, collapsing on the edge, with his upper torso resting on the level ground - safe at last!

After catching his breath he sighed, "I don't know who you are, or how you got here, but you saved my life. Thank you."

"I'm Brice, and this is my son, Blaine, from Nebraska. We've been studying glaciers in Alaska, and wanted to see what you were doing?"

The ranger, now sitting up, but still stunned, explained, "I was trying to find where the melt water was going, and I found a torrent of water cascading down this crevasse."

"We found the same thing on the Columbia Glacier. They're melting all over," added Brice.

Blaine picked up on the conversation with, "We even had to save some sled dogs that fell into one of these," as he pointed to where the ranger had just ascended. "We did the same thing as we did with you," as he grabbed the now limp rope.

The ranger, now standing up, said, "We'd better block off this crevasse. It's too dangerous for the tourists, including you. But there must be a reason why you were here."

"Yes, God works in mysterious ways," said Brice as Blaine and he walked back to the safety of the snow coach. "Where have we heard that before?" as he gingerly poked his son, who returned the ribbing (no pun intended).

As they disembarked, Brice turned to Blaine and said, "We've had enough excitement in this park. First the bear, and now this. What say we head to the other park, and see what excitement awaits us there?"

"Drive on, Dad."

More Impacts of Global Warming

They then headed south on Highway 93, driving with their headlights on in midday. On the map, they passed the highest mountains in the Canadian Rockies, but their view was obscured by the smoke from the many surrounding forest fires. Blaine, looking intently for any sign of these peaks, suddenly spotted one as the wind briefly provided an opening in the haze.

"Look, Dad, this must be Mt. Columbia, at 12,294 feet the highest point in the province of Alberta. This mountain looks barer than Mt. McKinley. There's not much snow at all."

"The drought must be really bad around here," concluded Brice.

And that was the only mountain they saw on their drive to Banff National Park, home of famous Lake Louise, the "Diamond in the Wilderness," one of the most photogenic places on the planet; still pristine with its glacial-blue hue and surrounded by jagged mountains. But even here climate change was having an effect.

While in the interpretive center, Blaine stopped to read a sign about something he had never heard about before: POPS, or Persistent Organic Pollutants. He read the sign while his dad was browsing the gift shop, looking for something for Tricia. Maybe he'd really changed.

When Brice rejoined him, Blaine explained what POPS were all about.

Pointing to the pictures on the sign he explained, "Look at this. Remember Dr. Hill telling us about the food chain in the Arctic Ocean?" Brice nodded in the affirmative.

"Well, the same thing is happening here, except this time chemical pollutants are carried from far away countries by air currents. Then they attach themselves to snowflakes that eventually make up glaciers. And here's where global warming comes in. When the glaciers melt into this and other mountain lakes, these chemicals are eaten by zooplankton. Do you remember Dr. Hill mentioning that?" Again Brice nodded, "Yes, go on, professor."

"OK, so then trout eat this tiny plant, and osprey eat the trout, so they're all affected. More bad news for the environment. But there's good news, too."

"What's that?"

"Well, the sign goes on to say that there is an international treaty to regulate these POPS, and Canada was the first to sign it."

Brice added, "That's what we need to see happen in Reykjavik. By the way, I wonder if Magnus made it back OK."

Blaine, checking his iPhone, had the answer, "Yep, he just texted me to tell us they got back safely, although they had to wait for a bad storm to pass in Alaska. He wants us to come to Reykjavik."

"Let's not worry about that now, son. Do you want to spend one more night in the mountains? The smoke has lifted for now. Maybe we could have a quiet night with a campfire."

"Let's do it. I'd like to do some hiking around here before it gets dark. You can tell the days are getting shorter down here."

They walked around the level path surrounding Lake Louise, dodging the many tourists. They heard many languages, but only understood English, and the Icelandic words they learned from Magnus. This place was indeed an international destination. But for how long? Could this beautiful setting be maintained in the face of POPS, melting glaciers, pine beetle disease, fires, and diminishing snowfall? Would they have to move the ski lifts higher up the mountain to catch the powder there? But for now God's Creation was in its glory here, and the "flatlanders" were enjoying it.

Their last night camping in Canada passed without a bear spotting. But in the middle of the night both men suddenly sat upright in their tent.

"Did you hear a crashing sound outside, and the sound of thundering hoofs?" wondered Blaine. "Or was I dreaming?"

Rubbing his eyes and rolling over Brice slowly answered, "You've been seeing too many cowboy movies."

Now curious, Brice clumsily crawled out of the tent, shined his light and looked around at the branches piled on the ground. Then, with his bear spray in one hand and the flashlight in the other, he traced hoof prints to the edge of a steep cliff. And then he turned around to see a large bull moose charging him. Was it another bluff charge?

This time he squeezed the trigger, releasing a cloud of red pepper spray that immediately stopped the huge beast, who bellowed, turned and charged toward the cliff.

Blaine, seeing what happened, ran to his dad. "Are you OK?"

Brice, taking a knee like he was back on the football field, simply shook his head up and down, muttering, "I'm still having close calls, but now God is with me."

Blaine grabbed his father's strong arm and led him back to the tent, where they both collapsed until dawn - without Spud's watchful eyes.

Heading down to the Plains

After packing, the duo headed east to the bustling metropolis of Calgary, stopped for a quick fast-food breakfast, and headed south on Highway 2. Their sight-seeing was over, except for noticing the dry and dusty wind-blown fields - many without crops. Would this severe drought extend to the lower 48 as well? They would soon find out.

They stopped at a rest area and noticed a sign, "BC Is Idle-Free," showing a picture of black exhaust emanating from a gas guzzling truck, overlapped by a big red X.

Brice quickly shut off his truck muttering, "These Canadians are serious about protecting their environment."

"Yea, echoed Blaine. "We can learn a lot from them, and not just about hockey."

And then it was time to go through customs - American style. They remembered the rough time they had trying to "smuggle" their wood into Canada, and this time they had none. They also remembered the last time they had to show the officials Spud's shot certificate - a bittersweet memory this time.

Once in the US they followed the same route home, traversing Montana, and its snowless mountains on I-90. Throughout the state they again noticed the red and green patches in the national forests, and trees standing bare and blackened by recent forest fires.

The observant Blaine turned to Brice and asked, "Do you remember seeing this many dead trees before?"

"Don't know, son. You're the scout on this trip. I'll do the driving.

He was immersed in his thoughts about Tricia as they entered South Dakota - still dry with the persistent drought. He was praying about how he should approach her. Would the gift he bought her be an "icebreaker?" But first he had to make sure she wanted to see him. After all, she did give him her phone number. He'd have plenty of drive time to ponder his next move before reaching his home state.

A Storm on the Prairie

As they drove through the Black - or now mostly red - Hills, they noticed the sky becoming the former color. The cumulus clouds were gathering in the West, with all kinds of eerie shapes. And then the wind started blowing the dirt from the dry fields over the highway, prompting Brice to turn on his lights in mid-afternoon. They had been through this before, and knew what was coming.

Blaine, grabbing Brice's iPhone from the dash, googled "Rapid City weather" to hear the following warning: "This is the National Weather Service. We have just spotted a massive tornado traveling northeast at 50 mph, with winds up to 150 mph. It is classified as an F-3 on a 5 point scale. It is a very dangerous storm. Seek shelter immediately in a basement or the doorway of a small room in your house. If in a mobile home, get out and run to your neighbor's sturdy home or the nearest building marked with a "T." If driving in your car, stop and get out and lie in a ditch. Oh my, it's coming . . . ." That was the end of the transmission.

Brice, looking in his rear view mirror at the approaching funnel, floored the accelerator in an attempt to outrun the storm, but it was coming at them diagonally, so the attempt was futile. He could barely see the road ahead of him as the rain was coming down in torrents, and the wind nearly blew their vehicle from the road. He slammed on the brakes, pointed at the ditch on the left side of the road, and yelled above the wind and rain, "Let's jump down there and see if we can find shelter."

Brice opened his door with both hands to keep the wind from blowing it away. He then jumped out, took several steps before the wind knocked him down, and, like he was tackled, rolled to the bottom of the ditch. Blaine slid over to the driver's side and did the same thing. They both ended up in the same pile (no penalty this time), with the rain soaking all their clothes. But fortunately the wind was not as strong, as long as they didn't stand up.

Brice, trying to regain his senses, started crawling through the ditch, with Blaine blindly following. They crawled for several minutes, pausing to shake the water from their heads so they could see ahead of them. Finally, Brice spotted a dry culvert running under the highway, and was blown into it by a gust of wind. Blaine, close behind, grabbed Brice's leg, and the father yanked him to safety - for now. And there they sat, waiting out the storm, and praying that the runoff water would not sweep them away. Brice remembered the Bible verse Magnus had quoted, something about the waters not passing over you, and that settled him down. Now they were safe from the funnel cloud, but could only wait for any water to start running through the culvert.

Finally they saw a trickle of water coming from the other end of the culvert. Brice and Blaine instinctively moved toward the dry end, but the flow intensified. Then they moved toward the end as the water rose several more inches. With the storm still howling outside, they would be blown away if they left their place of safety. Brice, looking at the rising water, now up to their knees, turned to Blaine and asked, "Are you ready to swim?"

Blaine looked nervously around as the water was about to sweep him away, then back to his dad with, "We don't have any other choice. We'll drown in here. You lead the way. We're both good swimmers."

"We'll see," said Brice as he pushed away from the culvert into the swirling, muddy cold torrent. At first his head went underwater, but then Blaine saw him surface, and they both floated on the wild waves. And after floating and trying to swim for about the length of a football field, Brice scored a "touchdown." He looked up in time to see a split rail fence, stood up to grab it, but was blown away by the erratic winds. After lying in the muck for a seemingly long time, he got up from the field and sprinted to the fence, clutching it with his football-carrying hand. And quickly he reached out his other hand to grab the crawling Blaine. They both hung on as if their lives depended on it. Finally, Blaine grabbed one of the rails, and they were both able to crawl through the fence and fall on the other side onto the muddy ground. And, as the Bible promised, the water did not pass over them.

They both lay on the soft ground, panting heavily, pondering their next move. The storm had now passed and only the remnants of wind and rain remained. They finally got up and started walking toward the road, looking for their truck. They heard sirens in the distance, and realized they were the fortunate ones. Maybe that seaplane pilot was right about guardian angels.

They found their pickup where they left it; and other than having a few scratches from flying debris, it was drivable. It was a good thing the tie downs held the precious cedar box containing their belongings. So they both got in and collapsed as the sun again shone. Maybe God was smiling down on them, and their escape was more than luck.

As Brice started the motor, after several sputtering tries, he said, "I didn't think tornadoes happened this late in the summer. Is this more extreme weather?" That's what the climate models they learned were predicting.

Thankful to still be alive, they resumed their journey, heading for the Nebraska state line, with the welcoming sign, "Nebraska - the good life."

Brice was about to see if that were going to be true in his life.

Brice wanted to see his former ranch in the daylight, so they decided to spend one more night under the stars and full moon. He turned to Blaine with this suggestion, "What say we camp at the Halsey National Forest again?"

"Good idea, Dad. That's where this trip started you know. Maybe we learned something about camping."

And this night was peaceful as they sat around the campfire, not worrying about bears. But it still would've been nice to have Spud curling up by the flickering fire.

Blaine remembered, "I wonder if we'll see Spike on our ranch.

Brice, knowing more about the situation, simply replied, "We'll see tomorrow."

Back at the Ranch

As the Nebraskans drove from their last camping spot to their ranch, they noticed that there were no crops growing. This is the time when the second cutting of hay would normally be harvested. The fields were a dry brown with dust devils circling about them. There were no irrigation pipes in the fields. They weren't needed now.

As they drove down the dusty road to their ranch, Spike was not there to greet them. Blaine, looking around at the abandoned buildings and burnt fields, cried out, "What's going on? Is this our place? What happened? Where's Spike?"

Brice, who had kept this tragedy from his son for his own good, now finally said, "Your mother told me about this when we were still in Alaska. But I didn't want to upset you. She texted me about the aquifer drying up and the fields burning up. She sold the place and moved to Lincoln. That's where we're going next."

He put his arm around Blaine's shoulder, but the son walked away from his dad. He needed to be alone to process this change. He was thinking, "I've already enrolled at the University of Nebraska. Am I still going to go there? Will I see my mother there?"

Brice waited in the pickup for his son to walk around the lonely place. As Blaine walked around the boarded up house, garage, and barn, Brice used this opportunity, not to text Tricia, but to call her as she requested. He had her number in his directory, took a deep breath, and dialed.

It rang several times before Tricia answered, not knowing the caller (Brice had blocked his number), with a faint, "Hello."

Brice paused before saying her name in a low voice. Tricia then paused, thought about hanging up, but remembered she had told Brice to call, so she waited to hear his voice, "I'm at our ranch. It looks terrible. I can see why you sold it and wanted to leave."

"Well, I had to make a decision, and you weren't around, and you didn't seem too concerned and all, with your sleazy love life in Alaska."

"Tricia, that's all over. I want to see you and make things right between us. I'm a different person now."

Again Tricia paused before stating, "I'll have to see it to believe it."

"Deal. I'm heading to Lincoln now to get Blaine squared away on campus. If you give me your address, we can stop in. We've got lots to share with you. When can we see you?"

"Call me when you arrive in Lincoln, and I'll see how my schedule is. I started teaching here you know. Maybe after school's out tomorrow."

Tricia complied out of curiosity, not expecting things to change. Brice loaded her street and number into his GPS. Blaine came back to the truck, still puzzled, and they headed to Nebraska's second largest city and the final leg of their journey.

Reconciliation

After spending the night in a nondescript motel, the Sutherlands motored east to Lincoln on I-80, passing more bare fields with irrigation pipes not even connected. It was mid-afternoon when Brice pulled into a rest stop to call Tricia, who had just arrived home from school. The invitation was still on. Brice, using his GPS, drove directly to a small white house on the corner, across from an elementary school. "How convenient for her," he thought.

As they pulled up to her house, Brice got out, grabbed a wrapped package in the cedar box, brushed his hand quickly through his hair, and said to Blaine, "This is where your mother lives. Let's see what's going on?"

Tricia, who spotted them coming up the walk, opened the door and immediately hugged Blaine, saying, "It's good to see you, son. Where's Spud?"

"That's a long story. I'll let Dad tell you when he's ready."

Blaine answered with another question, "Where's Spike?"

"He's not a city dog, you know, so I gave him to the Humane Society, and told them to give him a home where he could roam."

And then she turned cautiously to Brice, eyed the package he was holding, and asked, "What's that? A peace offering?"

"You could say that," as he held it out for her to take. "Go ahead, open it."

Tricia sat down and took the slim rectangular package and carefully unwrapped the paper to reveal a framed, wooden, hand-carved poster with these words: "God grant me the Serenity to accept the things I cannot change; Courage to change the things I can; and Wisdom to know the difference."

Tricia sat and stared at it, and finally said, "Did you find God in Alaska?"

"He found me after I stopped running from Him. And that's where Spud comes in."

And so for the next hour, the males in the Sutherland family related their harrowing adventures in Alaska, showing pictures on Brice's iPhone that included their close calls with the sea-plane crash landing, and the emergency landing in Anchorage after flying over Mt. Redoubt. They talked about their friendship with Magnus, and then got to Spud. That's when Tricia perked up, Brice choked up, and Blaine picked up the story.

Tricia looked empathically at Brice, thinking, "I've never seen him like this before. Maybe he has really changed."

Blaine talked about the walks they had with Spud by the sea, and got to the last time when he chased the polar bear into the water.

Tricia interrupted with, "And what happened?"

"Well, the bear turned and chased him into the water where he couldn't get away. And that was it."

"You mean he died?"

Not looking up, Blaine silently shook his head slightly.

Tricia again, "And what did you do with him?"

Brice, regaining his composure, finished the story about the burial and the funeral in the cave by the ocean.

Now Tricia softened as a tear fell from her eye. "That was worse than me having to give up Spike."

And finally Brice got to the main point that he wanted to share. "But something good came out of it. It took this tragedy for me to find God. Magnus helped me to see that as Spud gave his life for us, so did Jesus. You knew I was an atheist, and in Alaska I picked up with the barfly you mentioned. Not a good choice. I had two brushes with death. But it was Spud's death that did it. I asked Jesus to come into my life and forgive me, and help me live for Him. And slowly but surely he's doing it. Magnus gave me some things to read, which I've been doing."

And then he surprised Tricia by taking her hand, looking into her blue eyes, and asking, "Tricia, I know I wasn't faithful to you in Alaska, and I broke my promise about keeping in touch, and I'm sorry. Will you forgive me and give me another chance to change with God's help?"

She pulled her hand away and picked up her present, and looked at it for what seemed like a long time. And then she also surprised Brice by standing up and stepping forward to hug him. They embraced in silence for a minute before she answered, "Just this one time."

And that was the start of trying to put the pieces of their rocky marriage back together. Maybe Humpty Dumpty could learn something from them.

Then they both came over to where Blaine was sitting, and sat on each side of him. Blaine, not knowing how to handle this true confession from his tough football father, looked down until his father said, "Things will be better now, son. We're all together again in Lincoln."

XI. At Home in Nebraska

Spud's Burial Plot

Ever since Brice's reconciliation with Tricia, he was looking for a place to keep his promise - to give Spud a decent burial. He figured by now Spud's temporary grave in Alaska had been washed out to sea. Besides, it would honor Tricia to participate in a civilized ceremony. After all, she got used to seeing Spud run on their ranch. And besides, this would be good for the Sutherland family.

One day as Brice was driving back to his apartment from his new temporary job as backfield coach for his former Cornhuskers, he passed a Pet Cemetery. He turned in and drove around the rows of graves of departed pets - some of them decorated with their favorite toys. As he drove out, he stopped at a kiosk that gave information on "Burying Your Precious Pet."

Then as he did frequently, Brice stopped at Blaine's dorm room to discuss this idea. The two of them decided they would select a plot for Spud, plan the funeral, and then surprise Tricia by inviting her to the ceremony. But in the meantime Blaine had his studies in environmental science (like his father), and Brice and Tricia had their jobs, so the ceremony was put on hold for now.

Brice Meets His Buddies

Brice couldn't hide from the Huskers very long after settling in Lincoln. As a member of Coach Osborne's national championship teams of 1994 and 1995, he was still a "big man on campus." And so it was, as he was walking to Blaine's dorm one day, he ran into one of his fellow Huskers, who ran up to him, shook his hand and said,

"Brice, remember me? I opened up the holes on the right side of the line for you. Good to see you, man. How are things going?"

Brice responded, "Zak, good to see you, too. What brings you here?"

"Football, of course. I'm the sports director for the college cable station. I've never left Lincoln like you did. Say, let's get our old gang together for old times' sake. What do you say?"

"Sure, that sounds fun. You name the place and time, and I'll be there. I've got lots to share."

As they parted on campus, Brice was thinking, "How am I going to tell them I've changed? They remember me as the life of the party. Magnus told me I was a new Creation. I guess I'd better pray about that."

The next weekend Brice got a text from Zak, "Meet at 'Husker Haven' on O Street, 9 on Saturday. Got the gang together."

As Brice walked in, he saw his entire offensive line, standing and welcoming him back. They did the "high five's" to the loud and rocking music. This scene attracted quite a crowd from the patrons, some of whom remembered this 1995 team as the greatest of all time, according to ESPN. And they were still handing out autographs, with Brice at the center, signing T-shirts, shoes, and textbooks. It was fun for him to get back into this college atmosphere, even though it wasn't game day.

Finally the raucousness subsided and Zak announced, "The first round is on me. Brice, do you want your usual highball? You used to down quite a few of these as I remember."

Overhearing Zak's loud voice over the music, the rest of the line nodded. They remembered the parties and carousing after the games, as long as Coach wasn't around.

Brice hesitated, and then said, "No thanks, I'll take a Pepsi, please."

That quieted the players.

They looked at Brice strangely. Finally, Tavaris, the still stout and fit offensive guard, chided Brice with, "What's the matter with you. Are you afraid of a little liquor?"

The square-jawed center Jackson chimed in, "Com'on, just one for old times' sake?"

"OK, just this time," conceded Brice. He felt bad that he gave in to temptation this easily, but rationalized, "Maybe they'll listen to my story now. And Lord, please forgive me this one time."

As the drinks flowed freely, the famous linemen opened up and shared their stories with Brice. Since the rest of the huge men lived in Lincoln, and drank together frequently, they didn't need to catch up on their lives. But they did with Brice. Just as he was on the field, he became the center of attention around the barstools.

And the questions came forward, "What've you been doing since you left our team? Did you graduate?" (Most of them acknowledged they hadn't). "What was your major, recreational leadership? Did you marry a 'babe'? Why did you leave Lincoln to live on a ranch in the middle of no place?" (that puzzled them). And finally, "You don't seem the same anymore. You used to be the life of the party. What happened to you?"

And that was the opening Brice was waiting for! All of a sudden the conversation stopped, and the entire offensive line was looking at their star player, wondering what his next play was going to be.

Brice, looking down at the half-empty drink he was sipping, raised his head, and started to recount his story. And for the next 15 minutes he related his trip to Alaska, and what he learned about global warming. When he got to that subject he could see some of their eyes rolling, like, "Get real, it's all a hoax." But no one said anything about it.

But then he regained their attention with his descriptions of his two plane crashes - the one in the seaplane and the emergency landing in Anchorage. He paused and then continued to explain the confrontation between Spud and the polar bear in the ocean. Even these tough football players felt Brice's emotion as he related his faithful friend's burial by the sea. Many of them no doubt had lost pets themselves.

Brice paused again and took a sip of his drink, and soberly asked, "And then you know what happened?"

"What?" asked Stu, the thick-necked tackle.

Brice didn't want to blow his answer this time. "I finally realized that Spud sacrificed his life to save me and Blaine. And my friend in Alaska explained that's what Jesus did for us on the cross. And then he led me in a prayer to ask Him into my life. And that's why I'm different now."

Brice looked around at the silent line, wondering how they would react. Several looked into their drink, seemingly thinking about their own lives. The others stared at the ceiling, shaking their heads in disbelief. Did anyone believe the way Brice now did? If they did, they weren't publicizing it.

Finally Curt, the tall and dexterous split end, got up from his stool, looked at Brice with a scowl, "Sorry, Pal, I can't buy that 'Jesus stuff.' I'm outta here. It's been good knowing you."

As he pushed himself from his stool and staggered out the door, he was followed by the rest of Brice's former blockers. This time they weren't in formation. If a referee would have been around, they would've been penalized for being off sides - and a little tipsy besides.

As Brice sat by himself and finally finished his one drink, he was stunned at their reaction. He silently prayed, "God, is this the price of being a Christian? Is this why I'm back with my buddies, only to lose their friendship?"

And then he had these thoughts, "Remember, I'm always with you. At least you tried. You planted seeds that may bear fruit later. Don't give up. I'll open up other "holes" for you."

Meeting Coach

Brice left the "Husker Haven" by himself, feeling lonely and defeated at his first attempt at sharing his faith with his now former friends. He wanted to share this experience with Blaine to see if he had the same reaction from his roommate. So the father again visited his son on campus to see how he was doing.

As soon as Brice opened the door to Blaine's room, his son asked his dad, "Where do you think I'm going tonight?"

"I hope not drinking. Just kiddin'. I tried that with my football friends, and it didn't work."

"What didn't?"

"I shared our story in Alaska, Spud's fight with the polar bear, and Magnus helping us to find Jesus, and they walked out on me."

"I'm proud of you for trying, Dad. Hey, I've got something that will cheer you up. I saw a poster in the union that Coach Osborne is speaking to the FCA group tonight."

At the mention of Coach Osborne, Brice lit up, but was puzzled, "What's FCA - a secret fraternity, or what?"

"No, it's called Fellowship of Christian Athletes, and you don't have to be in sports to attend. It's open to anyone. I'm bringing Jim," as he nodded to his roommate. "Do you want to come with too, Dad? We can grab a pizza in the SUB before the meeting - you paying, of course."

"Of course," agreed the father. "Let's do it."

As the three of them were "chowing down," Blaine glanced up to see a tall, fit, lanky and brownish gray-haired man walking briskly toward their table, carrying several books under his left arm. He turned to his father and whispered, "Look, that's your coach! Do you think he'll recognize you?"

Brice quickly turned his head toward Coach Osborne's direction, and didn't have to wait long for the answer to Blaine's question. He stopped in his tracks, turned toward them, and extending his right hand to Brice as he stood up, said in his usual mild-mannered voice, "Well, if it isn't Number 24 from our championship teams. Good to see you, Brice. Say, I'm on my way to speak to the FCA group. Why don't you join me, and we can get caught up afterwards?"

Brice, looking like he'd just been hit by a defensive tackle, didn't know what to say. He just got up, motioned to Blaine and Jim, and they followed Coach, who was striding out - not wanting to be late to the meeting.

The Meeting

A standing room crowd was already assembled when "24," "24's" son, and Jim arrived. They found a vacant part of the wall on which to lean. Brice quickly looked around to see if any of his drinking buddies were here. He was surprised to find Curt, the first one who left the "Husker Haven" the night before. Brice thought, "Hmm, maybe I did plant at least one seed. I hope Coach has a good talk for him."

The crowd was buzzing at the speaker, whom everyone knew as the Nebraska legend. Then the crowd quieted as a muscular student, currently a member of the Cornhusker Black Shirts, stepped to the microphone for a lengthy introduction, recounting the many victories and championships of Coach Osborne's teams.

The MC concluded with, "But that's not why Coach Osborne is here. He came to talk about what's beyond the final score, incidentally the name of one of his books, available at the Nebraska Bookstore. Coach Osborne."

At once a sea of red stood and applauded enthusiastically, but they didn't perform the wave. That was reserved for Memorial Stadium on Saturday afternoons.

Brice, staring with rapt attention at his now much-older coach, wondered if he would reminisce about the Husker's glory days that included him. Coach focused his remarks on the different roles he himself had played - on and off the field - player, coach, athletic director, politician, mentor, family man, and even fisherman. But the last role he mentioned was the most important to him - servant.

When he mentioned that, the crowd quieted. The humble coach began, "I've been blessed with athletic and mental abilities, a wonderful family, fame, some fortune, and good health - even in my

84th year. The question I want to leave with you is, 'What's beyond all that?' We can come to the end of our lives thinking one of two ways. I'll give you two examples from the Bible."

When he mentioned the "Holy Book," some people fidgeted, while others opened their Bibles, ready to turn pages.

"How many of you have heard the phrase, 'the wisdom of Solomon?'" About a fourth of the crowd raised their hands. The others looked around, wondering what they had missed. So much for Biblical literacy at UNL!

The coach continued, "Solomon had it all. He was both the richest and wisest man of his time. He undertook massive building projects, such as the temple and his palace. He acquired slaves, silver, and gold; drank wine; and had 700 wives."

That last phrase got a "Yea!!" from a few skeptics.

Without being phased, Coach Osborne began again, "And then King Solomon tried hard work. But as he looked over his life, he characterized it as, 'Vanity, vanity, all is vanity. It's like chasing the wind. All is meaningless.'

"But he did have a few words of wisdom at the end of his life: It was to fear God and keep His commandments.

"And then there's the Apostle Paul, a highly educated and respected man, who gave it all up to serve Jesus and others. In doing so he suffered persecution and hardships after his encounter with Jesus. And when he came to the end of his life in prison - before being beheaded - he summed up his work this way, 'I have fought the good fight. I have finished the race. I have kept the faith.' Sounds like what a dedicated athlete would say after a winning season, right?"

With the crowd quieted, the Coach concluded with this question, "Someday - when you're old and gray," as he brushed his hair, "how do you want to have lived your life - for yourself, or for God and others? The last choice is being a servant. My prayer is that you choose the latter. Thank you."

Again a standing ovation. Since Coach mentioned seeing Brice afterwards, the three of them stuck around while the crowd thinned out. But several students came up to speak briefly with the person they had only seen on TV. The coach, now turned counselor, took time to encourage them, answer their questions, and even sign his books.

And then Brice noticed Curt standing in line, waiting to see his former coach. He prayed a quick prayer to give Coach the wisdom of Solomon in dealing with this agnostic. Brice was too far away to hear the conversation. Besides, it would remain confidential. But he did see Coach reach under the podium and hand Curt a book. Was it the same one Magnus had given Brice? A coincidence?

Finally the crowd had dispersed, and Brice, Blaine, and Jim walked to where Coach Osborne was standing. He spotted them and, not forgetting his invitation, said, "Let's find a quiet spot on campus where we can talk - just us. Know any place?"

Blaine looked at Jim, and they both mentioned one of the study rooms in the library. "And they even have free coffee and pop in there," said Jim.

As they walked to the library, Dr. Tom asked Brice, "Well, Brice, briefly tell me what you've been doing since you left football?"

Brice took the "ball" and ran with it, relating his desire for the land and ranching, his rocky relationship with Tricia, and his graduate work, culminating with his trip to Alaska and his new passion

- climate change. They reached the library, quietly found an empty study room, helped themselves to coffee and pop, and found three comfortable chairs.

With the Coach finally having a chance to relax after a long day, he reflected on his coaching days, remembering Brice as the star on the greatest team. But he wasn't thinking about football. Finally, he looked at Brice with his penetrating eyes, "Tell me Brice, why did you come to FCA tonight? Was it because of me or was it something else?"

Remembering his coach as a man not wasting words, Brice began, "Of course I wanted to see you after all these years. But I've changed since my off-field days, as you probably remember."

Dr. Tom, his long legs stretched out on another chair, simply smiled at Brice's comment, and asked, "Tell me about your change."

Brice's heart skipped a beat as he realized this was his chance to again share his faith. He related the same story as he did the night before in the bar with his buddies, but this time he added, "Magnus gave me your book, *Beyond the Final Score*, which I've been reading. Reading how you handled your many roles as coach, Congressman, AD, and mentor helped me to learn about my new faith."

The Coach asked, "Which role in my book did you like in particular?"

Brice thought a minute and said, "I guess the ones where you weren't in the spotlight, like your private time with your family. That was funny when you tried to teach your wife how to troll for salmon."

Tom smiled and said, "Yea, I'd better stick to catching trout."

His coach rose from his comfortable chair, gave Brice a "high five," and said, "Congratulations, brother. Now make sure you read the Bible daily, pray, and find other Christians with whom to fellowship."

And then the proverbial "light bulb" came on as Dr. Tom leaned forward and asked, "Brice, why don't you consider getting involved with FCA? All the kids remember you on the field, and look up to you. You could use that connection to connect them with Jesus. It would help both of you. I've been doing that for years with young people, and it's rewarding. Think and pray about it."

Brice was taken aback by this suggestion. His only thought was, "If Coach says it, I'd better do it. He knows how to win on the field, and in life."

All Brice managed to mutter was, "Who me? I'm just learning this stuff myself. But since you suggested it, I'll consider it."

And that was the end of his conversation with Coach - for now.

Spud's Decent Burial

Brice and Tricia were now dating again - trying to reignite the "spark" they had during their courting days many years ago. They were feeling comfortable with each other, but there were still the fleeting romances they both flirted with last summer with which to deal. But as they discussed them, they both agreed to forgive and try to forget their pasts. But only time would tell if they could again live together as husband and wife.

During one of their dates, they talked about a faithful friend they both knew - Spud. And now the time was right. Brice revealed his surprise, "Trish, do you remember the story Blaine and I told you about Spud and his burial by the sea?"

"You bet. That must've been traumatic for both of you."

Brice nodded silently before saying, "Since you weren't there, Blaine and I would like to invite you to a decent burial for Spud at the Pet Cemetery on the Cornhusker Highway. You up for it?"

"Sure, as long as I don't have to dress up," she said with a smile.

That suggestion "broke the ice."

The next Saturday, Brice and Blaine pulled up in the pickup in front of Tricia's house. With Blaine in the rear seat, Tricia climbed in the front, staying by her window. No sliding over to the driver's seat in this truck - at least not now.

Upon arriving at the cemetery, Brice unrolled the tarp covering the truck bed to reveal a cedar box - the packing box brought from Alaska. And it still retained its fresh aroma. Simultaneously, Blaine took his mother's hand, saying, "Close your eyes, Mom, and hang onto my hand."

With trepidation Tricia asked, "What's going on here? Are you going to bury me, too?"

"Don't worry. Just follow me."

Brice grabbed the burial box from the truck bed, and showing his football speed, sprinted to Spud's plot and gently lowered the box into the hole he had previously dug, with the top open. By that time Blaine and his trailing mother arrived.

Blaine, looking at Tricia, said, "OK, Mom, open your eyes."

She first looked around at her surroundings and then focused on the box in the ground. It took her awhile to take it in. Inside were some of Spud's toys - a Frisbee, tennis ball, stick, and a half-eaten deer leg. And there were pictures of him chasing the cattle on their ranch, herding sheep in a contest, and riding in their truck. But no pictures of him in Alaska. And no polar bear.

Slowly Brice closed the cover so Tricia could read the inscription on top:

"Spud Sutherland: Karelian Bear Dog

Born in Wyoming, February 15, 2018

Died saving his friends in Alaska, August 15, 2021.

"Greater love has no one than this, that he lay down his life for his friends John 15:13"

She silently looked at the two elongated crosses along each side of the top of the box, and holding back tears managed to say, looking at Brice, "You and Blaine really loved him, didn't you?"

Brice, with a lump in his throat, silently said, "Yes." Blaine, standing on the other side of the plot, confirmed what his father said.

And then Tricia popped a surprise question, "And will you love me like that?"

Brice walked over to her, gave her a hug, and said, "Will you let me?"

This time Tricia nodded in the affirmative, and arm in arm, they both walked over and hugged their son, who had some tender feelings of his own.

As Tricia stood looking at the carved box, Brice and Blaine

grabbed their shovels and slowly scooped the loose dirt on the box. The only sound was that of the fine particles falling gently until they completely covered the inscription. But as a testimony to the humans who will visit this site, Brice also ordered a small gravestone with the same inscription etched in granite for all to see.

The Sutherland family would be visiting this cemetery often, either together or separately. So, even in death, Spud served as the catalyst to bring the Sutherlands together again. Maybe he'd be frolicking with them in heaven someday.

XII. At Home in Iceland

Magnus' New Job

L ittle did Magnus realize, that by the time the leaves dropped from the trees in Iceland, he would be a national celebrity - but not of the stature as their famous singer, Bjork. Ever since he returned from the IPY, the Reykjavik press picked up on his CO2 phone, which was now being marketed - not only in Iceland - but worldwide.

And his fame was helped by his new position in the government as a student representative for the Department of Sustainability. Minister Jonsdottir remembered her promise to contact Magnus upon his return to his native country. She used her influence to convince her department to create a new part-time position, post a job description (that just happened to match Magnus' background), and, lo and behold, offer him the job, which he quickly accepted. Not letting this new influence "go to his head," he remembered to thank God and his parents, in that order.

Magnus' first task, with help from the government, was to create his own website, "CO2 phone.is," which had video demonstrations of how to use the phone, together with a link for free ordering. The Ministry of Sustainability also advertised this invention on their government TV station.

Next, Magnus "hit the road" to demonstrate the phone to students, eager to try out the latest gadget. Using the athletic model of competition, he sponsored contests between schools to see which ones would reduce their carbon footprint by the largest percentage over the school year. He even built in a playoff system, and bracketed schools by size. At the end of each school year, there would be a CO_2 champion, awarded with a "green trophy" for their efforts in helping Iceland reach its goal of being a carbon-free country by 2025.

Remembering his promise to Brice and Blaine, now 5,000 miles distant "across the pond," Magnus sent two CO_2 phones to their new addresses in Lincoln, with this note, "My phone is taking off here. Blaine, see if you can get something started on your college campus. Looking forward to seeing you in two months."

Another Close Call

Even though he was busy with his new job and his studies at the university, Magnus was still able to keep in contact with his friend Erik. Mainly they just texted each other, but there's no substitute for seeing each other "eye to eye." But guys don't like to just sit around and talk. They want action. So another hike was born.

This time Magnus wanted to hike on a glacier, anxious to see if what he learned at the IPY was applicable in Iceland. He checked his iPhone for the closest glacier to Reykjavik, and found pictures of the gorgeous Myrdalsjokull, Iceland's fourth largest icecap, looming above the quaint village of Vik in southwest Iceland. Besides, it's close to the Ring Road, and you can hike on the glacier without booking a tour.

Since Erik was driving to Reykjavik anyway, they linked up, and drove to Vik, where they stayed overnight in a hostel situated below the imposing glacier - approximately 700 meters thick and covering approximately 700 square kilometers. They could look out their bedroom window and wonder what would happen if part of it calved over the cliff. Goodbye, hostel! But they slept well, and after a hearty breakfast, were ready for a new challenge.

Magnus remembered the IPY presentation on volcanoes by the three Icelandic scientists who discussed the recent massive Katla eruption of 2014. This eruption of hot lava, ash, and rocks came up through the glacier on which they were to hike. And because the glacier's mass was shrinking, Katla's lava had an easier time of reaching the surface. The resulting melt water rushed through tiny Vik, rushed out to the ocean, and boomeranged off a basalt cliff rising from the ocean, causing a 25 foot tsunami to rush inland, destroying many buildings. However, a series of earthquakes before the eruption gave the rescue personnel ample warning to evacuate the townspeople safely to higher ground. Even though many shoreline buildings were devastated by the tidal wave, they were rebuilt, and the city is still a tourist destination - pretty as ever.

So Magnus and Erik weren't worried about another eruption so soon. They didn't want to be caught like the last time they hiked on Hekla, the "Gates of Hell." They had their climbing gear consisting of crampons, ice picks, and ropes, and were ready to go. At least in wasn't crowded in October, so they had the glacier to themselves.

After about an hour of slogging through the mushy snow, they noticed a rushing waterfall rushing down the cliff, and cascading into a river running into the North Atlantic Ocean.

Magnus commented, "There's a lot more water coming from this glacier than the last time I saw it ten years ago."

Erik picked up with, "Is that what you saw in Alaska, too?" pointing to the water around them.

"Yes, it's happening all over the world with the increased warming."

They each used their ice picks to pull themselves on top of the glacier, and gazed toward the head, still miles above them between the black mountains, which had seen many volcanoes over the ages.

Erik again, "I'm surprised at how rough this surface is," as he stepped on both ice and rocks broken and turned topside by the glacier's force.

"That's another sign the glacier is melting, uncovering what's underneath it."

Magnus enjoyed being the "expert," gaining credibility with his closest friend. "Maybe that will help me with my Christian witness to him. He had a lot of questions the last time we hiked," he thought.

The duo kept hiking toward the toe, watching for crevasses. Since it had recently snowed, they had to walk slowly, and occasionally test their path with their ice picks. Magnus shared his story of the dogsled that about crashed down the crevasse on their glacier hike in Alaska.

"And you know what, Erik; I got to hold an injured husky as we sledded back to the vet. And he even licked me. I don't mean the vet!" That got a laugh from his serious friend.

Magnus, ever observant, noticed the many moulins that indented Myrdalsjokull. Pointing to the one in front of them he explained, "These holes collect the water melting on the surface. Sometimes the water disappears overnight. At least that's what's happening in Greenland."

"So where does the water go?"

"Good question. That puzzled scientists for quite a while, until they discovered, by accident, that this water is actually going through the crevasses all the way to the bottom. This acts as a lubricant underneath the glacier, and speeds its journey to the sea."

"Do you think that is happening here?"

"I don't know, but there's lots of water around here."

No sooner had Magnus finished his last sentence than they heard a deep rumble beneath their feet. Flashing back to their hike on Hekla, he shouted to Erik, "We'd better get out of here. Maybe this is an eruption!"

Magnus immediately did a 180, and they ran back toward the head, following their tracks. He looked back to see a steaming geyser spewing water, sand, and tephra behind them. Magnus, in the lead, yelled, "Let's see if we can outrun it, but be careful for the crevasses."

Alternately looking back at the approaching boiling water while dodging the crevasses, the two sprinted and jumped over the small cracks in the ice. With their speed they were putting distance between themselves and the melt water, now increasing because of the hot eruption. Both men paused briefly to catch their breath. Erik, sounding optimistic, said, "I think we've outrun it.

"Maybe for now," concluded Magnus. "But we better keep jogging at a steady pace. Ready?"

Erik, still breathing heavily, nodded his head, and they were off again.

Suddenly a burst of steam enveloped them, but they kept going even though they were temporarily blinded. And then it happened. Magnus heard a yell from behind him, immediately stopped, and started running back from where the sound came. As the steam drifted away, he looked for Erik, but couldn't see him. And then he heard a blood-curdling cry, "Help. I'm in a crevasse."

Magnus ran to the edge and looked down to see Erik perched on an ice outcropping. With both hands he was holding on to his ice pick, firmly embedded in the ice above him. In this position he was in no danger of falling further, but neither could he climb out, since he had no footing above him. He was stuck with no place to go. He was 20 feet from the top, and 100 feet from the bottom. But how long would his flimsy piece of ice hold before it would topple to the bottom? And how long could Erik hang on?

Magnus quickly surveyed the situation, took his rope from around his waist, tied a loop with a bowline knot, and lowered it down to Erik. The stranded climber let go of the pick with one hand and quickly grabbed the rope, and lowered it around one shoulder. He did the same thing with the other hand, and the rope slid down around his waist.

In the meantime, Magnus wrapped his part of the rope around his waist, and made another bowline knot. He then planted his right foot firmly in the ice and yelled to Erik, "When I start pulling the rope, start climbing up, using your ice axe. Give it all you've got, and I will too," and he said a prayer.

Magnus leaned back and used the leverage of his crampons, and pulled with all his might, but the rope was not moving. He took a deep breath, and tried again. Still no movement. As he paused to catch his breath, he turned around to see a tall, husky, bearded man walking toward him.

This stranger realized the calamitous situation unfolding at the other end of the rope. Without saying a word and with both hands, he grabbed the end of the rope behind Magnus. Magnus also grabbed the rope, and they pulled simultaneously, with Magnus grunting and groaning. The other man remained silent. This time the rope steadily moved away from the edge as the two men continued a steady pull. Magnus was actually pulled along by the man behind him, as was

Erik. Finally, Erik's motionless body appeared on the edge, where it was dragged through the snow, rocks, and ice to safety.

Magnus, lying beside his friend and breathing heavily, looked intently at the mysterious man, who lifted his huge arms toward Erik, turned, and started to walk away.

Magnus managed to softly say, "Who are you? Thanks."

The stranger turned and smiled, and without saying a word, vanished into the steam, leaving no tracks on the ice! Was this Magnus' answer to his prayer? Could it have been an angel? Magnus, like the silent stranger, kept these thoughts to himself, knowing that with "God all things are possible."

Erik's Procrastination

Magnus crawled over to where Erik was lying and lay his head on his friend's chest, listening for a heartbeat. Finally Erik slowly sat up, looked around, and shook his head, muttering, "What happened?"

And then the two of them heard a loud crash in the crevasse. Crawling over to look down, Magnus saw that the ice outcropping on which Erik had been standing was gone. Just like a glacier, it had calved, and tumbled to the bottom.

Magnus turned and crawled back to where Erik was sitting. "Erik, that could've been you down there," as he pointed toward the crevasse, "Dead."

"Yea, that was another close call, like the one we had on our last hike," reflected Erik.

Looking directly at Erik, Magnus asked, "Erik, are you ready to die?"

"I'm too young to think about that now. I want to enjoy life. When I'm old and gray, I'll worry about that?"

"When we were hiking Hekla, do you remember the story I told you about one guy going to heaven and the other to hell?"

Erik, his memory now refreshed, said, "You mean the one in the *Bible*?"

"Yea, that's it. Did you read it?"

Erik shook his head.

Magnus, in one more attempt to help his friend with this subject, offered, "If I give you a *Bible*, will you read that story?"

"Scout's honor."

Magnus turned to his friend and said, "Are you ready to head back?

Grabbing both of Erik's hands and lifting him to his feet, Magnus asked, "Do you think you can make it back to the car?"

"Let's do it."

They retraced their steps in silence - just the two of them. Maybe the seriousness of the situation was sinking into Erik's head. But if it was, he wasn't saying.

As they reached Magnus' car, he reached into the glove compartment and pulled out a copy of the New Testament, opened it to Luke 16, dog-eared the page, and gave it to Erik saying, "Here's what you promised to read - before the next time."

As they drove back to Reykjavik on the Ring Road, Erik kept his gaze on the huge glacier they had just climbed, precariously perched on the hill above them. He wondered if what they had experienced on their hike portended another eruption. Time and the seismologists would tell. In the meantime it was back to school for him. When would the next adventure come?

Part Four: Extreme Weather

❧

XIII. Special from the Weather Channel: The Extreme Weather of 2021

"Good evening. I'm Clare Keller. 2021 is going down as the worst year ever for extreme weather events. Next month delegates from 195 countries will gather in Reykjavik, Iceland, to try again to forge an international agreement designed to limit the greenhouse gases that are mainly responsible for the continued warming of our planet.

"Tonight, you will see our correspondents all over the world reporting on the most catastrophic weather events of the year. It's not a pretty picture we are painting, but one that needs to be presented. Stay tuned after our commercial break."

New Zealand

"Welcome back. First let's go to Dan Owens, high in the sky in NZ-TV's Sky Copter."

"Thank you, Clare. We're flying over the Southern tip of New Zealand's South Island, and what I'm seeing below is total devastation. Boats are strewn randomly on land like matchbox toys. Houses have been knocked from their foundations and are floating in the ocean. Litter from stores and houses is everywhere. Trees have been uprooted and are clogging the roads leading inland.

"We've been hearing for years about the melting ice in Antarctica. Climate scientists were surprised when the Larsen Ice Shelf broke up in two weeks back in 2002. And now the Wilkins Ice Shelf, the size of the U.S. state of Connecticut, broke loose, creating a tsunami with 75-foot waves racing toward our coast at jet speed. Fortunately, our alert system allowed most citizens to climb to higher ground, but they don't have much to return to. You can see the devastation far up both coasts. If anything good can come from this disaster, it's that Christchurch – the largest city on the island - was spared another disaster like our recent earthquakes. Back to you, Clare."

Australia

"Thank you, Dan. And now let's go to New Zealand's neighbor. Come in Kevin McCarthy."

"Thank you, Clare. This is Kevin McCarthy from the Australian Broadcasting Company. I'm live from the *SS Kangaroo* next to the Great Barrier Reef. This wonder of the world graces our Northeast coast for 1,600 linear miles, covers 133,000 square miles, and is composed of 2,900 separate reefs on 900 islands. Even though it's beautiful from space, as you can see on your screen, it may be completely white by 2030. Will tourists still come to visit this wonder of the world? Will there be any fish left to harvest? Those are the billion dollar questions.

"What's causing this possible catastrophe? Climate scientists say several factors are to blame. The most damaging is the increasing level of acid in our oceans. This results from the carbon dioxide in the atmosphere that eventually sinks into the upper part of the ocean. This increase in acidification decreases the ability of the corals to build their skeletons (screen shows emaciated corals), and this decreases the ability to create a habitat for the marine life that depend on the reef for their survival. It's even possible that the shells already made will dissolve - a "double whammy."

"The other impact on our reef is from the rising, sea-surface temperatures (on the screen is a schematic of a thermometer rising in the red zone). This is caused by human-caused CO_2 in the atmosphere, lack of cloud cover, and freshwater run-off. Warmer waters can break down the natural processes needed for the animals and algae living on the reef. It is projected that by 2035 the average sea temperatures will be higher than any previously recorded, and they have been increasing every year this century. Not a good sign."

At this point the camera pans the Coral Sea, writhing with the wind whipping whitecaps 35 feet high. Kevin nervously looks behind his shoulder at what the camera is capturing and begins with a shaky voice, "Well, as if on cue, the last reason for the reef's possible demise relates to extreme weather. A picture is worth a thousand words, so I'll be brief. Besides, we'd better head the *Kangaroo* back to shore to escape this oncoming cyclone, which is predicted to achieve a Category Five status.

"We've had a lot of these intense storms lately. Climate scientists hypothesize a link with global warming. In any case, these storms batter the reef and can even break up the dying coral. Not only does this damage the reef further, but it leaves our coastline vulnerable to erosion by the waves."

As the *Kangaroo* yaws to try to escape the coming cyclone "Susan," Kevin, facing the camera with his wind-swept rainhat flapping, signs off with, "We'll have more on this storm after it batters the reef, and I'm safely ashore. Good day mates!"

Peru

"Thank you, Kevin. Let's stay in the Southern Hemisphere and go to a city high up in the Andes Mountains. Let's bring in our correspondent in Peru, Bonita Chavez."

"Thank you, Clare. I'm standing in a dry irrigation ditch on a farm outside the City of Huaraz - a city of 100,000 that has seen its water supply dwindle as the glaciers have been rapidly melting. Furthermore, this city at 10,000 feet elevation is also subject to heavy flooding."

The screen now shows Jose Gonzales pointing to his dry ditch. "My family has relied on water from the glaciers to water our crops all year. Now we're lucky to have water in the spring. The rest of the year the ditch is dry like it is now. So when our crops dry up, I can't feed my family. I have nothing to sell to earn a living. Now we have to live off the government, and who knows how long that will last. I've heard there are food riots in the city. I don't know how long we can keep going," as he wipes a tear from his eye.

"So how can you be flooded out when your ditches are dry?" asks Bonita.

Jose answers, "Well you see, the melting glaciers have created lakes below them," as he points up the mountain. "And then one day a huge chunk off a glacier fell into one of these lakes, causing it to overflow its banks and run downhill to our farm. We managed to escape the waters, but our land is ruined more than it was. I don't know what to do now."

Bonita summarizes, "And if this "double whammy" wasn't enough for Jose and his family, the villagers are trying to farm higher up the mountain where there is still some water. But they have to cut down trees to clear their land, causing erosion downhill, and more flooding because of the intense storms.

"Climate scientists predict these glaciers will be completely gone this year. And then what will happen to families like Jose's? It's not a bright future for them. Will these residents be added to the climate refugees already fleeing the ravages of global warming?

"From outside Huaraz, this is Bonita Chavez reporting."

China

"Thank you, Bonita. And now let's go on location to Tiananmen Square in Beijing, China, where Connie Chang is reporting."

With the camera panning this huge public expanse, Connie begins, "Westerners remember this place as the site of deadly demonstrations back in 1989. Today another type of death has appeared, and it has nothing to do with protests. It is carried by the deadliest killer in the world - the malaria-carrying mosquito.

"And this small insect has killed people strolling in this peaceful square. This disease, which used to be only in and around Yunnan province on our Southern border with Vietnam, has now migrated North to our capital on the wings of this pesky insect. Let's interview one tourist who was stricken with this disease.

"I have with me Don Bates from London. Mr. Bates, were you surprised to have contracted malaria this far North?"

"Yes, I was taken off-guard. I've traveled to Africa and always took my pills before traveling, but I didn't think I needed them here."

"What were your symptoms?"

"The usual fever, chills, shaking, and vomiting. I was taken to one of your hospitals for observation. They gave me an experimental anti-malaria drug which didn't work. Later, when I returned home, I contracted jaundice, and was treated successfully for this. I'm OK now, and got my malaria shot before I returned this time. After all, I have business to do here in this modern city."

"Thank you, Mr. Bates. Climate scientists see a link between a warmer world and more cases of malaria worldwide. Our government officials are striving to reduce our greenhouse gases in the hopes that malaria will not spread any further North from here. They are not proud of being the world's largest contributor to global warming. This is Connie Chang from Tiananmen Square."

United States

"Thank you, Connie. Now let's travel to the Midwestern U.S. with Joe Anselmo. Joe, come in."

"I'm standing over the famous Ogallala Aquifer, or what's left of it, in the Nebraska Sandhills, which used to be a lush green in the spring. But now you can see the brown, barren hills," and he points behind him.

"I have with me Jeb Carlson of Ainsworth, Nebraska. Jeb, tell us what's the situation on your ranch?"

Jeb, dressed in his customary cowboy hat and boots, looks down at the ground and points, "This used to be my primary source of irrigation, this deep well, producing 100 gallons per minute when I started ranching 30 years ago. Now I'm lucky to get 5 gallons, not enough to water my cattle, let alone my crops. I have no choice but to sell off the livestock and switch my crops from corn to raising sunflowers, which need little water. Do you think there's a market for these (the camera focuses on Jeb's rough hands holding sunflower seeds)?

"And if that isn't enough to worry about, there's that *#@!%* Keystone Pipeline, which we fought so hard against, crossing my property. They've already had three breaks in the pipe, due to the dry ground sinking. You can still see the black stains on my pasture," as Jeb points to the East. "It's ironic that our soil used to be that color before the aquifer was depleted.

"I guess I'll have to move to Lincoln and become a Cornhusker fan like everybody else in this red-crazed state."

Turning to the reporter Jeb sarcastically asks, "Say, I got some land in the Sandhills I'll sell you."

The reporter smiled and then signed off with, "And that's the situation as the climate continues to warm in the Breadbasket of America. This is Joe Anselmo reporting for Cornhusker TV in Ainsworth."

The Bering Sea

"Thank you, Joe. And now we're North over the Bering Sea where an intense storm resulted in a massive oil spill. Our correspondent is on board an Alaska Rescue seaplane surveying the damage. What are you seeing, Rachael?"

"We are flying over a Russian oil rig that was hit by a 1,200 foot Russian tanker the *Pravda*. The ship, with a reinforced hull, ran into the 'mother of all storms.' The ship battled 60-foot waves for several hours as she headed to the rig - trying to tie up to ride out the storm. The Pravda's navigation system picked up unusually high winds, strong ocean currents, and an enhanced air pressure pattern called the Iceland-Azores - all signs of ominous things to come.

"The *Pravda* finally reached the rig when she was hit broadside by a 120-foot high rogue wave that broke the ship in two. Several of the crew were fortunate to be thrown onto the rig, where the workers rescued them. But the rest of the crew was washed out to sea, along with the millions of gallons of heavy, black, oily crude.

"We are circling the oil spill and you can see it moving slowly toward the Alaskan coast. In the distance you can see its effects - the dead seabirds, sea otters, seals, dolphins, and even a Humpback

Whale caught by the oil while migrating south.

"Now the Inuits in their villages face another challenge. Their eroding coasts have lost their ice protection during the fall storms. Will there be any animals left to hunt? Should they relocate like other villages, or hope the Russian oil company would take responsibility for the clean-up, which could take years? Would the U.S. government or the State of Alaska help out? Tough decisions lie ahead for these villagers striving to keep their culture intact.

"This is Rachael Welch reporting above the Bering Sea off the coast of Alaska."

Iceland

"Thank you, Rachael. We will now go to the country that is hosting the International Climate Change Conference - Iceland, which has also seen changes in its weather patterns. On the ground in front of the Parliament Building is Ingvar Ingvarsson."

"You're right, Clare. The last several years have seen drastic changes in the weather during our nation's Independence Day celebrations on June 17. Usually the crowds are dressed in shorts, T-shirts, tank tops, and wear hats to protect themselves from the 20-hour sunlit days. Now they are wearing their winter coats and rain gear.

"Our forecast for today is for a high temperature of only 5 C, far below the 25 C average for this time of the year. And with today's clouds, which is unusual for this time of the year, we may even see a combination of rain, sleet, hail, and even a few flakes of snow. The good news is that we may be able to view the fireworks without resorting to our harbor ships raising their high tech black sails that partially block the sun.

"I have with me climate scientist Dr. Joanna Jonsdottir from the University of Iceland to explain what's behind these cooler temperatures."

Dr. Jonsdottir: "Although we can't be sure at this point, we are speculating that the so-called conveyor belt that circulates warm and cold water ocean currents is changing. One theory is that the Irminger Current, which has brought us warm water up from the Gulf Stream for 100 years, is changing. Another ocean current, the North Icelandic Jet, studied by two of our scientists, may also play a role, as does the increasing melting of the Greenland ice cap.

"So bundle up and enjoy the festivities. This may be the new normal."

"Thank you, Dr. Jonsdottir. Back to you, Clare."

"Thank you, Ingvar. We'll see you in Reykjavik next month. Stay warm. This concludes our live feed from around the world for this year. Now, as we close, you will see on your screens what extreme weather events have been happening in other parts of the world this year. The pictures, narration, and even the somber music will speak for themselves. I'm Clare Keller. Good night."

"**Pakistan** holds the world's highest recorded temperature in a populated area - a sizzling, stifling, and suffocating 150 degrees Fahrenheit. People were literally dropping like flies in the streets, and the morgues couldn't keep up with the burned and decomposed bodies (picture of decomposed bodies), even though they had refrigeration compartments."

"The 40-year-old drought continues in the **Sahara Desert** - its relentless dry and dusty march southward has now doubled in the last 50 years. Haboobs - violent dust storms that sweep across the desert - are becoming more frequent and intense, blinding and choking people and animals alike (picture of people and animals in the Haboobs). The nomads who formerly eked out a living from the land either fled farther South to find grasslands for their animals and crops, or became climate refugees in countries who would resettle them.

In the **Gulf of Mexico** the frequency and intensity of Category 5 hurricanes has increased every year since 2012, due to the warming of the oceans. Now Katrina-sized storms are the rule, and not the exception (picture of devastation with destroyed buildings and uprooted trees). Even though the U.S. and Mexican governments spent billions 'shoring up the shores' with seawalls, people were abandoning the cities in droves for the higher ground inland - the first southern climate refugees in North America."

"And in **America's Midwest** the storms with the highest wind speeds were growing in intensity and frequency. Whereas meteorologists can give ample warning to prepare for hurricanes, tornadoes can form and descend suddenly, destroying everything in their path (picture of buildings, cars, and debris scattered over miles). The increasingly unstable weather resulted in a record number of F-5 tornadoes and deaths each year, with the total of all tornadoes reaching a record number of 999 in April of 2020. More climate refugees?

"In **Brazil** the problem was frequent flooding, due to the continual deforestation by the indigenous tribes living in the Amazon rain forest. With little vegetation clinging to the bare soil, the frequent rains became torrential, causing mudslides to wash away entire villages (picture of village washed away). As a result more climate refugees fled to the heavily-populated cities on the east coast, living in squalid conditions. These urban centers were fighting the rising Atlantic Ocean by building massive seawalls. These residents could themselves become climate refugees. Where would they flee?"

"**Europe** seemed to be experiencing schizophrenic weather patterns. While the Atlantic coast was unusually cold in the winter and summer - due to the changing of the warm Gulf Stream - the interior countries were suffering through prolonged heat waves and dry spells that produced massive wildfires in Siberian Russian and the Scandinavian countries (pictures of forests burning). As a result their lucrative summer tourist season, especially in the Mediterranean countries, ground to a halt."

"Nowhere were the melting glaciers more apparent than in the world's highest mountain range - the **Himalayas.** In a strange weather phenomenon, the glaciers in the higher elevations of this 'Rooftop of the World' are melting faster than those at lower levels. This melting, at whatever level, is causing two major disasters. The glacial lakes formed by the melting floods careen down on villages, often completely destroying them (picture of destroyed village). As a result of the shrinking glaciers, the water that supplies millions of mostly impoverished people is literally drying up (picture of empty river bed). More climate refugees.

XIV. Rendezvous in Reykjavik –International Climate Change Conference

December, 2021

E ven though the darkness shrouds Iceland's capital city for about 20 hours per day in December, there was a bright sun shining briefly as the delegations from 195 countries arrived to hopefully negotiate a binding agreement to reduce greenhouse gases - a goal that had eluded them in previous conferences. This was the largest group of foreign dignitaries to ever descend on this small but advanced island – strategically located between North America and Europe.

Reykjavik was ready with its new Icelandic Cultural Center, equipped with stadium seating and a state-of-the-art sound system. The many modern hotels, scrumptious restaurants, and fashionable shops wanted to demonstrate why Iceland has consistently been one of the most livable countries in the world. And the tour buses were waiting with agendas that included Iceland's volcanoes and glaciers, geothermal and hydroelectric plants, and the Golden Circle tour highlighting the country's history and natural features. If the foreigners wanted to venture out on their own, they could select from a wide array of nonpolluting hydrogen vehicles. After a difficult day of negotiating, the delegates could relax in Reykjavik's many thermal pools as the snow fell softly through the steam rising from these natural hot springs. And their trip would not be complete without a visit to Iceland's main tourist attraction, the Blue Lagoon, where they could enjoy soaking in the pure wastewater from an adjacent geothermal plant, and at the same time take in the breathtaking Northern Lights. It couldn't get much better than that!

Because of the momentum generated at the IPY by the developed countries' desire to curb their greenhouse gases, the delegates convened in Iceland with an air of optimism. But there still remained large differences in how to save the world, and there was an **urgency** to do so.

Ever since the first two international climate change conferences in Bali in 2007 and Copenhagen in 2009, delegates have met annually in different parts of the world to wrestle with the divide between the developed and developing countries. The latter countries, including China, India, and Brazil believe it's their turn to pollute as their economies are expanding rapidly. After all, they state, the developed countries, including the United States and those in Europe, have been spewing greenhouse gases into the atmosphere since the Industrial Revolution in the early 1800s. The advanced countries counter that they are the ones taking steps to curb their emissions, and have the technology to switch from fossil fuels to renewable energy. And besides, they argue, "We're already giving funds to assist the emerging nations to combat deforestation and adapt to climate change."

President Palin summarized the argument, "Two wrongs don't make a right. Let's get off the 'blame game' and work together." But China counters with, "Even though we are the world's largest emitter of greenhouse gases, we are also the world's largest manufacturer of wind and solar energy." Finally, the host nation says, "We are the world's leader in geothermal energy technology, and are on our way to become the world's first carbon-neutral nation."

The arguments and posturing continued, leaving the issue in doubt whether or not this conference would finally be able to bridge these differences. In the meantime the world has been warming at an increasing pace, the weather has been becoming more extreme, and the sea ice, glaciers, and permafrost have been melting rapidly at the Poles.

Day 1 - Opening Ceremonies

The protocol for previous climate change conferences was to have the host country's political leader open the conference. And so it was that Prime Minister Fredric Karlsson thumped the gavel on the podium and proclaimed, "The opening session of this Climate Change Conference is now in session." Setting aside their previous differences, the delegates rose to give each other a standing ovation. At least they were starting on a positive note.

Minister Karlsson continued, "It's dark here in Reykjavík, but you people are the bright lights as you convene to try to reach an international agreement to reduce our carbon emissions. This may be the last time we can avoid catastrophic harm to the earth. Iceland is proud to host this conference, and we are willing to share our technology to achieve our mutual goals.

"Several working groups have been meeting before this conference to set an overall goal for reducing carbon emissions. Previous climate models have calculated that a reduction of 80% by 2050 would be adequate to prevent the most catastrophic changes to the earth. However, these models did not anticipate the rapidity of global warming, and the consequences we have been seeing for several decades. Consequently, these groups have set the following goals for each succeeding decade to 2050." The giant screens surrounding the arena displayed the following numbers:

By 2030 a CO_2 reduction of 60% from 2000 levels

By 2040 a CO2 reduction of 80% from 2000 levels

By 2050 a CO2 reduction of 100% from 2000 levels (Carbon-neutral)

There were mixed reactions from the delegates as the last line was highlighted on the screens - from applause, to cheers, to "Oohs", "boos," and "wows." The bar was set high for this conference.

As the noise subsided, the Prime Minister continued by yelling, "Are you up to the challenge?" This time the answer was of one accord, with the delegates standing and applauding in unison, interspersed with chants of "Yes, we can. Yes, we will."

The Prime Minister concluded with this charge to the delegates, "And so the task at hand is a question, not of 'What are the goals?' but 'How will the goal for each decade be achieved?' Therefore each country needs to decide what is the mix of carbon-reducing measures your governments will implement; be it energy conservation, carbon sequestration of fossil fuels, various types of renewables, taxes, or market incentives. Let's work together for the good of the planet and future generations.

"The delegates will be divided into the following six working groups, as shown on the screens:

* Developed countries, divided into subgroups by population
* Developing countries, divided into subgroups by population
* Indigenous people groups
* Island nations
* Technology transfer programs from developed to developing countries
* Nonaligned nations, primarily from Africa

"And now for the parade of nations." As the Bose-like sound

system cranked up the old theme song from "Rocky," one flag bearer from each nation, and the rest of their delegation, proudly paraded around the arena in alphabetical order. As they passed the podium, each flag was briefly lowered in deference to the conference presider. And each time that was done, Prime Minister Karlsson showed his appreciation by his applause.

As the countries marched around the arena, Magnus, Brice, and Blaine, seated in the spectator seats, watched the proceedings through their binoculars. These seats were difficult to obtain, but Magnus had an "in" with his position in the Ministry of Sustainability. Since his parents weren't able to make the trip to Reykjavik, these tickets went to his two friends from America. Since leaving Alaska four months ago this trio had been communicating via Facebook and Skype. And now Magnus was anxious to show off his "green" country to these "flatlanders."

Brice wasn't just here as a tourist though. With his new position in the University of Nebraska's Department of Sustainability - thanks to the "pull" of his former coach - he hoped to take back innovative ideas to his native state. And Blaine, now on semester break from UNL, wanted to see his Icelandic friend, and get caught up with their lives in person.

As the three spectators, wedged in with many others, waited anxiously for their countries' flags to appear before them, they quickly caught up since their Alaska goodbyes. Magnus wanted to know if Spud had a decent burial in Nebraska. Affirmative. Brice wanted to know how Magnus' CO_2 phone was selling. Like hotcakes.

Before they could continue, Magnus, in the corner of his eye, spotted the Icelandic flag. As any patriotic citizen would do, he arose with many of his countrymen, who had the "home court advantage," and cheered when the flag was passing him. In fact the applause was so sustained that the procession briefly came to a halt.

Knowing that it would be awhile before the U.S. flag passed before them, the "Q and A" conversation continued. Magnus asked Brice how he got his job, commenting, "It sounds like we're doing the same thing in our own countries."

Brice recounted his "chance encounter" with his famous football coach, the FCA meeting where Dr. Tom spoke, and their talk afterwards about the book Magnus had given him in Alaska. Brice was starting to "connect the dots" when he mentioned, "You know, Magnus, it wasn't a coincidence that you gave me the same book Coach Osborne talked about at the meeting Blaine and I attended. And he encouraged me in my Christian walk. I'm even an FCA sponsor, and I occasionally give talks about my faith and football. And these young kids even listen to an 'old goat' like me."

Magnus asked Brice, "Do you ever see your old teammates?"

Before he could answer, Blaine nudged him and said, "Our flag is approaching. Let's be patriotic."

They both stood at attention as their version of the "Red, white, and blue" passed below them. This time the applause was mixed with a few "Boos." Would the still most powerful country finally lead this time?

As the Nebraskans sat down, Brice, remembering Magnus' question, recounted his bar meeting with his buddies, and his failed attempt to share the faith he found in Alaska. But then he put a positive spin on it by quoting a Bible verse Magnus had texted him: "And we know all things work together for good to those who love God and are called according to His purpose." "And guess what happened? The guy that led the walkout in the bar was at the FCA meeting when Coach Osborne was speaking. And he even went up afterwards to talk to him. I don't know what they said, but I'll pray that he finds Jesus as I did. All you have to do is ask in faith, as you know."

Magnus complimented Brice for his concern for his former team-mates by saying, "I saw a sign in one of the independent churches in Reykjavik that said, 'Eternity is at stake.' That puts things in perspective, doesn't it?"

"Yea," blurted Blaine, "You never know when your time is up."

Magnus, sensing the proper timing, shared the tragic story of one of his friends. He recounted the hikes he had had with his friend, Erik; first when they dodged the Hekla volcano, and more recently when Erik fell into a glacial crevasse and was pulled out by what must've been a strong angel.

Magnus concluded with, "And both times I talked about dying, and gave him a Bible. But he wanted to wait and think about making any decision for Jesus. Well, just last month his parents called me to say he was racing down a narrow mountain road, and his car hit a boulder that had fallen down on the road. He flipped end over end three times. By the time the rescue crew arrived, he was already dead. It's too late for him now. I only hope and pray that he made his decision before that happened. You never know."

In a sign of true friendship Brice and Blaine put their arms around Magnus as the procession continued. While these spiritual **urgencies** were being played out in the stands, the global **urgencies** were being paraded about in the arena for the whole world to see. The targets were set. Now the serious work was about to begin.

Day 2 - Seeing the Aurora

On Day 2 the conference broke into their working groups to begin the behind-the-scenes work, far from the clamor of the world media. Daily progress reports were to be given to the press, so there was nothing for the spectators to see. There was time for them to be tourists, with Magnus the gracious host for his American friends. And he would take advantage of the long winter nights.

After spending the short day strolling through the shops on Reykjavík's main streets, the trio was ready to sample the local cuisine. Magnus treated his friends, - if they would eat it - to whale meat, saying, "I know this is controversial, and your country can't understand why we still hunt whales in spite of the ban. Let me tell you. We don't kill very many whales, anyway. And besides, we don't like other countries telling us what to do. And it's delicious. Try it."

Brice, after staring at his dish for a minute, finally said, "I'm game. Are you, Blaine?"

"You go first, Dad. What's that saying, 'When in Iceland, do as the Icelanders do'?"

After silently blessing the food and this magnificent animal they were about to devour, the three of them enjoyed the taste, but Brice commented afterwards, "Well, that's one new experience for me, but I won't be eating it again very soon."

Magnus commented, "You're both game. Now let's catch a late night tour of the most spectacular thing you'll ever see. Good thing we're owls."

The three of them boarded AB Tours and headed away from the lights of Reykjavik to a remote and dark open area about an hour away. The passengers were ushered from the bus into a large log lodge with many windows and skylights, with the floors heated by natural geothermal energy. In the center of the room was a large fireplace giving off additional warmth.

As the trio warmed themselves by the roaring fire, several large screens displayed previous auroras, with their changing colors of green, magenta, blue, and violet dancing across the night sky, accompanied by Gustav Holst's "The Planet's" adding to this "heavenly feast." Below the screens were informative panels providing various ancient beliefs about what these lights portend - both good and bad omens.

However, the modern scientific explanation revealed by the screens is more prosaic. It starts with our sun that spews its solar wind toward earth at fantastic speeds. When these charged particles reach the earth's atmosphere, the magnetic field carries these particles around the poles. At an altitude of between 60 - 400 miles, the particles strike the gases in the ionosphere, causing them to glow and form the Aurora Borealis in the Northern Hemisphere and the Aurora Australis in the Southern Hemisphere. This phenomenon is limited to the Polar Regions.

In the North this "aurora zone" extends over northern Scandinavia, Iceland, the southern tip of Greenland, northern Canada, Alaska, and the northern coast of Siberia. Coincidentally, these countries and territories were all represented at the 2021 IPY.

As they were walking outside to wait for the display, Blaine explained to Magnus how they had seen the Northern Lights when they were traveling to the IPY, and that he saw them before his father did.

Brice, overhearing the conversation, said, "Yea, I told Blaine it was the gods acting up again. Now I believe it's something different, like God showing off His Creation."

"And they are even mentioned in the Bible," added Magnus.

Before they could continue their conversation, the sky was suddenly immersed in an array of moving green mist that was constantly changing shape. It didn't seem to have definite boundaries as it swayed and danced back and forth across the sky. And then it would suddenly disappear, only to return in another form and color, this time a bright magenta.

With every head turned skyward, the onlookers were mesmerized. They couldn't predict when the "show" would come flashing at them, so they didn't even want to look down or move. The best the spectators could do was to move from one foot to the other to keep warm in the dark cold.

Words couldn't describe the beauty. The oft-used phrase "totally awesome" was appropriate in this setting. This spectacle of total darkness followed by instant illumination was repeated several times from midnight to 2 am until the show was over for the night.

As the tourists walked back to board the bus, Blaine asked Magnus, "I suppose you see this all the time in the winter?"

"Yea, I do, but each time is different. You never take Nature for granted. I hope that's what the delegates are thinking, too. Maybe some of them will see these lights during their stay, and it will remind them to protect the Arctic."

The bus ride back to Reykjavik was in total silence, with visions of dancing lights in their heads.

Day 3 - An Apology? And a Protest

The men slept in late after their night excursion and didn't attend the conference. But they checked the press reports to find out that negotiations between the developed and developing groups had been occurring. But few details were provided, except those by way of a leak to the press by an anonymous member of the American delegation. It seems some sort of apology was being formulated in exchange for a pledge by the developing nations. That kept the "talking heads" and bloggers busy trying to unravel this riddle.

But what was happening outside the arena on the streets of Reykjavík was more visible. A group called "Indigenous Peoples of the World" stole the spotlight. They were clothed in their native dress, from furs and skins to loincloths, even in 0 degree C. weather! And they were playing their traditional music on instruments made from whale bones and gourds. They weren't dancing, but slowly moved in a circle around the arena holding signs that said

"P L E A S E H E L P U S"

and

"P L E A S E H E L P, U S"

Brice was the first one to recognize these signs on their TV. "That looks like the signs we saw when we were touring the refugee camp in Alaska! They look the same but have different messages, remember?"

The three of them kept staring at the screen until Blaine finally picked it up with, "Now I remember. One sign is directed to all the countries, but the one with the comma after the last letter 'p' is directed to our country. I wonder if the same guys we saw there are here?"

"Well, let's find out," suggested Magnus, as they hurried to the scene.

Blaine's conjecture proved true when they arrived on the scene. A large crowd was gathered around the peaceful protest. Magnus spotted a tall, dark man dressed in seal skin boots, fur seal pants and shirt, and a white, polar bear hat. With a bull horn he was shouting, "My village was destroyed by the warmer temperatures in the Arctic that melted the sea ice that used to protect us."

Magnus suddenly said, "That's Simon from Kivalina!" He turned to Brice and Blaine, saying, "He's the guy that gave us the tour of the refugee camp, remember?"

They both nodded as Simon continued; "Now we are living in Climate Refugee Camps in Alaska that are vastly overcrowded. More and more villages have been wiped out and fallen into the ocean. And Alaska isn't helping us anymore. We need your help desperately - now!"

The protesters kept circling the arena and chanting, "Help Now, Help Now, Help Now," until their sound faded as they marched from view.

Inside the arena the delegates were watching the events on their jumbo screens. The Indigenous Working Group was proposing a series of lawsuits against the world's biggest polluters. As one delegate stated, "We're the group contributing the least to global warming, and suffering the most. Those companies burning fossil fuels should pay for us to relocate our villages. We don't want to raise our families in these supposedly temporary refugee camps."

The daily press reports highlighted this group's efforts, both inside and outside the conference. But would the developed nations heed their cries for help?

Icelandic Social Life

As the afternoon sun dropped below the horizon, it was time to enjoy Reykjavik's favorite pastime – soaking, in one of their many thermal pools. The Nebraskans followed Magnus to one located only a few blocks from the conference center. On the way Magnus explained the protocol.

"These pools are the center of our social life. Instead of going to the bars, which happens on Friday nights, we get caught up with each other's lives and gossip here. We're a small country so we know who's related to whom. Everybody will be talking Icelandic, but I'll try to translate."

Brice responded, "Well, I don't cruise the bars anymore, so this sounds fun."

Magnus again, "And one more thing. We want to keep our pools clean. This means no shoes in the locker room, and you must shower in the nude. Don't be embarrassed. Everyone's doing it. Brice, does that sound like your football days?"

"Yea, I've been in many group showers. No big deal. Blaine, are you OK with this?"

Blaine nodded with, "As I've said before, 'When in Iceland do as the Icelanders do.'"

As the trio arrived at the pool they dutifully showered as requested and followed Magnus by slowly sliding into the first of three hot pools of varying temperatures. Brice let out a contented sigh as they relaxed while light snow fell on their heads. It was too early to view the Northern Lights from the cozy comfort of their pool. That would be an ideal combination of outdoor activities.

As Magnus was talking with his friends, laughing and gesturing toward the sky, Blaine turned to Brice and asked, "Is this heaven or Reykjavik?"

The trio tried out each of the pools and then entered the sauna for a final warm up. And then they cooled off with a swim in the Olympic-sized pool. With no chemicals in any of the water, their bodies were thoroughly cleansed. And they slept soundly that night.

Day 4 - Floating a Trial Balloon

With no breakthrough in the negotiations between the developed and developing countries, a creative approach was needed that would satisfy both groups. And it came from the continent caught in the middle of the world's CO2 emissions - Africa.

In a surprise move a delegate from Kenya slinked to the main podium. She began, "My country has been suffering years of drought caused by the pollution of the atmosphere by both the developed countries in North America and Europe, and the rapidly developing countries in Asia. Greenhouse gases don't stop at the nation's borders to show their carbon footprint passport. They continue to disrupt our land with poor crop harvests, higher prices, and record-breaking temperatures every year. This forces us to become refugees like the indigenous peoples we saw protesting yesterday.

"So here's our novel approach. It seems like nothing happens unless the legal system is involved. But this one is very different. My country is prepared to be the plaintiff and file a lawsuit before the International Court of Justice in The Hague that would declare the world's atmosphere a public trust that must be protected. We set aside public lands and even protect parts of the ocean. Why not the atmosphere?"

She was interrupted by hoots and howls and outright laughter.

Someone from the audience shouted, "So how do you protect it? Put a fence around it?" That elicited more laughter.

Said another, "Who's going to enforce it? The atmosphere police?" The laughter continued.

The delegate regained her composure with these words of warning, "So you think it's funny, huh? Is it funny to see our children die in our arms from lack of nutrition? To see our land literally dry up and blow away before our very eyes? And then there are our animal parks, with the watering holes drying up, leaving animal carcasses rotting in the hot sun."

She concluded with, "OK, this plan is 'way out.' Maybe the indigenous people's idea of a lawsuit against the polluters has merit. Do you have a better plan?"

With that she stepped from the stage to a round of applause. Maybe this radical proposal would help bring the disputing parties together. If so, the embarrassment she felt would be worth it for her country and the world.

The Island Nations Speak

Day four of the conference was devoted to the serious problems facing all island nations. A newly-released report to the delegates added **urgency** to their work. Because of the rapid melting of the Arctic, Antarctic, and Greenland ice cap, the Union of Concerned Scientists was doubling the projected sea level rise this century from three to six feet. An increase to approximately one inch per year doesn't sound like much, except to those most directly affected, including not only the micro islands but the larger islands as well. And what about all the nations bordering the world's oceans? Indeed, this single effect of global warming could be the most damaging to the world's population.

While the delegates were debating this report and its implications, there was plenty of action going on outside the convention. And Magnus, Brice, and Blaine were there to witness the twin protests. In a shrewd political move the Indigenous Peoples and the Island Nations Groups pooled their resources as a show of strength. And the cameras were rolling and the reporters were "spinning."

Simon, representing the indigenous peoples, was again marching with his bull horn, and the same signs asking for H E L P were visible. But this time there were signs identifying the largest island nations. Leading the charge was the large continent-country of Australia. Their aboriginal spokesman - scantily clad, even in Reykjavik - stepped from the protest line to address the crowd, "You've heard about our record heat waves, droughts, and floods. Now our coastlines are disappearing under water. Our people are being forced to move inland. Our crops are ruined. We need help now."

Once again the two groups joined in the now familiar chant of "Help, now! Help, now! Help, now!"

It wasn't just the indigenous peoples that were being affected by the rising sea. Wealthy landowners and resorts on beachfront property were also in danger of losing their property and livelihood. And these people were also in Reykjavik protesting.

A Japanese man in a business suit stepped forward to address the crowd. He held up a picture of a seaside resort and said, "This is my business in 2000. You can see the white sand beach enjoyed by many guests over the years." He then held up another picture explaining, "This is my business now. The beach has been reclaimed by the sea, the building is flooded, and the guests are gone. What am I to do?"

Another older, poorly-dressed woman took the bullhorn and said, "I survived our triple tragedy of earthquake, tsunami, and radiation in 2011. And as you can see, my body is ravaged by cancer. We're expecting another 'big one' soon. This time it could be worse because of the rising sea level. No telling how high the tidal wave will be this time."

While viewing the protest Magnus turned to Brice and said, "The same thing is happening to our island. If our shoreline is eroded, the people can't move very far inland, since our interior is uninhabitable."

One by one, representatives from the larger islands of Greenland, New Zealand, the Philippines, Indonesia, New Guinea, and Madagascar stepped forward to share their personal stories of flooded homes, eroded beaches, and forced migration inland.

Finally an Icelandic family, all blue-eyed and blonde, decked out in their red, white, and blue native dress, stepped forward to tell their story. The father began, "I'm Einar, a farmer who has tilled the same land my father and his father and his father have worked. The rich volcanic soil has yielded abundant crops in the past. But lately the salty ocean has covered our fields, making the land useless. We'll have to move to the city, where the government will retrain me for a high tech job. It will be a big move, but things will work out."

Einar's speech was greeted by applause from the locals, including Magnus, who turned to Blaine saying, "That's our optimistic outlook on life."

But things don't look that rosy for the smaller island nations. This time pictures told the story. One islander, dressed in a brightly-colored shirt and shorts, held a sign with a hologram taken from an airplane above the waters. Surrounded by the vast blue and emerald Indian Ocean was a crowded city of high rises, surrounded by a massive concrete seawall. Written beneath the picture was the question, "How long can we hold out?"

Simultaneously, inside the convention hall the delegates were watching the demonstrations outside. In a surprise move, the delegate from Maldives stepped to the podium to address the delegates..

"On your screens you see the most crowded capital in the world. Our city, Male, consists of 125,000 people packed into two square kilometers. You can also make out our concrete seawall completely surrounding the city. This island is one of 200 where our people live only one meter above the rising ocean. We know we will have to evacuate eventually. The question is when.

"And here's the irony. You rich countries that are causing the most pollution: you fly to vacation on what's left of our beautiful, white, sandy beaches, which you are helping to erode. We are striving to be carbon neutral by 2030, if our country lasts that long. We could literally sink into the sea before then, if another massive tsunami doesn't get us first.

"We've even raised two of our populated islands by one meter, but here's another irony for us. We had to use part of our coral reef as a base. So far we haven't seen any damage, but the continued warming of our ocean could further weaken and bleach these reefs, causing them to collapse. So either way, we're in a fix.

"Right now our greenhouse gas emissions are only one one-hundredth of one percent of the world's total. Our Mali Declaration calls on all developed countries to take immediate action to use alternative sources of energy. This injustice must be righted at this convention!

"Furthermore, we have developed a Population Resettlement Plan in case we have to leave our homeland one island at a time. But the question remains, 'Where are we to go? Who will take us in as refugees?'"

The delegate from Australia jumped up and interrupted his speech with a cry of "We will." Several other countries also echoed the same response, bringing a smile to the face of the Maldivian.

As he left the podium, the demarcation was clear. Standing on their feet and applauding were the delegates from the developing countries, while the developed countries remained seated. What would it take to break this logjam?

Meanwhile, south of the Equator, an even smaller island was facing possible submersion due to the rising ocean. The tiny nation of Tuvalu, situated between the Fiji Islands and Samoa, was also represented in this demonstration. A native islander, in a tailored black suit and red tie, held a sign juxtaposing two images - one showing a coal-fired plant belching black smoke while the other showed water washing over an airplane parked on the runway at the airport in Tuvalu's small capital city of 6,000 residents. Below the picture was the caption,

"We Want Climate Justice: Take the Polluters to Court"

In an orchestrated event - both inside and outside the arena – the delegate from Tuvalu took the podium to provide credence for the demonstrators.

"Our main island, which you see on the screen, is only 50 meters wide at its narrowest point, and 700 meters at its widest. It is only 13 kilometers long. Our whole nation is composed of four reef islands and five atolls, and covers an area in the Pacific about the area of France and Germany combined. Our average elevation is only two meters. How long can we last?

"You may be wondering, 'Why don't we just move to a bigger island?' Would Australia or New Zealand take us in as climate refugees? They would if the courts would give us legal status as refugees. That's why we need to pursue this avenue.

"So we have joined forces with the indigenous peoples to bring a charge of environmental persecution against the biggest polluter - the United States and Europe and its oil companies. They're making record profits. Let them help us."

Once again the arena was divided in its response to yet another small island nation. And they were making the evening news in the capitals around the world. But would their case have standing in the courts, or be dismissed as had previous attempts to sue the polluters? And would the developed countries come to their aid?

Free Time in Reykjavik

The three spectators had seen enough demonstrations for a while. Now Magnus became tour guide again, showing the Americans the culture of his modern capital city. And the first stop was Reykjavik's most famous landmark.

As the three walked briskly to Hallgrimskirkja - the huge tall concrete church that serves as a landmark for the tourists - Magnus explained Iceland's religious system to Brice and Blaine.

As they walked down the long aisle with rows and rows of pews on both sides, Magnus explained, "Unlike your separation of church and state, we have a Lutheran state church that everyone pays taxes for. But here's the rub. Very few people attend these big churches. They're more like museums, like this church. But the churches that make it on their own pack the pews. Go figure."

Blaine asked, "So when you're working here, where do you go to church?"

"It's an independent Lutheran church in the industrial area called Kristskirkjan, which means Christ Church, and it is. They get no help from the government, but the people are good supporters. And the pastor preaches from the Bible, and the people are friendly. Would you like to go with me Sunday? What do you think?"

Brice spoke up, "Sounds like a deal. Right, Blaine?" The typical head nod gave his tacit approval.

Magnus changed the topic with, "Let's take the elevator to the top to see the city before it gets too dark."

They rode the fast elevator up 75 meters to the enclosed walkway with viewing windows. The sun was just setting over Reykjavik Harbor as the three gazed over the many crowded buildings and high rises in brightly painted colors of red, blue, yellow, green, and gold.

Magnus again, "People look down on our city from here and think it looks like a movie set that will be taken down and carted away for another set. It doesn't look real."

Magnus pointed toward the sea wall by the harbor, saying, "That's what's keeping our city safe from the rising ocean - so far. At least we're not as bad off as those island nations we saw today."

As the winter sun set over the harbor, reflecting the stillness of the night, the men descended to the busy streets of Reykjavik in search of a restaurant serving an Icelandic delicacy, and a test for the tourists.

As they walked down the main street, Magnus walked into a restaurant to check the menu, came out, and motioned to Brice and Blaine to enter – not knowing what they were to experience.

When they were seated, Magnus looked at the menu and issued this challenge to the Nebraskans, "There's an item on the menu that separates the true Icelanders from the others. Are you game to try it?"

Curiously Brice asked, "Try what?"

"Rotten shark meat. We eat this delicacy during our Thorrablot Festival in late January that celebrates one of the Norse gods that helped the farmer provide food through the winter. Since you won't be here then, I'm giving you the opportunity to try it now."

"You're a real friend," said Blaine sarcastically.

"Well, we tried whale meat. We might as well," said Brice hesitatingly. It can't taste as bad as it sounds. After all, we eat Rocky Mountain oysters at home."

As they were waiting for this exotic dish to arrive, Magnus explained the process. "You wouldn't want to eat shark right after it was caught. There's too much urine in them, so you have to let it dry out for a while, to get rid of the ammonia. And then it's yummy!"

Brice and Blaine looked at each other in disbelief.

So when the food arrived, Magnus offered the prayer, this time really for the food, and he dug in while the Americans watched with trepidation. He took a bite-sized piece and ate it without winching, pointing to Brice's plate, "Try it, you'll like it."

Brice took an even tinier bite, tried it, made a face, and then gulped down his water. He motioned to Blaine saying, "Your turn."

After staring at his plate for a while, Blaine obediently followed suit, and did the same thing, and made the same icky face.

But then Brice, being game, matched Magnus bite for bite while Blaine ate only half his meat. Both Nebraskans filled their water glasses repeatedly to douse the taste.

When they were finished, Magnus congratulated them with, "Now you are full-fledged Icelanders."

Brice was quick to reply, "We did it for you - just once. If you visit Nebraska, we'll have a surprise for you."

And that was their cultural cuisine for the night. And they all survived.

Day 5 - Technology Transfer

And now the scene shifts to inside the arena where the real negotiations were taking place. So far there had been no dialogue between the developed and developing countries to reach an accord that would "save face" for both groups. The chief negotiators for the developed countries' largest emitters were drafting a carefully-worded apology for their "contribution" to greenhouse gases over the years. But that wasn't enough for the developing countries. They wanted more than words. They wanted something tangible.

And then the chief negotiator for the U.S. hit upon an idea. He called a closed caucus of the countries that had presented at the closing ceremonies of the recently concluded IPY in Alaska, plus France and Germany.

John Bancroft began, "Ladies and gentlemen of the IPY. Good to see you again. I want to present an idea that might break the stalemate with the developing countries. I know they want a formal apology from us, but how about this idea instead? The negotiators leaned forward, eager to hear Mr. Bancroft's next words.

"All of us in this room have developed a specialized technology or unique idea that, if implemented, would significantly reduce CO_2s. Let's develop a competitive grant system whereby developing countries would apply to use whichever technology or idea would work for them. These proposals would be judged by a special U.N. Committee made up of developed and developing countries. It would be up to us to furnish the expertise, funding, and follow-up to make sure our contributions are reducing emissions in the winning nations."

Mr. Bancroft continued, "The hope would be that the winning countries, once they have been successful in using our technology, will share it with their neighboring countries, thus creating a ripple effect throughout the developing world. What do you think?"

The first question from the Norwegian delegate was about the special U.N. Committee. "Who's going to determine what countries are on this committee? Since it's our technology we are providing, I think the West should have the majority of representatives."

All heads nodded before John could speak. "I agree, and I'll meet with the U.N. Secretary-General to see what we can work out, and let you know. Fair?"

"Fair," came the reply in unison.

Not to be outdone by her smaller neighbor to the west, the next question was from the Swedish negotiator: "But do we have time for this type of sharing? You know what the models are predicting."

Mr. Bancroft again: "It's better for these countries to see their neighbor's success and want to try this technology in their own country than for us to mandate emission reductions. Remember, the goals Prime Minister Karlsson announced during our opening ceremonies here are only voluntary. Besides, if this 'carrot approach' does not reduce emissions by our goal for 2030, we have no choice then but to impose mandatory limits to save the world. The situation is that **urgent**."

The German negotiator piped up with, "As you know, we are known for our thriftiness, and, as a result, our economy is booming. We have even been called stubborn." With that a few heads nodded silently.

"Why should my country share its success with countries that may not put our technology to good use?" Several other negotiators murmured the same thing.

Now Mr. Bancroft seemed to be in the proverbial frying pan. How would he jump out?

"I imagine others have the same, 'What's in it for us?' question. But I think the question should be, 'What's in it for the world?'

"You've all seen the first picture ever taken of our earth from space by our Apollo astronauts - a beautiful, blue planet set against the blackness of the universe. You didn't see national boundaries. Everything seemed so serene. Our mission here is to keep the picture that way, even though we know CO2 is invisible and is in the atmosphere and oceans. That's what is in it for all of us. This may be our last chance to keep it blue.

"That said, you have a point. Our grant could include a verifiable pledge to use our technology for its intended purpose - to reduce emissions to the 2030 target we've set. Also included could be periodic on-site inspections. Technology is not a panacea for these countries. They also need to become more efficient in their homes and industries through basic energy-saving measures that we all practice, right? And their transportation system must do the same thing. We could also monitor their progress in these areas. So, it's a two-fold approach, involving every citizen and the 'techies.' Our emphasis is on the latter. Does that long answer make sense?" Mr. Bancroft looked at the German questioner, who nodded in the affirmative.

After talking amongst themselves, the negotiator from Denmark said, "This sounds good for the developing countries that win these grants and use them, but how will this help reduce worldwide emissions? Isn't that our goal?"

Mr. Bancroft quickly responded, "Good question. And, yes, that is our goal. Let me answer your question with another question. How many of you are familiar with the ripple effect?"

"You mean like throwing a pebble in a pond?" asked the Russian negotiator.

"Exactly," affirmed Mr. Bancroft. "Now, here's how it can work with my proposal. Let's assume we are ten, big boulders in a large ocean. We each 'throw our technology into the ocean,' creating ripples that reach ten developing nations. These nations in turn use our technology successfully, and then 'throw their rocks into the sea,' reaching ten more nations. These nations in turn 'throw their pebbles into the water,' reaching ten more. This 'rule of ten' continues until all developing countries are reached, and they meet the goals outlined at our conference.

Before Mr. Bancroft could continue, the negotiator from Britain stood up and interrupted him with, "But why should these countries want to share their new technology with others? What's in it for them?"

"Another good question," responded Mr. Bancroft. "Two reasons. The first is practical. That's one of the conditions for receiving our technology grants. The second is altruistic. They, and we, need to realize we are in this thing together. CO_2 doesn't respect territorial boundaries. Either we save the world together, or all suffer the predicted consequences if we fail to act collectively."

"Here's a practical question," said the negotiator from Canada. "Most of us in this room can afford to share our technology. But what about the poor, nonaligned countries and the developing nations? Where are they going to get the money to share their new technology with their neighbors?"

"Another good question," responded Mr. Bancroft. "From the International Carbon Fund, which has been steadily increasing the price of carbon since it was established in 2015. Countries can apply to use these funds, based on their plan to share their technology with their neighbors. After all, that's what the ICF is for."

Seeing no more questions Mr. Bancroft concluded with this creative idea.

"You know that tonight the Blue Lagoon, Iceland's premier tourist attraction, has reserved the entire facility for our delegates. This may be a good time to contact the delegates you know from other developed countries, and feel them out on our proposal. After all, we need their support to make this thing work worldwide. How many of you are planning to soak under the stars?"

Seven of the ten nations represented in the room raised their hands.

Lobbying at the Lagoon

Busses were lined up at the cultural center waiting to take the exhausted delegates to soothing waters. As the procession speedily left Reykjavik via its modern freeway, enhanced by its many roundabouts, the terrain changed to a stark moonscape. They seemed to be in another world.

Suddenly the moonlit-sky silhouetted a smokestack belching pollution-free steam from a geothermal plant. The delegates had reached the Blue Lagoon. And they were in for a relaxing treat.

Once disembarking and entering the ultra-modern lobby, a blue-eyed blonde guide explained the procedure. "As you go through the turnstile, you will receive a wristband that has a sensor that will open and close your locker. No longer do you need the old-fashioned number you must pin on your suit. In the courtyard you may purchase food and drinks with your sensor. When you leave, swipe your wristband in front of another sensor, and it will automatically charge your purchases. We're a cashless society here.

"And one more thing. We protect our pristine waters, so we insist that you shower in the nude. Don't worry; we don't have shower police, so enjoy your soak." Pointing down the hall she explained, "We have a gift shop and restaurant here, so you can sit and enjoy the view, if you choose not to soak. We even have luxury, overnight accommodations for a complete retreat. Enjoy."

And the race to the pool was on! After squeezing through the narrow turnstiles, and trying to figure out this high-tech method to open their lockers (hold the white, round sensor on your wristband against the sensor on your locker and, "Voila", the door opens. You close it in the same way). With fear and trepidation they doused themselves in the same-sex showers, trying not to look around. One of the men said to no one in particular, "This is no big deal. We did this in our soccer locker rooms all the time."

And finally, they entered the hot waters of the Lagoon with sighs of "Oohs" and "Aahs." After sitting and soaking on the side, the delegates slowly moved throughout the lagoon with only their heads above the water. This surreal atmosphere was enhanced when one of them discovered boxes on the side of the pool. The delegate from the U.S. was the first to scoop the white, silica mud from the box and plop it on his face, creating a ghost-like figure silhouetted against the moonlit sky.

Mr. Bancroft shouted to those around him, "This is supposed to be good for your skin. Go ahead and try it."

After several embarrassing laughs the Chinese delegate stepped forward to whiten, not only his face, but his neck, arms, and upper torso. And that's all it took for the rest of them to follow suit. They had fun plastering each other with the soothing mud, and laughing at everyone else but themselves.

These two delegates that started the fun then disappeared into the steam, and were seen talking quietly at the far end of the pool for the rest of the evening. Throughout the lagoon, in the poolside restaurants, in the steam baths, and even under the waterfall the delegates were conversing in various languages. Reminiscent of the talking heads on television, these were floating heads, bobbing and weaving across the pool. Since there were no cameras or press allowed, no one will ever know whether the topics were about the experience of the moment, small talk, or the lobbying that Mr. Bancroft had proposed.

Deals that are made on the golf course by political and corporate leaders are commonplace. Was this the Icelandic version of conducting business under the steam and stars? In any case the conversations continued on the busses back to Reykjavik. New friendships were made. And they certainly slept soundly after this relaxing night rendezvous in the volcanic landscape. Would this rapport carry over to the convention?

Day 6 - Sharing the Technology: The Proposal Becomes Public

The delegates were abuzz as they filed into the convention hall. The talking heads at the Lagoon were still mulling over what they heard about the American proposal. Some seemed confused. Others wanted to hear more. They got their wish when Mr. Bancroft took the podium and held up a copy of the "Beijing Times," with the headline, "What Are the Americans up to in Reykjavik?"

After the murmuring subsided, Mr. Bancroft began, "Well, obviously our closed caucus proposal has been heard around the world. Reminds me of our own revolution with our 'shot heard around the world.' Let me explain.

"I know many of you, especially in the developing countries, want us in the West to apologize for our large, carbon footprint in past years. But that is indeed past. I am putting forward a proposal for the future that will use our technology to benefit the world."

Mr. Bancroft then projected on the screens the proposal he outlined in the caucus of IPY countries, plus France and Germany. First he listed each country and the technology they were to share with developing countries as:

Iceland - geothermal energy; hydrogen fuel cells
Norway - electric cars; environmentally-friendly oil drilling practices
Finland - reforestation practices; replacing wood cook stoves with charcoal; making buildings more energy efficient
Sweden- recapturing heat from public buildings; bike paths
Denmark - wave energy; floating cities
Canada - hydroelectric power; carbon tax
Britain- carbon footprint reduction; walking paths
France - safe nuclear power; bike rentals in cities
Germany - solar and wind power
U.S. - last-ditch technology in space (mirrors to reflect sunlight back into space; creating more clouds for cooling); painting rooftops white; planting rooftop gardens

Mr. Bancroft's next graphic was of three bodies of water:

* a large ocean with large waves created by boulders
* a lake with waves created by large rocks
* a small lake with ripples created by pebbles

John concluded with: "This is how our 10 countries can impact the entire world, one wave and ripple at a time."

As he left the podium, there was only a smattering of applause, mainly from the "Gang of 10." Now the rest of the countries had a chance to weigh in on the biggest polluters' proposal.

Reaction from the Developing Countries

Presiding Officer Karlsson didn't have to ask for comments from the floor as he spotted a delegate hurrying to the podium. It was the Chinese delegate Peng Huan who spoke without notes as he began:

"This speech is intended for my friends in the developing countries. First of all, we don't appreciate this characterization of our condition. My country is now the largest economy in the world, surpassing that of the previous speaker. Furthermore, my country is the world leader in the manufacture and technology of solar and wind power. Do we really need help from the West?"

A cacophony of "No, we don't. We can do it ourselves," came from the developing countries' delegates scattered around the arena. And then these delegates began stamping their feet in unison, drowning out their own chants.

Mr. Karlsson hastily jumped to the podium and began pounding his gavel repeatedly for quiet. After a few minutes the noise subsided enough for him to ask Mr. Huan if he had further comments in keeping with the decorum of the convention. Mr. Huan, in a somewhat subdued mood, again took the podium and began again.

"All we want from you so-called developed countries is an apology for your years of spewing greenhouse gases into the atmosphere. We don't need your help or "strings" telling us how to run our countries. We are perfectly capable of using our own technology to solve this climate crisis. And to show we are serious about this, I am asking all countries who agree with me, whether rich or poor, large or small to walk out of this convention hall until our demands are met. Are you ready?"

Again a chorus of "Yes, we will; yes, we will" as the arena resounded with hundreds of feet heading for the exits into the night air, illuminated by the TV cameras. Maybe Reykjavik would be hosting two conventions.

Minister Karlsson, unflappable in the face of the walkout, pounded the podium again and proclaimed, "Seeing a quorum is not present, I declare this convention in recess." He thumped the gavel again, and strolled from the stage into the remaining delegates milling around and wondering what to do next.

Meanwhile, the convention in exile outside in the cold winter was basking in their newfound publicity. These delegates found willing allies from the previous demonstrators, including the indigenous peoples and the island nations.

Mr. Huan, conveniently climbing up a series of steps, addressed the cheering demonstrators and the media with, "Look around you." (He paused and glanced at the crowd). "There's strength in numbers. China will transfer our own technology to help you. So will India, Brazil, and Indonesia - the largest and most advanced countries in our block. And we won't make you compete for our help. We're in this together. And we will meet the goals of the convention without the help of the West."

At that there was a tremendous roar of approval as the camera panned the audience. The demonstrators kept up their chants of "We can do it ourselves. We don't need the West's help. We'll save the planet ourselves."

Even though the unarmed Reykjavik police were in position to quell any possible violence, there was none.

Meanwhile, Magnus, Brice, and Blaine, heading to their hotel after eating in one of Reykjavik's fine restaurants, came upon the noisy crowd outside the convention center. They hurried to the glare of lights and TV cameras to catch the action - of which there was plenty.

Pointing into the crowd, Magnus exclaimed, "There's Simon again."

Brice followed with, "Yea, I see him, and he's still here."

Blaine chipped in with, "And he's still trying to make a difference for his people. I hope he does."

The trio watched as Simon, bull horn in hand, implored, "We've asked the U.S. for help, and they haven't responded. Now we're asking you, Mr. Huan. You claim to be a rich country. Use some of that money to help us relocate our villages before they are all washed away."

As soon as they reached their hotel room, Magnus clicked the remote to catch the latest news. And there was Simon again, being interviewed as a celebrity, asking Mr. Huan for help. While he was talking, the crawler beneath the picture screamed the headline, "Climate Change Convention in Chaos. Delegates Walk out. Fate of Convention in Doubt. Stay Tuned for the Latest Information."

After seeing this scene, Magnus suggested, "We'd better stick around and catch the action. Enough sightseeing for now. OK?"

The two American heads nodded in agreement as they all "hit the sack." What would tomorrow bring? Could the planet still be saved?

Meanwhile, back outside the convention center, after several demonstrators willingly gave interviews to the members of the press, the crowd dispersed into the city. And maybe they would find geothermal pools in which to unwind and relax after a hectic day. Or maybe they would be back in the streets.

Day 7 - Secret Soaking

John Bancroft was now back in his hotel as well, disillusioned by the Chinese-led walkout precipitated by Mr. Huan. After all, they had struck up a conversation in the Blue Lagoon, getting to know each other as individuals. Even though they didn't talk "shop," they had at least established a relationship that must count for something. Maybe a bridge could be built that could salvage the convention and still save the planet. After all, there was no Planet B to save.

So, with BlackBerry in hand, John scrolled down the cell phone numbers of the delegates, and found Peng Huan. He would make an overture. After all, what did he have to lose?

Peng answered to hear John say, "Peng, do you remember our conversations at the Blue Lagoon?"

"Yes, of course. That was a relaxing getaway from the hectic convention."

"How would you like to meet me at the largest geothermal pool in Iceland, and it's close to your hotel. Your GPS will direct you to the Laugardalslaug. It's got indoor and outdoor pools, hot pools, a whirlpool, and even a water slide. And it should be private this time of night. What do you say I meet you there in a half hour?"

After a long pause Peng answered, "Sure, but don't bring your laptop unless it's waterproof."

John confirmed, "Don't worry. We'll just talk and see where that takes us."

"See you in a while."

In the Laugardalslaug

John and Peng arrived at the same time, and the former bought the passes. Honoring the Icelandic tradition of pool cleanliness, the duo deposited their shoes on the rack outside the men's locker, took the customary nude shower, and made their way to the first and coolest of the hot pools, and silently slipped in. The moon was full, and even a few snowflakes were falling, creating an idyllic setting to try to save the world.

After uttering the sounds of relaxation, John broached the silence with, "Do you remember when we talked at the Blue Lagoon?"

"Of course, it was mostly small talk and getting to know each other."

John probed, "Exactly, but I'm curious about one thing."

"What's that?"

"Did you know then you were going to take the podium and criticize the West and orchestrate a walkout?"

Taken aback by this penetrating question, Peng turned and looked directly at John. "Like I said in my speech, our country is now the largest economy in the world. Therefore we have the resources to help our allies in the developing, or should I say rising world. That sounds better. We want to do our part to save the planet, too."

John acknowledged China's willingness to help but followed up with the American patriotic saying, "Yea, but if we don't hang together, we'll all hang separately in a polluted world."

Peng, feeling the thermal and political heat, grabbed the railing to leave and go to the next and hotter pool, with John following.

After the men settled into the second pool, and got used to the higher temperature, Peng asked, "So what do you want me to do, call the countries that walked out back to the convention? You saw the demonstrations, and they weren't just putting on a show for the media. Maybe they won't listen to me anyway."

John, trying to bridge the gap, made the first attempt at a deal by stating, "What if I go back to my caucus and ask them to draft an apology that was mentioned on the floor?"

After a long pause, with only the sound of gurgling water, Peng spoke again, "Do you think these words on a piece of paper or computer can make up for years of spewing your harmful gases into the atmosphere?"

John quickly shot back, "Well, that's what you're doing now with all your coal plants - bringing two online every week. Now that's pollution."

This tit-for-tat exchange was getting as heated as the third pool, into which they now slid. Peng could come back with their crash program in renewables. John could say the West finally placed a price on carbon and was working to sequester their coal plants. But these debating points wouldn't restore a quorum in the convention. A breakthrough was needed.

The Spirit of Reykjavík

As the two continued their standoff, and headed to the fourth and hottest pool, John looked up at the snowflakes that melted on his face, and had an "Aha!" moment. All of a sudden his mind flashed back to his foreign policy course at Harvard in 1986. The professor, whose name now escaped him, was discussing the Reykjavik Summit that year between U.S. President Reagan and Soviet Premier Gorbachev. The professor's point was that, even though there was not an agreement to limit nuclear weapons, progress was made that led to an agreement the following year.

The two soaked in silence, each waiting for the other to make the next move. Would it be bellicose or conciliatory? John again decided to open the conversation with, "Peng, I'm testing your world history. Do you remember a significant political event that took place here in Reykjavik in 1986?"

After a long pause he responded, "Of course I do. We were worried that your country and the Russians would destroy the world with their nuclear weapons. After all, we weren't a strong military power like we are now. At least the leaders of the two most powerful countries in the world at that time were talking instead of lobbing missiles at each other."

"Good. You get an 'A' in world affairs. Peng, do you see any parallels between what happened in this city in 1986 and what is happening now?"

This time Peng answered quickly with, "Maybe we're in danger of destroying the world in another way, with CO2s instead of radiation."

"Peng, I know we're rivals in the world. Some countries follow us, and others look to you for help. That means what we - you (John pointed at Peng) and I (pointing to himself) do here will affect the outcome of this convention, and the future of the planet. Do you realize this?"

Peng, now becoming reflective, answered, "Yes, I do. Now it's my turn to propose a solution."

John suddenly sat up in the pool and inquired, "What's that?"

Why don't we both go back to our respective caucuses, and tell them we've agreed to work together to salvage this convention. And I'll tell the delegates that walked out to come back and work with us to reach an agreement. How's that?"

"Good idea, Peng. I'll do the same. How about calling our night in the pools 'The Spirit of Reykjavik?'"

"That could be our little secret."

"At least for now. Maybe the world will find out soon enough."

John led the way to the swimming pool, where the two cooled off with a few laps, showered, dressed, and disappeared silently into the cold, dark, and snowy, Reykjavik night. Perhaps this city would become famous again.

Day 8 - Closed Caucuses: The West's Strategy

The hastily convened caucus took place in a meeting room in John Bancroft's hotel, away from the continuing demonstrations at the convention center. No members of the press were present, and the doors were closed and guarded.

The ten delegates from the previous technology transfer group filed into the meeting with quizzical looks, wondering what this was all about. John was already seated in one of a circle of chairs when the others sat themselves in no particular order, and with no identification by country. John, still seated, began, "You've all seen the demonstrations the last several days, and the spin from the world press. From their reports it sounds like we may as well pack up and go home. But not so fast CNN, BBC, and the rest of you. The 'Spirit of Reykjavik' is about to be resurrected."

The delegates were really puzzled now, some even scratching their heads and staring at the ceiling. John revealed the secret conversation he had had with the Chinese delegate, reviewed the Reykjavik summit, and told of their commitment to try to salvage the convention.

John began again, "The way I see the current situation, we have two choices. One, we can wait for the Chinese delegate to make the first move, and that could be until hell freezes over. In the meantime we could be inviting hell on earth. Or, two, we could make the first move to break this stalemate."

This time there was stunned silence. Finally, the Norwegian delegate spoke up; "Our country is known for the Nobel Peace Prize. Perhaps we could throw out an olive branch."

Intrigued, the Canadian delegate asked, "What do you mean? We're already meeting them more than half way with our technology transfer proposal. What else should we do?"

"Well, since I mentioned my country," reiterated the Norwegian, "Maybe our olive branch should be our apology. It's been talked about by some neutral countries."

Picking up on that idea the French delegate chimed in, "This is the time for statesmanship. The stakes are too high for political games and trying to save face."

"Yea, but an apology implies we did something wrong," said the British delegate. "Sure, we burned a lot of coal in our day, but look at how that helped us modernize the world."

After listening intently, the German delegate said excitedly, "How about this? Let's have the nonaligned block draft an apology for us, allowing us to save face."

John, looking around and seeing some heads nodding in agreement, asked, "Do we have a consensus on this? Will this allow us to save face while still admitting what we've done in the past?"

The Swedish delegate concluded, "Well, compromise is the name of the game. Sounds like we'd better do something here, or it will end up like another Copenhagen or the other conventions that have come to naught. Nothing personal," as he looked at the Danish delegate, staring at the floor.

John, sensing an agreement by the delegates' body language, and not wanting to risk a vote, concluded, "OK, it looks like we've formulated a plan. I'll contact the neutral block and ask them to draft an apology like we've discussed. When they've done that, we'll meet again, and go from there. Thank you for your cooperation. I'm reminded of a verse in the Bible I learned as a kid, 'From whom much is given, much is required.' Maybe that applies here. Enjoy Reykjavik, and its spirits."

The Chinese Proposal

Now it was Peng's turn to reignite the "Spirit of Reykjavík." In order to enhance his negotiating strategy, Peng decided not to call in the demonstrators. They were losing steam anyway, so maybe they would quietly stop after garnering enough publicity.

Instead, he decided to call a caucus of just the most influential rising nations, who also happened to be among the biggest emitters of greenhouse gases. He could meet in secret in his hotel room, and still keep an eye on the demonstrations. And he would meet at night with the delegates from Russia, Brazil, India, Indonesia, and South Africa - the fastest growing and most polluting of the rising nations.

In order to be unobtrusive, the delegates arrived at staggered times, orchestrated by Peng, who welcomed each one quickly and quietly. After all five had arrived covertly to Peng's room, he began by asking the Russian delegate to summarize the Reykjavik Summit. Not surprisingly, Mr. Kozney mixed fact with opinion, blaming the United States for its failure. But he ended on a positive note by mentioning there was an arms agreement a year later.

Peng piggybacked on this positive comment by expressing his hope that an agreement could be reached this year.

He concluded his general remarks with, "We now know that extreme weather events are driving climate change, in addition to the burning of fossil fuels." He then turned to the small group seated in a semicircle in comfortable leather chairs, and knowing the answer beforehand asked, "How many of your countries have experienced extreme weather events recently?"

Immediately all hands shot up, and they were talking at once about their landslides, tsunamis, floods, fires, droughts, diseases, and earthquakes.

Peng interrupted them with, "You've made my point. It's **urgent** we act now, and put aside our differences with the West. This time the room quieted.

Finally, Peng started to put forth his proposal. "I know you don't like the West, and in particular the U.S., getting the limelight with their technology 'ripple-in-the-pond' transfer idea. But I think we can help them with it, and use it to our advantage."

And now the Indonesian delegate asked the question on everyone's mind, "What do you mean? Cooperate with them when our bloc is demonstrating?"

"Yea," the Indian delegate affirmed, "You know saving face is important in our culture. So how can we do that?"

Peng held up his hands, signaling no more questions, and, raising his voice, shouted, "OK, just listen to me. The reason I called you here was because your countries all have the technology to reduce your greenhouse gases. And if the price on carbon keeps going up, there will be more of a demand for our products. Furthermore, if this convention adopts the reductions stated by Minister Karlsson during the opening ceremonies, countries will be clamoring for our renewable technology. We don't want the West to have a corner on this market do we? Besides, there are some nonaligned countries here that we could win over with our products."

Now the delegates looked at each other with approving grins, sensing their countries' GDPs rising.

The Brazilian delegate summarized Peng's proposal with, "This sounds like a win-win proposition for us, don't you think?"

This time all heads nodded in agreement.

Peng, sensing the consensus in the room, proposed the next step. "OK, here's what I'll do. I'll convey our willingness to cooperate to John Bancroft, and see what he's willing to concede in return."

"One more thing," added the delegate from South Africa. "What about the demonstrations?"

Peng answered, "I think they should continue. That will give us more leverage on our proposal. What do you think?"

"Sure," said the Russian delegate. "And I think I'll join them," and he rose to do just that.

Peng turned to the remaining delegates, "Feel free to join him. In the meantime I'm going down to the demonstrations. Perhaps they need some encouragement during these long, cold, winter nights.

A Courier in the Night

John Bancroft hesitated and then arose from his comfortable chair to answer a knock at his door. Before opening, he asked who it was, and a muffled voice replied, "It's important - about the convention." After looking through the peephole, John slowly opened the door to find a black man with a turban and an attaché case draped over his shoulder.

The mysterious man looked behind him and then quickly entered, and John closed the door behind him just as fast. "I'm bringing a message from the delegate from the Democratic Republic of Congo, representing the nonaligned nations." He fumbled and finally pulled out a manila envelope with five seals, handed it to John, opened the door, and stealthily disappeared.

John, surmising the contents, carefully pulled apart the seals, sat down again, and began reading the "neutral apology." He put it down, stared at the white, sterile ceiling, drummed his fingers on the arm rest, and pondered his next move. Finally he drifted to sleep with the "tube" still blaring. Would it be enough to pacify the rapidly-growing emerging nations that were now major polluters?

Day 9 - Another Soaking Summit

To keep their identities secret, John and Peng chose another of Reykjavik's thermal pools, this time at the Sundhollin, Reykjavik's oldest and only indoor pool. Since it was snowing heavily, this seemed to be a good choice. And it was private and uncrowded. Could the "Spirit of Reykjavik" continue?

While on the bus, John texted Peng the apology. After showering separately, both men walked out and eased into opposite ends of the pool, and gradually drifted toward each other in the nearly empty pool.

Finally John broke the silence with, "Well, what do you think?"

Peng, gazing at the steamed glass ceiling, uttered, "It's not much of an apology. It looks more like a progress report and a promise not to pollute."

"Well, isn't that why we're here, to concentrate on the future and not the past? Your history isn't so rosy either, but I won't go into that."

Whether Peng's face was flush because of the heat from the pool or from John's comment, he thought of the "Spirit of Reykjavik" again and finally said, "OK, this is getting us nowhere. I'll take it back to my caucus and see what they think of it."

"Remember, Peng, the West didn't write it. Be sure and tell that to your caucus. Now what did you come up with?"

"We decided we would help you with the technology transfer as long as we had input in choosing the countries that would use our products. Sound reasonable?"

"I'll have to do the same thing as you, run it by our caucus. At least we have specific proposals to present. In the meantime, I do have one request for you?"

"What's that?"

"Use your influence to call off the demonstrations. They've gone on long enough."

"Ok, I'll see what I can do."

With that the two leaders of their respective blocks swam laps separately, showered in silence, and again slipped out into the snowy night.

Would the convention finally be convened?

Day 10 - More Caucuses

Each day since the walkout and demonstrations began, Minister Karlsson would take the podium and call the roll of nations, knowing that there was no quorum. He would perfunctorily pound the gavel and announce the absence of a quorum, and again adjourn the convention. But serious business was being conducted behind closed doors that could determine the fate of the conference.

This time the developed and developing/rising nations were holding simultaneous closed caucuses in separate rooms on either side of the huge arena. The press awaited eagerly in the middle for any late breaking news, with each network trying to "scoop" the others with a dramatic headline. But wait they did, and did, and did.

The "Gang of 10's" Caucus

The "Gang of 10" was back to discuss - not technology transfer - but a proposed apology. As they filed into the small conference room, there it was on the white wall, above where John Bancroft was seating. They glanced at it on the way to their seats - saying nothing - yet.

John seized the silence, stood up, and pointing to the wall said, "Here's what the so-called nonaligned nations came up with as a compromise apology. What do you think of it? Is it something we can live with?"

All eyes starred at the terse statement: "Since the dawn of the Industrial Era, certain nations have harnessed the available technologies to better the standard of living for their citizens. However, other nations have not benefited from these labor-saving devices. Moreover, the advanced nations have willingly polluted the planet with their burning of fossil fuels. They now pledge to use their technology to reduce their greenhouse gases and assist other nations in developing renewable sources of energy. The fate of Planet Earth is at stake."

The German delegate, who proposed the idea, was the first to speak. "We all know our industrialization and technology has increased the standard of living of our countries, and has been the envy of the rest of the world. But we also know every invention has unintended side effects - such as polluting the atmosphere. But to say we have willingly polluted the planet goes too far. I don't think we should go along with it for this reason."

"I agree with my southern neighbor. Maybe I'm a stubborn Swede," began the delegate from that country, "But why should we agree to an apology at all?"

Seeing several heads nodding in agreement, John felt his "gang" was turning on the apology delivered to his door by the African courier. Maybe it could be used as a bargaining chip in the debate. He'll have to wait and see.

The Icelandic delegate addressed the other side of the proposed compromise with, "OK, if we agree to this apology, what's the other side willing to concede?"

John, not wanting to reveal too much of what Peng said at their last soaking session, simply stated, "They are willing to help us increase the ripples in a larger pond by sharing their technology, as long as they have a say in it."

The French delegate, showing his characteristic emotion, said, with a reddened face, "No way. It's our technology, and we should control where it goes."

And everyone shouted "Yes, Yes," in their native language before John could gain the floor. Finally the affirmations subsided and he began, I told you I would meet with the U.N. Secretary-General about this issue. Even though I conveyed our desire to have a majority of our member nations on the U.N. Special Committee, Mr. Mobotu said the representation should be equally divided between developed and developing nations. That means we would have to reach a consensus on the grants, who would get them, and which countries would provide the technology. Otherwise any votes would probably deadlock and nothing would get done. Compromise is the name of the game, and it's a serious one. Can we live with it?"

This time there was no visceral reaction, but thoughtful reflection by the West, who were now holding the fate of the planet in their hands.

Finally the Canadian delegate spoke up, "I guess that's why we have a U.N. Both sides can blame them and not each other. They can be a scapegoat if the convention fails like it has before."

This time John exercised his leadership prerogative, "Seeing no more questions, I'll walk across the floor to convey our position to the other side, and see what they're up to. Maybe all these closed door sessions will prevent floor fights. But it's up to us in this room to keep the rest of our troops in line. Otherwise any agreements Peng and I make won't mean anything."

After his "gang" left, John didn't have a good feeling about the meeting. He felt his original proposal was co-opted by the U.N. The delegates didn't like the apology. John understood the key role he was playing in trying to reach an agreement, but any deal could unravel during the floor debate in front of the media and the watching world. And now the planetary ball was in Peng's court with his gang. Would they "buy" the deal John worked so hard to "sell' to his caucus?

A Surprise Invitation

Usually a well-organized diplomat who arranged his appointments well ahead of time, John decided to try a different approach - being spontaneous. So, without calling or texting Peng, he slowly strolled to the other side of the arena to see what was going on with the emerging nations. He arrived just as their caucus was recessing at one of the many food stands. And there was Peng, standing by himself talking on his cell phone. His eye caught John's and Peng motioned for him to come over. Surprised at his luck - or was it more than that - John waited patiently for Peng's full attention, and then said, "I took a chance I would find you, and here you are!"

John started relating the latest developments in his caucus when Peng cut him off with, "I've got a wild idea. Wait here," as he pointed at a vacant chair. "I shall return."

"OK, MacArthur," but Peng had already headed back to his caucus.

John ordered a cappuccino, checked his e-mail, and picked up a Reykjavik newspaper with the headline, "When will they be done?" Glancing through the article he realized he was one of the "theys." This reinforced the **urgency** to reach an agreement as Peng and himself were desperately trying to do.

Finally, Peng hurriedly returned, smiling with, "Here's what I worked out. My caucus would like to hear from you firsthand. Maybe that would expedite an agreement without any more secret meetings or caucuses."

John reached down to grab the newspaper he was reading and held up the headline he had just read. Peng glanced at it, gave a thumbs up sign, turned around and started walking back to his caucus. He looked back and called to John, "Follow me into the lion's den."

John hesitated at first, but then quickly caught up with Peng, thinking "I'm not Daniel. Hope I can get out alive."

In the Dragon's Lair

As John walked in with Peng he thought, "Am I walking into a trap? Will I be vilified? Well, here goes. I'm breaking protocol."

John was surprised to be greeted with handshakes from all five of Peng's "gang" that had previously met with Peng in his hotel room. After a glowing introduction from Peng, he sat down and motioned for John to begin.

John opened with sarcastic, self-deprecating humor, "So this is what I get when I spontaneously strolled to your side of the arena. A pleasant surprise."

Eliciting a few chuckles, his introduction seemed to disarm any hostilities for the time being; so he got right to the point. And he had no prepared speech for this audience.

"Look outside. The demonstrations are still going on despite the bitterly cold weather. But the world is warming faster than the models have projected. We can't wait any longer for an agreement. You in this room represent the emerging nations that will become more powerful in the future, and I know that.

"Our bloc has both led in modernizing the world while we unwittingly released greenhouse gases, and…"

Before he could finish the Indonesian delegate jumped up and shouted, "What do you mean unwittingly? You knew you were harming the planet, but you were too concerned about the bottom line, weren't you?"

Taken aback by this hostile comment, and realizing he was trying to put a favorable "spin" on the apology his "gang" had just discussed (using unwittingly instead of willingly), John stepped back, took a deep breath, and looking directly at his accuser, replied, "And what do you think you are doing by cutting down your forests, even though the West is paying you not to do it?"

Now Peng jumped up and held out both hands, "OK, that's enough. Accusations won't get us anywhere. We need constructive proposals to reach an agreement."

After what seemed an eternity of silence, John spoke up. "OK, here's what I'm prepared to offer you, subject to approval by our own gang."

After saying that, this "gang of six" became quiet and all the delegates leaned forward to hear the offer.

John continued, "We know we both have to give a little to reach an agreement. Peng and I have kicked around - or should I say soaked some ideas," as he smiled at Peng, letting their secret out of the bag. "So here it is.

"Our side will accept an apology for the Western countries' burning of fossil fuels since the Industrial Revolution began, while acknowledging the technological contributions we have made to the world.

"And here's another concession from our side. The whole idea of technology transfer was our idea. We wanted to determine which countries we would benefit from our 'ripple-in-the pond effect.' But I decided to give the authority to a U.N. Technology Transfer Committee. Even though I initially wanted the West to control the committee, the Secretary-General suggested, out of fairness, to balance the 10-member committee with 5 delegates from the West and 5 from the emerging nations, with each caucus determining their own members. And I agreed out of fairness to you."

At that point Peng turned and looked at his delegates, trying to read their body language. Did they think John's "gang" was giving up enough for their "gang" to reciprocate in kind?

And then he began, "Thank you, John. Now what do you want us to give up?"

And this time John was ready to walk through the "door" Peng just opened.

"Our side realizes your emerging economies are growing faster than ours, and you are making technological breakthroughs that used to be the province only of the West. So we want your side as an equal partner in adding to our ripples that will benefit the whole world. And that means contributing more of your new wealth to the technology transfer fund."

Finally John got to the bottom line. "We know China, India, and Brazil are growing rapidly and are rushing coal-fired power plants online to provide power for your increasing populations. However, this dangerous situation for the planet can be remedied by requiring all existing and new plants to be equipped with the latest technology to capture and sequester your carbon emissions (CSS). And if you need help in creating artificial limestone to store your CO_2s, check out Iceland's state-of-the-art technology. You need to have large volcanic storage areas for this process to work.

"We in the West are also using coal, but are trying to phase out its use by 2030. And we already require all new coal plants to be equipped with CSS technology. Furthermore, we're experimenting with Iceland's novel idea by storing CO_2 in our lava beds."

Now John directed his gaze again at Peng, "And Peng, you can do something right now. Call off the demonstrations, and get a quorum inside so we can get this convention over. We've all got work to do at home."

As John started to leave the room, to no applause, Peng followed him out the door and again into the food court. "That took a lot of, what do you say, guts, to address our group. As you would say, you laid all the cards on the table. Now I'll see if our delegates will buy your offer. I'll be in touch," as Peng shook hands with John and returned to his lair. He still had a lot of convincing to do, as did John as he left in the opposite direction. But their paths were sure to cross again, but when and where?

Day 11 - More Sightseeing

With the caucuses still continuing, Magnus, Brice, and Blaine – having seen enough of the continuing demonstrations - decided to venture outside Reykjavík to see some of the beautiful country. With their resident tour guide and a government vehicle, they were off to tour a state of the art geothermal plant. After all, the Nebraskans came to learn about sustainability the Icelandic way.

As the trio headed east, they noticed streams of grayish white clouds emanating from the earth. Blaine was the first to speak, pointing to his right, "That looks like the pollution we'd see back home coming from factories."

Magnus was quick to answer, "The only factories we have around here produce steam that is carbon-free, and we're coming to one now" as he pulled his red hydrogen vehicle into the Hellisheidi plant. Thick clouds of steam rose that could also be mistaken for producing rain, but the sun was still shining at midday.

With Magnus leading the way, the three were greeted by a friendly Icelandic guide speaking perfect English. "Welcome to the first geothermal plant in the world that is carbon-free. And I'll be glad to explain why after our tour."

Oddur led the three to a schematic drawing explaining how the engineers use directional drilling to a depth of over one mile to tap the hot water from the molten lava that lies beneath the surface.

"Then we run this steam through turbines to produce electricity for Reykjavik and surrounding areas. And now I'll explain why we're completely carbon neutral, with assistance from America," as Oddur looked approvingly at Brice and Blaine.

He led them to a small room with the walls surrounded by movie screens, but with no seats. "In order to show you this process you have to walk through each section as it is being explained. You'll better understand it this way."

With that, he dimmed the lights with his remote, and the program "Using Lava to Create a Purer Planet" began. The sound and light show first gave an overview of the Hellisheidi plant that Oddur had just explained. Then the movie stopped to show a huge cloud of CO_2 (even though it's invisible) coming from the earth during the drilling process. On the screen flashed the question, "How can we get rid of this greenhouse gas so it won't harm the planet?"

The next screen displayed several cartoon characters trying to shoot the CO_2 down; cowboys attempting to lasso it to the ground; and finally a guy with a shovel digging to bury it - all to no avail. The next screen showed an Icelandic scientist with a light bulb turning on above his head saying, "By George, I've got it! We've got lava, lots of lava. Let's put it to work."

The mad scientist then took out a bottle of seltzer water, sprayed it on a piece of basalt, and presto, limestone was formed as if by magic!

The next screen showed a real scientist explaining what had just happened. "By pumping the C02 underground into our vast volcanic lava, and forcing the seltzer water into its pores, we can create artificial limestone which will permanently hold this harmful gas. This makes not only our geothermal plants carbon neutral, but this process will soon be used in other areas where there is volcanic lava, including under the oceans. The possibilities are endless. This process will insure that these harmful gases will never escape to warm the planet. We in Iceland are once again proud to be a world leader in this area. Hope you enjoyed the show."

By the end of the show, Magnus, Brice, and Blaine had walked an entire circle, and came out amazed at what they had seen. Brice commented to Magnus, "Well, this wouldn't work in Nebraska, but it would in Hawaii, Alaska, and some Western states. It gives me reason for hope as we return, right Blaine?"

"Yea, it just about makes you want to live by a volcano," as he looked at Magnus, who laughed as they climbed back into their car for the return trip to Reykjavik. As they drove through the city, they could see pockets of steam rising in the dark sky from the many geothermal pools. Were they all carbon-free as well?

The Courier Returns

Exhausted from his day of trying to negotiate with both "gangs," John was "vegging out" in his hotel room, "surfing" the TV channels for news of the continuing demonstrations and the approaching storm when a knock on the door caused him to spring up, check the peephole and ask, "Who's there?"

John recognized the voice, "It's me again. I have a proposal for you."

With the door still closed, John asked warily, "What kind of proposal?"

"Let me in, and I'll tell you."

John hesitated, and with his curiosity peaking, opened the door and the mysterious man from the Congo quietly entered, shut the door, and with his short frame, stood before John.

John, trying to guess, said, "Is it about the supposedly neutral apology you delivered? It didn't sound very fair to me."

"Well, that's what our neutral block came up with. I only delivered it to you."

"So now what do you want from me?"

With a whisper the black man said, "More money from the West."

"For what?"

"You know our continent is suffering the worst effects of global warming that your countries have heaped on us. Because of our record droughts, our land can't produce the crops it once did. And so our people are cutting down trees to clear more land. We know it's not good for the environment, but we blame the West. And the apology I delivered to you isn't enough to satisfy us."

John, now suspicious, sneered, "And what if we don't agree to give your countries more money?"

Hoping John would ask that question, the Congolese was ready, "I'll go public with the apology I delivered to you. And the world will finally find out what you've been doing to our planet for 200 years. And they won't like it."

Upon hearing that John blurted, "That's blackmail. That's no way to get what you want.

Without responding the Congolese turned, headed for the door, and walked hurriedly into the moonless darkness.

The game of "climate chess" was now under way, and it was John's move.

Day 12 - Hobnobbing at the Perlan

John decided he would get to the bottom of this "African bribe" by another secret meeting with Peng. This time he chose a "top-of-the-line" venue. What better place than the "Pearl," as the locals called it - a revolving restaurant with a beautiful view of the Reykjavík skyline and nearby mountains? And so he reserved a private table for two on the fourth floor and waited for Peng to arrive.

Finally Peng hastily appeared, sat down, and apologized, "Sorry, I'm late. I was meeting with our group to try to convince them to accept the deal. It's a hard sell. We don't want you Western imperialists, as one of our delegates said, telling us what to."

John interrupted him, "And that's why I proposed the 5-5 split on the U.N. Committee. Our group doesn't like it either. But you have probably heard this saying in politics, 'If neither side likes it, it's probably a good idea.'"

Without acknowledging John's perceptive observation, Peng continued, "And another thing. Why should we agree to CSS on our existing coal plants when you're only using it on your new plants? I realize we have more plants than the West, but we also have more renewable energy.

John interrupted, "But you're a bigger country. Touché!"

As soon as he said this cutting (pardon the pun) remark, John caught himself, "I guess if we're going to apologize, I'd better practice by apologizing to you for what I just said."

And then the proverbial "light bulb" lit in John's mind. Excitedly he approached Peng with, "How about this idea for another compromise? Instead of an agreement requiring you to retrofit your existing coal plants with CSS capabilities, why don't you send that amount of money to assist Africa cope with the extreme weather they have been experiencing due to climate change. We know you have been buying up natural resources there for security reasons. It makes sense you would want to protect your investments, right?"

Peng, after thinking a minute, slowly arose from his chair, and walked to the window to view the setting sun. He then turned to John, "Interesting proposal. OK, here's what I want from you. You know our country has been planting millions of trees while countries like Brazil and Indonesia are cutting theirs down. And the REDD fund is depleted. Why doesn't the West contribute an equivalent amount to this fund to match what we contribute to Africa?"

Now the rook was on John's side of the chess board. And it was his turn to view the setting sun casting its tentacles of red and pink over the snow-capped, black, volcanic mountains.

He then turned to Peng, "Remember the picture from space of our blue planet?"

John hesitated and then continued, pointing toward the horizon, "Well, this is a close up of what Earth still looks like in 2021. Don't we want to preserve this beautiful Creation for our children and grandchildren? This time Peng nodded approvingly.

"Well, let's try one more time to sell what we talked about here, in confidence, to our caucuses. And here's your sign to me that you're ready for floor debate. When I look out my hotel window and see no demonstrators, then I know you have your troops in line."

Peng, now fully engaged, "And what's your sign?"

John thought for a moment and then recounted a bit of American history. "Have you heard about Paul Revere's famous ride to warn our side that the British were coming?"

"Yes, I'm a student of your history, especially during your Revolutionary War."

"Good. Can you see my hotel window from yours?"

"Yes, but I haven't been a, what do you say, 'Peeping Tom.'"

"Good. But this time you can. I don't have any lanterns like Paul Revere used, but I did bring a portable LED light. I'll put it in my window when our side is ready for the floor debate.

"And one more thing, Peng. You and I have invested a lot of time together trying to make this thing work. And as you know, our agreements could all fall apart once a few delegates that haven't been in our gangs start grandstanding."

"What do you mean by that?"

"You know, the cameras will be rolling, and delegates from the so-called countries may want to make a name for themselves back home."

Peng asked, "So what can we do about it?"

The two thought for several minutes as they took in the changing scenery as the restaurant slowly revolved away from the setting sun.

Finally, John had an inspiration. "Let's use our 'ripple-in-the-pond idea,' and each of our gangs set up a text tree to notify everyone in our blocs of our agreements."

Peng picked up on that with, "You mean I text our agreement, assuming we have one, to everyone in our gang of five, and each of them in turn texts someone else, and the next ripple does the same, until everyone is contacted."

"Exactly, and I'll do the same. We can use an app that would order the developed and developing countries randomly, and then the program would choose the order. Do you have that program on your smart phone?"

Peng scrolled down his menu until he came to "Scrambling Countries," pushed a few buttons, and, presto, up came the names of the countries. He noticed John had the same program up on his screen.

Both men were thinking, "Who invented this program, us or them, or vice versa?" But no one claimed ownership. They had more important things to solve.

By the time they had their respective programs ready for texting, and finished their "volcanic dessert," the restaurant had completely revolved, and the sun was hidden behind the black mountains. Both men texted their bill to the restaurant's computer, which approved their credit, and they walked out into the night separately. When would the signs appear?

As John walked slowly back to his hotel room he felt good about this last meeting with Peng before the debate. He had avoided any discussion of the apology, and appeared to have an agreement about helping the Africans as the Congolese wanted. But now he would have to sell this new compromise to his caucus again. Hopefully the "Spirit of Reykjavík" was still alive.

Day 13 - Remembering the Sabbath

Since the conference was still in official recess - hoping that the closed caucuses would result in a consensus - Magnus decided to fulfill his promise of taking Brice and Blaine to his church. And it happened to be Sunday, a day of rest and relaxation for Icelanders, and, for a few, a day to attend a service at one of the state-sponsored Lutheran churches. Even though the buildings were large and ornate - thanks to the taxes of the residents (no separation of church and state here), a typical service would only see 20-30 parishioners in attendance. Not so at Magnus' church.

Even though his church was Lutheran, it was considered independent and not dependent upon a state subsidy. And ironically, the small warehouse church was filled to its capacity of 200 each Sunday. What attracted them? That's the question he hoped the Nebraskans would ask as the three stepped from the hydrogen-powered bus to the front of Christ's Lutheran Church, in the shadow of the huge Hallgrimskirkja church.

With the guitars and drums already "revved up" as they entered, they were greeted with a hearty handshake and "Hallo," given a bulletin, and ushered into a front row seat. Magnus quipped, "I guess that's what we get for being late."

Magnus, after settling in, glanced at his bulletin and noticed this was "Creation Care Sunday." He knew this wasn't a coincidence that the pastor chose this topic during the conference. After all, his church was a member of the World Evangelical Alliance, committed to mobilizing Christians to combat climate change. Magnus shot up a silent prayer that Brice and Blaine would be stirred by the service.

The worship team was playing songs that were familiar to Magnus as he was singing the words which were "PowerPointed" on the screen. The first song was appropriately chosen - as the congregation started singing "God of Wonders beyond our galaxy," the screen illuminated the Milky Way Galaxy. A laser pointed to the earth, a tiny speck on the outskirts of this mass of stars. The song ended with "Hallelujah to the Lord of heaven and earth," and a smattering of applause.

This was followed by another song that painted word-pictures of Creation. "Indescribable" sang about the "depths of the sea," the "heights of the mountains," the "colors of Fall" and "the fragrance of Spring." Scenes of majestic Mt. Everest, the churning waves of the North Atlantic, multi-colored leaves in New England, and lilac bushes in Ireland were choreographed with the words.

At the end of the singing, the pastor asked, "How many of you are ready to take care of God's Creation that you just saw on the screen?" All hands, including that of Brice and Blaine shot up.

And then unexpectedly Pastor Ingvardsson stepped down from the stage, went over to where Magnus was seated, and asked him to introduce his friends. Magnus, taken aback, looked at Brice and Blaine and said, "These are my friends Blaine and Brice Sutherland from the State of Nebraska in the U.S. They became Christians in Alaska, and are visiting me while we attend the conference here." As the pastor motioned for them to stand, the congregation also stood and gave them a rousing round of applause.

Before they sat down, the pastor looked at them and gave them this charge, "Please go back and tell your citizens and government to get serious about saving the planet. We're trying to do that here, but our population is only one one-thousandth the size of your country. Your nation holds the key. We'll be praying for the convention."

The pastor bounded back on stage, the lights darkened, and the familiar melody of "This Is My Father's World" served as the backdrop to scenes from Nature. This time a collage of animals paraded across the screen, from the hawks, eagles, and ravens soaring in the sky, to a massive hippopotamus and crocodile in the water, and a breaching whale in the ocean. God's zoo was a veritable variety of His Creation on display at Christ's Lutheran, and this "show" impressed the Nebraskans, and even Magnus.

Pastor Ingvardsson started his sermon by holding up his Green Bible, commenting, "In honor of the climate change conference, I will be using this environmentally-friendly Bible, with this all-natural cover," as he rubbed his hand across the cover, "and printed with soy inks. Furthermore," as he leafed through the pages, "you will notice verses printed in green. These refer to God's Creation, and include animals, land, water, and the sky. And, of course, it's the inspired version!" That remark elicited a few chuckles.

"So why should Christians be concerned about caring for the planet and what happens at this conference?" the pastor asked as he looked at Magnus and his friends. "Doesn't the Bible teach that soon Jesus will come and take us to heaven?" A few heads nodded their approval. "Doesn't 2nd Peter say the heavens and earth will be destroyed? And doesn't Revelation talk about a new heaven and earth? So why don't we all go hide out in our volcanic caves and wait to get outta here?"

The pastor started reading from his Green Bible, starting in the first book of Genesis. "And God saw that it was good. And God saw that it was good. And God saw that it was good. And God saw that it was good. And God saw that it was good. And God saw all that He had made, and it was very good. I know, I'm repeating myself, but I want to emphasize that every aspect of God's Creation - the light, the atmosphere, the land and sea; plants, vegetables, and trees; the sun, moon, and stars; the sea creatures and birds; the land creatures; and last, but certainly not least, us. You get the point.

"And now I'm going to read a verse that many Christians take as the right to plunder God's Creation." He paused as he found the correct page. "And God said, 'Let us make man in our image, in our likeness, and let them rule over the fish of the sea and the birds of the air, over the livestock, over all the earth, and over all the creatures that move along the ground.'

"Many Christians take this verse to mean we should dominate the earth and all that is in it. But the correct interpretation actually means dominion. In other words, we humans are partners - not lords - over the creatures of Nature. Another passage in Genesis gives Adam the responsibility to cultivate and protect the Garden of Eden. And that's not just about the first man, but is a command for all of us to care for God's Creation and not harm it. Thus the concept of stewardship of the planet is the duty of us all.

"But as we read further into Genesis, we see the Fall of Adam and Eve, resulting in our own sins. As a result the Garden of Eden today has been trashed by corporate greed and our own conspicuous consumption. So we are all to blame for the crisis we are facing today."

And now Pastor Ingvardsson spoke in a subdued and solemn tone. "Today we see the planet heating up because of human activity." Looking again at Magnus, "And you know the science behind this, and we in the religious community have to listen to it. The scientists tell us what is happening, and that gives Christians the facts and possible solutions, and, along with the commands in the Bible, the reason to act responsibly. We should be the leaders in the environmental movement. That's what Jesus would want us to do." With that a smattering of applause erupted, led by Magnus.

"And to help you with practical ideas to combat global warming, ushers will hand you a list of what we can all do. As the Chinese expression states, 'The journey of a thousand miles starts with a single step.'"

Pastor Ingvardsson then closed with a prayer of commitment [see Appendix B], asking those who are serious about protecting the environment to first make sure they are serious with God by repenting of their own sins of polluting the planet, asking Jesus to forgive them, and asking Him by faith to come into their lives to give them the power to be stewards of God's Creation, and to be an example of Jesus' love to others. As the music softly played, "Indescribable," many people went forward and knelt at the altar as the pastor prayed for them. Even Magnus, Brice, and Blaine joined in, thinking another prayer wouldn't hurt, especially with the fate of the conference still in doubt.

As the three left the church, they walked back to their rooms and noticed it was eerily quiet, even for a Sunday. And then Brice figured it out first, "Guess what? I don't see any demonstrators. I wonder if they took Sunday off, or are they done for good?"

Magnus replied, "We'll just have to wait and see. Maybe the convention will convene again. Maybe the pastor's prayers will be answered."

They hurried back to their room and checked the local news channel and, sure enough, the camera crews were outside the arena looking for some demonstrators to interview, and there was no one in sight.

One commentator speculated, "Maybe the demonstrators took Sunday off. Or maybe their demands were met. Or maybe they are trying to beat the oncoming storm, which we are covering. Tomorrow we'll be inside the arena to see if the debate will finally begin. Good night."

Meanwhile, John Bancroft also noticed the absence of the demonstrations. Was this Peng's sign? He anxiously waited for to-morrow as he was glued to the Weather Channel. He arose from his comfortable recliner and turned on the LED that he had placed in the window - up to now unlit. Would Peng notice?

Day 14 - The Debate Begins

After a week of sightseeing, soaking, and secret caucuses, the delegates were ready to wrap up the convention - agreement or no agreement. But there was an air of apprehension as they filed back into their seats. Many questions were on their minds: What effect will the demonstrations have on the debate? Will the developed and emerging nations be able to work out an agreement? And what about the predictions that the "storm of the millennium" was bearing down on Iceland?

Minister Karlsson received a standing ovation as he pounded the gavel to again convene the conference. To insure a quorum, he called the roll of the nations, finding that 170 nations had returned, enough to conduct business. Did the other 25 nations stage their own protest, or did they want to beat the terrible weather headed to Iceland? They left in haste, without requesting permission from the chair. So much for civility.

He then explained the rules for floor debate. "Ladies and gentle-men of the world, welcome back. In Iceland we respect the right of peaceable protest, which you have demonstrated. Now it's time to get back to work.

"We all realize the **urgency** of reaching a binding agreement this time. In order to facilitate this goal, our parliamentary committee has decided to move from previous efforts to gain unanimous agreements to something more possible. So, for the first time, all amendments and the final vote on an agreement will require only a ¾ vote of the total of 195 delegates, whether present or absent. That computes to 146 affirmative votes on any proposal. Looking at it another way, with the present total of 170 delegates, 25 negative votes would defeat any measure. So we'll still have a formidable challenge to pass the proposals before us. And finally, *Robert's Rules of International Order* will apply during the debate. Any discussion?"

Hearing none, the Minister continued, "The issues that have been discussed and need to be addressed before adjournment are as follows:

* Topic 1: Protecting the Atmosphere as a Public Trust
* Topic 2: Demands by the Indigenous Working Group
* Topic 3: Assisting the Island Nations with Their Population Resettlement Plan
* Topic 4: Ratifying the Technology Transfer Plan
* Topic 5: The REDD (Reducing Emissions from Deforestation and Forest Degradation)
* Topic 6: Ratifying the CO2 Reductions through 2050

A Special Treat

Minister Karlsson continued, "But before we proceed with the debate, we have a special treat brought to you by the children of the world. They have composed a song just for this occasion. Let's welcome the Climate Change Choir and its director, Kendra Mobotu from Kenya. The delegates all stood and cheered, whistled, and clapped as 195 children, all in their native dress, suddenly appeared from all sides of the arena, spread out and holding hands.

The director also suddenly appeared in the middle of the arena as she was slowly raised by an elevated platform. And this ministage slowly rotated clockwise so she could direct the entire choir. It wasn't the revolving restaurant at the Perlan, but it was the same principle.

Magnus, Brice, and Blaine slipped into their seats as the choir was about to begin.

As he was looking through his binoculars Magnus whispered to Brice, "I can pick out our Icelandic child. She's the blue-eyed blonde with the red, white, and blue dress. And she's pretty, of course. Here," as he handed the glasses to Blaine. "See if you can pick out the American."

After rotating the lenses, and himself, about 180 degrees, Blaine exclaimed, "That must be him. He's wearing a cowboy hat and cowboy boots, and dressed in red, white, and blue chaps. The only thing missing is a bull," he joked. "We start 'em young in Nebraska."

The somber, slow music started and gradually became louder and more intense. On the screens appeared an ocean with rough waves that gradually covered a small island. Choreographed were the children first running, and then frantically appearing to climb to higher ground. Finally, they all stretched their necks and heads high as if to stay above the rising water.

The next screen displayed a parched desert, with huge cracks in the ground, and cattle carcasses rotting in the blazing sun. This time the children put their hands to their throats with their tongues hanging out mouthing the words, "Water, water, I'm thirsty."

The final screen, with the steady cadence of a drum roll, showed a huge electric plant ravenously gobbling up coal on conveyer belts, and belching thick black clouds into the atmosphere, darkening the sun. The children were coughing and sneezing, and some of them even lay down.

And then everything was quiet for a moment. And then on the screen could be heard the sounds of birds, the whistling wind powering fields of windmills, noiseless electric cars on the freeways, rows of homes with solar panels on the roofs, a bullet-train riding on a cushion of air, and the steam of a geothermal plant with people soaking in a surrealistic pool. It was the Blue Lagoon, immediately identified by the audience.

And then with music that slowly builds to a crescendo, the children slowly arose from the floor; and with their hands in the air pointing to the sky, they began to sing:

"I see blue sky, clouds of white; what a delight." Now, extending their arms outward and moving them ever so slowly, they continued with "I see oceans of pretty blue, what a peaceful hue."

Now they all bent down as if they were sitting and moving their fingers over their iPads: "Here I sit in my super-fast train, watching the terrain speed by; and I don't have to fly."

Now they pointed at the delegates seated in the front seats, singing to them: "Please listen to our request, and give us a world that for us is the best. And remember, your children and grandchildren are counting on you."

With the music still playing "We are the world," the children bowed gracefully and then spread out throughout the arena, all carrying in their hands lollipops shaped like the blue earth. And then with assistance from the ushers, the children delivered their colorful suckers to the delegate from their country. The delegates, taken by surprise, took their gift and held it up for others to see. Some were laughing and smiling and even hugged their child. And then the children headed for the exits as the audience was clapping in unison to the song.

A little emotion couldn't help but move the delegates to action. At least the final session started on a friendly note.

Minister Karlsson, quickly wiping a tear from his eye, again took the podium.

"Let's remember the sweet faces of these children as we begin the debate, which will be led by two floor leaders; John Bancroft representing the developed nations, and Peng Huan representing the emerging nations. As determined by a flip of a coin, Mr. Bancroft will speak first."

Mr. Bancroft stepped to the podium.

"My esteemed colleague from China Mr. Huan and I have put together a package of proposals that, if passed, would be the most significant international agreement to date in seeking to avoid the 'tipping point' that would trigger catastrophic events caused by global warming. And yes, you have heard right. The two biggest polluters, instead of waiting for the other to agree to binding emission reductions - as has happened in previous conferences - are now working together to pass the package of proposals we are now presenting to the entire assembly.

"I will now yield the balance of my time to Mr. Huan."

After stepping to the podium beside Mr. Bancroft, Mr. Huan said, "This conference will be unlike any we have seen before for two reasons: First, it will be the first one that is proposing a binding agreement with sanctions. And second, Mr. Bancroft and I have worked together to break down the divisions between the developed and what I will call the emerging nations. If we can work together, you can too."

Applause interrupted Mr. Peng's remarks. The delegates were starting with a united front - for now.

"After all, the blue earth lollipops you were given have no boundaries between nations. The earth belongs to us all."

Again applause erupted throughout the arena.

Mr. Bancroft again stepped to the podium and started the debate with a motion. "Mr. Chairman, I move the six proposals you mentioned at the beginning of this session (he pointed his laser at those proposals on the screen), all within the framework of mandatory reductions, with the final goal of a worldwide reduction in emissions of 100% by 2050."

Minister Karlsson stepped to the podium, gavel in hand, hoping for a civil debate when he was interrupted by the delegate from the Democratic Republic of Congo.

"Mr. Chairman, I rise to a point of personal privilege."

Minister Karlsson, taken aback by this motion, hesitated and then asked, "Is there any objection?"

John, trying to comprehend the motive behind this unusual move, yelled, "Objection. Mr. Chairman, according to our rules of parliamentary procedure, points of personal privilege are reserved at the end of each day's session."

After conferring with his parliamentarian, Mr. Karlsson responded with, "Objection sustained. Proceed with the debate."

John immediately recognized the speaker as the mysterious courier who had visited him at night. "What's he up to now? Was he trying to 'take the floor' to make the apology public, and embarrass the West?"

In the meantime, discussion started on Topic 1 with the Minister recognizing the sponsor from Kenya, who had originally proposed designating the atmosphere as a public trust, free from pollution. As the debate droned on about whether any international organization, be it the International Court of Justice or the U.N., could catch polluters of the unseen CO_2 pumped into the sky, John stealthily hurried through the rows of delegates to where Peng was seated, texting his "gang."

John, whispered in Peng's ear above the blaring microphones, "I think the Congolese delegate was going to make our apology public with his point of personal privilege. Has your 'gang' agreed with the compromise we discussed at the Perlan? I need to know by the end of today's debate."

Peng, trying to be helpful, "That's what my texting is all about. But sometimes it's better to be old-fashioned and meet face to face like we've been doing, but not necessarily in the hot water," he replied with a smile. "I'll tell you what I'll do. During our lunch break I'll get our gang together in one of the conference rooms and see where they're at on this. Fair enough?"

John nodded and gave a thumbs up as he hurried back to his seat.

Meanwhile, the Kenyan's proposal on the atmosphere was running into difficulty. It's one of those ideas that sounds good in theory, but how do you implement it? And once again, delegates rose to ridicule the proposal with references to fencing the CO_2s and even lassoing the pollutants to the ground.

A British delegate stood up and brought howls of laughter with, "If George Bailey wanted to lasso the moon for his honey in *It's A Wonderful Life*, why can't we?"

After order was restored, the Congolese delegate rose to speak in favor of the proposal, and John suddenly perked up.

"Mr. Chairman and fellow delegates, what's so funny about the so-called developed countries polluting the atmosphere with their smokestacks and factories? If it wasn't for them, my colleague from Kenya wouldn't be offering this proposal, and trying to save our continent from further devastation by global warming."

Now John was trying to put 2 and 2 together. Were these two delegates really neutral? Or were they trying to embarrass the West? He had to find out today.

The other speakers on this topic were more serious, and raised questions such as: "How would this proposal be enforced, and by whom?" "What part of the atmosphere would be safe from CO_2s?" "How can you draw boundary lines in the sky?"

With the questions continuing, the Kenyan delegate spoke again, "Mr. Chairman, I see the handwriting in the sky, and it says, 'Withdraw your proposal. You've made your point. Perhaps another time.' Mr. Chairman, I move to table Article 2021-1."

Without discussion, Minister Karlsson called for a vote and the electronic board lit up with a total of 150 green buttons and 20 red buttons. "The results of the vote are 150 nays and 20 ayes. The proposal is tabled. We will now recess for lunch until 13:30," as he pounded the gavel.

And like a Pavlovian dog, John bolted from his seat to try to find the mysterious courier. And time was of the essence.

Fish and Chips in the Delegates' Cafeteria

The line was long, and the time was short. What chance would John have to run into his courier? While picking up his tray, he looked around to see if he could spot him. No luck. And then he heard a soft voice behind him, "Mr. Bancroft, looking for me?"

John whirled around and looked up as if to say, "How could you do this?" and then back down to the Congolese. After he regained his composure, John, putting his loaded tray on the conveyer belt leading to the cashier and pointing toward the far wall, turned around and said, "There's a table over there. We need to talk. Follow me." And the Congolese did.

Eating and talking at the same time, John blurted out, "I'll get to the point. What are you trying to do with that point of personal privilege?"

Staring down and poking at his fish, the Congolese looked up, "We've waited for years for the West to help us. In the meantime, our people lack the basic necessities such as clean water, sanitation, and enough food to eat. And we're tired of waiting. It seems like nothing happens unless there is a deadline. So I'm giving you one. If you don't make a public commitment to send more funds to our nation by the end of the debate today, I will exercise my point of personal privilege and make public the apology I delivered to you. I've already alerted the press that they may have a headline for tomorrow's news, and I'm not talking about the monster storm heading our way."

Now it was John's turn to stare at his plate. He finally looked the Congolese squarely in the eye and said, "That's blackmail. I thought your nations were nonaligned at this conference."

"Desperate times demand desperate measures."

"OK, I'll see what I can do. But I'm not making any promises. Threats only boomerang back and hurt you in the long run."

"Time is short," prophesied the Congolese as he hurriedly gathered his tray and left, leaving John still seated, pondering his next move. He sat in the cafeteria until it emptied, and then the "light bulb" went on. Now he hurried out and went straight to Minister Karlsson's office. Perhaps he could catch him before the debate resumed.

A Backroom Deal?

John spied Minister Karlsson in his office, just finishing his lunch. He knocked and heard a hearty, "Come in John. What's on your mind, other than the brewing storm?"

"Aha," thought John. Another light went on.

"Minister, I have a way to end this debate so we can all get outta here to beat the coming storm."

Mr. Karlsson pushed his tray aside and leaned forward, "I'm all ears."

Hurriedly John blurted it out. "Instead of taking each topic separately, let's combine them into one package, and have one final vote."

"Are you suggesting we circumvent the democratic way of giving everyone the chance to speak? Don't you believe in freedom of speech?"

"Of course I do. But any agreement will ultimately come down to money to help the indigenous peoples and the islanders relocate, to transfer technology to the developing nations, to pay certain countries not to cut down their trees, and to help all countries reach the reduction goals you yourself set out when this conference began."

"OK, where do you intend to get the money for all that? The U.N. doesn't have it. These are hard times for most nations in the world."

Looking out the window and seeing the snow-covered trees, the minister sarcastically said, "And I don't see any money growing on these trees."

John, ignoring the minister's last comment, got serious with, "You remember the Stern Report issued over a decade ago, don't you?"

"Of course. He 'threw down the gauntlet' for nations to spend money now in order to prevent a worse disaster later."

"Yea, you're right. And he raised the ante from 1% to 2% of GDP because of the seriousness of global warming. That's what I'm proposing we do here. This may be our last chance to act boldly."

"Where are the poor and developing countries going to get the one or two percent, let alone rich countries like yours that still have struggling economies?"

"Well, if they're serious about combating global warming, they'll find the money. Maybe it'll take a crisis," he said as he looked out the window at the dark clouds and heard the wind that was increasing in intensity.

"Sounds like a tough sell to me, but more power to you. That's why we're here - to make the tough decisions that haven't been made before."

Trying to bring the conversation to closure Mr. Karlsson asked,

"So what do you want me to do about it?"

John was ready with, "Call on me first when the debate convenes, and I'll propose the 'grand bargain' to end this conference quickly, so we can get outta here with a binding agreement."

Minister Karlsson turned in his chair to face his computer, leaving John hanging as he left, thinking, "Well, at least he listened to me. I'd better be ready when the debate begins."

Storm Central: Reykjavik

The lunch recess found Brice and Blaine with Magnus at his office, only a few blocks' walk from the arena. He wanted to show his American friends how Iceland tracks storms with state-of-the-art technology.

The Nebraskans stood in Magnus' small office as he moved to the far wall and looked at a large flat screen which lit up immediately, displaying a blue earth from space. Then, with hands at his side, Magnus stared at the screen and the picture zoomed in on the European coastline, revealing a gigantic whirling cloud stretching from the Mediterranean Sea to the northern tip of Scotland and even west to Alaska. And finally, with Magnus remaining motionless in front of the screen, a 3D image appeared underneath the cloud showing a Category 4 hurricane with torrential rains uprooting trees and lifting houses from their foundations. And through the enhanced speakers connected to the flat screen came the sounds of howling winds and incessant rain. Magnus turned around and sat with Brice and Blaine, both bewildered by what they observed.

Finally, Brice blurted, "This beats the Weather Channel. How did you do that?' as he pointed to the screen. "You either hid the clicker or didn't have one."

Magnus looked directly at Blaine and moved his eyes from right to left. "With my eyes. We don't need a mouse or a touch screen any more, thanks to this Swedish technology. It's like being there, isn't it?"

And now Blaine reacted, "And I wouldn't want to be in that eye," as he motioned to the whirling image on the wall.

"And here's the bad news. This hurricane Olga, which originated in your Gulf of Mexico - thank you very much - is on track to hit our southeast coast and follow it to Reykjavik in 2 days. We can track her path by the minute, and predict the exact spot where she will hit. And even though most hurricanes lose their intensity when they hit land, this one is predicted to gain strength to a Category 5. Minister Karlsson knows this, and wants to end this convention so the delegates can fly home before we have to close Keflavik Airport.

"And one more thing. Our climatologists think this extreme storm is caused by two converging anomalies. The first is the changing Irminger Current, which brings us our warm climate for our latitude. The second is the Arctic Oscillation, which alternates between high and low pressure. During the positive phase, the higher pressure drives ocean storms farther north and changes the ocean circulation pattern to bring wetter weather to Alaska, Scotland, and Scandinavia. So that's what's happening."

Thoroughly impressed with Magnus' technical explanation, Brice blurted, "So how do you know this stuff?"

Magnus, with a sly grin, answered, "I watch our Weather Channel without a clicker."

"We'd better get back to the convention. Maybe we can do something to get you outta here. Nothing personal, of course," he said as the three headed back to the convention. What Magnus didn't tell his friends was that he was the main one monitoring the storm in Iceland, and was sending real time reports to his boss, Minister Karlsson. Only the two of them really knew the seriousness of the impending storm. Meanwhile, back at the convention.

Making the Motions

Minister Karlsson gaveled the afternoon session into order and immediately recognized John Bancroft, who rose and began,

"Mr. Chairman, we are all watching the weather and want to end this convention, but we have a lot of work to do. In the interest of saving time, I am proposing we consolidate topics 2, 3, 4, 5, and 6 into one amendment with one vote and a thorough debate."

Quickly the Minister called for objections, and, hearing none, ruled in the affirmative. This ruling caused much commotion as the delegates were trying to assess what they were about to debate.

Minister Karlsson calmly clarified the motion by reiterating the 5 topics to which Mr. Bancroft referred: Topic 2: Demands by the Indigenous Working Group; Topic 3: Assisting the Island Nations with Their Population Resettlement Plan; Topic 4: Ratifying the Technology Transfer Plan; Topic 5: The REDD Plan to Reduce Emissions from Deforestation and Forest Degradation; and Topic 6: Ratifying the CO2 Reductions 100% by 2050.

And then a point of clarification was raised by the delegate from Peru, "Mr. Chairman, this motion doesn't address how we are going to pay for all these proposals."

John, anticipating the question, rose to be recognized, "Mr. Chairman, I propose we review the Stern Report that came out last decade to see if this esteemed British economist has an answer to your question," as he looked at the Peruvian delegate.

Mr. Bancroft continued, "And Mr. Chairman, I move that we adjourn until 0900 to discuss this question in our caucuses."

These comments from one of the leading delegates to the convention caused a commotion in the arena, as the delegates tried to find the Stern Report on their BlackBerrys.

Seeing further debate was futile the Minister stated loudly, "We are adjourned until 0900 tomorrow," as the heavy thump of the gavel resonated throughout the arena.

And John breathed a sigh of relief, knowing that his motion preempted the Congolese's point of personal privilege. Two birds killed with the proverbial stone.

And now the stampede to the exits began. The delegates were on their phones, laptops, and scurrying toward the TV monitors around the arena, anxious for any storm news. In the meantime, John texted Peng to see if he was also calling a caucus of all the emerging/developing nations. If the two of them could agree on the "grand bargain", maybe they could beat the storm home. But the "wild card" in this "rush to adjournment scheme" was with the nonaligned countries, over which he had no control. Maybe the bargain wasn't so grand after all.

Counting Votes

Immediately after adjournment, John texted Peng on his BlackBerry with,

"Check the Stern 2% recommendation, and count votes for it in your caucus. I will do the same. Remember the 'Spirit of Reykjavik!'"

Then John hurriedly corralled his "Gang of 10," who were conveniently seated together. They found a side conference room where they could talk above the din. Unfortunately the "Gang" had been whittled down to 6 because of Olga. John was troubled to learn that all the Scandinavian delegates (except Iceland, of course) from Denmark, Finland, Norway, and Sweden had flown north from Keflavik to beat the storm. The "magic number" to pass was still 146.

After this shock, John heard the news about another one. Air Force One carrying President Palin to Reykjavik had to turn back to Washington because of Olga. "This storm must be serious," John thought.

He checked his BlackBerry to find a text, not from Peng but from President Palin, that read, "Sorry I couldn't help you out, but I want you to know we are committed to a binding agreement, even if it costs us 2% of our GDP. Keep the troops in line. Sarah."

A Special Appearance

With airline flights still arriving in Keflavik from the East, the Chinese Premier, Wen Xing Chou, arrived in Reykjavik for a special mission at the urging of Peng, who had been briefing him on the convention developments via a secure transmission. He arrived with great fanfare and press coverage, basking in the limelight as now representing the world's largest economy - displacing the U.S. Still China maintained its dubious distinction as the world's largest emitter of greenhouse gases, but also the largest producer of renewable energy - a seemingly schizophrenic distinction.

Upon arrival at the airport Mr. Chou was hustled into one of Iceland's hydrogen limousines and rushed to the arena, where Peng was waiting to escort him into the caucus room, crowded with delegates from 85 developing/emerging nations. Since the caucus was closed, the press corps was forced to wait outside for any important developments. But Peng invited one VIP in - John Bancroft, and Peng introduced him to the Premier.

Peng then introduced Mr. Chou to the delegates, who enthusiastically applauded his arrival. John sat in the back and stoically took in the proceedings.

The Premier began, "Fellow delegates, Peng has been apprising me of the latest developments going on here. It seems you are at a crucial point in both the voting and in trying to avoid the storm, which fortunately I weathered."

A few subdued chuckles were heard over this unintended pun ("weathering the storm?")

"Unfortunately, President Palin, flying from the opposite direction as I, couldn't make it."

That comment raised John's ire. "Was the premier playing the game of 'one-upmanship,' or was it merely a statement of fact?"

But then the Chinese leader surprised John with, "The world's two most powerful countries are, at this convention, doing something different. Instead of being rivals, as we have been, we are working together here to try to save the planet. After all, we both have to live on it. There's no planet B (by now a familiar line at the convention). Some of the delegates were even sporting a 3-D button with the blue Planet Earth and underneath, "Save Planet A.""

"That's why Mr. Bancroft is here. We have no secrets and want to work together."

John, remembering the last caucus to which Peng invited him, didn't expect any recognition, but this time he received a warm smattering of applause, which he acknowledged with a wave of the hand.

The premier continued, "It doesn't matter what label we call ourselves - emerging, developing, newly industrialized, or developed; whether we come from the East, the West, or in the middle; we need to stand together. This may be our last chance for a binding agreement before we reach the 'tipping point.' That's why I'm here, and if Olga tarries, I'll be here for the final vote. I encourage you to listen to Peng and Mr. Bancroft, and to throw aside your prejudices. I won't be counting votes, but Peng and Mr. Bancroft will. Remember, Earth First."

This time everyone was on their feet with sustained applause, with even John rising to his feet in the back as the Premier was escorted out to a special VIP room to await the final vote. Would he be "twisting arms" behind the scenes?

John's Caucus -Again

Meanwhile, John had his own counting to do. This time he called a caucus of the remaining 28 developed countries to "nail down" their votes for the 2% (of GDP) to finance the "grand bargain."

John stressed, "We need everybody here for the final debate. Hang in there one more day, and we'll all get outta here safely. The Icelandic airline authorities have contingency plans if need be."

I've checked with Peng and he's already had 11 that have left."

Finally the delegate from Cyprus spoke up, "What about the nonaligned nations? Can we count on their support for the 2%?"

John replied, "I don't know. I'll see what I can find out. He had an idea but didn't want to reveal it now. Something about not counting your chickens until they are hatched.

Sheepishly, the delegate from Greece stood up and spoke, "You all know the financial problems our country is facing. We have an austerity program to get us back on track, and our people would riot again if we earmarked money for this so-called bargain. Our crisis is now, not way into the future."

John didn't say anything until the delegate from Portugal simply raised his hand, "Ditto for my country."

"That's two," stated John. "Anyone else?"

The Italian delegate stood up and stated, "And you know our situation. We're on the brink of financial collapse. We don't have any money to spare either."

And finally the delegate from Ireland stated her case. "As you know, we're still recovering from the austerity plan the EU foisted on us," as she glared at the German delegate. "The bailout plan didn't give us any discretionary money for something like this in the future."

This time, silence.

John, keeping these four countries in mind, said, "OK, that's it for now. Let's see how the other caucuses are going."

He walked out with a dejected look, knowing the final vote would come down to the wire. But he still had another trick up his sleeve.

As he dismissed the "gang" he thought of previous conventions where the cry was, "We're waiting for the U.S. to lead." And now he was trying to lead, but his followers were few. How ironic. But maybe there was hope from the East.

Another Meeting with the Congolese Courier

John knew where the non-aligned caucus was meeting, so he headed that way, and, as in the cafeteria, there was the Congolese man leaving the caucus on a break. John caught his eye and beckoned him to a back bench hidden in an out of the way alcove. No lunch this time.

John started the conversation with, "I don't expect any inside information from your caucus, but I'm trying to put together a coalition that will support the motion I made yesterday."

"Which one? You've been busy on the floor."

"Well, I want to get this convention over so we can all head home safely. The press has labeled my proposal to consolidate the remaining topics as a "grand bargain.""

Not impressed the Congolese replied, "It doesn't sound so grand for our Continent. Show me the money."

"OK. You've come to me in secrecy. So am I, and in confidence. Agreed?"

The black man nodded in agreement to the white. Mutual trust was of the essence here.

John continued, "I'm sure you've gotten wind of the 2 percent deal between the developed and developing countries to fund the 'bargain'?"

"I have my sources." But now the Congolese got animated,

"So do you expect us to ante up the same percent? Don't you remember our previous conversations that we need help from you rich guys? We're the poorest of the poor; hurt the most by your pollution. Our people are starving right now. You don't think about the future on an empty stomach, only where your next meal will come from. Where are we to get that kind of money?"

When he quieted down John thought for a long moment before speaking.

"OK, here's what I'm proposing. We need the 2% to prevent the catastrophe we're already seeing from getting worse. Otherwise we might as well leave now and forget about trying to save your people and the planet. Here's what I'd like you to do. Go back into your caucus and see how many votes you have for the 2 percent proposal, with the proviso that your poorest of the poor, as you call them, can use 1% of their GDP for climate change mitigation in their own countries. The other 1% would go for funding Topics 2, 3, 4, and 5 that the Minister mentioned. He concluded with, "Here's my iPhone number. Text me with the results today. We need to count votes before the session tomorrow."

Without saying anything else, the Congolese slowly arose from his bench and went back to his caucus, pondering the proposition. But would it fly among the 42 nonaligned delegates that were left? Twenty-one had already returned to their countries, giving up hope for any help at yet another failed conference.

It was getting late and John was beat from his meetings, caucuses, and the press "hounding" him to reveal his strategy. Already there were leaks that the convention would end without an agreement, as the delegates had a more immediate concern - leaving Iceland.

John had heard the stories, but, being an optimist, thought there could be a silver lining behind the clouds. He remembered that saying as he slowly trudged back to his hotel room, facing a strong wind and horizontal rain.

What would his next strategy be? Let his "lieutenants" continue the lobbying for votes? Let the Chinese premier exert his new economic muscle? And what of the Congolese? Could he be trusted to deliver his votes?

He called his wife, checked his plane reservation, glanced at the Reykjavík Weather Channel, and dozed off immediately to the sound of the howling wind. In a strange way it was comforting. Zero900 would come soon enough, and he needed a good night's sleep.

Checking Olga Again

This delegate-caucus day found Magnus, Brice, and Blaine back at the Icelander's office to eye (literally for Magnus) Olga's progress - if you want to call it that - since their last visit. Once again Magnus faced the wall, motionless, with Brice and Blaine standing beside him watching his eyes move.

Immediately the sound and light show began. The storm track had moved northeast considerably in the last day, and the wind speed had picked up to 150 mph, or, as they record wind speeds in Iceland, 65 meters per second (m/s). Olga was still a Category 4 storm but was picking up speed.

The screen showed the devastation all the way up the coast of Scotland, including the Shetland Islands which are, fortunately, sparsely populated. And with adequate warning, these coastal lowlands had been evacuated. Would the delegates be as fortunate as it approached Iceland?

Magnus moved his right eye and the screen zoomed in on the picturesque Icelandic town of Vik, midway on the southern coast. The town had already put into effect its emergency evacuation plan, this time not for glacial flooding but for hurricane devastation. Even the Lutheran state church on the hill overlooking the city, now only used for a museum, was packed with citizens praying for deliverance. And Magnus offered up a silent prayer on their behalf.

And now Brice and Blaine were becoming concerned if they would be able, with the remaining delegates, the press, and others, to escape the storm. But Brice didn't want to say anything to Magnus. After all, he was a tough football player.

Magnus moved his left eye as the screen predicted Olga would indeed hit landfall at Vik as a Category 5 storm with sustained winds of 175 mph, or 80 m/s; with a storm surge of 20 feet striking its rocky coast, which might mitigate damage to the town.

Magnus, after studying the picture, concluded, "Olga is set to follow the coast north to Reykjavík, arriving at 1200 in two days. That means tomorrow better be the last day of the convention if everyone wants to escape our lovable country," as he silently laughed. And then he moved both eyes and that sent this report directly to Minister Karlsson. Here was another **urgency** to add to the others.

That wasn't funny for the Nebraskans contemplating their trip home. Brice thought better of calling Tricia. Hopefully, she wasn't following this hurricane, since it was off the normal Gulf Coast track, and the US didn't yet have the tracking technology of Iceland.

Day 15 - Last Day?

As the delegates gathered promptly at 0900, there was both an air of apprehension and excitement. By now the press had picked up rumors that this might be the last day, and that behind-the-scenes deals were being made - all with a wary eye on Olga picking up strength as she charged up the Atlantic to strike landfall on the southern Icelandic coast.

As usual, Minister Karlsson called for a quorum call, and to his surprise, only 155 green lights lit up. Fifteen more delegates had left the country, and the arena was near panic with the "double whammy" of unfinished business and the approaching storm, with minute-by-minute updates by the Icelandic Meteorological Society. Quickly calculating in his head, he deduced a mere 10 negative votes would shipwreck the convention to end as all previous ones had ended. Hopefully the day of caucuses would prove productive.

Finally, the debate on what the press is calling "the grand bargain" began with the Minister setting the procedural rules with,

"Ladies and gentlemen, in order to expedite the debate today, for obvious reasons," as he looked at the dark clouds through the back windows, "I am limiting speeches to one per delegate and to no more than five minutes. We will discuss Topics 2, 3, 4, 5, and 6 as a package with no amendments, concluding with one final vote. I propose this concession to unlimited freedom of speech in a country that values this right in normal times. But these are **urgent** times", as he looked through the rear windows to the black, morning clouds. "And I will not allow any recesses for food, restroom breaks, caucuses, or other reasons. Any objections?"

He paused as the delegates also turned and looked out the rear windows, confirming what the Minister also saw. And now the rain was starting.

Hearing none, the floor was now open for debate, with a maximum time of 775 minutes, or more than 12 hours. Would it go that long?

The first thing John had done upon waking from a good night's sleep was to get a firm count of the remaining delegates in this fluid situation. His "lieutenants" texted that there were still 28 delegates in the arena with 24 yes's.

He checked his BlackBerry to find 2 text messages. He scrolled down to find the first from Peng, which read, "Five more delegates left. Down to 85. Premier working hard for the "bargain," but have 5 no's and 80 yes's."

And what about the nonaligned vote? John hadn't heard from the Congolese. He quickly counted that there were 104 votes for the "2%" plan – far short of the 146 needed. From where would the other 42 come?

"These countries were as mysterious as the Congolese courier in the night," John thought. But then his "trick up his sleeve" came back to him. It was worth a try.

More Maneuvering

The debate droned on, with each delegate taking his or her 5 minutes in the limelight. Now that it was approaching 1200, and with no break scheduled for lunch, John decided to go "behind the scenes." He snuck between the rows to where Peng was seated. The two then disappeared into the VIP room where the Chinese Premier was still seated, waiting for the final vote.

Mr. Chou stood and bowed with Peng and John. The Premier spoke first, looking at John, "Peng has told me how the two of you have worked together to get an agreement here."

John looked over at Peng, looking down at his shoes.

"Yes, that's right, sir. But we're still short of votes. My 2% idea doesn't go over well with the poorer countries, and I can understand that."

Mr. Chou again looking at John, "Peng and I have been discussing an idea that may help."

"I'm open to anything. Go ahead, sir."

"I've been sitting in this suite talking to some countries in our bloc about the 2%, and you're right; those that need help the most don't have the money for it. So I'm willing, with approval from my cabinet, which I will get, to fund the 2% plan for the 25 poorest nations in the world according to the U.N. Development Index. They are all in the nonaligned block."

John had to ask, "Mr. Premier, I don't want you to divulge any secrets, but from where will the funds come?"

Surprisingly, Mr. Chou put his hand into his pocket and pulled out a U.S. Treasury bond, holding it up for John to see that it was real. "We have trillions of these, and it's no secret."

John, now blushing, had no further questions. He thanked Mr. Chou, bowed again, and departed, thinking, "China is definitely targeting Africa with its new economic muscle. And money does speak. And it buys allegiance. We know how that works. We've done the same thing."

And now to find the Congolese. There he was in his seat, texting furiously.

John knelt down (not out of humility but so as not to be seen) and whispered, "Well, what's your count?"

"For what?"

"The 1 plus 1 plan."

"We have 25 committed to the 2%."

John, quickly adding in his head, came up with 129 votes, still

17 short. He also wondered if the 25 votes were "bought" by China, but he didn't ask. Votes were votes.

John, still mentally counting, "What about the others?"

"We have 16 left that say they can't commit any funds with the drought showing no signs of stopping."

"Don't they realize they can keep the 1% that would go to the Sub Saharan drought relief in their countries?"

The Congolese surprised John with this statement, "Have you heard of Maslow's Hierarchy of Needs?"

"Well sure, it's required study in most of our universities," as John wondered if this black man was educated in America.

"These countries, including my own, are at the basic needs level, where food, water, and shelter are the most important things in their lives."

He asked another question, "You do remember the apology I delivered to you in the night, and that our bloc drafted it to be neutral?"

"Our bloc didn't think it was. Can an apology be neutral?"

No answer from the Congolese.

John didn't say anything but thought, "I figured I had outmaneuvered him on that. Is this coming back to haunt me?"

The Congolese again, "Maybe your apology would convince these 16 that the rich Western countries are serious about helping us."

And now it was John's move in this verbal chess game. "OK, I'll tell you what. If you can deliver all the votes from your bloc to pass this thing so that we can all escape the storm, I'll stand up on a point of personal privilege at the end and read an apology. According to my latest count, we need 17 votes for the 'grand bargain,' but that may change. During the debate I'll text you if anything changes."

In another surprise move, the Congolese, saying nothing, reached out his hand to where John was and grabbed it. John grabbed his in an integrated hand shake, turned and left, sneaking back to his seat, thinking, "I played my final trick. Let's see if it works."

As the debate continued, it became apparent that the repetitive speeches were mainly for press coverage, and not to change votes. Most delegates had decided in their caucuses, and wanted to keep their commitments – but not everyone. The noise level arose as informal conversations started to drown out the formal speeches. Was it to make deals, convince wavering delegates, or nervous talking about the storm threat?

But the biggest voice was ready to howl outside the arena, and her name was Olga - and she was furious.

Magnus had more important matters on his mind. He motioned to Brice and Blaine, and they followed him back to storm central to check Olga's track. With a blink of the Icelander's eye, the screen appeared on the wall, this time in 3D, showing the damage done to Vik in real time. The sound was like that of many freight trains rumbling, with glimpses of rooftops and splinters sailing through the air, and water washing out to sea. No, Toto and Dorothy weren't there, but there were a few casualties that hadn't heeded the evacuation order.

Magnus' right eye moved to the right and the projected storm track showed Olga actually gaining strength as she rolled along the rocky and surging coast, projecting a direct hit on Keflavik at 1100 - an hour earlier than the last prediction - with wind speeds in the Category 5 range and a storm surge of 25 feet. And with another blink, the screen showed the high protective sea wall recently built to hold back the rising sea. This would be the first test of this reinforced concrete and titanium wall.

Magnus stood motionless in front of the wall, not even blinking for a time. Then he pulled out his BlackBerry and texted Minister Karlsson with the latest news. Perhaps he could speed up the debate, but the rules had already been adopted. What would it take? He knew.

Extreme Weather Reports

As soon as the 50th speaker finished about 1300, the Minister pounded the gavel and gave the following announcement, "Ladies and Gentlemen, I have just been informed by the Icelandic Meteorological Society that Olga has just devastated our scenic city of Vik on our south central coast. Fortunately there were only a few casualties. She is predicted to hit Keflavik Airport at 1100 tomorrow as a Category 5 hurricane."

With one accord the delegates turned around to face the window showing the oncoming storm with its thick, black clouds, howling winds, and increasing rain. And suddenly the **urgency** increased.

Minister Karlsson continued, "I urge those who have not spoken to choose your words carefully, and not to repeat what previous speakers have said, although our temporary rules do allow 5 minutes each. Let your conscience be your guide. We would like a final vote as soon as possible. Thank you."

And all of a sudden the debate's focus changed. It started with the delegate from Peru, holding up the report from the Intergovernmental

Panel on Climate Change (IPCC) that established a high correlation between extreme weather and climate change.

He began, "I'm sure you remember this report," waving it in the air. "When it first came out, I was skeptical, since weather patterns can be erratic and vary from year to year. But the IPCC included the melting glaciers in my country, with the prediction they would disappear by 2020. And I'm sorry to report it has already happened as they predicted. Farmers' fields are drying up for lack of water. Whole villages are deserted. Poverty in our country is high."

He concluded with, "And for the sake of my country, I will support the grand bargain."

As he sat down there was a smattering of applause, muffled by Olga.

And now the floodgates (not literally!) were open. With one eye on the storm and the other on the IPCC report, other affected delegates rose to tell their countries' stories.

Next it was the delegate from Pakistan trying to explain the highest temperature ever recorded in his country. "I'll use Fahrenheit. It sounds more dramatic - 150 degrees. Factoring in the heat index, it's 175. You've seen people frying an egg on the sidewalk. We can bake bread, and this is from the streets of Karachi," as he held the loaf in his hand. "I'm supporting the plan. Our country needs help."

And now from the developed world, the Australian delegate arose to speak.

"Advanced countries like mine are not immune from weather extremes. God sends the rain on the just and unjust alike. I don't know what we are, but we've been experiencing record floods on the coasts, and record heat waves and drought in the interior. And you've probably seen the pictures from space that show our national treasure, the Great Barrier Reef, bleaching from the increase in ocean temperature and acidification.

"Now we have a carbon tax that generates revenue to try to mitigate some of these problems, but we need more resources to combat our environmental problems. That's why I'm supporting the 2 percent plan, and I hope you will also."

Not to be outdone by her larger neighbor "down under," the delegate from New Zealand wanted his turn.

"Ladies and gentlemen, we've had earthquakes as you know, but never a devastating tsunami like we had earlier this year, caused by another break off of an Antarctic ice sheet. Ours made the ones in Indonesia and Japan in the last decade look tame in comparison. And like my neighbor said, advanced countries are not immune from disasters.

"We don't have a carbon tax yet, but are seriously considering it. In the meantime, committing a fixed amount of our GDP to the topics we are discussing seems like prudent planning for the future."

With countries from his bloc telling their disaster stories, John could certainly relate some of his own; from the flooding and tornadoes in the Midwest, to the intense hurricanes like Olga, and to the continuing drought in the Southwest. But he decided not to speak yet. He'd rather be texting Peng and the Congolese for his latest vote count. There were a few more yeses, but not enough for passage. Maybe the storm needed to get closer. He remembered the political reality that nothing gets done unless there is a crisis. Maybe this was it, and just in time!

Slowly the turbaned delegate from Afghanistan rose, and, looking out the window, began, "You know the tough times we've been through for the past 40 years. First, war with the Russians," looking at the Russian delegate, "and then contending with the Americans," as he looked directly at John. Both powers left; failing to improve our country. That's why we're called the 'graveyard of empires.'

"But a worse disaster is now facing us with the rapid melting of the Himalayan glaciers - our lifeblood. It's not like war, where you die quickly; but losing our water supply is just as effective in killing our people. We're still a poor country, but will support the compromise, the 1 percent plus 1 percent plan. That's the best we can do right now."

And then a lady with a brightly colored dress from Ghana slowly stood. "Mr. Minister, ladies and gentlemen, I represent the countries comprising Sub-Saharan Africa. You've heard much about our 30 year drought that shows no signs of letting up. But that's nothing compared to those our people faced during the 'Little Ice Age' in the Middle Ages. They lasted for centuries and killed hundreds of thousands of our people. And the predictions are that it could happen again.

"This 2 percent plan, or 1 plus 1 plan, sounds fine if you're not starving, but our countries don't have any extra money for the future. We need to feed our families. Therefore, we can't support these plans, no matter what they are."

Now John was wondering what was going on inside the non-aligned bloc. Were the remaining 17 nations, all in the Sub-Saharan region, following Ghana's lead? If so, the "grand bargain" was done. Now what?

A Flashback

All of sudden the "light bulb" went on as the sky was darkening outside. John remembered meeting the South African delegate 10 years earlier at the climate change conference in Durban, a modern coastal city on the Indian Ocean that had also hosted the World Cup soccer games. This Afrikaner, Peter Dejager, was also here in Reykjavík. John remembered striking up a friendly conversation in Durban, which ended with the exchange of business cards and pledge to keep in touch. "Maybe I'll take him up on it" John thought.

While the extreme weather reports from all over the world were being related by the speakers, John again took off to find Peter, whom he had greeted on the opening day. Time was getting short for another try, but try he must.

It happened again. As John walked into the men's room, Peter almost bumped into him, walking out. Chance, again?

After a brief discussion of the topic on everyone's mind (how are we going to get home?), John followed up with, "You know, Peter, you could help us all wrap this convention up?"

"How's that?"

"Do you know the delegate from the Congo?"

"Yea, I ran into him several times here."

Not wanting to reveal his previous negotiations with the same person, John nonchalantly said, "Would you be willing to talk to him now?"

"About what?"

"Have you been following the discussion on the 2% plan to fund the topics we are discussing?"

"Sure. The developed countries like yours can afford it. And the emerging countries like mine and the developing countries are for it, with a little help from China."

John didn't say anything, but thought, "The Chinese are certainly doing a PR job here." Then he spoke, "Yea, you're basically right, but the problem is with the nonaligned bloc, made up mainly of Africans. You heard the speaker from Ghana denounce all the plans. I'd like to know if she is speaking just about her country, or other poor countries. By my count we need 17 more votes to pass the grand bargain."

"So you want me to find that out?"

"You got it. And try to convince them of at least the 1 + 1 plan. Remind them 1% of their GDP will benefit their country directly and the other 1% will benefit the planet on which they live."

Now Peter asked his bottom line question, "What's in it for me?"

John, disappointed he would ask that question, simply replied, "How about a world worth saving."

They stood in silence, each looking out at the ever darkening sky. Peter tapped John on the shoulder, turned and said, "I'll see what I can do."

John's last word was, "Text me what you find out, and quickly, please," as he pointed to the trees swaying in the wind.

As John hurried back to his seat, he noticed the digital clock on the wall. It read 1515. The sun, hidden by the ominous looking clouds, was about to set. What did that portend for the convention?

Finally . . .

John slowly trudged back to his seat thinking, "This is the last chance to pass the 'bargain.' All I can do now is wait and hope Peter can convince them. After all, he's one of them, and his country is good at negotiations."

The debate continued with more stories of natural/manmade disasters from all over the world. Even several European delegates rose to describe their erratic weather from extreme heat to bitter cold - both temperatures setting records. And then there were reports of snowfall in Rome - unheard of before.

Then the Russian rose to speak, "Ladies and gentlemen, you don't know heat until it is coupled with massive forest fires breaking out in Siberia. Not only does it kill people and animals, but methane is released from the tundra, polluting the skies much worse than CO_2s."

Next it was the Brazilian delegate. "Our precious trees, which take tons of CO_2 from the atmosphere, are being ravaged both by fires and desperate tribes trying to eke out an existence in the jungle. If our Amazon is gone, there's not much hope for the world."

To John's surprise Peng stood up to speak. "Fellow delegates, even the world's largest economy is being buffeted by massive floods in one part of our country, drought in another, and a new strain of malaria in the South. Fortunately, we have developed a vaccine that is holding it in check, at least for now. But who knows where this devastating disease will spread next to harm the world's children."

With the sun setting and the sky steadily darkening, John figured he'd better get a vote count - this time from his seat. He first texted his Icelandic assistant to see if there had been any changes as a result of the debate. Next it was to Peng, and finally to Peter. He also texted Minister Karlsson to see if he could speed things up by giving an updated Olga report. And then he waited - restlessly. It was now 1630.

Then it was Simon from Kivalina up next. "Ladies and gentlemen, you have seen our indigenous people demonstrating outside. Now we're asking you to support the 2 percent plan that would help us relocate our villages that have been devastated by the fierce Arctic storms. Every year since 2007 the sea ice has been shrinking to where today the summer ice is down to a few floating chunks. Our coastlines have no protection anymore. Our only choice is to relocate, and not to the refugee camps. We want the same services we had before the big melt. And the right to hunt and fish like we've done for hundreds of years. Support the 'grand bargain,' please."

There was a brief pause and Minister Karlsson, seeing no other flashing LED lights on his console, stated, "We will now move to debate on the vote on Topic 2, dealing with the indigenous peoples; Topic 3, resettlement of the island nations; Topic 4, ratifying the technology transfer plan; Topic 5, the REDD plan, and Topic 6, ratifying the CO_2 reductions by 2050. Is there any discussion?

"And I have just been informed that Olga is now moving back out to sea, and is picking up strength, and is expected to make landfall close to Reykjavík at 1000 tomorrow - one hour earlier than predicted. So choose your words carefully, if you choose to speak at all."

With that warning several delegates, standing, sat down again. But one remained.

The delegate from Thailand began, "Fellow delegates, I have from reliable sources that some secret negotiations are going on that don't seem fair. Some countries are cutting special deals on the 2 percent plan. The rich countries, as he looked at Peng, are helping the poor countries, and some of us that are struggling have to pay the entire 2 percent from our own treasury. And furthermore, some countries can use half of the 2 percent for their own climate mitigation instead of helping everyone. And I'm opposed to this unfair plan."

This news caused grumbling that could be heard above the howling wind outside. The Minister, taken by surprise, pounded the gavel, saying, "We will take a short recess." He immediately texted John and Peng to come up to his office, while the other delegates milled around, most of them on their BlackBerrys checking the conditions outside. The delegates were ready to call it quits, but who wanted to brave the storm howling outside?

Last Ditch Effort

John and Peng arrived in the Minister's office to find him already conversing intently with Mr. Mobotu, the U.N. Secretary-General. With all four seated around the round, mahogany table, the Minister threw out the basic question, "How are we going to save the 'grand bargain?' As you just heard, some countries think it's not fair that some have to pay the entire two percent while others get to keep one percent for themselves. And furthermore, some are being helped by others," as he looked at Peng, "while others aren't getting any help at all."

Silence ensued, and finally the Secretary-General spoke. "Gentlemen, I may have a solution."

Everyone leaned forward in their chairs.

"The International Carbon Fund was established for such a purpose – to help poor countries cope with the ravages of climate change, and we've heard a lot about that today," he said, pointing out the Minister's picture window, "and we're seeing it here firsthand."

John asked the first question, "But how do we determine who gets help and who, like many of our Western countries, can afford the two percent?"

Mr. Mobotu again, "The U.N. Development Index is an objective measure that ranks all countries in the world by their GDP."

Peng piped up, "But is there enough money to help most of the African countries that need help? We've already helped some, but even we don't have enough money for all nations that need it."

John was getting tired of hearing about China's new wealth, but then he thought that's how many people still perceive his country. No time to bring his negative thoughts up. We need positive solutions - and fast!

Minister Karlsson, trying to end the meeting, summarized the conference with, "If we pass the 'grand bargain,' the price of carbon will skyrocket as our CO2 reduction measures go into effect. This should make more funds available to those who need it."

Mr. Mobotu, "We could set up a grant system similar to the one for the technology transfer program. That way we don't need another bureaucracy."

With all heads nodding in the affirmative, the Minister closed the conference with, "OK, let's go out and use this plan for our closing remarks."

Looking at John and Peng the Minister said, "As soon as we resume the debate, I will call on both of you to summarize what we just agreed on. And then we'll proceed immediately to the final vote, and trust that it will pass, God willing. OK?"

Looking around and seeing no objections, he said, "Let's get outta here. I want to get home and prepare for Olga. My family is getting worried."

John and Peng, walking out together, stopped for one last check.

Peng, "How are your numbers holding out?"

"So far, so good. No more defections, and everybody's hanging in there, as you say, until the final vote."

"Good. Same here. It's up to the non-aligners. I guess we'll just have to wait and see."

John hadn't heard from Peter, and was wondering how he was doing with the African nations. Without them the "grand bargain" was dead.

Taking time to briefly rehearse their closing remarks, John looked at Peng, "Thanks for sticking with me through this all. We've proved the two largest economies can work together."

Peng jokingly, "And we were in a lot of hot water, as you would say."

John loosened up, "You're learning our slang. Maybe I should learn yours."

"Come on over, and I'll teach you Mandarin. Maybe someday it will replace your language."

As they left, John pointed at Peng, "Remember the 'Spirit of Reykjavik.'"

With a thumbs up both men left to their respective seats to await the final vote.

It was now 1700 and it was pitch black outside.

Evacuation Plans

In the meantime, as the delegates were anxiously checking the minute-by-minute reports Magnus was sending to them, much feverish work was being done outside the convention. How were the Icelandic Airport Authorities to fly 155 delegates safely from their country? Ever since Olga first became a serious threat to their country, creative minds had been devising a two-pronged solution.

First, all nonessential air travel to and from the country had been grounded, freeing the Icelandair fleet of 15 Dreamliners on the tarmac at Keflavik International Airport, which had won many awards for being the best small airport in Europe, particularly for their high level of service. These accolades would be tested in this looming crisis.

The second option was one that was never used. Ever since 2006 the huge American military base, established during the Cold War in 1951, had been closed on Reykjanes Peninsula. After being vacant for years, NATO had converted this vast area to use as a strategic air base - a convenient location between the East and the West. And with no looming military crisis, many fighter jets were available to whisk the delegates to safety.

All plans on the outside, including the logistics of assigning delegates to specific planes and routes, were in place. Now, if they could only adjourn in time.

Closing Remarks

Once again Minister Karlsson gaveled the delegates into session - hopefully the last one.

"The chair recognizes the delegate from China for closing remarks."

Peng arose, adjusted his headset for the maximum volume, and began, "Fellow delegates, we've come a long way since the opening ceremonies 15 days ago. With demonstrations, negotiations, and now Olga," as he turned and looked at the back windows - only seeing black - "we are finally ready to vote on the package put together by the world's two largest economies," as he again turned and looked at John, sitting and texting.

"By committing 2 percent of your GDPs, you are, for the first time saying we will NOT allow global temperatures to rise more than 2 degrees Celsius since the industrial era. And we're just about there now."

He tried to continue but was stopped by a standing ovation - at least by most of the delegates.

Peng, after politely pausing, continued, "Every climate change conference has set this as their goal, but we will do it."

This time there was delegate applause from their seats.

Peng continued again, "Your 2% will allow the indigenous peoples to finally leave their refugee camps and be relocated in their native settings, where they can resume the ways of their ancestors."

This time it was Simon and his Inuits who applauded and cheered from the balcony.

Peng then turned to another group in the balcony, pointing, "And you island nations, also displaced by the rising seas, will be able to relocate to friendly countries that have agreed to take you in."

This time it wasn't applause. The islanders, dressed in their colorful costumes, stood and did the wave that started on one side of the balcony and spread to the other, with spectators in between joining in. How appropriate!

While Magnus was back in his office checking on Olga, Brice and Blaine were among the spectators. When the wave started, Brice rose, stood and raised his hands and swayed by himself. He motioned to Blaine, who reluctantly stood and joined in.

Brice, with arms still raised, turned to Blaine and shouted, "I've seen this many times in Memorial Stadium, and always wanted to do it. So there."

Blaine finally grabbed his dad's shirt and gently pulled him down, saying, "We're not in Lincoln, you know."

And that was their "Big Red" demonstration, 4,500 miles from home.

Peng continued, "You may be wondering how this plan will benefit our country. We are the world leaders in solar and wind energy, and are reducing our carbon intensity significantly. But we are still relying on coal, which we hope to eventually phase out. But now, with this plan, we will be able to sequester the CO2s from all our existing coal plants.

"And with our new plants we will be using the technology, pioneered right here in Iceland, that pumps CO2 into basalt rock below our lava fields, creating artificial limestone which will remain in place forever - and out of the atmosphere."

He looked in the balcony to a waving Icelandic flag, and cheers from the locals, proud to have produced another innovation to help save the planet.

Finally Peng turned again to John, extended his hand, and said, "And I want to publicly thank the delegate from the U.S., Mr. John Bancroft, for showing that we can work together to save the planet. And our Premier for braving the storm to support our efforts here. He's now safely back home awaiting with eagerness the final vote."

John raised his hand in acknowledgement to the sustained applause. But he knew the deal wasn't done yet. And neither was Olga.

"He had to say it," thought John, "just because our President couldn't make it."

As soon as Peng sat down, Minister Karlsson recognized John.

John slowly arose, looked around, and addressed the delegates. "Brave delegates who remain, I too want to thank the gentleman from the People's Republic of China for his cooperation, and the help provided by the Premier. President Palin sends her regrets at not being able to attend.

"Now for the rest of the 'grand bargain.' Remember it's a take it or leave it proposition. One vote, up or down, that will decide whether this convention is a success.

"And now for the technology transfer plan. The media has characterized it as a plan hatched by the West and for the West. That is not true. Yes, some of our countries did ..."

John was interrupted by a question from the delegate from Sierra Leone. "Will the gentleman from the United States yield to a question?"

Stunned, John looked at the Minister who reluctantly agreed, "Just this time."

The African delegate, with her high-pitched voice heard above the howling wind, said, "Mr. Bancroft, you've talked a lot about the 2% plan, but not about the 2 degree temperature increase your countries have foisted on us poor countries. And now you think your technology will help us? Don't you and your cohorts feel guilty about what you have done to our continent?"

A hush fell over the arena as they waited for John's reaction. With it getting late, the storm increasing in intensity, and no time for another caucus; he played his last hand.

Ignoring the questions, John looked straight ahead and said, "An apology from the West will be forthcoming. It will be texted into the record of the convention …"

A visceral reaction from several other African delegates erupted, but before they could speak, the Minister banged the gavel and recognized John with, "You may proceed, Mr. Bancroft."

As he proceeded to explain the technology transfer plan and the REDD plan, with the developed nations contributing the bulk of the funding, a huddle developed in a small conference room. Peter, the South African, and the Congolese courier were conferring earnestly.

"I thought we had all 17 votes locked up," said Peter. "It sounds like we're losing some."

The Congolese, not revealing his deal with John, simply said, "I'll go talk to her," and he left hurriedly with Peter still standing.

John, not knowing what was transpiring away from the limelight, continued with his remarks, "To address the delegate from Sierra Leone's concern, the technology we are using today is pollution-free. If you are awarded a grant, your country may see solar panels and windmills on your land, and even the ability to harness the waves in the Atlantic. Let bygones be bygones."

This seemed to satisfy her for now, and she had no further questions.

As John was continuing, all of a sudden the big screens in back of the Minister's seat and in the back of the arena went black. And next the LED lighting was extinguished.

But how to vote? The electronic board, with all countries listed, was also blank. As the delegates milled about aimlessly, John texted Peng with, "Any changes in your vote count. We need every one."

The Minister was also in a quandary. He was on his iPhone, looking nervously at the dark ceiling and the dark skies. However, the exits and stairways were still lit, powered by quiet hydrogen generators.

After several minutes of waiting, the Minister, still able to use the backup power, blared into the microphone, "Please remain calm. This isn't Olga yet. There's no need to leave. I have been assured that the power will be back shortly, and then we can proceed to the final vote. Thank you."

John used this time to check the vote count in his bloc, as he hoped Peng was also doing. What if some delegates had left, especially the yes votes?

After all, there was no proxy voting: something else about which to worry.

And then a cheer erupted as the lights flickered and then resumed full power, and the voting board came to life. The hydrogen backup had prevented a convention blackout. The digital clock crowed 1800 - past the normal adjournment time. But this wasn't normal.

The Minister resumed his chair, banged the gavel with these in-structions, "Fellow delegates, thank you for your patience. We will now resume closing remarks. The chair recognizes Mr. Bancroft for 5 minutes."

Up again like a yo-yo, John gave one final pitch for the "grand bargain" Peng and he had worked so hard to craft.

"Fellow delegates, we don't need any more speeches about ex-treme weather and climate change. Just look outside."

And they did - again.

"What we need now is the political will to commit ourselves, for the first time, to reducing the global greenhouse gases by 100% in just 29 years. How will you do it? With technology, conservation, renewables of all kinds, carbon taxes, cap and trade, cap and divi-dend, public-private partnerships, and creativity. Each country can decide what type of mix will best achieve your goal.

"We all have a natural tendency to avoid decisions that require sacrifice in the near term to achieve a longer term goal." But as my friend Peng knows, "The journey of a thousand miles begins with a single step. Let it began here, and maybe in 2050 those of us who remain on this blue planet can bring our children and grandchildren here and show them where we turned the corner and the hockey stick graph started downward. Thank you."

John sat down, not to applause, but to stunned silence. All was quiet except for the ever-present raging wind and splattering rain.

The Final Vote

Hurriedly the Minister, turning and checking to see that the vot-ing board was lit, posed the question to the convention, "All those in favor of Topic 2, Topic 3, Topic 4, Topic 5, and Topic 6 as written and discussed will signify by voting in the affirmative. All those against the previously-named topics will vote in the negative. A total of 146 is required for passage. The voting board is now operational and open for your vote for 15 minutes. Proceed."

John and Peng, in order to leave no doubt for the other delegates, had previously agreed that they would vote immediately. Besides, maybe they still needed time to do last-minute lobbying. And so two green lights lit simultaneously, one for the People's Republic of China, and the other for the United States of America. But their task wasn't done yet.

John, with one eye on his BlackBerry and the other on the board, was checking to see if his predictions matched the actual vote. After a few minutes of tense waiting and watching, the 28 remaining developed countries votes were recorded. True to their caucus "pledges," there were 24 ayes and 4 noes. In spite of his lobbying; Greece, Portugal, Ireland, and Italy still voted no.

"They must be more concerned about their immediate financial problems instead of what the world will look like in 2050," John mused.

Now John surveyed the board for the rest of the votes as he anxiously glanced at the flickering board. Was it because of the changing votes, or was it another power outage? And again the board went blank, throwing the arena into chaos. Delegates were milling around in the dark, with only the light emanating from their iPhones and BlackBerrys. But maybe there was a silver lining behind the literal black clouds looming ever closer.

With his LED flashlight John shined his way over to where Peng was sitting - patiently waiting.

"I wonder why I haven't heard from him," he thought as he tried to avoid the chairs and delegates wandering around in the aisles.

Finally he found him and shouted over the incessant wind, "Have you lost any more votes?"

Looking downcast Peng replied, "The delegate from neighboring Mongolia is upset that our Premier didn't include her country in the 25 nations we helped. She's threatening to vote against the package. That would make six of us against. How many do you have against?"

Quickly John held up four fingers, did a quick calculation in his head, and replied, "That means even though all 42 non-aligned nations vote yes, we'd still be one vote short. There goes the 'Spirit of Reykjavík,' after all our work. Is there anything you can promise her to get her vote?"

Peng sat there motionless, head in his hands, like Rodin's "The Thinker." "I'll see what I can do?"

John, figuring he had pushed him enough, lightly touched him on his shoulder, re-illuminated his BlackBerry and walked in a zig zag fashion back to his seat, waiting for the lights to resume, as were the other 154 delegates, press, and spectators.

It was now 1830, and you could feel the anxiety level building. Would they ever finish?

Finally the lights flickered back on and the board lit, but all votes were erased. Now what?

Immediately the familiar voice of the Minister boomed over the microphone,

"Fellow delegates, thank you for your patience. I have been assured by the Icelandic Power Authority this will not happen again. Their geothermal backup kicked in when the hydrogen generators failed. However, we need to revote, as you can see by the blank board. I will reset the clock for the full 15 minutes. You may proceed with your votes."

Again John and Peng lit their green buttons immediately. John again counted four noes in his block. Simultaneously across the arena Peng was counting his negatives. There were five red lights, all belonging to five Asian countries that were part of the former Soviet Union. Maybe the old Sino-Soviet split in the Cold War era was getting in the way of today's warming planet.

However, the one he was concerned about, Mongolia, voted green.

"Whatever Peng did, worked," thought John. Somewhat jealous, John concluded, "China is exerting its new found influence in the 21st Century like we used to in the last."

But what about the non-aligned bloc? John scanned the board to see if any of the African countries had voted. And there were none. There was no yellow light for "abstain" or "present." The adopted rules didn't allow for vacillation. So what was going on? There were only five minutes left in which to vote. More anxious moments.

This time John, now with the lights on, made a mad dash to the South African seat. Out of breath he saw Peter, seated and calmly watching the board.

John shouted over the howling wind, "We need all 42 votes. Did you deliver them?"

Peter, without saying a word, pointed to an empty chair and motioned John to sit down. Without lifting his eyes from the board, he said, "Watch this."

John slowly sat down, and the two of them were fixated on the board, showing 104 ayes and nine nays, with an elapsed voting time of 13: 26.

Finally, a slow string of green lights lit the board, until the count was 145 ayes, and nine nays, with an elapsed time of 14:32. Only one light was dark - the Democratic Republic of the Congo.

Just like in some crucial movie scenes when time passes in slow motion, John's mind flashed back to his meetings with the Congolese courier - first in his hotel room and then in the conference cafeteria. He even recounted his words, "Maybe your apology would convince us you rich Western nations are serious about helping us."

Suddenly the buzzer indicating the voting was closed jolted John back to reality. He looked up and there it was. The final green light was lit! He didn't know whether to cheer or cry - both eliciting the same emotion.

So John sat in his seat stunned as he heard the familiar voice of the Minister, "The final vote on the 'grand bargain' is 146 ayes, nine nays. The measure having received the necessary ¾ majority vote of the total delegates is declared passed. Congratulations on becoming the first climate change conference to seriously attack global warming!"

Before the Minister was finished, all the delegates, even those who voted "no" stood in sustained applause, turning to look at John and Peng, who were also applauding. They were joined by the spectators, including the Nebraskans, student activists, and even the protesters. It was truly a time to celebrate as the press continued to upload their stories across the world instantaneously. The "Spirit of Reykjavik" was alive and well - at least for now.

Would this historic agreement be enough to prevent the "tipping point" of 2 degrees C. from being reached? Only time would tell. But for now it was a time for brief celebration even as Olga was still howling outside. Maybe she was mad at the agreement. No more extreme weather?

After the applause subsided, the Minister rapped his gavel before speaking. Ladies and gentlemen, thank you for persevering under difficult conditions. Normally we would hold closing ceremonies with national leaders in attendance. But because Olga prevented most of these dignitaries from attending, we will suspend these festivities.

"I'm sure you all want to pack and prepare for the evacuation plans the Icelandic Airport Authority have prepared for your safety. And one more thing. I have just received this Olga update from the Icelandic Meteorological Society: she is expected to turn into a Category 5 early tomorrow morning. But the good news is that Olga's eye will be over the Reykjavík area also starting then. That means light winds and clear skies for a short time. That's the window we need to head home. Bon voyage, and thank you for sticking it out."

"I declare this convention adjourned," and Minister Karlsson banged the gavel for the last time.

And with that, the delegates scrambled to the waiting underground hydrogen light-rail that would carry them safely to their motels for one last night - albeit a short one.

Among the scramble were Brice and Blaine, who exited through a tunnel to where Magnus was manning the latest weather report. They found him staring at the wall map, which projected the middle of Olga's eye right over the convention arena at 0712.

Magnus heard a noise outside the hall, and excitedly ran to open the door for the Nebraskans.

"Come on in and look at the map."

He blinked his left eye, and a close-up showed the arena with the eye directly above it. He then turned to Brice and Blaine, pointing to the map,

"Do you see that?"

Then he pointed his laser, circling the eye and the arena.

"Do you remember the Christmas story we heard at the church we attended last week?"

Both of the Nebraskans half-heartedly nodded.

Magnus, answering his own question, "This is like the Star of Bethlehem, staying over the stable where the Baby Jesus was. Is this our sign of safety?"

But then Magnus enlarged his circle to reveal a ring of dark, towering thunder clouds.

This is the eyewall surrounding the eye. That's the really dangerous part of a hurricane. You may get out of Iceland, but you've got to get over these clouds."

This time Brice and Blaine didn't know what to think, other than they needed to head back to their motel and join the packing frenzy. As they turned to leave, Magnus said, "Be at Keflavik at 0600, and I'll see you off."

Evacuating the Island

After a night of throwing things together and trying to sleep through the howling winds and incessant rain, Brice and Blaine took the hotel's escalator down and down to the light-rail - crowded with harried delegates and other foreigners heading to Keflavik. At least underground they were escaping Olga - temporarily. And it gave them a temporary reprieve from the extreme weather they were sure to face.

As the train quietly sped along, Brice turned to Blaine with this astute comment, "Maybe what the delegates did here will prevent this extreme weather from happening to your generation."

This reflection was short-lived as the rail rolled into Keflavik, and the passengers boarded the escalators to the terminal - crowded with potential passengers. But the airport authorities were ready with their plan.

As the Nebraskans reached the main floor, there was Magnus anxiously waiting. "Follow me," he said sternly as he pointed to the flashing digital sign reading, "Westbound passengers."

Magnus grabbed Brice's carry-on bag as the Nebraskans wheeled their luggage swiftly, trying to catch Magnus, who again pointed to another sign, "Convention spectators." Out of breath, the former football star and his son joined the long line to await the next step.

Magnus explained, "You see the sign for delegates," as he pointed at a 45 degree angle up and toward the left. "Some of the delegates get to ride on NATO jets which flew into Keflavik before Olga hit. We have furnished corporate jets also. These will be taking off first."

And then he turned and made the same gesture to the right, "And this sign is for the press. They will be boarding their own company jets that have been at Keflavik during the convention."

Turning his head back and forth Brice asked, "And what about us?"

"You get Icelandair's newest fleet of Dreamliners, made in the USA."

Brice, looking out a window, pointed and exclaimed, "Look, the sky is clearing. The eye must be upon us," as he waxed poetic.

"But how long will it last?" Blaine asked worriedly.

"We don't know," answered Magnus. "The authorities have added extra staff to handle this crisis. Remember our excellent rating for service. Just relax and be patient."

As the line was moving, Brice asked Magnus, "Where are you going to ride out Olga?"

"All of our government officials, including our Office of Sustainability, have been assigned underground shelters below our offices. They are stocked with food, water, and supplies to last for two weeks, so don't worry about me. I'm more concerned that you arrive safely home. Besides, I want to visit Nebraska, and even take in a football game as you call it."

"Now you're talking," as Brice lightened up. "And I want to introduce you to Tricia, Coach Osborne, and my fellow workers in my Office of Sustainability."

Blaine continued, "And I want to show you my world at UNL and my friends."

"We'll be in touch," concluded Magnus as the line started to move rapidly. "But first we'd better get you home."

This was the lull before the storm that was sure to follow.

"Boarding Passes, Please"

And now it was crunch time as the 155 remaining delegates, members of the press corps from all over the world, and the global spectators moved through the lines to their directional destination. Keflavik had never moved so many people through its gates in so short of a time. Their high service ratings would now be put to the test.

As the trio moved toward the front of their line, they could see the first of the jets streaming toward the sky in a 90 degree ascent. They were part of NATO's Response Force that is used for non-combatant evacuation operations, and this one would certainly qualify.

Blaine pointed, "Look at that plane. It's climbing straight up like a helicopter. What is it?"

Magnus replied, "That's a British Harrier Jump Jet. It's a VTOL."

"OK, smarty, what's that?" asked Brice.

It stands for Vertical Take Off and Landing. They are used on aircraft carriers, and NATO sent them over here to climb quickly over the eyewall."

"How do you know that?" puzzled Blaine.

"I used to build model planes and hang them from the ceiling in my bedroom. This plane was one of them. And for fun I blew it up with a firecracker. But I have nothing against the English. In fact these jets with only a short range are going to deliver the European delegates safely, I pray."

"Please do," requested Brice, "and for us too."

Magnus nodded in agreement.

"So how are the delegates from the rest of the world going to get home?" asked Brice.

"NATO has enough jets to get them up and over Olga. Then they will land at civilian airports to connect on regular flights to their destinations. They're just like regular passengers - like you guys. And it's the same process with everyone else, but you're not VIPs."

"Thanks," muttered Brice sarcastically.

Again Blaine asked, "So how do you know all this?"

"Our office has worked with the Icelandic Airport Authority and Emergency Evacuation Department to coordinate all this, and it's been quite a challenge. We'll see the results soon."

Finally, the three arrived at the gate where they would part company – at least for now. The line was now moving so fast there wasn't time for any goodbyes. Besides, the wind was picking up again, and they could see streaks of rain on the windows of the airport.

Magnus, who had a special security clearance, followed the Nebraskans to the ramp leading to the plane. Before they were ready to walk down the ramp to the plane, Brice and Blaine turned to Magnus, and they "high-fived" each other, just as Brice had done with his teammates so many times at Memorial Stadium.

"See you in the States," shouted Brice.

"And thanks for everything, and please pray for us," followed Blaine.

Magnus gave a thumbs up, turned and walked away with a tear in his eye as he headed back to his office to monitor Olga - this time without his American friends. But he would see them again, he reasoned.

The Ride Home

The passengers, who all seemed to be speaking English, streamed down the aisles to find their seats with the assistance of the friendly attendants. Each passenger was given a bottle of water and a souvenir of Iceland – a small replica of a glacier that was a hand warmer.

As Brice and Blaine found their seats in the massive plane and settled in, they checked the overhead monitors tracking Olga. It looked ominously black as the eye was closing and the eyewall was looming larger. And this plane somehow had to fly over it, and it wasn't a VTOL.

With their seatbelts fastened and the huge plane slowly bouncing down the runway, the safety instructions repeated thousands of times by the flight attendants seemed to take on an extra **urgency**. And it was 3,000 miles of churning ocean before reaching the U.S. coastline. Flotation devices, anyone?

And now it quickly quieted as the pilot came on.

"Ladies and gentlemen, this Dreamliner is the most storm-worthy plane in our passenger fleet. It will get its finest test today, and we will land safely. We've added extra thrust to climb quickly so make sure your seat belts are fastened securely. Radar has indicated a window of calm air within the eyewall. It's an unusual cloud formation that's called an eye within the eye of a hurricane. We're going to aim for that opening, but it will be a bumpy ride getting to it. I suggest a brace position upon takeoff until I give the all-clear. And one more thing. If you're a praying person, now would be a good time. Flight attendants, prepare for takeoff."

Brice and Blaine looked around to bewildered looks as the plane was picking up speed down the runway. And then people started putting their heads down with their arms braced on the seats in front of them.

Brice quipped, "Why don't they hand out football helmets?" And then after checking Blaine's position, he nervously asked, "What was that Bible verse Magnus used for protection?"

Through a muffled voice came the reply, "Something about God being with us when we pass through the waters."

And then the plane was airborne in a smooth takeoff. Brice raised his head and looked out the rain-spattered window for one last view of Reykjavík, bathed in dark clouds. He looked down at the waves crashing over the seawall that had been raised for protection. It would have to be raised again if the extreme weather were to continue. "But maybe what happened at Reykjavík this month would buy time for the construction," he thought.

A sudden pitching of the Dreamliner brought Brice back into his brace position. There were peals of lightning and crashes of thunder seemingly in stereo around the plane as it jolted back and forth. Brice flashed back to the close calls he had experienced in Alaska - first with the seaplane crash and then with the forced landing after being hit with volcanic ash from Mt. Redoubt. But this time something was different. Instead of panic there was peace. Instead of being overwhelmed by the storm, he was strangely still. He looked over at Blaine, who also seemed calm. Was he praying or sleeping? Either way he seemed OK.

The violent shaking continued as the plane kept a gradual upward trajectory. The cool Nebraskans heard their fellow passengers yelling, crying, and even crying out to God in desperation. One man even screamed, "Go ahead, God; take me. I'm ready."

Finally, just as quickly as the turbulence began, the plane leveled off in a glide path, and a ray of sunshine surrounded the plane. Brice lifted his head and looked back at the black clouds swirling over Iceland. Now his thoughts were for Magnus and his countrymen. But somehow he knew they would be OK. They had braved worse crises in their 1,000 year history. And besides, the "Spirit of Reykjavík" would prevent a worse calamity from occurring in the future.

And this was the hope of all North Americans as they headed west to their homelands. Would the alliance between the two largest economies – and polluters - delay the "tipping point" and buy time for Reykjavík's reforms to work? Only time would tell.

Author's Note

You have just experienced a fictional account of climate scientists in Alaska during the International Polar Year of 2021, using their expertise to warn the world about a looming global catastrophe. You have read their formal presentations, and have come along with them on a series of field trips.

I have used many sources in telling this story. I relied heavily on the following books dealing with climate change: Alun Anderson's *After The Ice: Life, Death, and Geopolitics in the New Arctic* for descriptions and projections of the changing Arctic; James Hansen's *Storms Of My Grandchildren: The Truth About the Coming Climate Catastrophe and Our Last Chance to Save Humanity* uses many charts and graphs to project a dismal climate for future generations, unless we act with **urgency**; Sir David King and Gabrielle Walker present solutions to the climate change problem in *The Hot Topic: What We Can Do About Global Warming*; Katherine Kahoe and Andrew Farley, *in a climate for change: global warming facts for faith-based decisions*, offer scientific analysis supplemented with a Christian perspective; and *Climate Refugees* by Collectif Argos use a pictorial narrative of extreme weather events across the globe. In addition I have synthesized numerous websites, NPR broadcasts, and periodicals in compiling evidence for my story. My projections of the climate in 2021 is based on the above information, as well as my own analysis. For Icelandic history and culture I used Terry G. Lacy's *Ring of Seasons: Iceland - Its Culture and History.*

You have traveled with the main characters, a former Nebraska football star and his son as they forge a friendship with an Icelandic student during their time in Alaska. The three of them "tag along" with the scientists to see the effects of global warming firsthand. Unexpectedly, these field trips often end in a crisis. Throughout it all you see the Nebraskans change their attitude toward God, due in part to the witness of their Christian friend. However, their "epiphanies" climax with a fight for survival between their beloved dog Spud and a hungry polar bear in the changing Arctic.

Brice, Blaine, and Magnus meet again, this time in Magnus' country of Iceland for a climate change conference in Reykjavik. They witness the political maneuverings and demonstrations as the world tries to reach a binding agreement to avoid the "tipping point" - against a background of extreme weather.

Throughout the discussions, both in Alaska and in Iceland, the term **urgent** becomes the battle cry. The scientists are venturing from their sterile lab to warn the world. Will 2050 be warmer than the world about which you have read? Will the measures enacted in Reykjavik keep our planet habitable for future generations of humans, animals, and plants?

But do we see this looming crisis as **urgent**? It's difficult when the major contributor to global warming - carbon dioxide - is invisible, odorless, and tasteless? And the changes to our planet, are, for the most part, happening gradually. Besides, we can rationalize to say that most of us reading this book won't be around to see if the scientific scenarios projected to 2100 will actually happen. But maybe the extreme weather most of the world is experiencing right now will be our collective call to action?

There's another **urgency** that has eternal implications that is woven subtlety throughout the narrative. Our stay on our still blue planet is very, very brief by geological standards. As the Psalmist says, "The length of our days is 70 years - or 80 if we have the strength." And then what? Do we - our body, mind, and spirit - R.I.P., decomposing in the ground, or does part of us live forever - somewhere? And where is that somewhere?

Magnus didn't want his American friends to encounter any more death-defying experiences without having the assurance that they would spend eternity in heaven. What if the polar bear had killed Brice instead of Spud? It would've been too late for him to pray the prayer committing his life to Jesus. The time for **urgency** and repentance would have passed.

But you may say, "I have things to worry about in the "here and now." I'll think about where I will spend eternity at a more convenient time. Besides, I can't see heaven or hell, but my problems are right in front of me now. That's the tyranny of the **urgent.**

But what if you encounter your "polar bear," and can't escape? What if you don't finish your "bucket list," but instead "kick it" as did Magnus' friend, Erik? Are you ready to meet your Maker? What's your wake-up call?

If you have a continuing interest in one or both of the **urgencies** portrayed in this book, I invite you to check the Appendices for additional suggestions on what you can do to help save the world and your soul. That way you've got both worlds covered - now and forevermore!

And let me know how you are doing on your dual journeys!

Jay Mennenga
jaymennenga@gmail.com

What You Can Do To Help Stop Global Warming

Opportunities abound . . . at home, with your car, while shopping and traveling . . . to help stop global warming. To assist you, check off those items you have done or are already doing. As you continue to decrease your carbon footprint, add more checks.

Your Home

___1. Get an energy audit for your home or business <u>www. eere.energy.gov/consumer/your</u> home/energy audits/index.cfm/ mytopic=11170

___2. Make sure your home is insulated properly.

___3. Invest in a programmable thermostat.

___4. Turn your thermostat down 2 degrees in the winter and up 2 degrees in the summer.

___5. Use your home air conditioning sparingly.

___6. Keep you fireplace/wood stove damper closed unless a fire is burning.

___7. Use kitchen and bathroom venting fans sparingly to reduce heat loss in the winter.

___8. Close doors and heating/cooling vents of spare rooms in your house.

___9. Open or close blinds on South-facing windows to let heat in or keep it out.

__10. As appliances need to be replaced, purchase energy efficient models.

__11. Turn off lights, appliances, and computers when not in use.

__12. Unplug electronic devices when not in use. Up to 75% of energy is consumed by "phantom draw." Plug into power strips with switches.

__13. Install compact fluorescent lights (CFL) or LEDS.

__14. Set the temperature of your hot water heater to 120 degrees. Turn it to the lowest setting when traveling.

__15. Install low flow showerheads, and take shorter showers.

__16. Use the energy saver setting on your dishwasher.

__17. Wait until you have full loads before running dishwashers and washing machines.

__18. Use cold or warm water to wash clothes. Hang them out on a clothesline when weather permits.

__19. Adjust your irrigation system for upcoming weather.

__20. Enroll in paperless billing for utilities and credit cards.

__21. Remove yourself from junk mail lists at www.newdream.org/junkmail/

___22. Read newspapers on line.

___23. Buy rechargeable batteries.

___24. Buy organic foods and clothes.

Your Car

___1. Drive less. Walk or ride a bike whenever possible.

___2. Carpool or use public transportation.

___3. Drive or buy a hybrid or electric vehicle.

___4. Drive slower. Energy efficiency decreases by 2% for every mph that you drive over 60 mph.

___5. Keep your tires inflated to recommended pressure.

___6. Follow the maintenance schedule in your owner's manual.

___7. Remove unnecessary items from your car to reduce weight.

___8. Use a tailgate net on your pickup to reduce wind resistance.

Reduce, Reuse, and Recycle

___1. Participate in your communities recycling program.

___2. Donate usable clothing and household items to thrift stores/ Salvation Army, and buy used items there.

___3. Buy products that have less packaging.

___4. Buy fresh foods instead of packaged foods.

__5. Buy local and from "Farmer's Markets.

__6. Take your own reusable bags to the grocery store.

__7. Use refillable water bottles.

__8. Bring your own coffee mug/cup to restaurants and filling stations.

Other Things You Can Do

__1. Plant trees . . . especially if you burn wood.

__2. Leave healthy trees standing.

__3. Buy acres of tropical rainforests. www.rainforest.org/help/save-an-acre.html.

__4. Compost food scraps so they are not transported to landfills.

__5. Stay at hotels/motels that are members of the Green Association.

__6. Use the courtesy van at your hotel/motel.

__7. Turn AC, heat, and lights off in your hotel room when leaving.

__8. Pack a night light for children instead of leaving the bathroom light on in your hotel/motel room.

__9. Lobby your local, state, and national policy makers to take action to reduce greenhouse gases. www.congress.org/congressorg/home/

Visit These Web Sites For More Information

www.theclimateproject.org
www.myfootprint.org

NOTE: This checklist adapted from a handout at a climate change presentation in Red Lodge, MT, March 2007.

Appendix B

Connecting With Brice's Epiphany

It took several death-defying crises for Brice, a self-proclaimed atheist at the beginning of the story, to start wondering why these strange occurrences were happening to him. Finally, because of the death of his faithful dog Spud, and assistance from his Christian friend, Magnus, Brice realized that's what Jesus did for him - sacrificing His life on the cross so that he might live and have a purposeful life on earth, and spend eternity in heaven with His Savior. *1*

But it wasn't enough just to believe what Jesus did for him. Brice had to reach out and accept this gift by faith, which in itself is a gift. *2* After he prayed this prayer, led by Magnus, he felt an immediate peace that things would work out for him. *3*

But that was only the start of his life as a Christian. Brice started talking to Jesus in prayer, reading the Bible Magnus gave him, attending church with Magnus, and telling his friends about his changed life - some whom bought his story, and others who ridiculed him. Brice eventually reconciled with Tricia, who saw the change in his life. *4* And his son, Blaine, followed steadfastly in his father's new footsteps. Their "journey" continues.

How about you? Where are you on your "spiritual journey?" Have you made the commitment to Christ that Magnus, Brice, and Blaine eventually did? Are you looking for the truth? *5* Are you wondering if there is more to life than you are experiencing? *6* Are you living day-to-day, and don't have time now to think deep thoughts? "Maybe later when I'm old and on my deathbed?" you rationalize. *7* Magnus' friend, Erik, didn't have time to make his decision - he died in an automobile accident. *8* Or do you want more proof about this "Jesus stuff?" before you make a decision to be a Christ follower? *9*

Hopefully the stories of the main characters in this book, along with the resources listed below, will help you on your "journey" to a personal relationship with Jesus Christ. And you don't have to be religious - just a faithful, humble, and receptive "seeker."

1   This is how much God loved the world: He gave his Son, his one and only Son. And this is why: so that no one need be destroyed: by believing in him, anyone can have a whole and lasting life. John 3:16

This is the testimony in essence: God gave us eternal life; the life is in his Son. So, whoever has the Son, has life; whoever rejects the Son, rejects life. 1 John 5:11-12

2   Saving is all his idea, and all his work. All we do is trust him enough to let him do it. It's God's gift from start to finish. We don't play the major role. If we did, we'd probably go around bragging that we've done the whole thing! Ephesians 2:8,9

3   Suggested prayer: Dear Jesus, I believe you are the Son of God and died for my sins and rose again. Please forgive my sins, come into my life, and help me to live a life that pleases you. I can't do it myself and need your help. Give me your power to love you and others. Thank you. Amen.

4   The old life is gone; a new life burgeons! Look at it! All this comes from the God who settled the relationship between us and him, and then called us to settle our relationships with each other. 2 Corinthians 5:17

*5   Jesus said, "I am the Road, also the Truth, also the Life."
John 14:6*

*6   I came so they can have real and eternal life, more and bet-
ter life than they ever dreamed of. John 10:10b*

*7   If there's no resurrection, "We eat, we drink, the next day we
die. That's all there is to it. I Corinthians 15: 32*

*8   Everyone has to die once, then face the consequences.
Hebrews 9:27*

Note: The above quotations are from *The Message: The New
Testament In Contemporary Language* by Eugene H. Peterson

9   I Don't Have Enough Faith to be an Atheist, by Norman L.
Geisler and Frank Turek.

*God, Actually: Why God probably exists; Why Jesus was
probably divine and Why the 'rational' objections to religion are
unconvincing,* by Roy Williams.

CPSIA information can be obtained
at www.ICGtesting.com
Printed in the USA
FSOW01n0453140115
4533FS